The Gift of a Daughter

Also by Emyr Humphreys in Seren

A Toy Epic
Outside the House of Baal
Unconditional Surrender
The Taliesin Tradition

The Gift of a Daughter

Emyr Humphreys

seren

seren is the book imprint of
Poetry Wales Press Ltd
Wyndham Street, Bridgend, CF31 1EF
Wales

© Emyr Humphreys, 1998

The right of Emyr Humphreys to be identified as the Author
of this Work has been asserted in accordance with the
Copyright, Designs and Patents Act 1988.

ISBN 1-85411-222-8

A CIP record for this title is available from
the British Library

*The publisher works with the financial assistance of the
Arts Council of Wales*

Cover image: Terracotta sarcophagus, Tuscania, mid-second century BC.

Printed in Plantin by CPD, Ebbw Vale

The Gift of a Daughter

ONE

i

He emerged shivering from the passage grave. I've no idea what he was trying to prove. My daughter ran towards him squealing with excessive delight. My wife looked the other way. What passed for a smile was frozen on her face until it became a grimace of distaste. I could hear their laughter on the breeze. Rhiannon was urging him to creep in again on his hands and knees. Then she turned to wave at me and order me to photograph Buddy's resurrection. My camera would record their merry prank at the cromlech. Rhiannon would pose as some sort of Persephone, offering the genius a helping hand. Or was it Orpheus and Euridice in reverse? I was raising my camera when I felt Marian's hand on my arm.

'Aled. Better not give the thing permanence.'

Caught between wife and daughter. Not easy to have a mind of one's own. Marian pointed to a shaft of sunlight striking the ruined church tower. An alternative picture.

'Buddy has risen!'

The same breeze that carried Rhiannon's shout made the genius shiver: a thin bearded creature in brown, inadequately clad. She put one arm around his waist to stop him shivering and she raised the other to insist I took their picture. Marian turned her back on the scene. I could barely hear what she was muttering between her teeth.

'What does Rhi know about music? She gave up the piano when she was twelve.'

I took two pictures. Rhi was so pleased with their prank she would have liked half a dozen. Not exactly a fairy-child caught by a hairy monster: but near enough to disturb. Buddy! What a ridiculous name. Why should it be ridiculous? Because Marian said it was. Certainly it didn't go with that outsized beard. He was cool. I would be cool too and implacably amiable: relaxed, not a stiff desiccated academic which is probably what Master Buddy Thwaite believes me to be.

At least he was interested in megaliths. That was something to build on. Our island had so many. We were proud of them. We forged our way through rocks and marsh to reach yet another one, described in my field book as 'much disturbed'. Rhiannon caught up with me to exert her charm in my direction and as is my wont I succumb.

'You should write a whole book about them, Tada,' she said. 'It's long overdue.'

Well of course I should. The question is how to find the time. There is this Stakhanovite pressure to publish in one's own field. The college gazette was the Principal's favourite reading.

'And you'd still have time for Boethius.'

She squeezed my arm before she left me to rescue Buddy who was floundering on the edge of a bog. This was my girl. I had to be proud of her. And this bearded creature she had brought all the way from Cambridge to sink up to his ankles in the mud. Was he really a genius?

Marian marched alongside me slapping thistles with a stick and murmuring a stream of protest.

' "Buddy has a special contempt for diminished sevenths." Would you believe it? What does Rhi know about diminished sevenths for heaven's sake? I can't bear it. "And Beethoven is played far too often." What's the matter with the girl? Hasn't she got a mind of her own?...'

We came to a more formidable obstacle of shrub and falling wall. It wasn't the best route we had taken and it seemed to me the genius was beginning to resent the effort he had to make. Rhiannon was determined to be cheerful.

'Buddy is only really interested in the world before the invention of the wheel.'

Marian seemed to see a chance. In any case she seized it.

'In that case he will have no objection to walking back.'

She bent to release her trouser leg from the barb of a young thorn.

'Back where?'

I was foolish enough to ask. Marian's head was lowered but Rhiannon could well have heard her vehement whisper.

'To wherever he came from.'

ii

Perhaps I took too much comfort from Buddy Thwaite's interest in megaliths. It was anything but academic. Like his reading. It was raining hard outside and he sat in my chair with a science-fiction comic rivetted to his face. He was at one and the same time totally absent and very much at home. In my role as host and Rhiannon's father I stood by the window and waited for his next gnomic utterance. Was the threadbare hole in his jeans a deliberate tear, the result of genuine wear, or a generation gap? If Marian could have been prevailed upon to take his presence more lightly, there was a range of word-play in that word 'jeans'. It needs a kindred spirit to share the sprightly notions that skip across one's field of perception.

'These are the plots that count.'

He licked his thick lips and shook his comic before lowering it to register his disapproval of the progress of the rain across the yard.

'You need cyberspace to give added music and meaning to the Stones.'

I had no idea what he meant or whether it mattered. He spoke as if I should be grateful for the information. I stared at the lurid brutalities of infantile technological warfare suspended in front of his hairy face. Every man likes to think of his home as an oasis of tranquillity. This intruder had transformed mine into a potential war-zone. Rhiannon pranced in from the kitchen and snatched the comic from her genius's hands.

I was impressed with her daring. No death-ray flashed from Buddy's pale blue eyes.

His large hands slumped limply to his lap.

'What about our Stones then?'

He was not disposed to respond to her challenge. He concentrated on fondly stroking his beard.

'Will there be music in the Ogre's Apron? Will there be symphonies in the stones?'

I was listening to my daughter. I thought I knew her. Was she under his spell or was he under hers? If I understood their clotted chatter it appears there are more intense vibrations in the stone circles of north east Scotland than anything we could offer. There were fifteen recumbent stone circles between the rivers Urie and Don in Aberdeenshire of great significance. Fair enough. Was that sufficient reason to buy a cottage up there? All that long way away? And did it mean he would take her with him? And if so when? And what about her Finals? I was much disturbed.

And so was Marian. She lay awake that night murmuring over and over again: "what on earth does she see in him?" I was unable to sleep myself and the repetition got on my nerves. I was considerate enough not to say so. I was given to understand that a mere father could know nothing of the depths of a mother's intuitive misgivings.

'Have you noticed his tone?' Marian said.

'What tone?'

'You must recognise it for goodness' sake.'

I could guess what Marian was referring to. That vestigial whinge. It meant that Buddy had complete access to that reservoir of excuses filled by generations of undergraduates in their tireless efforts to exonerate themselves.

'Whatever goes wrong will never be his fault. Ever.'

We were both teachers, Marian and I, and this was a practice we were long accustomed to detect. My wife had given up her own career for the sake of her family, but she had not lost any of her analytical skills. This gave added weight to her judgement.

'It's a disaster. Can't you see it? A complete disaster.'

I suppose I could but not in such stark uncompromising terms.

'You can hear it. She's making his excuses, hers. She's taking them all on. The whole load. And what possible good will that do her?'

After midnight I tip-toed to the landing. They were in my study. The door was open and the light spilled into the hall. She was making him free with my inner sanctum and no doubt he was casting a bleary eye over my desk. It wasn't that I could be bothered with whatever he chose to think. As Marian said the well-being of our daughter was our only concern. In the stillness of the night I heard a strange sound.

Buddy was singing. If you could call it singing. A noise that came through his nose rather than his mouth. I strained my ears to catch any meaningful pattern to the melancholy ululations. It was always possible he had some brilliant orchestration lurking in his brain and the noise he was making was more than an extended whimper of self-pity on my daughter's breast.

I was overwhelmed by a sudden sense of loss. She had been ours for twenty years. Our bright daughter was in her second year at Cambridge. We were ready to be astonished by her sparkle and wit when she came home. She would freshen the stale air of approaching middle age with new insights, exciting perspectives, thrilling discoveries, revelations, prospects... All she did was bring home Buddy.

I struggled to be objective. After all I was a scholar. I could understand a longed-for child would bring you pleasure and pain in equal measure. Perhaps he was a genius. Perhaps she had acquired new knowledge; an extended organ of perception. Parenthood like scholarship was a lifetime's exercise in patience. As a Reader in Classics I had chaired the business of the Faculty through difficult times. My role in life was to introduce a level of rationality into every discourse, if possible laced with a little humour.

I returned to bed in a more stable frame of mind. I found Marian sitting up in bed.

'I can't sleep,' she said. 'How can I sleep.'

She spoke as though I were in some way responsible. Some inadequacy in my character made me incapable of dealing with this crisis. Had there been a burglar downstairs it would have been my duty to confront the intruder. By the same token I should contrive to rid our premises of this undesirable foreign body.

'He's been married before,' Marian said.

'How can you tell?'

'You've only got to look at him. He's probably got a wife and children. He's been married before. Dozens of times.'

'Dozens?...'

I tried to make a face to denote comic exaggeration. It was important that we should be able to laugh together. Marian was in no mood to be amused.

'The rubbish that girl is talking,' she said.

'If it's rubbish it's not worth remembering.'

' "Buddy hates cars." Did you hear that? "The human race is speeding along the road to extinction". "Schubert is all bang, bang, bang." She hasn't got a mind of her own any more. I can't bear it.'

Marian was staring at me in the semi-darkness. She had stopped complaining, but her silence demanded to know what I was going to do about it.

iii

Things don't just happen once. At the Porter's Lodge I was all set to take a photograph. I had 'the millstone' which is what Marian calls my Pentax, hanging from my neck, and there was Rhiannon chatting with a group of female undergraduates on the path across the lawn of the college court. She would be pleased to see us. We were loaded with gifts. Home-made this and that. A suitcase containing jam, cakes, marmalade, biscuits, enough to withstand a siege: and books and magazines in Welsh we thought she would want to keep abreast with. My idea was to take a succession of stills at each step she took towards us and register a sequence of shocks of puzzlement and surprise, recognition and delight. I actually began to photograph as she turned to look at the Lodge. She ran towards us and right past us, just as Marian's arms were rising to embrace her. We both swung around and clapped eyes on Buddy for the first time. A passer-by among passers-by who had stood still on the pavement to wait for her and no one else. Within inches of our faces she hadn't seen us because she had eyes only for him. In fairness to the child, as I had pointed out to Marian, we had moved to one side to improve the camera angle and it was likely we were obscured by the shadow of the Porter's Lodge. There we were, and there, across the street, they were. Tall as he was, he was more in her embrace than she was in his.

We moved and he saw us before she did. It amazed me even in that first moment that such a willowy, almost emaciated figure, that seemed to prefer to allow the wind to pass through it than offer solid resistance, could contain so much adhesive power. Rhiannon was already a satellite caught inside an unaccountable force of gravity. When at last she saw us, she dragged him by the hand to introduce him to us. She made all the effort. Being negative had to be part of his magnetism. Or was it lethargy? Before taking his hand I was already rubbing pins and needles of disquiet out of my fingertips with my thumb.

'Mam! Dad! How wonderful! I hadn't seen you.'

She was bubbling over with confidence and excitement. She was in control of the situation and was full of benevolence towards each one of us. Buddy's baptismal names were Lawrence Arthur, but as a composer the world would know him as Buddy Thwaite which rhymed with 'great' – which is what we were, she said; the greatest, the best, the sweetest and so on. Our only child ... how could we resist her?

Our Rhiannon was baptised by Marian's great-uncle, a venerable retired minister with a flourishing moustache and a bald head and twinkling blue eyes. That was the way we both wanted it in spite of our doubts and disbeliefs. We would adhere to our traditions until something better came along. "Do you promise to bring this child up in the nurture and admonition of the Lord..." I wasn't sure what it all meant but I answered 'I do' firmly enough so that Marian had no need to give me a nudge. She was smiling so beautifully at the old man holding the precious bundle and I reminded myself to ask her exactly what was meant by 'the admonition of the Lord.'

She was more likely to have the explanation at her fingertips. Her talent for lucid exposition was always superior to mine. Our marriage was based on admiration and respect as well as any impulse of physical attraction. How else could we be so frank and so supportive with each other?

'She takes after you,' I said to Marian.

The cafe table in Silver Street was between us and I leaned across it to reinforce that second person singular which brings us that much closer together. 'You were a real rebel, you know. "Running wild".'

I quoted a family joke. I was struggling to dispel the foreboding that was making it so difficult for her to smile. I wanted to protect her.

'The very first time I set eyes on you, Madame, you were being dragged by the hair along the floor of a Post Office by a policeman. A dirty floor it was too. Not the best way for a well-brought-up girl to behave.'

The first links of our love had been forged in a time of turbulence; protests, rallies, sit-ins, marches, hunger-strikes, fines and imprisonments. It didn't really suit us then, any more than it would now. To be dragged by the hair across the street on a wet November morning and be poked at by the points of old ladies' disapproving umbrellas. To be pushed into a dock in a Magistrates Court and be given a fine and a prison sentence for stubborn militance went clean against the tender respectabilities of her chapel upbringing. Marian was a minister's daughter brought up to respect the Law and not to defy it. We could smile about it now, but as I gazed at her troubled face across the cafe table in Cambridge, I saw those same eyes shining with bewildered excitement under the black curls that escaped from the demure woolly cap as she sat with the other students on the Post Office floor. They waited their turn to be dragged across the floor.

'That was for a Cause', Marian said.

She sounded impatient and unwilling to dwell on the past. When it was all over at least as far as we felt compelled to act, we were able to marry and resume our academic careers with the necessary degree of concentration that our quietened consciences allowed.

We had our reward. PhDs and halcyon days. Work supported by love and comforting affection.

'He'll ruin her life,' she said. 'It's awful. Can't you see it?'

A daughter can look so like her mother and in moments of tranquillity there is an abiding pleasure in perceiving fresh aspects of the resemblance, but in practice it is the differences that matter. I had to draw her attention to what in my view was patently obvious. For Rhiannon at twenty, Buddy was a Cause with a capital 'C': a combination of misunderstood genius and lame dog. What could be more fatally attractive?

'We've got to nip it in the bud.'

She frowned in a way that withered my witticism about bud and Buddy before I could utter it. She was still so beautiful in my eyes. And clever. In those early days there were one or two waspish colleagues who hinted that the sweetness of her smile had saved her several months rewriting on her thesis and had helped propel me into a Senior Lectureship at an unusually early age. We called those things academic irritations and we rose above them with ease. It was out of a repletion of success and happiness that Marian's desire for motherhood gradually overtook her. At first it was a quiet joke. In those days we were still young enough to giggle. "Think of all the holiday jaunts we would have to give up," and "I'm a career woman aren't I? So can't have my cake and eat it can I? But there's no harm in trying, is there?"

Success was important to us both. We spoke openly of "legitimate ambition". Marian had to prove to her father who was a male chauvinist as well as an extremely idealistic person, that a woman could flourish in an academic environment originally devised exclusively for men. He would have liked to have been a professor himself.

She grew quite cross when he puffed at his pipe and declared that women were superior to men because providence had designed the estate of motherhood to incline them towards spontaneous unselfishness. I was never entirely clear why Marian took such fierce exception to the phrase "naturally unselfish", but in this as in any other argument I was invariably on her side. It never mattered to me if colleagues occasionally muttered that Aled Morgan was totally under his wife's thumb. We were comrades bound in the emotional proximity of marriage able to assert with confidence that all reliable knowledge is based on love. But since love is notoriously blind – I saw Marian stretch herself in bed and wave an index finger and giggle to announce what she liked to call a "silly syllogism" – all such inside knowledge is inherently unreliable. *Quod erat...* So where does that leave us?

The enunciation of her mental processes became notably less sparkling after the first of her two miscarriages. At the same time she became more critical of the verbal exuberance of others, as though all the deeper truths of life were drawn towards brooding silence. The medical verdict decreed the first miscarriage as less serious than the second, but it was then that she began to laugh less often: that infectious giggle faded with the soft peach-like bloom that used to visit her cheeks each summer. It could have been no more than the natural ageing process, but I witnessed her acute analytical intelligence being diverted from linguistic scholarship to an intense study of the functioning of her own body. From bed I would catch her stare at herself naked in the mirror as she made morose pronouncements concerning physical decay and the progress of the soul that I would be obliged to dismiss with simulated abruptness. She took to weighing herself as much as two or three times a day. A new caution supervised the things she ate and even the way she slept. She moved around as though unseen weights were dragging her whole being closer to the ground.

Our doctor of that time was a burly young Cardiffian who still played rugby and modestly assured me that he had studied many books on the "interdependence of physiology and psychology among females." 'You've got to accept that a miscarriage is like a death in the woman's family.' His face was close to mine as he said it. 'You should treat it as a bereavement.' He seemed to be accusing me of a lack of basic understanding: I was yet another case of an incompetent and insensitive male trampling the flowerbeds. I restrained myself by thinking the man meant well. I showed the outward signs of gratitude by paying the ponderous full-back the closest attention. Marian had suffered wounds in the mind as well as the body and it was my mission to make our life together a healing process. It was an on-going treatment and it continued through the precarious course of her next pregnancy. I was resolved to make the sequence of months as comfortable as possible. I made myself a master of light-hearted diversions. In spite of my unflagging zeal, where she had once been active and critical, she became passive and mute. She listened to the doctor with reverent intensity as he issued his predictable directions. Scholarly works that she had once devoured with analytical concentration she now let slip from her listless fingers.

Rhiannon's birth was such a triumph. The midwife disentangled the umbilical cord from the folds of her glistening neck and out of a welter of blood and membrane and mucus emerged a new beginning: a simultaneous birth and rebirth. In a matter of minutes I saw my Marian undergo yet another transformation. A canopy cot had been prepared for the baby. It had lurked in the shadows for many weeks, more of a threat than a promise. It had been made to a design Marian had derived from a painting by Berthe Morrisot during her previous pregnancy. Now it emerged as the centre of the universe and its calm radiance was reflected like sunlight in Marian's face. This was a different beauty. The long silences of her pregnancies had also been extended meditations on the nature of motherhood. While I had been lost in the byzantine and unfruitful intricacies of college politics, she had been formulating the precepts and patterns that would govern all aspects of behaviour appropriate to a perfect mother. From that first day of triumph to this cold cup of coffee on the cafe table Marian's life had been dedicated to the well-being of our daughter. In the shadow of the Porter's Lodge the nurture and the admonition appeared to have reached an abrupt end.

iv

It was for Rhi's sake that I put myself out to entertain the bearded Buddy. Marian had become abnormally attached to the chrome rail of her Aga stove and was lapsing into impenetrable silences. I imagined that Rhiannon had given her hairy friend many fervid evocations of her island home. True, it was less isolated than appeared – a mere nine mile drive to the college the other side of the suspension bridge – but most sensitive people were quick to recognise its numinous quality. Nothing seemed to surprise Buddy. He behaved as though he had seen everything before and had long since decided it was unworthy of his complete attention. Rhiannon moved on tip-toe to introduce him to the moorhen that haunted the thick thorn bush overhanging the duck-pond half way up our lane, and I saw him yawn without bothering to put his hand over his mouth.

He usually looked as though he was struggling to wake up or about to fall asleep. "Drugged", was the word I heard Marian muttering under her breath. As the cloud cleared, he stopped blinking to stare at the mountains across the straits; but when

Rhiannon started naming them one by one, from left to right, (a time honoured party-piece she had been performing since she was eight years old) he slunk away from her side before she had reached half way. Those mellifluous names meant nothing to this great composer's ear. All the same she ran after him, grabbed his arm, gazed up at his bearded face so that it became painfully obvious to me that for our one and only daughter, Lawrence Arthur "Buddy" Thwaite was the most precious specimen of homo-sapiens treading an earth made joyful by his presence.

I set aside a lecture that needed urgent attention to take the happy pair on yet another tour of pre-historic sites. As they bumped up and down on the back seat, holding hands, I put the shock absorbers of my car through their paces to get as close as I could to one site after another. He paid reasonable attention as I suggested that the given central area of a henge had been used for ritual purposes rather than burial. I regurgitated a colleague's fanciful theory, assuming this might appeal to the creative impulses of our musical genius, about the passage pointing towards the sea to facilitate the return of the soul to a primordial form of infinity; but his only response was to raise eyebrows above those unnervingly pale eyes. On another site Rhiannon traced with her delicate fingers patterns cut into the upright stones. She wondered how much they might have meant in the light of their burning torches. Buddy held up his head then, as though he could hear archaic music filtering though the quiet. Rhiannon touched my arm. Did she want me to share the awesome spectacle of genius at work?

It seemed to me that with an attention span of such limited duration, a chap like this could never be capable of sustaining the effort needed to produce anything that could claim to be a work of art. I felt I knew the type. I had seen so many students like him. He displayed a brief attachment to the standing stone in the field visible from our guest bedroom window. He even went as far as trying to embrace it and rubbed his beard against the rough edge. He pronounced it lacking in vibrations. It could be nothing more than a cattle rubbing stone. He turned away and that was final. It was a fact that store cattle tended to congregate at its base. I have seen them in silhouette against the setting sun in winter approaching the stone in single file and it has seemed to me the remnant of some prehistoric ceremonial. Buddy ignored the important fact that our stone farmhouse was called Maen Hir because of this very stone.... Having him slouch about the place diminished the legendary status of the site we were privileged to occupy. He also showed a certain silent disdain at the fact that the island could no longer boast of any unbroken stone circles. Our cherished habitat was much inferior to that talismanic rectangle in north east Scotland between the rivers Urie and Don. He took no interest in the thesis that our island had been the headquarters of an exceptionally large and influential body of Druids. He had no time for Druids. "Just a bloodthirsty gang of media manipulators" was the verdict pronounced with unusual clarity, which made me think he had had occasion to use the phrase before. In fact from Rhiannon I learned later that Buddy had no time for Celts either. He disapproved of them. They had disturbed a Stone Age Arcadia that had flourished for three millennia: much longer Rhiannon repeated solemnly than Anni Domini. This was the gospel according to Buddy. In her bright eyes he saw the reflection of his own glory. Whenever, if ever, he was assailed with twinging doubts about the authenticity of his genius, there she would be, eager to reassure him.

On the third day as I lay in bed, I was visited with a sudden inspiration. Marian had been reduced to taking a sleeping tablet and she was snoring gently at my side. Muzio, I said to myself. Muzio Bianchieri! He would come to our rescue. He would enjoy an innocent imbroglio. He had always had a soft spot for Rhiannon. I could see them now walking down the *Via Torre di Lavello* and Rhiannon dancing back to inform her mother that she hadn't heard a single word of English all day. 'Ah' says Muzio, 'But you haven't heard a word of Etruscan either, have you?' That became their little joke. And the old Marchesa that everyone including her son Muzio said was so difficult, she let Rhiannon dress up in fantastic costumes and loaded her with antique bracelets and necklaces and took her out in the ancient limousine on trips to Orvieto and around the lake. For years the girl idealised the place. All we had to do was rearrange her career pattern and get her out there as fast as we decently could and as far away as possible from this would-be-genius. Thus, bring forward the year at the University of Rome and throw in a preliminary vacation at the *Villa Vignola* on the pretext ... no, no ... the bona fide purpose of getting some first hand work experience on Etruscology.

I sat up in bed. It was so simple, so imperative. I shook Marian. I had to tell her. She resented being woken up.

'What's the matter?' she said.

'I'll write to Muzio,' I said. 'That's all there is to it.'

Her response was less than enthusiastic.

'I'll never get to sleep again,' she said. 'He won't thank us for dumping our troubles on his doorstep.'

'These things can be arranged,' I said. 'I've seen it done in all sorts of ways before. Anyway courses of study should be flexible. Tailored as far as possible to the particular need of the student. I'm going to write him a letter this minute.'

She laid her hand on my arm.

'Sleep on it,' she said. 'He's married, remember.'

'What's that got to do with it?' I said.

'It's shaky,' Marian said.

'Shaky?'

I was puzzled. Why should she know more than I did? Muzio had always been my friend. Long before he got married.

'Prue is a very reasonable person,' I said.

'What's reason got to do with it?'

'She's English,' I said.

I felt the bed begin to shake. In spite of her drowsiness Marian was laughing.

'Since when has that been a guarantee of sanity?' she said. 'Her dogs and her singing are all she cares about.'

I sank back under the bedclothes. It had seemed such an easy option. This kind of humorous cynicism was more off-putting than outright opposition. It was distressing to be sinking into a predicament from which there would be no escape; all the same I would write to Muzio. I saw his hands make those harmonious gestures. I could hear his husky voice and that lilting inflexion. Between us there is no wall ... so we can say what we like, because we understand each other. That was the essence of friendship. But he never told me anything about his marriage being shaky. So what about all this business about speaking freely and the privilege of total frankness? The bond that is between us and the depth of honesty that should belong to unadulterated friendship. I was closer to Muzio than to any of my friends and colleagues in or out of college. But I didn't know his marriage was shaky and Marian did. Perhaps he didn't know? His wife must have murmured some feminine complaint when the women were alone in the music room or in the kitchen. All the same I am going to ask him for his help even if it is too much to ask.

V

My dream was a deranged chaos at the bottom of a swirling sea. People had become fish with broad flat heads and tapering tails,

19

small hungry mouths that opened and shut with fatuous persistence. They crawled about on top of each other driven by unassuagable appetites that slowly turned the opaque waters into trembling red. Because their teeth were so feeble they tore at each other with their claws. I woke up resentful at being consumed with such a meaningless nightmare. The house was so silent I heard the creak of a naked foot on the landing. In theory I had no objection to them sleeping together. Marian had put him in the guest room. Rhiannon was in her own room that was like a museum of her childhood. This was more than vestiges of my wife's puritan upbringing or bourgeois inhibitions. She was adamant that they should not couple under our roof. It was the same determination that made her stop photographing Buddy's mock resurrection from the passage grave. She withheld her blessing. What else could she do?   I wont have them behaving as though they were already married. I won't have it. This was the fourth night. How long did she imagine they would abstain in an age and at an age when most forms of sexual abstention were considered unhealthy inhibitions? Every paper and magazine they fingered boosted its circulation by waving the multicoloured flags of sexual liberation. Restraint was cowardice; hesitations despicable. The glamorous mores once the prerogative of artistic bohemians had become the inalienable right of the young and so on and so further until an explosion of ecstatic fulfilment would ravage the spawning grounds at the bottom of the ocean.

I caught her in a beam of light about to open the door to Buddy's bedroom. She was momentarily startled. As soon as she understood it was my hand that held the torch, she smiled and raised her finger to her lips, confident that with me she could do as she pleased. She held that smile until she felt certain that she had drawn me into their benign conspiracy. Then in she went.

I went downstairs. I made myself a cup of tea and shuffled to the study, tempted to practise some calligraphy. It was a soothing hobby. I could add to my commonplace book, my codex as I called it. Take out my battery of pens and coloured inks. There was a passage from *De Consolatione* I was keen to finish. But it was more important to finish my letter to Muzio. I was finding it extraordinarily difficult to write. What was the Latin for other people's business? And what made his marriage "shaky". And why hadn't I questioned Marian more closely? Were her reservations valid scruples, and should I be sharing them? When I wrote I only spoke for myself, but the matter concerned Rhiannon, who was as much hers as mine. If only I could have spoken to Muzio face to face. The letter became impossible to write. I would ring him up first thing in the morning. I made a list of points as a guide to have in front of me as we spoke on the telephone. I framed proposals in brief succinct sentences that he could answer with reasonable ease. It was late when I got back to bed, hours wasted it seemed to me with fruitless effort and worry.

The raised voices were already reverberating in my brain before I woke up. In my mind's eye, as I shrank under the bedclothes, I saw Marian's hand clutch at the curtains and tug them back and the naked pair blinking in the intrusive light. This was no way to proceed. I wanted to take Rhiannon aside and talk to her about Rome and the *Villa Vignola* and the *castello* and the lake and the enticing prospect of studying and working under Muzio's direction. I would appeal to the pride she took in her scholarly prowess. It was my duty to prepare the ground so that when the offer came from Muzio she wouldn't be able to refuse it. Conflict would follow confrontation and conflict inevitably breeds conflict.... To some irreparable point of destruction. When I arrived downstairs Marian was standing with her back to the Aga trembling with a form of venomous righteousness I had never seen before. My first thought was how to calm her. She was pointing a finger at me.

'Did you know that this man is married? Did you know he has a wife and two children?'

I shook my head. I didn't know, but it didn't surprise me. I knew of several colleagues and academic acquaintances who had deserted their families to cohabit with younger women. A commonplace of our Time, but this wasn't the time to say it. We usually agreed that men were more feeble and pliable and fallible creatures than women. But how did Marian know about Buddy? Searching through his things when we were out visiting cromlechs and meini hirion? That was very unlike her. To such lengths had she been driven by God knows what misery and desperation.

'What are you going to do about it?'

Suddenly I had been elevated into the traditional role of master of the house. The young people were watching us. They were witnessing my innate inclination to avoid confrontations and it looked just like cowardice. I had to make my position clear. I didn't think it mattered so much whether he was married or not. What mattered was Rhiannon's career. As I put it in one of the letters to Muzio I had tossed into the waste paper basket, sexual love was an abiding form of insanity and much of civilised behaviour consisted

21

of attempts to restrain the implacable fever and contain the infection. What was I expected to do, confronted in this irrational way? It had always been a point of honour with me to insist how much more brilliant Marian's early academic record had been than mine and how right I was to continue to defer to her superior critical judgement. In this ridiculous situation there was no way I could say as much without giving her further hurt. There was no time to compose considered formulations and in any case none of the parties concerned appeared in a condition to take them in: what I wanted to say, and would have to say in one way or another was that compromise might be an inferior form of reconciliation, but if civilisation was to continue it had to be resorted to sooner rather than later.

'I'm off anyway.'

Buddy had spoken He had already packed his rudimentary belongings. A sheaf of science fiction comics stuck out of the mouth of his haversack. Wherever he went they would go with him. And so would Rhiannon.

'You stay here! Do you hear me?'

Marian's voice was approaching a scream. I was appalled by the primitive nature of their clash. Rhiannon was shouting back at her.

'I'm not a child you know. Do you think I didn't know?'

I had to speak. I had to say something. Buddy was out of the kitchen and already trudging down the lane. I could see the sag of his shoulders through the window. He would not allow emotional upheavals to impinge on his elevated level of consciousness. He had his genius to roll in front of him like a dung beetle.

'Why don't we sit down,' I said. 'Let's sit down and talk calmly about this.'

My effort was useless. Marian's face had begun to crumble. Still holding on to the chrome rail of the Aga she sank in a sobbing heap to the floor. Rhiannon was in a hurry to leave. She barely had time to pity her mother.

'It's no use, Mam. I've told you. If he goes, I go. That's all there is to it.'

vi

There she was on the kitchen floor, moaning. The place was never untidy, but that sound reduced it to quivering disorder. She should be back in bed. I should re-lay the table, put the porridge back in the microwave and see the whole ritual of breakfast re-initiated. They couldn't have gone far. All I had to do was bring them back. Apologise if need be. Certainly construct a sequence of explanations. One possible line of reasoning would be the stubborn nature of our innate puritan reactions, or at least Marian's and my supine subservience to them. It was her Sunday School background, I could say that lightly, that had brought about this untoward encounter. I shouldn't lay all the blame on her though. The sound of her distress un-nerved me. I would put more emphasis on misunderstanding and the biological source of such disconcerting clashes of affections. This was no time, I would say, to make futile reproaches. All the arguments forming in my head were scattered by the thin moan of an animal in a trap. Action was called for. The longer I lingered, the wider the breach would become. I could not bear to contemplate Marian's condition should all contact be lost.

I found them on the far side of the main road. They had taken up the position of experienced hitch-hikers. Hitch-hiking was something we had always advised Rhiannon to avoid at all costs. She was never to venture anywhere without more than enough money to cover her fare. I left the car in our lane and crossed the road to talk to them. I didn't run or shout. I imagined there was a conciliatory smile on my face. I kept my right hand in my trouser pocket to prevent myself from giving a cheerful wave. It would have been out of key to pretend that nothing had happened however much I wished that to be the case. When he saw me approach, Buddy turned, stretched himself and climbed to the top of a limestone stile. Rhiannon was peeling an orange. Buddy reached out into the hay field and pulled up a stem of long grass to examine it in greater detail. I had no choice. It was up to me to speak first.

'I don't know how these things happen,' I said. 'I honestly don't. The last thing we want is for you to leave us. The very last thing. It was a mistake this morning. A complete mistake. I'm sorry. We're both sorry.'

That was my apology. I would repeat it if necessary. Vary it even. But I would prefer it if they said something. Buddy manipulated the stem of grass so that it bent without breaking. Rhiannon reached up and popped a section of orange in his mouth. I thought I heard him mumble with his mouth full.

'I know when I'm not wanted.'

That is what I thought I heard. It was a fact: or had been. It was

23

possible after all that we had treated him badly. He had this way of inviting antipathy. All the same we had behaved as correctly as we knew how: at least until Marian's early morning invasion of their bedroom intimacy. He was an individual that took a lot of getting used to. Having him in your home, Marian whispered quite early on, was like having to put up with grit in your shoe. Well this was the moment to take the shoe off and let the air reach between the toes.

'I've written to Muzio,' I said

I was smiling fondly at my daughter. It was true only in the sense that I had composed several letters to him without posting them. In this critical situation I had to improvise. Yet another plan was burgeoning in my mind. I was so taken with it I could not easily distinguish between desperation and inspiration and I was so intent on putting together an acceptable formulation I did not at first take in her question.

'Who's Muzio?'

The name meant nothing to her. That is what she was saying. A spurt of anger flared inside me. How dare she ask and how had this creature contrived to take such absolute control of my child as to wipe out at a stroke some of the fondest memories of her childhood? Perched on that stone stile, he had never looked more repulsive. A grimacing gargoyle would have been less disturbing. It was monstrous and yet it was a state of affairs I had to accept. To think that they were looking at me with equal suspicion and hostility as I struggled with the presentation of a scheme I had devised entirely for their benefit.

'I think it's a splendid idea,' I said. 'I'll supply the cash and so on. I don't know whether Buddy would want to go as well. That's up to you of course. But the thing is, you could have all the time in the world to see how you felt. Feel your way around the problem so to speak and do some Etruscology with Muzio at the same time. I'm sure Buddy would be fascinated by the proto-Villanovan stuff. Nothing in the stone-circle line I'm afraid. It's all more microlithic than Neolithic: but equally interesting when you come to look at it. Then you could take up your year at the University of Rome and come back to Cambridge later. It's simply a matter of re-tailoring the course as they say, to fit the circumstance.... I've written to Muzio about it. He'll see to things at that end without any fuss or bother. It couldn't be easier, could it?'

She was gazing at me pityingly and shaking her head.

'You don't understand anything, do you?' she said.

24

This was my daughter. Our only daughter. In an earlier age we would have claimed she was possessed with an alien spirit or a demon. I couldn't bring myself to say 'evil'.

'You don't understand, Tada, because you both live in a closed contained little world.'

Those were her fingers grubby with orange peel that were confining her own parents into a suffocatingly small space. The nest was being transformed into a cage. Our own child!

'You live in a farmhouse and you never have muck on your boots.'

Buddy was smiling secretly into his beard as he listened to his ventriloquist doll. My words had difficulty in emerging from my throat.

'You know what we stand for,' I said. 'Your mother and I.'

'Yes, but you've turned it into a Refuge though, haven't you.'

I don't know why she had to sound so triumphant. Did I have to recite to her all over again how much her mother and I had been made to suffer in the course of our protests on behalf of the language: fines and imprisonments and discrimination. Second class citizens in our own country and all that?

'I mean how much did you really gain? And what have you done in the end except turn the language into a vested interest?'

A complete travesty. A total reversal of the truth. Black propaganda issuing from the innocent lips of our cherished only daughter. And she was smiling at me as if she expected me to share her delight in the flash of insight that had revealed to her bright eyes her parents' feet of clay. Where could I begin to demolish her argument and tear up a false agenda that would never lead us anywhere. Had I no choice except to stand on the edge of the road and listen to second-hand ill-informed nit-picking above the sound of the traffic delivered from the mouth of my own daughter as she prepared to forego the blessing of a privileged education in order to throw in her lot with this self-regarding, self-pitying ignorant egomaniac?. It was more than I could bear and yet I had to bear it. My skin was on fire. I had to bear it. To abandon love was the ultimate mutilation. Without it, what would there be left to live for? I had to allow her to abuse me as much as she chose.

'Think of St. Brendan, Tada,' she was saying. 'And all the *peregrini*.'

Another change of tack to make me short of breath in trying to keep up with her. But this didn't sound like him. Didn't he disapprove of Celts? He certainly wasn't listening any more. He was drifting down the road and taking more notice of the passing traffic. I meant little or nothing to him, even as Rhiannon's father.

'Where will you go?'

I moved closer to plead with her. At least she could take some pity on me.

'How will you manage?'

'Drift with the wind and the tide,' she said. 'You remember.'

She had a voice of her own and a mind of her own and yet she was ready to follow him anywhere.

'What are you talking about?'

I was the petulant child and she was smiling as she made her first essay at parental patience.

'I'm quoting you, for heaven's sake,' she said. 'Don't you remember? Megalith tombs and Celtic chapels. Those stone builders and the Saints with just three thousand years between their identical tracks. That sort of thing.'

Suddenly she kissed my cheek.

'Don't worry,' she said. 'I'll keep in touch.'

She turned to call out at the bearded genius.

'Buddy Thwaite! You wait for me. You hear me?'

He turned to look at us and raised a limp hand. Rhiannon shook my sleeve.

'Tada. Listen. There's nothing more important than being free. You know that as well as I do.'

I stood there watching until they were out of sight.

vii

I sat at the steering wheel of the stationary car struggling to bring a turmoil of thoughts and feelings under control. It seemed a futile process. There was no technique I knew of that could bring the menacing mists of the immediate future into any semblance of a settled text susceptible to analysis or prolonged study. The present was more than I could cope with, like the hedges on either side of our lane that badly needed cutting. Rhiannon may have had a point. We should pay closer attention to the practical necessities of country living and spend less time on vacuous academic speculation. I should have invited Buddy to join me in tackling the hedges: except that he appeared to regard all forms of physical labour as obsolete. He could sit around long enough for lichen to grow on

26

his trousers. I might have pointed out to him that the reward of hard work on the land was an exultant appetite. Not much point. The creature had more than enough appetites already. When they came to drift in the wind and tide without food or water, he would just turn and eat her.

Or would she eat him? Not so much a notion as a spasm of comfort. She was the one who mentioned drifting with the wind and the tide. Whatever his interest in megaliths, he would never have perceived any connection between the paths of the builders and the Celtic saints. There was a residue of sense in that girl. There had to be. But how could it prevail against a tidal surge of folly? I could sit in front of the steering wheel groping beyond words for a metaphysics of meaning that would fit the case. And never find it. Speculation was more poisonous that inertia. The longer I slumped in front of the steering wheel the more vulnerable I would become. Already the overgrowth in the hedges were threatening to link up with the ferment inside my head. The machine and I would be discovered a century hence buried under brambles. Activity was the only avenue left open. What needed to be done was to attend to Marian and somehow bring her distress under control so that she could bring some order into mine.

I took her a cup of tea. Her head was tightly shrouded in the bedsheet. As I prised it off I fingered the damp patches left by her tears. She was still in shock. The tea would revive her and I had to reassure her.

'I thought it was a good sign,' I said. 'Helpful in a way. Megalith builders and Celtic saints.'

'What are you talking about?'

She screwed up her eyes against the pain of the light. This was my girl too.

There were grey streaks in Marian's hair and lines on her face of course, but the eyes and the voice hadn't changed. She was the same person. Capable of being as youthful and serene as her photograph in profile.

'What saints?'

'At the last minute,' I said. 'Between the stirrup and the dust so to speak ... she wanted to draw attention to the abiding bond between us. It hadn't been broken. It was being stretched, that's all.'

'What did she say?'

Marian's voice was husky with her own kind of despairing scepticism. She wanted the evidence set out before her so that she could examine it with her own practised forensic calm.

'That's what she was saying in effect. " Don't worry, I'll keep in touch."

'Were those her actual words? Were they?'

'Yes. They were.'

Marian gave a massive sigh. Her hands trembled and the brown liquid churned into a small storm in the tea mug. I urged her to drink it. I longed to conjure a smile on her pale profile.

'He'll poison her mind against me,' she said. 'I've lost her for ever.'

'Nonsense,' I said. 'And you know it. And I'll tell you something else.'

It was some kind of comfort to be assertive. I had sound practical points for her to consider calmly. It was important not to be helpless. We had this house, these fields, this view of the bay and the headland across the water. We had to draw strength from these things.

'It would be a sensible move to approach his parents. That's what I think. We might not find much in common with them of course, but at least there would be a community of interest.'

'That would be difficult,' Marian said.

I must have looked too pleased with my own agenda, like a politician. There was undisguised sarcasm in her voice.

'His father was in advertising. He died from over-eating. The senior partner swallowed what was left of his portion, leaving Master Thwaite's mother almost penniless. However she was personable, well preserved and resourceful.'

It was at least encouraging to hear my Marian recovering so much of her accustomed lucidity and discernment.

'She rescued herself by marrying a prosperous stamp-dealer in Chislehurst in the county of Kent. He conducts his business from a large house in its own grounds and he won't allow his wife's impossible offspring anywhere near the premises.'

At least they had been talking. I assumed Marian hadn't passed the information on because she had been confident it would be irrelevant once she had brought Rhiannon around to our point of view. The girl had to be persuaded that Master Buddy was just another of the army of malcontents and misfits slouching out of the eccentric quagmire of suburban sprawl, looking for some romantic spot to be reborn. And now he had drawn our daughter into his unsufferable orbit. Where the hell would he take her? I shifted to look out of the window. The sea and the sky were blue and should have been consoling and pleasant. Where would they go? It was important not to infect Marian with my irrational agitation.

'Anyway she said we shouldn't worry. She said she'd keep in touch.'

It was an order. An instruction and a piece of monumental thoughtlessness. We had always taught her to be considerate and thoughtful.

'I suppose I should get up.'

Marian held out the cup. I took it and she swung her long legs over the side of the bed. She sat with her hands under her thighs and her head lowered as she summoned up the strength to continue.

'She'll keep in touch anyway,' I said.

'How?'

'Write. Telephone. One or the other. Or both.'

'Or neither.'

Her shoulders had slumped. She had to be consoled, comforted. The world could wait. I pulled her nightdress over her head. She did not resist. She was limp, helpless. I pressed her gently until she lay naked on our bed. Her body was as perfect as it had ever been. Only the expression on her face was tired and vulnerable. I should comfort her and thereby comfort myself. We were together. Our bodies could be in contact and bring understanding and comfort while our minds were too exhausted to drag up any more conjecture, any more surmise. We had each other. While we made love there should be nothing more we could want.

A car horn hooted in the yard outside. Marian froze under me. Instantly she pushed me roughly aside. With surprising speed she moved to the bathroom.

'Whoever it is,' she said. 'Don't you dare bring them into the house.'

There was more impatient hooting, forcing me to get up when all I wanted was to lie on our bed.

From our bedroom window I recognized the battered shooting-brake in the yard. Sockburn had already turned the car around in case I was not readily available with my usual sympathetic attention. I could see his fingers drumming on the steering wheel. He gave a sour smile as he saw me approach from the back door.

'You're a lucky sod, Morgan,' he said.

We were friends and colleagues and this entitled him to address me with mild forms of abuse. I repressed any flicker of resentment by recalling his wife had had both her breasts removed and that he had twice been denied a Readership. I had only to glance at his rugged face to envisage the trail of misfortune that had dogged the Sockburn name since his father was drowned off Murmansk in 1943, and his uncle Cuthbert had died of pneumoconiosis when the young Daniel Sockburn was sitting his finals in 1962. The result was a loquacious Northumbrian whose despondent view of the world was given an interesting edge by a cultivated capacity for unrestrained critical comment.

'I look at this place and it seems bloody idyllic,' he said. 'I said to Phyllis before I set out, "I'm off to Maenhir where that lucky bugger Morgan sits in the middle of the nearest thing to a bloody Welsh Arcadia." And d'you know what she said? You've got to admire her guts – "Bring back a load of Maenhir rocks and we'll stick 'em in the garden. See if they'll bring us some luck." Bloody great, she is.'

He stared at me to evoke an enthusiastic response. Phyllis was brave. I had to avoid inviting him into the kitchen for a cup of coffee. I behaved as though I had set aside a selection of rocks for him and they were waiting impatiently to be collected. I made too much of the process of guiding him to the heap beyond our pig-sties where the stone troughs held rose bushes instead of pig swill. It was a sanitised Arcadia. On the low roof Rhiannon in her early teens had cemented a cheap bust of Beethoven who was then her hero. Buddy had ignored it and I had begged her not to knock it down. The soft stone had begun to weather but you could still see the token frown of genius on the master's brow. Kitsch as well as roses. Sockburn was picking out the shapeliest rocks and ferrying them with both hands to the tail board of his vehicle. The springs sank under the weight. I joined in to help him.

'You can have as many as you like,' I said. 'But you mustn't bust your shock absorbers.'

'This Italian chum of yours,' Sockburn said.

He paused for breath and leaned against the pig-sty wall. He was bent on having a chat. I wasn't going to get rid of him so easily. I had no idea how long it would take Marian to recover sufficiently to be able to face everyday encounters. He would be bound to ask after Rhiannon. He always did when he saw Marian. And remark on some aspect or other of their striking resemblance. "I can see it. Don't you see it, Morgan?" We were always prepared to put up with his prolonged pantomime out of sympathy for his catalogue of misfortunes.

'D'you think you could get him to give a couple of talks at the

Summer School? What d'you think?'

He could see my face brighten. My letter would be an invitation, not a cry for help. Once Muzio was here I could talk to him for hours at a time. Life always provided tides of opportunity: the trick was to seize the chance when it came.

'I could write him if you like,' I said.

Sockburn screwed up his eyes as he stared at me. I solemnly suppressed any sign that I had spent so many hours of the night composing and destroying one letter after the other to this same 'Italian chum.'

'He's a Marchese or something-or-other, isn't he? That'll go down well. There are more snobs to the square inch in Academia than anywhere else in this Vale of Tears. And I'll tell you something else. The storm cones are up, comrade. If we don't make a success of it we're out on our ear. And even if we do, we may still be in for exceptionally early retirement.'

He had vast quantities of resentment to unload, but I couldn't ask him in. Blunt as he was, he would never invite himself. It was too simplistic to categorise him as the kind of chap who blurted out his thoughts more or less as they occurred to him.

He was not encumbered with wavering lengths of Cymric antennae that sought out what other people desired to know before speaking: but he had his own variety of Anglo-Saxon awareness. Sockburn was staunch. He picked up rocks with a grateful grunt and called a spade a spade.

'It's going to be a bloody reign of terror I can tell you,' he said. 'This new chap is a Philistine of horrendous proportions. It will be good-bye Philosophy, goodbye Classics and Medieval Latin and welcome welcome to the twin chairs of Tourism and Business Studies.'

'You must be joking,' I said.

I looked concerned. I was concerned. Even in the midst of domestic misery one should never lose sight of larger issues. If I asked him in, he would talk about college politics for the rest of the morning.

'*Dies Irae*,' he said. 'It's the kind of world we are living in, comrade. I'll tell you this: we've got to counter-attack. On all fronts. Otherwise we're done for.'

I demonstrated physically that I could not agree more.

'Look Daniel,' I said. 'I've got to fly. You take your time. And help yourself.'

He was looking at me with a disconcerting quality of scepticism on his face. He knew I rarely "flew" anywhere on a Saturday morning. I improvised.

'A bit of a family crisis. Over on the mainland.'

He waited for me to amplify.

'You know what it's like,' I said. 'Cousin this and cousin that. Marian's relatives by the way. Not mine.'

'I'll trundle this lot home, anyway.'

I stood back to take a critical look at the size of the load.

'That lane of yours,' he said. 'It's got a crest down the middle like the backbone of a dinosaur.'

I laughed with a surplus of appreciation. This was the well-known Sockburn frankness.

'Not to mention axle-breaking potholes. Listen. You get him. It could make a difference. This new chap's spouse is a howling snob from all I hear and she wears the trousers. They say she won't rest until her hubby gets his 'K' and she's Lady Kingsley Cross-eye Jenkins.'

'Sockburn the subtle,' I said. 'How devious can you get?'

He grinned at me.

'Are you sure your chum isn't a Principe? That would look really good. You get him Morgan. Without fail.

'Well, I'll do my best,' I said.

TWO

i

I had forgotten, or I had chosen to forget, Prue Bianchieri's capacity for bringing out the worst in Marian. The word "shaky" should have alerted me. She could whisper something into my wife's ear and transform her into a person I didn't really know. "Shaky" indeed. Who was this Yorkshire lass as she liked to call herself, to mutter her variants on the theme of what women had to put up with? Just by marrying my friend Muzio, Prue Cooke from Pudsey had snatched the glittering prize of estate and title. Who was she to complain? And who was she to shove her elbow in my back?

'Come on,' she says – does the Yorkshire Marchesa. '*Forza*, Dr. Morgan! It's only a piece of wire.'

That may well be so, but the twisted wire was also a pathetic symbol of the vestige of sanctity that belongs to this deserted chapel. Marian hasn't moved out of the back of the car. She seems to be enjoying my dilemma. My scruples are entirely on her behalf. This was her great-grandfather's chapel. That is to say he supervised and paid for its renovation and extension in 1881. Briefly, and not too successfully it has to be added, her grandfather was minister here: so this building had been a source of family concern, and muted pride, for well over a century. And now it was decaying with holes in the windows and slates missing from the roof.

'Look. If the pigeons fly in and out as they please, why can't we?'

Prue has this nerve-wracking English disposition to consider brutal frankness a demonstration of pristine virtue. She was standing too close to me – breathing down my neck in fact. Her person was designed for public appearance even when there was no one looking: solid and engaging without being particularly beautiful. Equally eligible for politics, the concert stage , or a shop window. The sculptured coiffure hovering behind me was maintained by concentrated daily ministration and a weekly visit to the hairdresser. She saw herself as elegance personified and Muzio seemed to regard her with the satisfaction of a gardener contemplating an herbaceous border kept in perfect condition.

I suppose I had to be grateful to see Marian nodding and smiling and encouraging us to break in. I had to thank Prue for that and marvel again at the way the two got on. What did they have in common, except this inclination to accept their respective husbands as unfailing sources of amusement? It wouldn't be any use me drawing Prue Bianchieri's attention to the state of this building symbolising a decay of faith. But Marian could say something apposite. How long could we sustain a meaningful identity without the conviction of our forefathers: that sort of thing. All she did was raise a thumb and forefinger and make a flicking gesture that caused Prue to nudge me hard in the back so that they could both giggle at the look of indignation passing over my face. Then I had to smile. Prue after all was the proverbial breath of fresh air able to dispel any cloud of mid-life melancholy threatening to settle about my Marian's pretty head. Since they had been staying with us, I even heard Marian responding to Prue's pleasantries with something like that girlish giggle I thought she had lost. This was a blessing. Having them with us at such a difficult time had to be a boon.

Muzio was moving about some distance away, apparently making an archaeological assessment of the isolated building in its relation to the undulations of the green landscape. I was eager to discuss the whole business with him. After all I had, so to speak, an inside knowledge of the decline and fall of Welsh nonconformity: of the strength and the weakness of a way of life that had in some senses been the high-water mark of community strength and civilisation in this corner of the globe. Muzio would provide a perspective: a more detached view. The first time I took him to see the interior of a nonconformist chapel he looked puzzled and even amazed. 'Is this a shrine?' he asked me in a subdued voice. 'I don't see any graven images.' And when I laughed, he barely smiled and looked around him muttering 'strange ... strange.'

'Come on,' Prue said impatiently. 'Are you going to do it or shall I?'

I untwisted the wire and put my shoulder to a half-door that was sagging on its hinges. The floor of the lobby was thick with dust and withered leaves. On a green-baize notice-board rusty drawing pins held up faded notices of meetings long ago. They read like dates and inscriptions on old tombstones.

'The hall of song becomes the haunt of the owl....'

I murmured the quotation. Prue didn't seem to hear me. I tried again as she pushed open a side-door. The interior echoed with the flapping of the wings of a startled pigeon as it flew about before escaping through a hole at the top of a tall window. I quoted more confidently.

'Bare ruined choirs where late the sweet birds sang...'

'Shat you mean,' Prue said.

She wrinkled her short nose with distaste as she indicated the bird droppings drying on the walls and on the pitchpine pews. A motto in blue and gold had been painted in an arch above the smudged plush of the pulpit: *Llawenychais pan ddywedent wrthyf. Awn i dy yr Arglwydd.*

'What the hell does that mean?' Prue said.

It was also her habit to tease us about our language and refer to it as outlandish and unpronounceable. It surprised me that Marian didn't seem to mind. She seemed to accept Prue's insensitivity as an uncovenanted blessing. At the end of the pews there were raised enamelled numerals. I polished the nearest with the palm of my hand as I translated the line from the *Psalms*.

'I was glad when they said unto me. Let us go into the house of the Lord.'

'Well there you are! What did I tell you?'

Muzio came in followed by Marian. They both looked around like sightseers equally stirred but for different reasons. I hoped Muzio saw a gaunt temple built out of local stone and not without a simple dignity. Marian moved down the right aisle towards the organ that was neatly housed in the centre of the front pew. It faced the railed dais where the elders used to sit and peer up at the elaborately carved pulpit that soared above them.

'I played this organ once,' Marian said. 'When I was a little girl. I was so small I couldn't see my grandfather in the pulpit.'

'Did you, love,' Prue said. 'Did you really?'

Muzio took a seat ignoring the dust covering the pew. He stared at his surroundings with concentrated interest and benevolence. His head was tilted to one side and he ran his fingers through his thinning hair. My heart warmed towards the solitary figure among the empty pews. In this light he, too, looked a faded remnant of his former self. I could have rushed to embrace him and reassure him that he hadn't changed a bit. For a moment an impulsive falsehood would become the quintessence of friendship.

'What will it be,' Prue said. 'Singing or preaching?'

She climbed up the pulpit steps more than ready to face an audience. She clapped her hands to test the acoustic and smiled and nodded to show she was pleased with it. Marian sat at the organ. She played a sequence of scales to see which keys were still functioning. We all raised our voices as we became more accustomed to the place. The noise we made no longer seemed intrusive or inappropriate. Prue filled her chest with air, and began a trial run of an aria from an opera I was unfamiliar with. She had no inhibitions about displaying the power of her lungs. Muzio was smiling at her, full of encouragement. Her vulgarity somehow nourished his anaemic refinement.

'*Chi sa, chi sa...* Try that my dear. In this acoustic it would sound good.'

'*Chi sa,*' Prue was singing. 'Who knows, who knows, what is best for me... Love, language of my heart / Guide thou my steps / Dispel these bitter misgivings / That trouble my heart...'

We heard feet stamping in the lobby and an ill-tempered voice shouting in Welsh.

'What the devil is going on in here?'

We turned around like guilty children. The quiet re-occupied the place, reducing us to delinquent intruders. An uncouth native had kicked open a side-door. From force of habit he snatched off his greasy cap. His frizzled red hair stood up as he stared at us. He broke into English at the sight of such a scattering of strangers.

'Don't you know that this is private property? Trespassing. That is what you are doing. Trespassing!'

He was dissatisfied with our lack of response and with his own vehemence.

'Cheeky devils!'

It was the best he could come up with in English. It was my responsibility, I felt, to soothe his anger. I moved towards him with a hand limply extended and spoke to him in Welsh.

'*Mae'n ddrwg gen i,*' I said. 'I'm very sorry. We came in to pay our respects, you could say. I had no idea it was private property.'

'You are Welsh then?'

The farmer smelt of cattle. He was staring suspiciously at Prue who showed no inclination to descend from the pulpit.

'More or less,' I said.

I glanced towards Prue and ventured a mild joke.

'She's English,' I said. 'You must excuse her.'

The farmer wasn't amused.

'Breaking in,' he said. 'Breaking the Law. That's what it amounts to. I don't see why I should put up with it.'

His stubbled chin jutted out.

'You can clear out,' he said. 'The lot of you.'

My companions showed no sign of moving. Muzio and Marian

36

were turning in their pews with expressions of equal innocence on their faces. The farmer was beginning to tremble with fury. He took particular exception to Prue's apparent defiance.

'Get that bitch down from there,' he said. 'Or I'll drag her down.'

His anger increased as if to make up for his diminutive size. His movements were arthritic and he carried a heavy stick which he now pointed threateningly at Prue. I spoke to her quietly in Italian.

'You'd better come down,' I said. 'Or he'll do himself an injury.'

Then I turned quickly to the farmer to dispel any antagonisms unfamiliar sounds might generate.

'Let me explain,' I said. 'And excuse. That's my wife sitting at the organ. She played it once when she was a girl. Her grandfather was the minister here for a short while.'

I made myself sound more enthusiastic.

'And her great-grandfather actually restored the place. There's a date above the door. 1881. So we felt we had to come in and pay our respects, so to speak.'

The farmer's suspicions subsided into smouldering discontent.

'I don't know anything about that,' he said.

He stirred himself to reassert his authority.

'It belongs to me now, anyway,' he said. 'Lock, stock, and barrel.'

I made an effort not to look appalled or even disturbed. This sort of thing was happening all over the country: and all over the country middle-class intellectuals with a feeling for tradition or whatever, were shaking their heads and telling each other how little they could do about it. I tried to be positive and polite.

'What do you intend to do with it, may I ask?'

The little farmer relaxed sufficiently to take hold of the back of a pew with one hand and lean more heavily on his stick with the other. He looked at me with a new interest. Did he see me as a possible buyer?

'I've had some good offers,' he said. 'There was a man from Liverpool who wanted to start something he called a Country Bingo. I wouldn't have that. I could see he didn't have the capital to develop it properly. Not to satisfy the Planning anyway. Do you know Dr. Banerjee?'

I shook my head.

'Very clever man, they tell me. He would like to turn it into a convalescent home. Old people and so on. Might end up in here myself.'

He grinned slyly and indicated the weakness in his hip.

'I'll have to do something, that's for sure. What with vandals and visitors. I don't know which are the worst.'

I looked as sympathetic as I could. The civilised thing would be to introduce him to Muzio and Prue and Marian. These were our friends from Italy who were eager to learn about our culture and our history. Their interest was probably much greater than his.

He followed us out and made a great play of retwisting the thick wire on the doors. For such a small man he had large hands. Before Marian took her seat in the car he called out to her over his shoulder.

'I'll tell you something.... You're not the only one.'

Marian put her hand against her breast to confirm that he was addressing her.

'Yes. You. This business about your great-grandfather restoring this place and so on. It's a funny thing. There was a girl here not so long ago saying exactly the same thing.'

Marian and I were instantly filled with the same misgiving. We moved closer to each other.

'Five or six of them,' the farmer said. 'Hippies I suppose you call them. A dirty lot I can tell you. They spent the night here, the cheeky devils. Shameless they were. When I set the dogs on them that's exactly what she said.'

'What?' Marian said. 'What did she say?'

'My great-grandfather something or other built this place. That sort of thing. Just like you did.'

'Rhiannon.'

Marian was staring at me. I held her hand. She had begun to tremble.

'This great-grandfather business. It's the same with livestock. If you go far back enough, we're all related, aren't we?'

He was pleased with the way his words were disturbing Marian. He leaned on his stick and stared at her as though he were waiting for her to collapse sobbing in my arms. This was enough to stiffen Marian. She would never accord him that much satisfaction. The farmer was grinning and his gums glistened with saliva.

'Quite like you she was,' he said. 'Come to think of it. Underneath the dirt you might say.'

'Come.'

Marian tugged my arm. Muzio and Prue hastened into the car leaving the doors open.

'Come,' Marian said. 'We've got to go. There's so much to do.'

Why should we take the blame? An insolent daughter puts father and mother to shame and will be disowned by both ... which was nonsense. It was my grandfather's husky voice I heard. In his old age he had taken to reading the *Apocrypha* with a magnifying glass. He liked me to listen to him. He wore a yellow night-cap on the side of his head and exuded contented pessimism. Things had been far better in his youth and would never ever be as good again. A man who loves his son will beat him frequently so that in after years the son may be his comfort... Pamper your child and he will give you a fright ... do not share his laughter if you do not wish to share his sorrow and to end by grinding your teeth.

The old man loved the sound of his own voice and the expression of puzzled disapproval on my face gave him endless amusement.

What constitutes insolence? The old man never had trouble with defining words. I seem to have spent my life pegging out definitions. What did he call it? Paying a tithe of mint and anise and cumin and omitting the weightier matters of the law, judgement, mercy, and faith... And I would say to myself: what does all that lot mean? Does insolence mean impudent? She was never impudent. A model child. Polite. Thoughtful. Attentive. Or shameless? Depends what you mean by shame. Never until now. So why should we disown her? How could we, as civilised, responsible, loving parents? Because she had chosen to disown us. Debating point and patently untrue. "Don't worry I'll keep in touch." Nothing could have been more thoughtful under the circumstances. So why are we distraught? A headstrong daughter keepeth her father awake and maketh him a laughing stock among his colleagues... Was that the old man again? Or did I make it up. Why should we lie in bed like effigies on a tomb, being bruised by the night and the darkness?

It had been a day of concentrated activity, sightseeing pursued with robotic intensity as we cared for our guests and they responded with circumspect concern for our stressed condition. From the ramparts of a thirteenth century ruin I watched Marian and Prue Bianchieri walking arm in arm on the shore and I felt an unexpected twinge of resentment. At such a distance from me, Marian looked more relaxed. It was likely that she took greater comfort from Prue's robust optimism than my painstaking rationalisations. Muzio was trying to raise my spirits with a detailed account of his experiences as an external examiner at Palermo. He knew how intrigued I was by the magic of the island and the people who live on it pierced by the sunlight and the dangerous sweetness of their existence. I spoilt his story by my hasty interruption of his account of a corrupt examination system. We ended up with an arid argument about how to overhaul tired systems of custom and practice in higher education.

I wanted to embrace Marian and to comfort her. And find comfort for myself. Why else were we lying in the same bed? I would hold her in my arms and worship her with my body if she would allow it. Happy the husband of a really good wife: the number of his days will be doubled... That was the old man again. Old age was his refuge. He was immune to this bitter adversity of the spirit and his flesh was incapable of sexual desire. Marian was the only object of tenderness left to me: the thought of the beauty of her naked body was more precious than ever. I brought my lips close to her eyelids determined to be as gentle as I could so that our physical embrace would ease the fears and anxieties that paralysed her. As soon as my lips brushed hers she began to speak. Her voice was so loud and penetrating, I was taken aback.

'Do you think it's some sort of revenge?'

Was this the conclusion she and Prue Bianchieri had arrived at as they walked arm in arm along the shore?

'Does she do it to punish us?'

'Good God, no!'

Too fierce a denial. I searched for her hand to take in mine. She seemed unwilling to give it. She would not be diverted from her line of reasoning.

'Why should she have gone there, to the old chapel, of all places? Why except to bring our name into disrepute? My name anyway.'

My wife had the strength to confront catastrophe with an unblinking stare while my inclination was to bury my head under the pillow if not in the sand. We should try and react more positively. That means our responses should complement and not conflict.

'It's because we are so stuffy and respectable,' Marian said.

'Are we? Who says so?'

Who else but the Marchesa Bianchieri. What were we supposed to do? Wear paper hats and blow toy trumpets? We could of course – the depth of my sarcasm gave me a fleeting solace – adopt the carefree raffishness of a would-be opera singer rescued from the doldrums of an unpromising career by the sympathetic charity of a congenitally benevolent if psychologically insecure Italian aristocrat?

'We have to face it,' she was saying. 'The truth is, we imposed a strait-jacket of belief and behaviour on her from the beginning.'

I could quote my grandfather. I could hear that hoarse voice teasing me. Those who fear the Lord do not disdain his words and those who love him find satisfaction in his Law. 'What Law?' I used to say and then he would lift that black *Apocrypha* and shake it as though he were Moses on Mount Sinai showing off the Tablets.

'Look,' I wanted to say to Marian. 'We went over all this before.'

It began when she was learning to talk. There was no choice for us, we were agreed, except the language of our forefathers. Anything else would have been a betrayal of everything we believed we stood for, including that memorable protest on the wet Post Office floor. And the innocent rituals that went with it. The whole box of tricks, we said, until someone came up with something better: this was our revolutionary conservatism.

'Will the children now come forward to say their verses...'

The society we belonged to. That benevolent tremolo in the old deacon's voice. His gnarled hand clutching the polished rail with democratic zeal, he half turns to address the congregation with that sheepish smile. A shy man doing his duty. I raise my knees so that our little one may pass and as she hesitates in the raked aisle I give her a gentle push in the back. She trots down the aisle in the direction of the deacon's pew just as her mother did at that same age and every silver cord unbroken.

The visiting minister picks her up and places his plate of a face next to hers as if they were about to have a photograph taken.

'Now then, little one, tell me your name. I should know your name, should I not? Aren't you very like someone I used to know?'

He smiles across the pews and Marian blushes as she is obliged to smile back. Democratic intimacies. It had its drawbacks but to the best of our knowledge we both agreed, no one had devised anything better. She was four and a half and didn't look frightened. There were other children in a row behind her waiting their turn. She was the smallest and he had lifted her first.

'Suffer little children to come unto me and forbid them not: for such is the Kingdom of Heaven.'

What was wrong with that? A familiar ritual much appreciated

41

by older members of the congregation: a small girl, pretty as a picture in her green coat and green bonnet, piping out her verse. Native customs. Welsh petit bourgeois elitism. Exploitation. To what hair-splitting cant we submit ourselves, when we wallow in excessive critical analysis. Perhaps I could offer that to Marian as some basis for comfort. She was droning on in the darkness as though conducting a seminar with herself.

'This competitive mode, it seems endemic in our culture. Eisteddfodic structures. They exist as a substitute for a more basic sense of security.'

She loved it. Competing. Or at least she did when she was younger. Singing. Reciting. Choirs particularly. She loved being in the school choir.

'We are so unaware of it that we accept it as a fact of life.'

'Aware of what?'

I tried not to sound impatient.

'The competitive mode. What else? It doesn't have to be, does it? Is that what she is trying to tell us? Not a nation but a sect of undisciplined achievers.'

Why would she need to tell us something we knew so well already? We had to survive inside moribund life-modes. We knew that. I overheard my wife's thinking as if I were reading the darkness.

'First, second and third and ribbons to match. And scholarships. Always scholarships. The bigger the better. If she hadn't gone to Cambridge all this would never have happened.'

'Cambridge, I hear.'

The hue of envy suffuses Hannah Mary's round face as her small lips mutter her congratulations. Like a rival mother-hen her sleeves ruffle in the breeze as she attaches herself to Marian on the school lawn. That at least was not my responsibility. They were in the same form long before I appeared on the scene. Hannah Mary claimed the privilege of being Marian's oldest friend and took precedence whenever the occasion offered, usually with a glint of resentment in her eye even as she smiled. She was always overweight and always reproached Marian for being too thin. She never caught up with Marian's academic achievements. And now their daughters were re-enacting the same unsatisfying scenario. Her Megan was consistently overweight and could never catch up with Rhiannon's results however hard she tried.

'Oh, she's done so well, your Rhiannon. I must congratulate

you.'

I was reduced to walking behind them – an attendant lord permitted to overhear a regal conversation. In Hannah Mary's view of the world there was nothing to distinguish between a school prize day and a royal garden party.

'We are pleased,' I overheard Marian say. She said it modestly enough. No one could accuse her of crowing. As for me I was obliged to lower my head to hide the smile of satisfaction on my face.

'She has her own ideas, hasn't she?' Hannah Mary said.

Her tone was nicely balanced between praise and blame.

'So Megan tells me.'

And of course Megan tells her everything. In this respect at least she is a paragon among daughters.

'She knows all the latest about everything. So Megan tells me.'

I could see Megan confiding breathlessly in her mother as they both crouched over a plate of chocolate eclairs. Rhiannon was at fault nibbling too ardently on the fruits of the tree of knowledge. And that would be my fault. I was a man who could never draw the line between raw curiosity and legitimate knowledge.

'So it's Cambridge, I hear.'

A note of gentle reproach. We had been disloyal to the University of Wales and, by extension, to Hannah Mary herself; since in her capacity as Marian's oldest friend, she should have been among the first to have been informed of what some of their friends, not necessarily Hannah Mary, would have regarded as a sly betrayal.

'I think I would have preferred a Welsh college myself,' Marian said.

She may well have meant it. At the time I imagined she was providing the most soothing retort she could think of. I may have cleared my throat or even sniggered. Hannah swung round to confront me. There was too much weight on that glossy heel and she almost toppled over. She had to grab Marian's arm to steady herself. She bared her teeth at me, stretching her rosebud lips to their limit.

'Dr Aled Morgan,' she said. 'Your influence without a doubt?'

I grinned back at her as cheerfully as I could.

'Dear Mrs. Williams,' I said. 'What could we do? They made her an offer she couldn't refuse.'

And the glittering prize was Buddy Thwaite's embrace.

iii

Muzio was already up. He was standing on the granary steps staring at a patch of lichen on the stone wall, as though he were estimating the sempiternal tempo of its growth. His inward stillness matched the sounds of early morning drifting on the thin clear air. It brought relief. I was able to breathe deeply with therapeutic intensity. He was here so that I could talk to him. Once again we could walk through the wet meadows, and the cool morning would free me from the prison of my own mind. There couldn't be a more agreeable companion. I heard hens cackling in the distance. We should be keeping hens at least. There was substance to Rhiannon's criticism, even if it were originally his and not hers. It wasn't enough for me to retort that he had a vested interest in dirt. There should be a sow in the pigsty and not a row of long-stemmed roses growing in the stone troughs. I would need to discipline myself to look after the animal. And I should do more gardening in the orchard. The apple trees all needed pruning. When she comes back I'll have hens scratching around and cackling in the sun.

'Have you been up there?'

I pointed to the granary door. I had to talk about her and this would be a suitable occasion. And Muzio was the most suitable interlocutor: a pose of objectivity would make things easier to bear. When our well-being and even our sanity depended on the whim of a girl, it was important not to give up hoping for what we had to persist in believing was best for her.

'This was her den,' I said.

I pushed open the door. Muzio turned around from studying the view from the top of the granary steps. Everything he saw seemed to interest him: even the way he stood suggested that the pursuit of knowledge was an end in itself, a religious exercise, and, if conducted with reverence, was assured of bringing its own reward. The light from the small latticed window was barely enough to make out the odds and ends scattered around the floor. Discarded treasures. When she was small she would bring a chosen friend here and they would create their own little world and lose themselves in it. Muzio had bent down to examine a shelf of fossils, all neatly captioned in childish capitals.

'That was when she had decided to become a palaeontologist,' I said.

I could hear my voice in the empty granary as though it were someone else's: cool and condescending, mildly amused at the recollection of a childish absurdity. It was so remote from the sensation of loss that made my pulse race. I saw her again on her knees in front of her little collection. The alchemy was in her fingers. When she looked up at me her eyes were pools of wonder.

'A museum of childhood,' Muzio said.

'Well, assembled by accident,' I said. 'Not by design. We've been at her for some time to clear it up. Do something about it.'

I talked about her as though she had just gone away for a couple of days. Cobwebs had gathered around her doll's house. Marian had suggested she should give it away when Rhiannon was doing her A-levels. We laughed at her indignant response, but we were secretly pleased. We took it as a sign that the emblems of her childhood were as precious to her as they were to us. We assured her that her doll's house would stay in the granary as long as she wanted it to. And here it was, inviolate and unravished, but where the hell was she? Muzio was making sensitive italianate gestures with his hands. He was searching for the appropriate words to express a discerning perception that could possibly bring me comfort.

'How do we know?...'

He began, but failed to continue. Or at least he gave up. He pointed at a mask and a head-dress hanging from nails on the furthest wall. Slanting eyes and knowing smiles peered at us through the gloom. The snakes in Persephone's head-dress writhed with life-like energy. They must have caught in her hair as she made her way through the damp earth to the Underworld. Muzio handled the mask with care and asked about the material they were made of.

'Fibreglass, I think,' I said. 'Or some sort of plastic.'

Muzio held the maenad mask up to the light.

'The *Portoneccio* temple in *Veii*,' he said. 'Quite well made too. A craftsman? Here?'

I shook my head.

'Ah, remnants of the days of college prosperity, my dear chap.'

This was the way I always seemed to talk to Muzio: as though I were using a code that I assumed all scholars had in common whatever their native language. Or was it merely that his English was better than my Italian and what we spoke was the dregs of some latinate *lingua franca*? It wasn't the words. It was the awkwardness of Rhiannon's behaviour that was putting up an unwanted wall between us.

'Chap in the Classics Department had a chum in the scenic section at Stratford-on-Avon. He made them for a production of *The Bacchae*. Or was it a pageant he did on Orpheus and Euridice? No expense spared. Those were the days.'

I sounded like a ventriloquist's doll. Whatever I said came from the minute area of my brain that remained uncontaminated with a continuous throb of anxiety. The gloom of the granary loft was no place to be in.

'Rhiannon inherited the bits. They were a great success at fancy dress parties. Of course she was mad on Etruscans in those days. Thanks to you.'

Muzio smiled at me sympathetically.

'She was bright,' he said. 'And charming. Always so enthusiastic.'

And cunning. And thoughtless. And selfish. And ruthless. In spite of myself I was engulfed in bitterness. This den of Rhiannon's had no comfort to offer.

'What's this?'

Muzio was on his knees examining a reproduction of a frieze of dancing mourners from an Etruscan tomb.

'I think I gave her this,' Muzio said.

'Of course you did.'

And this was the way she looked after it. Footmarks all over it gathering dust on the granary floor. Just one more token of thoughtless ingratitude. My urge to discuss the imponderables of her academic future with Muzio had evaporated. She would only do what she wanted. I had to let her go. Perhaps I could suggest a walk. The morning had everything to offer. Only yesterday in the hazel hedge lining the stream at the bottom of our meadow I saw a greenfinch. Its bright eye declared me the intruder into a world that was perfect balance until my big feet blundered into it. While we were descending the stone steps, the Post Office van with its bilingual badges rattled into our yard. The driver's door hung open and Tommy Post planted his right boot on the yard. The engine was still running. He waved at me excitedly. His thick lips seemed designed for oratorical utterance. His hair-line had retreated to underline the capacity of a large white forehead for profound thinking. He had a postman's cap but he never wore it even when it was raining.

'Dr Aled. Dr Aled! You were quite right.'

He paused, beaming, to give me time to realise what it was I had been so right about.

'She came equal first in the under-fourteens. And the adjudicator said it was the choice of piece. So unusual. "Classic" that's what he said. "Classic".'

He was talking about Eirlys Mair, his daughter, who specialised in dramatic recitation and penillion singing. Marian and I thought the poor girl went through agonies of nervousness as her parents trotted her along from one local eisteddfod to another. The fact is we were probably wrong. Away from the platform she was glued into silence by some obscure form of arrogance, rather than what we had assumed to be shyness. This was because she had won so many little pots and prizes. She kept her fair hair long and let it hang over her left eye until she faced her audience and raised her head to sing or recite. I should explain all this to Muzio. He took an interest in our democratic culture; unlike Prue, who was inclined to dismiss it with a patronising smile.

'Remind me,' I said to Tommy. 'What was it again?'

'Manawydan hanging the mouse,' Tommy said. 'It went down a treat I can tell you. And thank you for your guidance, Dr Aled.'

He was looking at Muzio with open curiosity. He wanted to be introduced to this distinguished looking visitor.

'This is the Marchese Bianchieri, Tommy. Here on a visit.'

There was no need to go into further detail. Tommy handed me the letters. My heart missed a beat when I recognised Rhiannon's writing. At least she had put the card in an envelope, otherwise the contents would already have become common knowledge. She knew that when cards came, Tommy often told us what we were about to learn. To all enquiries about Rhiannon's welfare or whereabouts Marian and I had always been cautiously vague. When it came to personal matters we kept more on the edge of this democratic culture than at the heart of it.

I gave Tommy a desultory salute as I moved down the yard to our garage. It was lower than the level of the yard and built of stone. Prue called it Aled's Stone Age car-port. Between the old workbench and the folded table-tennis top I read the card. I had to prepare myself before I prepared Marian to digest the message. The picture was the corner of a neolithic circle showing the cupmarks on a recumbent stone and a bare tree against the sky. It was somehow more reassuring than the message. *I met an old colonel fishing in a lake near here. Smoking a pipe with a bowl like a bath-tub and a silver band around it. He said he never caught anything except curious young girls like me. He had a motto 'Don't worry-Be silly' So I pass it on, underlined. Love to you both and see you soon (When I've solved the mystery of these cupmarks) Ciao.*

47

iv

We looked as though we were celebrating, the four of us. Prue led
the way up the shallow stairs to the dining room on the first floor.
The White Horse flaunted its antiquity and Prue looked around
beaming her approval. She paused to examine framed prints on the
wall and the scent she was wearing mingled with the smell of
beeswax as it drifted down to where I brought up the rear and
waited patiently for them to move. Muzio and I were more casu-
ally dressed but Prue and Marian were decked out in finery that
was on the verge of formal evening dress. Marian was more heavily made-up that I could recall seeing before. This had to be Prue's
influence. The pair of them looked distinctly theatrical in the tinted
lights of the hotel. If it was an illusion it was pleasing enough.
Marian looked as dark and as handsome as a film star, as though
the make-up she was wearing imposed an artificial stillness on her
features and the gold collar around her white neck was placed there
to reinforce the effect.

Our table was in a bow-window that leaned precariously over the
street. It gave us a view of the moated castle and in the distance
the cliff that overlooked the Straits. It was a warm evening. The
window was open and we gave the large menu-folders the closest
middle-aged attention.

'Absolutely anything you fancy,' Prue said. 'It's my treat. And I
know what I'm having to start. Yum-yum.... Arbroath smokies.'

Muzio looked puzzled, but not displeased with her enthusiasm.
There were enough people dining to provide Prue with the basis
of an audience. Her determination to cheer us up gave her sufficient excuse for bursts of extrovert behaviour.

'What we need is a bit of *Stimmung*,' Prue said. 'Do you know
what I mean?'

With her elbows on the table she clasped her hands together and
looked around her with eager anticipation.

'You know this place quite reminds me of the *Till Eulenspeigl* in
Salzburg. Except there, I seem to remember we had to climb miles
up the turret of a tower. Or am I thinking of the right place? My
God, I hope I'm not getting confused before my time. We were
rehearsing *Der Rosencavalier* and there was this gorgeous Swedish
baritone who seemed to take a particular interest in me!'

Prue sighed romantically.

'I think if I had encouraged him a little more, my career might just have taken off at that point. It just might. And think of the vast amounts of money I'd be earning!'

Suddenly she took hold of Muzio's hand.

'A miserable life though,' she said. 'From one airport lounge to another. Living out of suitcases. Portmanteaux anyway. You have to be tough you know. I just didn't have it in me. I'm such a sensitive plant.'

Her excessively musical laugh made heads in the dining-room turn in our direction. Muzio didn't seem to mind. Other people were welcome to admire his most prized possession.

'So you see what my hero rescued me from,' Prue said. 'A fate worse than death.'

Marian was smiling at her. At least my wife was amused and that was something to be grateful for. At the last minute in our bedroom I saw her slip Rhiannon's card into her handbag. In the two days since it arrived, it had become the centre of her existence. In the study, she brought out our most powerful magnifying glass and pored over the postmark. She could make nothing of the place-name, and all that was visible of the date was the year. It was difficult for both of us to avoid talking about it.

'Rejoice, you two!'

Prue had caught us gazing wistfully at each other.

'We have come here to enjoy ourselves. Isn't that right?'

Marian nodded rapidly and smiled her plea for forgiveness. Prue bent forward and lowered her voice as she took us into her confidence.

'If you ask me, I think that girl has more sense in her pretty head than the four of us put together.'

It was the kind of pronouncement we were so eager to hear. We paid Prue the most respectful attention. I wondered if Marian still took the view that this marriage was "shaky". Perhaps there had been some spectacular reconciliation and this trip to our island constituted a renewed lease on their attachment? It would, I suppose, be some form of consolation to reflect that our misfortune had brought this about. It is a plain fact that without some unspoken meeting of minds all marriages are "shaky". And in spite of her "hard boiled professional pose", Prue had a gentle heart: or at the very least, her operatic view of life drew its nourishment from a core of genuine sentiment. And who am I to devalue sentiment when my present existence trembles on a sea of molten feeling?

'What a girl!' Prue said. 'What guts she's got when you come to think of it.'

She spoke as though Rhiannon's misguided adventure had the makings of an opera libretto that would provide her with a powerful singing role.

'She's a bit like me, you know, when you come to think of it. Scorns convention. Finds things out for herself. A new female breed for a new century perhaps. I tell you she's exactly the daughter I might have had. If I went in for that sort of thing.'

Another burst of silvery laughter. Muzio was still smiling benevolently. There was no reason why he shouldn't. He told me years ago he had no wish to perpetuate the Bianchieri name. The title would die with him, and more or less good riddance. "A discontinued line...." He used the phrase to show he understood the commercial connotation. This among other things was what so infuriated his mother. I was always astonished at the cold distance between them, in spite of his unfailing politeness. And her barely disguised loathing for her daughter-in-law. Weighed in the scales of impartial judgement, this evening as we sat around the pink table-cloth with its elaborate setting, glittering and gleaming in the candle-light, it was possible that their domestic situation was more permanently fraught than ours. Prue's high spirits could be concealing a desperation that made our worry look no more than a minor irritation. He was looking at her lovingly enough now: even closing his other hand over hers. How far was this a role directed by class and custom?

In Italy life was a prolonged ceremonial and all that: but I found it difficult to believe that he could listen to her expressing the crudest opinions without an occasional shudder of distaste. Now I was being insufferable myself. Since I shrank back at the least excuse from any descent into the depths and darkness of my own psyche – Muzio was choosing the wines now with a quiet authority that had the grumpy little *maître d'hôtel* paying an unusual degree of respectful attention – how could I ever hope to plumb his? In his case the unknown depths had to include the trace elements of ancestors for an indeterminate number of generations, stretching back to those lethargic Etruscan aristocrats who made their peace with Rome.

A procession of waitresses was assembling around our table. Marian sank back in her chair. It was an attitude of exhaustion rather than relief. For her part Prue was drooling dutifully over her sole with champagne. She took a cheerful interest in what each one of us had chosen. I made my own inept joke about her being the life and soul/sole of the party to encourage her. She clapped her hands before picking up her fish knife and fork. I was grateful to her when she made Marian smile. We need people around us who can laugh. Muzio's retiring good looks and world weary smile were all very well for a sheltered life of scholarly contemplation.

'*Nouvelle cuisine*,' Prue said. 'What was the name of that chef from Lyons? To think his gospel has penetrated as far as this little island. Nothing like this in Viterbo, is there Muzio? Only one thousand and one varieties of pasta. You know, I think if we had any sense, my dear, we'd move to Provence. I could sing in the opera at Aix and you could be my manager. How about that? But then I suppose you'd be too far away from the Etruschi. And think of your poor dear mother. She'd die of boredom without her daughter-in-law in front of her eyes to stimulate the venom she thrives on, and survives on.'

She had every right to insist on our attention. She was intent on entertaining us and we needed to respond with nods and smiles. I had a clear view of the street past her left shoulder. There was a pink sky over the sea which gave the street-lighting a luminosity that verged on the supernatural. Passers-by seemed to float in it. With unusual clarity I saw a cyclist lose his balance and wobble into an old man dragging an empty trolley basket behind him. The cyclist sat on the pavement, a bewildered look on his face as the ancient pedestrian sprayed his head with spittle and curses. My jaw stiffened and my knees trembled under the table as I recognised the bearded Buddy gazing up at the street lighting.

Prue was intent on an anecdote about Agostino, one of her mother-in-law's retainers, who held an umbrella over his wife's head as she opened a ditch between the vines on the hillside behind their small-holding. If Buddy was here, Rhiannon had to be around. I had to contact him and do it without disturbing Marian. To stand up and shout and wave my arms about would have been the height of folly at this juncture. There was no point in raising expectations without being able to fulfil them. I waited for a pause and excused myself from the table. I moved through the dining room without conspicuous haste until I reached the stairs. On the landing I took the wrong turning and found myself in the saloon bar which was crowded and yet appeared unnervingly silent. All the faces that looked at me were tense with curiosity. I had emerged from a doorway that was little used and I stood there like a visitant form another planet.

Which of course was what I imagined Buddy to be, whether dream or reality, and I had to get hold of the slippery bastard. He had fallen off his bike because he had never learned to ride one.

He was an obstacle, an outsized piece of litter, but I had to get at him in order to get at her. The street was deserted. My anger made me shake. In the distance I could hear the sea displacing the pebbles on the beach. I raced in that direction convinced that I would find her sitting on the water's edge and gazing across the straits at the clear outline of the mountains as I had seen her do on countless occasions in the past. The mountains meant just as much to her as they meant to me. Maybe she had a bicycle too? Goodness knows how they had acquired them. Or how they had removed themselves from the land of stone circles back to this familiar habitat. There was no sign of them.

I rushed up and down the dark alleyways leading from the High Street to the Green in front of the Promenade. If they were there I would find them. I was desperate to find them. I was in a profuse sweat before it dawned on me I would have to account for my prolonged absence. Muzio had come down to search for me. He was waiting in the dimly lit entrance to the hotel. I took his arm and shook it.

'They're here,' I said. 'I saw him. I could see him from where I was sitting. The idiot fell off his bike. I didn't want to upset Marian. That card from Scotland and so on. She carries it around in her handbag. They've vanished anyway. God knows where. So let's not say anything. Right?'

Muzio was nodding solemnly. At least he was reliable. I realised how tightly I was gripping his arm and apologised.

'We won't say anything,' I said. 'What's the point? I mustn't raise her hopes. That would be cruel. I've got to lie, haven't I? I'll say I bumped into someone from college. We'll say that. Old Button Hole. She knows about him. He used to go into cinemas to concentrate on his logic and fall asleep. That one. She knows about Button Hole. And you came along and rescued me.'

'Button Hole,' Muzio murmured the name like an actor going over his lines.

'Button Hole.'

Here was an Israelite indeed in whom there could be no guile. The one reliable fact in a chaotic universe of conjecture.

V

It was a bit of a showpiece occasion. The Principal and his wife and members of the College Council were in attendance. The

Treasurer fell asleep after the first quarter of an hour. I saw his chin sink over his golf-club tie. I wouldn't say I made a mess of the lecture but it wasn't the rousing success I intended it to be. These things needed to be meticulously prepared for public consumption: the arguments hammered into bold relief, signposts all the way, illuminated by highly polished illustrations, even the most casual aside structured for elegant delivery. Who the hell could concentrate on all that with a daughter missing and a wife flitting to the window at the least suggestion of a Post Office van bumping into the yard? I had to live with that look of yearning disappointment on her face. Her hair was turning grey before my eyes.

It could have been my indifferent performance that made Sockburn look so pleased with himself. 'Go for a catchy title,' he said, so I called it "The Mystery of Boethius". I had too much material and an uneven balance between fact and conjecture. When it was over, Sockburn lost no time in damning it with the faintest approval. 'Not bad old boy,' he said. 'More mystifying than mysterious though, if you don't mind me saying so.' He smiled as if he were personally responsible for the morning sunshine pouring through the open casements of the Oak Room. His beloved Classical Summer School was fully subscribed and Trefignath Hall which had been bequeathed to the college on the expressed understanding that it would become a 'centre for advanced antiquarian studies,' was bursting at the seams. Such a convenient condition, the Principal said with his customary jovial smirk, since it allowed for the maximum academic flexibility. Sockburn said the man was flexible because he was made of india-rubber. The great man was standing with his broad back to the open fireplace. The coat of arms carved in the overmantle above his head could have been hovering there in anticipation of his knighthood. "Sir Kingsley and Lady Shirley Jenkins request the pleasure...." Sockburn said Kingsley Jenkins reminded him of an old-fashioned paraffin lamp. He couldn't wait for me to ask why, and chuckled to himself before delivering the answer, "because he oozes an unmistakeable smelly warmth." Which I didn't find so funny. Considering the sour comments he indulged in, Sockburn himself was shamelessly obsequious in the Principal's presence.

Sockburn waved a half-nibbled digestive biscuit and invited me to look around the room. '*Monumentum mihi circumspice*,' he muttered and dipped the biscuit into his coffee. They were all teachers of one kind or another. It could have been my imagination but the ones from Eastern Europe had fallen on the refreshments with greater speed and zest than the others. I even spotted one balding scholar slip a couple of digestives into the pocket of his linen jacket.

'More *fressen* than *essen*,' I murmured to Sockburn, but he didn't hear. He was bursting to speak himself.

'I can tell you this much Morgan...'

I had to wait while he darted to the table to help himself to another biscuit. I shuffled back a step or two into the shadow of the oak panelling.

'They couldn't care less about Latin and Greek, old boy. It's English they're after.'

I don't know whether it was true or not. They all seemed dedicated scholars to me. Sockburn wanted to enjoy some form of primaeval triumph as though his All England team had won the ultimate trophy outright. I could make points about the *lingua franca* of instruction books and the language of the machine, but it wasn't worth arguing about. Perhaps Sockburn felt himself a reverend senator of ancient Rome as he gazed around the room at the varied specimens of subjugated Barbarians.

'I see your Italian chum is getting along nicely with our Principal's better half,' he said. 'What's the betting it's all about California?'

Shirley Jenkins's cheeks were glowing. There was every possibility she would invite Muzio to view the slides of their trip. He, too, of course was at it improving his English. He could be listening for idioms instead of tedious details. Kingsley Jenkins had made a reputation in the early days of printed circuitry and had thrived on it ever since. Sockburn said our Principal had filched his one contribution to human understanding from an unsuspecting colleague, and this made him uniquely qualified to practise the backstairs intrigue that passed for wisdom and vision among the higher echelons of educational administration. I gave ear to Sockburn's unrelenting animadversions because they were at least preferable to the sour melancholy of my own thoughts.

'She's a one, isn't she?'

He wasn't referring to the Principal's wife. He gave me an exaggerated wink and I was inclined to resent it. He was talking about Muzio's wife. Out of the goodness of her heart, Prue Bianchieri had accompanied Marian on a quick visit to Phyllis Sockburn before they set out on their shopping trip to Chester: to cheer her up and see if there was anything she needed.

'She's been around,' Sockburn said. 'I can tell you that much.'

It occurred to me if I had been in his place at that moment I would be expressing profuse gratitude. My mother used to say "never take any kindness for granted." She walked through this world fully armed with such exemplary instructions. I used to dismiss them as stereotyped ingratiations, but now I would claim they were the unmistakeable marks of civilised concern for others. All Prue did was liven things up to entertain his ailing wife. And this was the reward of her liberality. His mouth was open now as he stared at Muzio, his face ravaged with curiosity: how did an Italian aristocrat come to marry a woman who would pass for a barmaid, when he could make the Principal's wife flush with the sheer joy of basking in his mute attention? In the field of human attachments the world was totally inexplicable.

'I've been meaning to ask you.'

The searchlight of his intelligence was adjusted in my direction.

'How did you two bump into each other in the first place?'

It was mildly cheering to learn that our close friendship was also a mystery to him. He found it rum, suspiciously rum, that two chaps from such different backgrounds should persist in taking pleasure in each other's company.

'In the queue for the bathroom,' I said. 'More than twenty years ago.'

'What bathroom?'

He was impatient. It was his prerogative to deliver cryptic utterances and my privilege to receive them.

'The Chateau. Near Grasse. In Provence.'

It was my turn to indulge in a burst of eloquence.

'When forest fires swept the Riviera, old boy,' I said. 'And the Beatles were driving their fans mad in New York or wherever! Brother Sockburn have you forgotten the swinging sixties? There was this German youth, if you please, locked in the bathroom. Taking a bath when water and time were rationed.'

The pleasure of recollection made me smile. Dear old Klaus. I shouldn't give him a bad press. After that momentous day of volunteer fire-fighting, the three of us became fast friends: Klaus, Muzio and Aled. There's something about the figure Three. As a Celt I have a predilection for triple groupings. A small lecture would not come amiss while I had Daniel's undivided attention. But more important was the memory of those days when unalloyed friendship warmed the heart and reaffirmed our faith in human nature. And there was Muzio across the room, as stalwart as ever, and as courteous, listening to that loquacious woman. And where was Klaus? Beavering away in his museum in Bremerhaven. "When shall we three meet again, in thunder, lightning, forest fire...?" I would admit Daniel Sockburn into the secret history of our excavations at Castro in '66 or was it '67? When Klaus slipped down a hole and landed in the remains of the papal drainage system and how it took us at least two hours to haul him out. I could still see those John Lennon specs gleaming in the damp darkness and as I tried to analyse the mixed emotions of that fateful morning, I became aware that Sockburn was no longer listening. He had closed the file. The connection between A. Morgan and M. Bianchieri was nothing more than one of those academic accidents that were bound to occur in an age of frenzied over-communication. Humans or molecules colliding could mean no more and no less than just one more collision.

Muzio's lecture went down far better than mine. I was pleased with this even if I suffered by comparison. The essence of friendship is to rejoice in the success of a friend. He had organised his slides with practised skill. He had taken most of the photographs himself and they fitted perfectly with a measured exposition delivered with the charm of a quiet but exotic accent. There were intriguing anecdotes about the activities of the Buonaparte family at Canino and the exploits of less exalted *tombaroli*. He gave a vivid first hand recollection of the *Carabinieri* occupying *Grappe di San Angelo*, bulldozing half a hill and calling in archaeologists from various universities to announce that they had discovered what the *tombaroli* were already robbing: an unexplored cluster of Etruscan tombs. If only Rhiannon had been here to listen. Her father's best friend had his audience sitting on the edge of their seats and the Principal's wife giving out stage whispers concerning her urge to get out there at the first opportunity to see for herself. Here was the chance of a lifetime on offer. A career in waiting. And all she could do was wander about with the bearded Buddy in search of God know what obscure and perverted source of inspiration. Where could that lumbering chthonic creature lead her except into a barren underworld?

My lecture did not pass completely unnoticed. On the way to the dining room I was approached by a pair of East German teachers who were intrigued by the comparison I had made between Sakarov and Boethius. I felt myself at the time the comparison was far-fetched but I couldn't help making it. The sight of our college treasurer's nose touching his golf club tie demanded some diversion to bring about his rude awakening. It didn't succeed. The woman called Grisela bent forward eagerly so that she could look me in the eye. Her hair was as blond as ever and her eyes as bright, but a thirst for truth had hollowed out her cheeks.

'The collapse of the Marxist state bears certain resemblances to the failure of Arianism to take over the West. Is that the point you were making, Doctor Morgan?'

The fingers of her thin hand were spread out before me and they seemed to tremble with the desire to grasp the essence of a problem. I had a sudden vision of the two women going hungry in order to buy books: breakfasting on thin porridge and reading late into the night wrapped in overcoats and scarves. These were people that needed to be helped. It was a pleasure to see them carry in their food from the self-service kitchen and take their places near the garden window. Their plates were piled high and who could blame them?

I needed to walk rather than eat. Muzio was not available for conversation – he was being monopolised by the Principal's wife and I had had enough of Sockburn for the time being if not longer. It was the duty of a conscientious academic, whatever his domestic difficulties, to think through the implications of his dimly perceived hypotheses. Washington was the new Rome, as Constantinople had been in Boethius's day. Theodora was the C.I.A. of the Emperor Justinian and I needed Muzio to bring his scepticism to bear on flights of fancy engendered by Procopius's secret history and the vivid mosaics of *San Vitale*. What greater celebration could there be of the petrifying power of hypocrisy! I had drawn his attention to the spectacle of Boethius's widow marching around Rome with a hammer, demanding the destruction of the images of Theodoric, and the wild attacks in Eastern Europe on the statues of Lenin and Stalin after the collapse of Communism. He found the comparison interesting in a journalistic sense but not necessarily significant.

My old friend made something of a fetish of scholarly caution. We were sworn-in jurymen at the court of verification. Which was true of course. Perhaps I found scientific restrictions more irksome than he did because I suffered from a more speculative nature. My cultural background for what it was worth allowed a greater range of imaginative freedom than the intensely private and conservative way of life of upper class Italians. The surface of their lives was so agreeable it needed a ritual obeisance to the sepulchre and the dark tombs. And with Muzio, a weary scepticism.

A weary scepticism suited his circumstances as much as his

scholarship. When we first knew each other he would often inveigh against his inherited wealth and title: a quarter of a century later he still had the use of both, however much he would wish the outside world to overlook the fact. The knowledge that I valued him for himself alone remained an important factor in our enduring friendship.

Somewhere in the trees behind the new kitchen area there was an inscribed stone I wanted Muzio to take a look at. It had been moved there by one of our antiquarian squires in the middle of the last century. He had discovered it being used as a chopping block on a tenant's farm. Presumably centuries before it had been taken from an abandoned burial ground. I located it among the shrubbery. It was a pleasant relief to see it safe and sound and out of harm's way. I sank to my knees on the fallen leaves of previous seasons to examine the inscription more closely. ...*iva sanctissima mulier...hic jacit...* A most holy lady lies here, who was the very beloved wife of Bivatig ... servant of God, a bishop and disciple of Paulinus. That was the exciting part! This could be that very Paulinus who left his name in Cornwall and Brittany and was trained by the great Illtyd alongside so many Saints and sinners. St. Samson of Dol and Maelgwn Gwynedd and Gildas the contemporary of Arthur who managed never to mention the hero's name and all flourishing in that same sixth century when Justinian and Theodora imagined they ruled the world. I had to submit all this material, along with heady speculations, to Muzio's critical scrutiny.

I wondered whether the stone needed attention or was better left in obscurity and peace. Redundancies and economics meant that large areas of Trefignath Hall were being allowed in one way or another to return to nature. The old kitchen garden had become a notable ruin: the long greenhouses were all rotting wood and broken glass. Saplings were taking over from nettles and thistles. When the sun came out, there was an atmosphere of sweet melancholy about the place. Also from the kitchens the smell of institutional cooking. Hardly appetising but a reminder that it was time to eat.

As I turned to face the main building I glimpsed the making of a genre-picture outside the kitchen windows. Two males in grubby jeans were being handed food through an open window by a sympathetic kitchen maid. The feverish activity in the kitchen was subsiding and the cheerful girl was finding time to feed the needy. She was transforming leavings from the Summer School menu into crumbs from the rich man's table. Viewed in the appropriate light, a typical situation from the everyday world could always be made to mean something. It was all worth mentioning to Muzio.

The two men shuffled off with their heaps of food towards an open coach-house where they could squat with their belongings on a load of timber and relish their free meal. It was by his gait that I recognised Buddy Thwaite. He had shaved his beard and his face looked as pale and defenceless as an empty plate.

vi

I stumbled through the shrubbery like a man looking for somewhere to hide.

When I screwed up my eyes with the effort of subduing the waves of guilty excitement that swept over me, I stubbed my toe against the very holy lady's inscribed stone and that to some extent brought me to my senses. The pain shot up my leg. It was real enough. He was my quarry and would not move away until he had filled his belly. But where was she? Was she too, reduced to begging for food? I had to approach the creature in a cool forensic mood. I had to prepare a case, extract all the relevant facts and set them out in Rhiannon's best interests and of course in Marian's and mine. I had to deal with the man dispassionately and set all prejudice and untamed emotions to one side. This involved a massive effort in self-control and rational behaviour.

I stood in front of the coach-house and waited for the creature to take note of my presence. He was chewing as he looked at me. It was possible that since I was silhouetted against the bright light he did not immediately recognise me. It was also possible he had stayed under my roof for so many days without actually seeing me. I abandoned my resolve to hear him speak first. In any case the element of surprise was not relevant. He was cornered in the coach-house. His companion showed more curiosity. This one had a battered fiddle-case at his feet and looked like a seasoned traveller: a kind of man you might see playing his fiddle in some echoing tunnel at the bottom of a moving stairway.

'Where is she?'

It was all I wanted to know. His mouth was full and he was in no hurry to answer. He spoke at last.

'Your guess is as good as mine,' he said.

This could be good news. I should be inclined to smile. Her innate good sense had reasserted itself. She had seen through this aimless vapid creature. A pathetic pair they looked, feeding in the coach-house, smeared with the same patina of greasy dust. She had re-established her powers of critical judgement and had left him flat... So where was she? Still in Scotland? Solving the riddle of the cup-marks. Chatting to that old colonel as he fished in the Loch?

'Wild, man.'

His mouth was full again and it wasn't easy to make out what he was saying.

'She was out to re-design the planet,' he said. 'Starting with me. I was all for it. Living in caves on next to nothing. No problem. We can sleep rough if we have to. Can't we Pete?'

Pete displayed a mouthful of teeth that were in need of urgent dental attention.

'Germany's the place,' Pete said.

He could have been presenting me with valuable information.

'There's a flip side to material prosperity. Get it?' he said. 'And that's the place for artists and art. And that's where we're off to.'

He pointed a fistful of bread at Buddy Thwaite.

'Unless you change your mind before nightfall,' he said. 'Hey! I like that line! It should go down in Germany too. We give them parts of speech, see. "The voice of the dream is sugar and always blameless". Man, I like it! "I looked upon it and found it fuckin good".'

'Look,' I said. 'Just tell me. When did you see her last?'

'She walked off,' Buddy said. 'She walked out on me.'

'When?'

'In the middle of the night. She left me.'

'Just tell me when?'

'Look mister...'

Pete was interfering and I was finding him more objectionable as each moment passed.

'Look. Can't you see this poor fucker's got a broken heart? Where's your human sympathy, for Christ's sake?'

'Where's my daughter?'

My head was beginning to shake. I was being drawn into a mauling altercation with a pair of drop-outs: the kind of thing you knew before it started would be at best a futile exercise. Buddy was wiping his mouth with the back of his hand. Pete's sympathy had un-manned him. There were tears trembling on his eyelashes.

'What could I do? She had visions,' he said. 'Maybe it came

from the stones. Do you know about visions? Heavy. They crushed me, man. I couldn't keep up.'

'Where? Where is she?'

I must have been shouting without knowing it. Was I dangerous and desperate? Pete brushed the crumbs from his lap and rose to his feet. He was big and intent on protecting Buddy. This was their set-up. The misunderstood genius and the indifferent performer. Something else for the world to ignore

'Look mate. If she went, she went,' Pete said. 'That's how some of them are. You don't know where they come from and you don't know where they're going. He's not responsible any more. If he ever was. So leave the poor fucker alone.'

My loss was immeasurably greater than his. If he was crying, why shouldn't I? Because I am a responsible father, a scholar, a civilised man, with a responsible position in society and a nature infinitely more sensitive than his, but under, what should I call it, under the yoke. I had the critical acumen to be aware of my own limitations which was almost certainly more than he would ever have. He would stumble into old age still trying to prance like a promising young man. All I wanted from him was one piece of inexpensive information and then we could turn our backs on each other for the rest of time.

They were both on their feet now, and ready to leave, and there was no way I could stop them. They had committed no offence. I couldn't have them arrested and grilled. Buddy was close enough for me to smell. He needed a wash. Marian was so right. What the hell had she seen in him?

'Ree,' he said.

At first I didn't realise who he was talking about. It was a sad plaintive bleat. My Rhiannon was never a Ree.

Buddy's head was lowered like a child ready to repeat a lesson only recently learned. 'She said every second we have to make decisions and it's always too late.'

He was ready to repeat it and mull it over for hours on end. He had lost his beard and acquired some kind of humility.

'What does that mean?' I said.

His eyelids lifted and I stared at those pale blue eyes and found them as off-putting as ever.

'I was hoping you'd tell me,' he said. 'She said we need a new faith.'

I had to encourage him to go on talking. I felt in my pocket for some money to give him. I knew I would need all the help I could

61

get to find her. It was a trial by ordeal I would have to go through by myself. No appeals to Marian. No chats with Muzio. Whatever this grubby messenger had to say I would have to keep to myself.

'What new faith? A new religion or what?'

'That's what I asked her. She said the earth was too small for our appetites. And human beings are too small. So you need a system to siphon off that excess of desire that can smother the little objects of affection.'

This was my little girl growing up at lightning speed. She was brilliant. The trouble was we had not kept up with her. Her mind was more delicate than mine or Marian's. And minds that are so finely tuned are delicately balanced. This shambling would-be genius had in some clumsy way functioned as a catalyst.

'You heard her yourself,' he said.

'Heard what?'

' "Drift on the wind and the tide.... Between the megaliths and the Saints." That sort of thing. She said she knew what she was looking for. I was lost. Anyway she didn't need me.'

Pete had gone to the kitchen window to scrounge for more food to take with them. I didn't want them to leave until Buddy had given me more specific information. But I could hardly beg them to stay. They lifted their shabby haversacks and Buddy took up Pete's fiddle-case. With his head on one side he took a long last look at me.

'She said I was like you.'

He was lying for some reason. It was such a ridiculous comparison. Just a fumbling parting shot. I could never imagine her making it. He was the only living link with her left to me. I had to delay his departure. Pete was already on his way.

'Did she?'

I tried to sound affable.

'In what way?'

'Too possessive. That's what she said.'

'Possessive?!'

He didn't wait to hear my expression of incredulity. They were off. And I made no effort to stop them. I was too disturbed by what he had said. Instead of going to the dining room I took another path to the woodland. I could only walk and make a painstaking survey of our past life and see if there was any truth in an accusation that threatened to cut me off from her with greater finality than her abortive elopement with Buddy Thwaite.

THREE

i

I was pleased and even flattered when Muzio and Prue both pressed us to accompany them on their trip home. They made it sound an alluring prospect. They would take their time. Prue was in no hurry to renew hostilities with the old Marchesa who had joined the elementary schoolmaster to make reactionary noises. That old Fascist bitch, she called her mother-in-law without bothering to check that Muzio was out of earshot. Muzio said he would like my help in tracking down relevant remains and monuments to photograph. He needed a decent range of Romano-Celtic iconography for his slide library and I was the very chap to help him. My mouth opened like a dog's having his head patted. I looked at Marian and hoped that she appreciated the invitation: here at least were people who valued our companionship. If our daughter so plainly could do without us, why shouldn't we stretch our wings and set off on such a pleasant journey?

We sat on the verandah after supper. The sun was already setting behind the hill and injecting the air around us with the colours of nostalgia.

'So why not come?' Muzio said.

He was filling his pipe as he made a broad gesture, the pipe in one hand, the pouch in the other. He allowed himself a smoke in the late evening.

'This place,' Marian said. 'It will be so quiet without you. So empty.'

She smiled and I wondered if there was any prospect of our making the trip.

'I'll miss the smell of Muzio's tobacco,' she said.

She wrinkled her nose.

'It stinks,' she said. 'But at least it keeps the midges away.'

Muzio pointed his pipe at me.

'Isn't it St. Michael de Valbonne? You know, the maenhir of the horseman, riding over five severed heads. It needs to be re-examined. We could go there after Entremont....'

The prospect was increasingly agreeable. It reminded me of a plan I prepared when Rhiannon was fourteen or fifteen to take mother and daughter on a jolly pilgrimage to Burgundy and even the Rhineland to pay our respects to the shrines of the horse-goddess. An exciting idea. Marian wasn't keen so I dropped it. They had other plans, mother and daughter. I gave way as usual. So who was being possessive? It would have been good for her. She was already showing a scholarly bent. It might have been a source of deeper inspiration. She was doing well but she might have done even better, spurred by a deeper interest ... and this was our reward.

'I'm after the Troubadours,' Prue said. 'Since they're not after me any more. How about a spot of Courtly Love? Toulouse, Nimes, Arles, Narbonne. Much more fun than grizzly graven images.'

'Tempting,' I said. 'Very tempting.'

'So why not give in?' she said. 'That's what temptation is for. Give in to it. You'd better come and save the Bianchieri from getting bored with each other.'

We all laughed but Prue's forthright pronouncements were more often than not truth spoken in jest. She rolled her eyes and I felt a twinge of concern for my friend which at least gave me a brief respite from the unprofitable process of licking imaginary wounds.

Later in bed Marian said I should go by all means if I wanted to. I said I wouldn't dream of going without her. A silence opened between us heavy with foreboding. I transposed her generous offer into a threat. I was being encouraged to separate myself from my wife just when our daughter had decided to separate herself from us. Why had I not told her about my encounter with Buddy Thwaite? Merely to spare her feelings? That didn't ring true. Conversation between understanding husband and wife should never need such close analysis. I was afraid of being cut adrift. I knew I hadn't the courage to drift with the tides because I doubted the existence of any destination that could be an improvement on what I had already. That's what made me so possessive. It allowed me to excuse myself from burdening her with the weight of my knowledge.

Foreboding was an affliction. Gloom engendered a panic of uncertainty. The spontaneity and comfortable exchange of confidences that had been the hallmark of our relationship from the beginning was suddenly out of reach. And what about that understanding that the poet declared was the seed and fruit of love?

'I know I'd find it too hot.' Marian said. 'But you go if you want to, Aled. You would enjoy it.'

This was Marian being as thoughtful and as unselfish as ever. Irritating speculation trickled into the vacuum created by the absence of our old familiar frankness with each other. Why should she be so willing to be relieved of my presence? Since I found myself unbearable it became reasonable to assume I was even more unbearable to her. Did she too find me too possessive? She was the host and I was the parasite. What other plan could she have in mind? It took me far too long to arrive at the obvious reason for Marian's reluctance to leave home. The daily visit of the red Post Office van. Her whole existence revolved around it. It was the vehicle of all her hopes that came bumping down the lane. If it didn't arrive one day she could look forward with even keener anticipation to the next. It was far more important to her than to take a valuable trip with me. I could accuse our cherished offspring of throwing up a barrier between us. Merely to suggest as much would create fresh difficulty. I had been conveyed without my consent into a condition where it was better to remain silent than to speak.

ii

The place became unnervingly quiet when they had gone. There was work to do but I couldn't settle down to it. Once the Post had been Marian became busy. In addition to her usual activities she took to visiting relatives and ailing members of her father's congregation still surviving in the old people's homes that seem to have mushroomed all over the island: she did anything to shorten the time between one postal delivery and the next. There was no Muzio around to discuss the distant or the recent past and I even missed the sound of Prue laughing in the kitchen or exercising her catholic taste in music. The weather was dry and there was no longer any excuse to postpone scything the grass in the orchard. I could hear myself making exaggerated claims about the pleasure of the sun on my bare peasant back and the sweat dripping off my brow into my eye-sockets. Prue pleaded with me to leave the grass alone. She wanted to stand in it waist high, lift her head, aim for the highest apples hiding in the green leaves and knock them off with a top C.

Working alone without an audience was tiring. With each season that passed, my arms seemed to get flabbier and my legs more knotted with varicose veins. I stopped oftener than was necessary to sharpen the long blade. Each time I wondered again if it had been set correctly on the handle; and speculated for the hundredth time why such a traditional instrument should have been imported from the United States of America.

Lying on the grass against the swell of the ground it occurred to me that I should make a bonfire. There were plenty of weeds around and rotting branches that were better burnt. This was my property and in order to maintain it in good heart I needed to foster the illusion of being master of all I surveyed. It was easier to scurry hither and thither than stick at one back-breaking job. Good husbandry meant keeping every corner of the estate in order, and it was time Rhiannon's den in the granary was given a thorough clearing out. The toys and the masks and the fancy dresses were broken and torn and gathering dust. She attached no value to them, so why should we?

I dragged the battered tin trunk to the doorway of the granary. In the daylight everything inside it seemed irretrievably dead: the teddy-bear with one eye, the pyjama case in the shape of a lion with a moth-eaten mane and rusted zip-fastener, the bonnets, the pink picnic set. Why on earth had we kept them? I was infected by their moribund condition. I gazed across the yard at the foxgloves and campion and vetch we allowed to flourish in the orchard hedge. They had a stronger title to the space they occupied than I had: a feeble imitation farmer. No mud on my boots, she said. Her contempt had robbed me of the right to enjoy existing here. I had the whole place to myself. People like Sockburn envied me. He even called me the Master of Maenhir. This most desirable ten-acre smallholding, tastefully restored and modernised in a secluded location with magnificent views of the mountains and the sea: an estate agent's dream. I was in imminent danger of discovering I didn't want it. No. The place was alright. The trouble lay in myself. There was an abyss at the centre of my being that needed to be filled with fire.

I would burn the doll's house too. There was woodworm in its floors. All this rubbish had to be dragged down the stone steps. It was a healthy activity. It gave shape and purpose to my hither and thithering. The column of smoke in the orchard had a ceremonial presence. It brought the whole of my surroundings to life. Under it was the earth, that state of being and becoming, a depth of fertility and living presence; and above the smoke, the infinite pale blue sky that covers all our concerns with a calm that could pass with equal ease for compassion or indifference.

'What are you up to?'

Marian had left the Volvo at the top gate. She was wearing a blue straw hat and squinting up at my efforts to manoeuvre the bulk of the doll's house down the granary steps. A white handbag dangled from her bare arm. I was aware of looking guilty. I gripped the sides of the house more tightly.

'Burning rubbish,' I said

'That's not rubbish. That's Rhian's doll's house.'

It was an absurd confrontation. Marian still didn't want her to grow up: wanted to keep her like a pet bird in a gilded cage of childhood. The most therapeutic course would be to burn it.

'It's riddled with woodworm,' I said.

She was ready with her answer.

'That doesn't matter these days. Don't they cook them or some-thing? There are processes anyway. These things get more valuable as time passes. Let her decide. It is hers after all. You'd better put it back.'

Possessive means possessions. It wasn't worth arguing about. Who was being possessive now? I had to give in as usual. I was filled with the conviction of my own rightness. I could let the damn thing tumble down the steps and shatter at her feet. That would be absolute conviction. I didn't have it. I never did have it. Only a flabby willingness to see every available point of view. No wonder Marian was so much stronger than I was. She was so absolute. All I wanted to say to her, as I manhandled the damned doll's house back into the gloomiest corner of the old granary, was: "give a little my dear. If you don't bend you'll break!"

iii

My room in college was chilly enough to be a prison. There are, as it happens, bars on the window. It is dim and dark and the light has to be on all day. An ideal place to sulk in. There were dozens of jobs that needed doing in Maenhir. There was no immediate hurry to make notes for the Dean on the proposed reorganisation of the Faculty. Sockburn was a scaremonger. All his talk about an academic reign of terror, and Kingsley Jenkins's determination to create a new chair of Tourism and Allied Studies. There was no hurry for the notes. I should be in Cae Garreg Lwyd cutting this-tles. The more I did myself the less we would need to spend on hired labour. Somehow I was estranged from the place for the simple reason I couldn't talk to my wife. My absent daughter had contrived to call my entire existence into question. What was I doing in this dungeon? Earning a living for God's sake, researching into the forgotten recesses of the Past and holding a candle for a dwindling band of students to stumble in my unsteady footsteps. What I needed was a superior intelligence who could put some order into the suffocating centre of my being. It was Marian who usually set me to rights. I stared at the sombre green walls of my cell. They totally failed to come up with an answer.

iv

She stood smiling in the door of our guest bedroom, waving a post-card.

'It's come,' she said. 'Here it is. What did I tell you?'

She hadn't told me anything. For two days we had barely spoken to each other as if we had both been stricken dumb by some invisible pestilence: all links of speech broken. We shared the same view of the sea and we were as distant as ships separate on the horizon. I was the one that was being put to the test by the silence and I would be the first one to give in. In any contest of will, she would be the one to emerge triumphant. Whether or not this assumption was true, it added to my unease. It was never my custom to sit up so late on the pretext of working. I had taken out my coloured inks and pen-holders to copy out that section in the *Consolatio* about Orpheus and Euridice. It was some form of comfort. I was so chilled when I gave up the lettering I crept into the spare bedroom, so as not to wake Marian with my cold feet. And I have to admit I slept like a log. I suppose the separate bed was some kind of haven.

Marian was restored to her usual affectionate self. She ruffled my hair, reached for my spectacles and sat on the side of the bed as I studied the postcard. An aerial photograph of the Outer Hebrides. The message I found irritatingly gnomic. *Illumination lies between the ferns and the water. Ask the moorhen. Leave a space in your lives so that it can come and look for you. Illumination I mean, not the moorhen. It's what we must all do. See you soon. Love R.*

'I had the most amazing dream.'

Marian was leaning against me all softness and confidences.

When the way was clear for our bodies to occupy each other, our minds could follow suit. I was eased and relieved, but still marginally resentful for no reason I could name or I would ever own up to.

'There was this telephone box squashed between two huge megaliths. Two enormous limestone pillars. And there she was. Our little girl. Struggling to get in. But the door just wouldn't open. Isn't there a postcard somewhere of a tiny cottage in Brittany stuffed between two megaliths? Hardly needs interpreting does it?'

This was the moment to tell her. Even with an elemental twitch of triumph, should I grin, or gaze with solemn depth into her eyes.

'She's left him.'

It sounded so banal, this secret that had weighed me down and struck me dumb. I could have been throwing away a remark about anybody. How else could I put it? Marian looked puzzled.

'She tried him out and found him wanting,' I said. 'So she went merrily on her way.'

I waved my hand with daring abandon. I might have some explaining to do. Any moment I expected her to reproach me, even bitterly reproach me, for keeping her in the dark. Instead she clasped her hands to her bosom with such delight and smiled so joyfully that I was filled with a renewed tenderness towards her. Her love for her daughter was so transparently pure, so unconditional, so vulnerable.

'I knew it,' she said. 'I knew it wouldn't last.'

Whatever doubts had tormented her evaporated in an instant in the heat of this newly acquired conviction.

'That girl has got so much sense.... I can't tell you. And perception. So much perception. How could she ever be satisfied with such an obviously secondhand specimen? I mean to say, how could she? Ever?'

This was as close as my disciplined Marian could ever come to incoherent happy talk. All morning she wandered around the place with a secret smile on her face. Each time she emerged from the house she wore a different straw hat or a different frock. It was amazing how her presence brought the whole place back to life. In the heat of the morning the bullocks were already sheltering in the shade of the trees and the tallest hedges. There were jackdaws squabbling on the outhouse roof and a green woodpecker performing its own balancing act on the telegraph pole by the top gate. As I worked around the place with sickle and scythe I felt part of an ordered flowering. Insects nibbled at the nettle leaves as I was cutting them down. Finches hid in the trellis on the gable-end and raided what was left of the lettuce in the patch of kitchen garden. Everything was appropriate. Such phrases as passed through my torpid brain turned around words like "oasis" and "earthly paradise". We were privileged. It hadn't been a mistake after all. We were married to the place. It was for this we had stretched ourselves to buy when Rhiannon was little more than a toddler. I needed to check those photographs of her in imperfect colour posed about the place as we worked to improve it. Now the stone walls warmed to another summer and grew thicker with custom. As Marian walked about, the cat followed in her footsteps, until it had found the perfect nest to sleep in the shadow of a bush with grey leaves and yellow flowers.

She came to me as I rested from my labours in the orchard under the apple trees. She brought refreshments in a basket. She had news of a pheasant's nest but she thought the eggs had gone cold. Somewhere a wood-pigeon was moaning softly in the dark leaves of the sycamore tree. I had not seen Marian so relaxed and carefree since that fateful day in Cambridge when we first set eyes on Buddy Thwaite outside the Porter's Lodge. The softness and seclusion of the afternoon in our orchard was itself a celebration. The tree as I looked at it became a solid fountain of joy and the spread of the branches and the position of each leaf a balance of understanding between earth and sky. Marian was ready to make love. The slow intensity of her passion brought me solace beyond words. She was a benediction in herself. My being inside her was sheltered and structured by the controlled power and energy of her blood. She was able to smile at my satisfaction as if I were a child. Something she had created. When I began to murmur about our lovemaking restoring our youth she put a finger against my lips. I closed my eyes to touch the peace that lies between life and death: I could be young as the petals of the flowers she planted or old and resigned and beautiful like bones bleached white among the brambles. I would leave my skull on the ground for the wind to use or a nest for ants.

I wanted Marian to share my repletion and placid calm. This place was ordained for our bliss. To lie side by side with no barrier between us was the happiest state. But she was restless. She dressed herself as though she had many duties to attend to, and beyond that, many intractable problems to resolve. I knew they were to do with Rhiannon. I had my own view about the girl and her unpredictable behaviour.

It seemed too simplistic to put to Marian. I always assumed her thinking was both more subtle and swifter than mine. But a simple view need not necessarily be mistaken. When you are young you instinctively protest against the imperfections of the world as soon as you come up against them. This is part of the rhythm of history, the essential ebb and flow of the generations. We know this first hand from our own experience: how fiercely we protested when we were her age. It is, after all, no more than an endemic condition among the oppressed, shall we say, the disenfranchised, beleaguered minority cultures. Out of a privileged upbringing and relative freedom, what our girl is protesting about is the absence of meaning: which is acceptable enough.

As I prepared it in my own mind, it seemed a case worth putting. Marian was standing between two apple trees, running her hand through her hair, restless with an excitement I couldn't share. Her passion was far from spent. Little use my talking about the consolations of maturity. Pedestrian projections about Rhiannon growing out of whatever sickness afflicted her and settling down with billowing grace to some bourgeois role, either independent career in some feminist mould, or as traditional wife and mother, would receive short shrift. Marian's eyes would narrow, her voice sharpen and the base and superstructure of my thesis would be systematically demolished. And yet to me as I lay on the grass and squinted at the sky such thoughts were comforting.

V

It is our custom to share work in the kitchen; even take it in turns to cook and be in command; but while Marian is engaged in such intensive research and meditation, I am very willing to prepare supper alone. You can learn a great deal about people from their culinary customs. We are both fastidious eaters. Marian has a repertoire of simple recipes so that she never needs to arrive at the table as she puts it "smelling of cooking oil". The freezer is stocked with stews and minces and soups and pies that she and Prue Bianchieri piled up during several mornings devoted to cooking.

Muzio has a special affection for Marian's chicken and leek pie and there are two or three left over. I would take one out and heat it up and we could have it with peas and new potatoes in butter. A mouthwatering prospect after a day's manual labour.

Now that our protective house guests had left us and Marian's despondency had so decidedly lifted, I was ready to suggest we did a little entertaining, albeit on a modest scale. There were several friendships in danger of lapsing or in need of repair. We had rather withdrawn from the world and in a place like Maenhir this was very easy to do. We needed to confirm that the withdrawal was not permanent. The longer we remained out of practice the harder it would be to get back into the swing of things. Over the last few years I had perfected cooking a leg of lamb and I could turn out a notable chicken with cream sauce. Marian of course could produce miracles when she felt so inclined. And she was the one given to quote La Rochefoucauld or whoever about the table being an altar raised to celebrate the cult of friendship.

I wanted to know whether Marian fancied a red or a white wine. I took pride in the coal hole I had converted into a small cellar. Fussing about wine Marian considered one of my less acceptable habits. I called out her name with a certain trepidation expecting to hear her call out, "Please yourself. You know what I like". She was not in the house.

I found her in an outhouse that had been a stable in the distant days before the advent of the motor car. She sat on an old three-legged milking stool looking through the books and magazines we had no room for in the house. They were mostly theological works from the last century. They smelt of mildew. Merely to look at them still gives me a sinking feeling. So much industry presumably based on so much certainty, exposition, textual analysis, and for light reading, the hagiographical biographies of departed pulpit heroes. Not wanted in the house and yet too sacred to throw away. What a busy world it was that revolved around those networks of denominations and chapels. I asked Marian what it was she was looking for.

'Illumination,' she said.

For a moment I thought she was joking.

'I can remember it distinctly. Tudor said it was the best thing he ever wrote. That's all I can remember.'

She was talking about her grandfather's literary efforts. He was suspected of "doubts" in the last phase of the age of certainties and took refuge in a brand of mysticism that alienated him from a congregation that still hungered and thirsted after full-throated pulpit eloquence. A search for a mystical heredity?

'It was in three parts,' Marian said. 'I've found two. There was to have been a fourth. Then came the Great War. He was so shat-

72

tered, so appalled ... the poor old thing sank into a condition of mental lethargy from which he never recovered. That was the family legend, so don't you laugh at it.'

She sensed I was capable of making a frivolous comment, even though I kept a solemn face. This, she would say was a conspicuous difference between our two families: mine had an irresistible tendency to tease and provoke and to compromise too lightly: hers was a breed of embattled puritans dedicated to a serious and unblinking contemplation of the human condition. Marian picked up the magazine with a faded green cover and shook it. There were other old volumes lying open on the cobble stones around where she sat. Her straw hat was on the back of her head and she looked charmingly bucolic. She could have been milking or spinning rather than reading.

'The one necessary condition is to find the will to believe.... There you are!'

She tapped her forefinger on the fading print.

'It's a question of language,' she said.

I gave her respectful attention.

'You have to pore over it, literally, until the meaning emanates...'

She made another gesture with her fingertips, an unconscious habit that I loved to watch.

'....Penetrates your brain like a perfume. It's such an effort sometimes to stay with it. You know what I mean? They talk so freely about God and all that. He was there because the word was a constant part of their discourse. They could go on at such length because they could assume that there were others, – a whole cross-section of educated humanity – who knew just what they meant. We can't. That's the difference. That's all.'

It cheered me so much to listen to her. The kind of spontaneous perceptions that she was so capable of could only occur when she was at ease, free of constricting anxieties. She sat in the stable intent on proving to herself that her daughter had reverted to type. I hoped she was right. The word "illumination" had taken hold of her.

'I'm sure she's not talking about the Cabbala or anything of that sort. I'll look it up to check on it of course. There is that business of the point of contact between the Finite and the Infinite. What I'm sure she means by "illumination" is "revelation". That's what she means. In the most literal sense. Those standing stones.'

'Twenty two letters,' I said.

I had broken into her train of thought. She frowned at me.

'What are you talking about?' she said.

'Just trying to remember. Twenty two letters of the Hebrew alphabet. You could rearrange them, de-construct and de-compose and discover hidden truths about the infinite and the finite. I always rather fancied that idea. Anyway you'll catch cold in here. Red or white wine?'

She closed her eyes to recapture her train of thought.

'Please yourself,' she said. 'You know what I like.'

vi

It was not possible for me to tell whether the dream set her off or she set off the dream. She sat up in bed in a state of excitement all the more disturbing for the effort she was making to subdue it.

'All it amounts to,' she said, 'is that we've got to go out and find her.'

I could see she found the notion immensely appealing, irresistible, and expected me to feel the same. Why not? A girl in a stone circle was better than a needle in a haystack. She had disposed of Buddy. She was alone and waiting for us. She had sent us a card and that was a signal. In effect an urgent summons.

'You are entitled to go away,' Marian said. 'A few days holiday. That's all it will amount to. You can leave a forwarding address. And if you miss one sub-committee it won't be the end of the world.'

She had little patience with my hesitations.

'Where do we start?' I said.

Not 'where', 'when' was her positive answer.

'Look. There are at least nine hundred prehistoric stone circles still standing in the British Isles.'

She brushed this aside. We had to arm ourselves with books and maps. It was a subject in which we had always claimed to take a deep interest. Less than one in twenty-five stone circles had any cup-marks or geometrical carvings on them. And we should start off north and aim for a circle in Aberdeenshire.

She spoke of her dream with unnerving precision. One moment her feet and mine were squelching through mud and heather and then suddenly the sun came out and we saw the ring on the crest of a hill. She would know it the moment she saw it. It was surrounded by trees with no leaves on them and a low crumbling wall, and there were twelve massive granite stones and there she was, our Rhiannon, dancing in the level circle with the new moon in her left hand and a painted globe in the other, and when she saw us she dropped the globe so that she could wave and call out to her mother. They both thought it was very funny and they both laughed, and they both laughed again, and pointed at me because I was trying to take a photograph, and I had a square stone in my hands instead of a camera.

One could call it an act of faith. History was a construct founded on dreams: that sort of thing. It's not only God that moves in mysterious ways: even the most secular, mundane human beings are prepared to wander the face of the earth, their eyes wide in anticipation of a wonder. In the middle of our fevered researches with ordinance survey maps covering the floor like a paper carpet, Marian caught the fleeting expression of despondency on my face.

'There's something about you, Aled,' she said.

'Me?'

It was too late to put up a protective covering of innocence. All my reluctance and scepticism was at the mercy of her penetrating stare.

'You avoid things,' she said. 'You never want to face up to reality.'

An impartial witness secreted in the back of my brain thought this was rich. Wasn't there a line somewhere about dreams being the source of reality that I could quote with sarcastic emphasis? I suppressed the flicker of rebellion and submitted.

'A bit of a coward, you mean?'

I spoke with judicious impartiality.

'Yes. I suppose so. In a way.'

Like an accused in a show trial I collaborated in the verdict. I was ready to condemn myself. All the same it wasn't a sugared pill I had to swallow. There they were, the two of them, wife and daughter, sitting above me on the bench. Well placed to observe my behaviour if not to search the secret reaches of my heart. I could expedite the due process by summarising the summing up: I was a possessive coward and the sentence decreed the phrase should be worn as an identification disk around my neck or P.C stamped on my forehead.

I was at the wheel as we drove northwards, eager to please. As usual I found driving on the motorway a dispiriting experience. The traffic most of the time was heavy and it was necessary to concentrate with such intensity that my whole being was transformed into an extension of the machine that encapsulated our trapped existence. It seemed to me that this was the experience of all our fellow travellers. We were all locked into a shuttle system, somewhat like robots in battle formation, and every life involved in the exercise depended from one second to the other on the unimpeded functioning of the myriad complex elements of a thousand machines. I was a peasant as well as a possessive coward and nervous peasants should stay at home, tethered like goats to their piece of land.

Marian did not appear to suffer from any such inhibitions. She took in the landscapes around us and theorised at length on the wealth and meaning behind the cryptic messages on Rhiannon's postcards.

'"Between the ferns and the water". That's fascinating. Live with nature, what else. But "ferns" and "water"? Ferns flourish and die within their season. Water flows on for ever. The same degree of contrast between a leaf and a stone. She's coming to terms with the transience of life, its agonising beauty, and she's finding her own way to cope with it and work with it. It's what you were saying the other day, or whenever. Where the finite touches the infinite, the growth area of art and religion. She's put her finger on the mistake we made. With all that brilliant percipience that belongs to the first phase of a maturing mind....'

'What mistake?' I said.

I did want to know, but it was also a way to save me from the tidal threat of Marian's over excited eloquence.

'Permanence,' she said. 'In a way. I'm not blaming you. I'm the female and I suppose I was even more intense on nest-building than you. Mind you, you are fond of routine, aren't you? The only way to get a job of work done, you say. And I agree with you. We are both alike there. Academic hard workers. Or ex-hardworker in my case. I'm not blaming you. I'm just saying how sharply she's spotted it. She's finding her own working relationship with life and with nature. That's what it amounts to....'

'Shouldn't we leave her to it?'

The comment escaped before I could stifle it. Marian started laughing. She put the fingers of one hand over her mouth and held on to my left arm. I became suddenly enraged.

'Look out!' I said. 'Don't do that. Can't you see I'm driving!'

Marian apologised and I apologised for shouting at her. We were quickly in accord.

'We have to learn from her,' Marian said. 'That's what I feel. It's most important that we should. As soon as possible. We are over the threshold of middle age, after all.'

'You're not,' I said. 'You are as beautiful as ever.'

'We mustn't sink into a rut,' she said. 'We have this chance through her to go on seeing life with a fresh eye and go on searching out its meaning.'

I derived no meaning from the M6: apart from getting and spending: and it was certainly wasting my powers. All that might have been acceptable persiflage with Sockburn or even Muzio: but not with Marian in her present mood. It wasn't a mood. It was a state. A feminine condition of expectation. Somewhere ahead of us she was convinced a great illumination lay in waiting.... My only course as so often in the past was to submit, no, more than submit, identify, espouse her cause, merge, melt into the dynamic combination of thought and feeling. It has always been a working precept with us that you can only feel precisely when you think precisely and vice versa. I grasped the steering wheel more tightly and renewed my inward pride in our partnership. Another axiom: two in harmony could always achieve more than twice one. The dynamic unit of the economic base.

We would first visit Long Meg and her daughters. The size of the ring in no way corresponded with Marian's dream, but she had noted down the fact that a spiral and a cup and ring mark were visible on Long Meg, a stone twice as high as a grown man. 'If a piece is chipped off Long Meg she is supposed to bleed,' Marian read with great delight. This was to be a holiday, a jaunt, a carefree excursion, more than a search she said: it would be a happy coincidence that could quickly turn into a celebration. I approved of that. It would go some way to absolve me from the dreaded charge of being possessive. We were combining work and pleasure, engaged in fieldwork. Looking for Arthuret for example: Arfderydd, Armterid, that elusive Dark Age battle, between the rivers Sark and Esk where Merlin was driven mad by the sight of bloody internecine strife and acquired the gift of prophecy. This was a chance to take a closer look at crucial areas of the Old North as well as to fulfil an old ambition to visit some of the most impressive rings of stone in the British Isles. We had a room booked in Carlisle for the first night and the best part of the day lay ahead of us.

Marian read the map. We left the M6 at Penrith and her finger followed the A686. After Langwathby I had to keep a look out for a sign on the left. It wasn't difficult but Marian was in high spirits and she behaved like an explorer as she jumped out of the car and made for the thin outline of Long Meg to check on the traces of prehistoric carvings. I was surprised at the sheer size of the ring: more than seventy stones marched immemorially around an area that could have contained hundreds of people. Who were they and what were they doing, and how many generations of curious amateurs had stood where I stood asking the same futile questions?

Marian waved her arms at me.

'Pre-history, my learned friend! That's the whole point.'

The weather was changing. A grey mist was advancing from the west: the Solway Firth: a name redolent with classroom geography. Marian's voice was a clarion call through the mist.

'Before history and by the same token before myths. A petrified ritual as permanent reminder of a stone Arcadia. And before that the golden Age. The Garden. The myths and the legends just reflect history's recurring fears. They say nothing about the stones.'

It was refreshing to see her so happy. The change in the weather wouldn't dampen her spirits. Once we got to Scotland our feet would be squelching through the mist and the mud and the heather as we trudged after our quest. I had to enter into the spirit of the thing. There were humorous remarks I could make but Marian had set off to walk the circumference of the ring. It sloped away to the north and I lost sight of her as the mist began to swirl around a dark line of trees. I put my hands on the bulky stone nearest to me and tried to submerge my own consciousness into the bulk and weight of the boulder, telling myself this was as close as I would ever get to an earthbound Forever. Pressing against the smooth hard surface of the megalith I could make some form of contact with the hands that dragged it into place six or seven thousand years ago.

Marian was out of breath when she reached me. She poked me in the ribs and accused me of being lazy. We walked arm in arm back to the car. There was a police car facing it with its headlights on. They glared at us out of the mist. Marian nudged me.

'Now then, Morgan. What have you been up to?'

A young police officer came to meet us. The policewoman with him stayed by their vehicle. She looked tense, as apprehensive as a novice before a solemn ceremonial. My blood was already running cold before the policeman opened his mouth. He took off his peaked cap and tucked it under his arm.

'Dr Morgan? Mrs Morgan?'

They had checked the number of our car. They knew where we

were and who we were. There was no escape. He took out a slip of paper from his breast pocket and read out our names and address before turning it over and reading the message.

'Please return at once. Body discovered in Gelli Wood believed to be that of your daughter.'

vii

Bleeding to death. My girl. Our girl. Within a mile or two of her home. This is a fact not a mystery. The world is made up of measurable miserable unbearable facts. The books on my desk are blocks of wood. There is nothing inside them that means anything. The world from one end to the other could not offer me any form of forgetfulness. What could I do except lock myself in, in my room in college, and leave my wife to carry on the unpleasant business of living. Her body was found in the ferns. I didn't see it but the images won't leave me: the flies buzzing over the pool of blood between her legs: the maggots already eating her mouth. At each end the first onslaught of decay. How am I supposed to bear it? How long? How long? The rest of my life.

'She wants to spare you.'

I watch our doctor Lydia's lips move and I read the message. Small plump lips in a small plump face. Does she use the same formula with Marian? This is a configuration she has danced before. To think we had once taken her lightly and dared to smile at the way she dressed and her confident waddle. A plump assertive little female, overdressed to the point of being feathered, but now the rock we clutched at to save ourselves from drowning: the cool efficient family doctor, and more: our staunch deliverer and shelter from the implacable storm. It was she who held Marian's hand. What am I good for? I could lie as cold as a corpse in a wood, but what use would that be? What am I good for? All I can do is crouch in my room in college and get no answer.

Our family doctor Lydia is engaged in a discreet but energetic exercise of disposal and concealment. 'All I need from you, my dears, is your co-operation and consent.' Marian gave that. Marian was able to cope with a range of processes that were outside my reach. She identified the body. Supported by Doctor Lydia. She was able to do it with superhuman unspeakable detachment. That was a thing and it was her. It had been Rhiannon, now it was a

79

thing. Bloated but still recognisable. At some undefinable point of change the Lord who gave had snapped the thread and our child was snatched away.

They conferred with the coroner. How to dispose of what was left with the maximum discretion, the minimum of fuss. Whispered consultations, murmurs, sibilations, conversations, telephone calls: and the inquest was expedited, the death certificate signed and the furtive funeral rites at the crematorium completed in a black blur. Sleep-walking is the most acceptable form of going through the motions of mourning. We have no wailing wall.

Doctor Lydia had her own urgent concern to maintain that the girl's death was not due to something objectionable she defined as 'self neglect.' A miscarriage in this case is an act of God and not self-inflicted. She was ripe with the future until the placenta praeva gave way and the prize-winner became the victim and bled to death in the ferns. She was homeward bound to have her baby we had to believe, in the bosom of her family: and the cliches grew out of the cold ground with the lavish abandon of an army of ferns re-occupying the earth. Coming through the wood so that she wouldn't be seen? Coming to surprise us? Or trying to escape from someone? Trying to avoid her fate and running to meet it? How could she tell us?

I jumped in my skin when the telephone bell rang. My room reverberated like an empty tomb. Telephones were just as danger-ous as the hiss of geese or serpents. It was an effort to pick the thing up.

'Jenkins speaking. Is that Morgan? My dear fellow, could I come down and have a word with you?'

Who was I to prevent him. The first thing I had to do was tidy the room and unlock the door. It wouldn't do for the Principal to discover he had a maniac on his staff. What on earth had I been looking up? I was still picking up books and papers when the discreet knock preceded the opening of the door.

'My dear chap, I can't begin to tell you....'

How could he? How could anybody? He looked around and found himself the most suitable seat. I have half a dozen chairs in readiness for my seminars. He could take his pick. They were in fact more his than mine. He was the master, and in the high-ceilinged cell his condolences were modulated and moulded so that he could enjoy the sound of his mellow baritone. There was no reason why he should stop. Life would be improved if by the effu-sion of syrup we could sit down and weep.

'Whatever you did would be up to you of course, my dear fellow. I must say I like the idea of a sojourn in Etruria. From the college point of view. We need to cast the net wide to sustain any impetus in classical studies. "Archaeology" and "Antiquities" sounds more attractive somehow, doesn't it, in this day and age, than plain Greek and Latin. I don't really know why this should be: but we are forced to keep up with the times in one way or another. And I'm sure the link with the Marchese Bianchieri is one we should do all we can to strengthen ... but it's up to you of course, my dear chap, to decide what to do with your Sabbatical, that is, if you decide to take it.... We mustn't hurry these things of course ... but if you let me know, say, by the end of the month what you have decided, in broad outline of course, I'd be most grateful....'

What was he up to? No occasion can occur in the Academe of Kingsley Jenkins that cannot be taken advantage of... What would happen to this room once my back was turned? Handed over to some unsuccessful expert in Tourism and Business Studies. He who can, makes a mint: he who can't chats to children about it. His smile is all sympathy and says, "get away my dear fellow until the smoke clears and the scandal dies down". He is lubricated with goodwill and his joints do not creak as he rises to depart. He's done his best for me.

I have no reason to be difficult or ungrateful. The desk is covered with invisible wreaths. My role is to bow and be grateful and suppress ungenerous and unworthy thoughts. He is going and soon will be gone and I must move slowly so as not to speed the parting guest.

'I'll leave the door open, shall I?'

Was that the gentlest of hints that I should not lock myself away, inter my being in the cold sepulchre of grief. I can stand in the doorway and watch his stately departure down the corridor towards the light at the end of the tunnel down the path of trodden phrases through the thickets of remorse. Will he turn and raise a hand in final salutation before passing out of my sight? A distant figure ever distant standing aside politely to make room for her return. She is coming towards me now, smiling, as fresh as ever, filled with the spirit of light as she moves down the dark corridor and its sepulchral echo. I am transfixed by the passionate strength of the girl. She abandoned the father of her child. He did not abandon her. She cast him out. He was unwanted. She made her way homeward, three months pregnant, to be with us in order to

81

reassess her existence as she waited with stoic patience for the birth of her child. She struggled back to the place where she belonged until she was caught in the wood by the beating wings of the angel of death. She had no right to shake the box in front of my face.

'Action Aid. Summer collection.'

She had no right to pretend to be Rhiannon or to smile at me so coyly. Flaunting her eagerness and her youth.

'We keep at it,' she was saying. 'Got to break last year's record.'

I don't know what she read in my stare. She didn't sense any unaccountable hostility. What if I said to her, 'What right have you to be alive?' She'd probably have an answer. Her head was cocked pertly to one side and her silly cap was ready to fall off. Did she expect me to count her teeth and dote on the rich perfection of her flesh?

'I've already contributed heavily,' I said.

I couldn't bear the sight of her. She was going to shake that collection box and coax me to give more.

'Too heavily,' I said.

I turned on my heel and closed the door on that smiling face.

viii

Marian has taken to visiting a cousin with an invalid husband. He sits in front of a large television screen and the women retire to a chilly parlour to look at old photographs and share reminscences of their childhood over a corner fireplace with a smoky chimney. She tells me this much when she returns as though the journey were made in order to provide us with crumbs of conversation. Myself I prefer the habit of lurking in my study, practising calligraphy like a secret vice. Boethius again: *Felix qui potuit boni / Fontem visere lucidum....* Happy was he who was able to look at the fountain of all goodness; happy to break/ loose/ dissolve – or whatever – the chains which bind him to the heavy earth....'

She made her own bonfire. Things that she had saved about which I barely knew: a trunk full of schoolgirl's clothes. She held up a gym-slip, dropped it on the flames and watched it burn. I wanted to take her in my arms in order to comfort myself. She was so stern and relentless with herself. I was nervous of the things she was liable to expose: always more likely to blame than exonerate. How culpable were we, except of doing our best, of trying too hard?

There was a knocking at the front door. It was late. I assumed that because of my obsession with locking doors I had inadvertently locked Marian out. With my shoelaces undone I had to hobble through the house like an old man to open the front door. I was faced with an uniformed policeman. I trembled so much when I saw him I had to hold on to the door.

'Dr Aled Morgan?'

I had to answer but my mouth wouldn't open.

'Are you alright, sir?'

There was at least an element of sympathy in his voice: enough for me to recover.

'If you could come down to the station, sir. It's Mrs. Morgan. She's had an accident; not too serious, sir, – she's not hurt. A case of shock, sir. The thing is, she won't say anything. She seems unable to speak.'

He was staring at me as if he were expecting me to provide an explanation. I swayed a little as I bent down to tie my shoelaces. Should I try to put my head between my knees? He was watching me too closely, taking into account any sign of abnormal behaviour. One never knew how much the police knew or didn't know. Was he counting the hairs on the top of my head? A policeman was a trained observer with the light of continual suspicion in his eyes. Appearances had to be maintained but the true agent of law and order was a surrogate of heaven, at all times well aware that human appearances were nothing more than an infinite variety of disguises.

'Ratings Lane is a dead end, sir. You may as well say she drove straight into a brick wall.'

In the back of the police car I kept my own counsel so that anything I said would not be held in evidence against me. Instead I made a conscious effort to anaesthetise myself against any further shocks that could be lying in wait to claw me. Marian used the Land Rover to visit her cousin because the lane leading to the farm we used to call 'Fossil Field' was pitted with prodigious potholes. The excuse was the farmer's invalid condition: but there was also a lifelong practice of parsimony to be taken into account. Marian's cousin was inclined to complain about her husband's failings when he turned up the sound on the television: bad temper and meanness were high on the list. They were childless and they used to rebuke us for not taking Rhiannon there often enough to visit them: now that was a cause for complaint that had ceased to exist.

At the police station Marian sat at a small table in the waiting area with a cup of tea going cold in front of her. I touched the policeman's arm.

'If I could have a word with the sergeant on duty,' I said. 'There is something he should know.'

The policeman was slow to understand that I wanted to make some kind of statement without my wife overhearing what I had to say. He could see with his own eyes that Marian and I shared the same melancholy pallor. He was making his own estimates of our age, weight, our jaded physical condition. In the back room I offered my explanation of the accident. The sergeant knuckled his moustache as he listened with close and critical attention. I chose my words with care as I outlined the nature of our recent bereavement. It was part of the nature of his duty that he should treat all forms of death as suspicious circumstance. He was understanding but firm.

'She shouldn't be at the wheel of a car, sir. I have to say that. In her condition. As we have to keep telling the public, sir, a car is a lethal weapon. The trouble is you see, she might have killed someone. And there's the danger she could have killed herself.'

There were notes to be taken; forms to be filled, private griefs and hidden facts that had to be withheld. I came as close as I decently could to making an open plea for sympathy. Marian's state of shock was more apparent than any damage to the wall or the Land Rover. I explained we were soon going abroad for a prolonged stay in a different environment. It would be part of a healing process. The sergeant sighed as he made the decision not to make a court order.

'The main thing, Dr Morgan, would be for your good lady to give up driving for the time being. On a voluntary basis shall we say, but I'll make a note of it. And you'll undertake to see to it, shall we say.'

Marian maintained her stubborn silence until we were back home. She marched upstairs and I followed her when the police had gone. I stood in the doorway. She threw herself on the bed.

'Bloody police,' she said. 'I should have done it.'

Her eyes were shining. She was in the mood for youthful protest. I smiled to encourage her. Anything was better than catatonic silence.

'My foot wouldn't stop trembling,' she said. 'I couldn't control it. When I was in the piano final at school it was the same. My foot shaking on the sustaining pedal. I should have killed him.'

She was too calm. It was dangerous.

'That creature. I'd got him there in the headlights. He soiled her. Made her pregnant. Took her life. He had no right to exist.'

I was appalled by her coolness. My wife had been on the brink of committing murder. This cultivated product of several generations of non-conformist rectitude was reaching out her hand and expecting me to offer to make her a cup of tea. I was angered by her coolness.

'There are so many of the beastly creatures around,' she said. 'I didn't stop to think what Master Thwaite was doing lurking around. There he was. Trapped. A chance. Not to be missed.'

'Beastly creatures' meant unwashed lay-abouts, piss artists, junkies, drop-outs, travellers. It was a theme of almost daily complaint, that I was more prone to indite than she. But did that mean we had to run them down, drive over them, using Land Rovers like tanks? It wouldn't have crossed my mind even to suggest it. And here was my demure and gentle wife taking the most extreme form of action, committing the unthinkable and I was reduced to excusing my own weakness instead of sternly admonishing her.

'We have no right to kill him,' I said, as if I were talking to myself. 'We can't take his life because Rhiannon lost hers. A life for a life. An eye for an eye. A tooth for a tooth. In any case. How could you be sure it was him?'

'I was sure,' Marian said. 'He'd shaved his beard. But I knew him. How could I forget him?'

We lay in the dark. Neither of us could sleep. When I ventured to touch her I felt the rigidity of her body. She didn't want comfort. Her voice was as disembodied as a recorded message from some unnatural source.

'I should have done it. I could have done it. Then he moved his head in the light and for just one second I thought it was you.'

'Me?'

I blurted the word out like a frightened child.

'Your face not his. Shaven. Exposed you could say. No more than a second. But it gave him enough time to scamper out of the way.'

ix

Where has she got to? Our firm agreement was to meet under the Departure board at the *Stazione Centrale* at ten o'clock. My uncertainties compelled me to be precise. Now the sun's great rays penetrate the glass and metal canopy to create a vast chiaroscuro of trains and a scurrying multitude that includes like a small blemish my shrunken foreign body. "Where is she" equals "who is she"? The sweet familiar figure the sweet familiar face. Where? In my mind's eye I saw her years ago, after a protest meeting, stop, raise her hand and prescribe a circle around her pretty face. I may look sweet, I may sound sweet, Aled Morgan, but underneath I am tough. Don't forget I told you.

I don't forget anything. Who was she trying to execute? He moved his head in the headlights and for a moment she saw me. No wonder the threat of violence appalls so much. It is there to prove I am a coward. And for her, an attempt at murder has reduced her grief to a manageable pain. The nerve-racking roar of the first rush hours have subsided. I have swallowed black coffee and bread, but the echoes and reverberations are still loud enough to terrify all animals other than gregarious humans. I am not gregarious. It is only Marian I want to see and keep in sight. We separated at her insistence. Who was she trying to punish? Herself? Or was she bent on exculpating herself from blame? How could I ever know unless I asked her? And this was the question I could never ask.

It wasn't my intention that we should separate. The bond that once held us so tightly together was being loosened against my will. Marian didn't seem to mind. 'You go there,' she said. 'And I'll go here.' And that was all there was to it. Find our divergent consolations. She was looking at herself in the mirror and seemed satisfied with what she saw. She was pleased, certainly with the *Locanda*. It was prettily decorated and tastefully old-fashioned with sufficient modern conveniences and within walking distance of places she wanted to visit such as the *Brera*.

'Off you go,' she said. 'If that's what you want.'

It wasn't what she wanted. To her, my projected pilgrimage was a naïve notion. I had an urgent desire to go to Pavia and touch, or at least gaze at, through a square of glass, the bones of Boethius in the crypt of the *Ciel d'Oro*. The relics of a saintly hero.

'Better for you to go alone,' she said. 'You're not responsible for the loaded gun so long as you're not carrying it.'

She was teasing me and I felt uncomfortable. How had she come to terms so quickly with her violent impulse? She would take two days to visit the large-scale exhibition of The Celts, set up at great expense in a Venetian palace. It touched on her special field at several points and she was ready to reactivate critical faculties she said had been too long dormant, and it was plain that she welcomed the opportunity to make the trip alone. That was the way it took her. She was looking for a renewal of rational disciplines and I was still looking for consolation.

I didn't find any in that gloomy crypt. I got wet walking from the station to *San Pietro in Ciel d'Oro* and when I stepped inside, a fat woman shook her wet umbrella in my face before proceeding to her candle-lit devotions. There were too many displays of oleaginous piety. The crypt was in semi-darkness and an American was reading a guidebook to his three restless children. He stopped suddenly when he discovered he was reading about San Salvatore. 'Holy cow,' he said. 'Are we in the wrong place fellers, or aren't we?' He was sceptical about Boethius's bones. 'They could be anybody's,' he said, inviting me to agree with him. I tried to remember the words of a hymn we used to sing in chapel about dry bones in a valley waking up to sing. It wasn't going to happen here.

Searching the faces of passers-by as though each one might reveal the secret of my wife's whereabouts, I was slow to realise that there were at least two other Departure boards in the grandiose interior for them to study. Possessed by a sudden panic I began to hurry from one to the other. I broke into a sweat. Our luggage had gone ahead. We only had so much time. Muzio and maybe Prue would be waiting for us at Orvieto, their ancient diesel Mercedes baking in the sun in the largest station car-park in Italy according to Muzio. Marian was being irresponsible. Our seats were booked. The train was already stretched most of the length of platform 14. Standing still was impossible. I charged down the stairs to the cavernous Booking Hall and charged up again. I was ready to search every nook and cranny and my persistence was rewarded. I found her seated calmly in the shabby interior of the waiting room where a pair of *Carabinieri* with a sniffer dog marched up and down between dismal rows presumably looking for drugs. The dim interior had the smell of the lower depths. Marian was seated opposite a couple of what we used to call hippies. The man's hair was longer than the girl's and tied in a pony-tail. They were both eating ham rolls that Marian had given them. The besotted blonde, her mouth still full, lifted a loose strand of the man's hair so that she could kiss his dirty neck. Marian was gazing at them with detached, clinical interest.

'For God's sake,' I said. 'Where the hell have you been?'

She rose lazily to her feet and smiled at me without a flicker of surprise.

'Ah, there you are,' she said.

I wanted to grab her arm and drag her away in the direction of *binario quattordici*. Cataracts of reprimands and protests would fall from my lips once I opened them. Was she in a dream or in shock?

'Other people,' she said. 'They're all over the place.'

She wasn't going to hurry. She was talking to herself and it didn't matter whether I understood her or not.

'That chap was awfully wrong,' she said. 'Heaven is Other People. That's why foreign parts are so delectable. It's obvious really when you come to think about it.'

It disturbed me to think that she was so close to being happy so soon. It was unseemly somehow in the light of our bereavement. The shortcomings of my character, so transparent, were always a source of amusement to them both, mother and daughter, as if I were a domestic animal that had to be fed and taken for walks and petted at regular intervals. I tried to summarise my more obvious defects as we moved along the platform in search of our reservations: excessive ambition, infantile misgivings, unworldly immaturity, nervous respectability, timidity, lack of courage.

When I took her travelling case she suddenly held my arm and pulled me down towards her to give me a kiss.

'You're a good boy,' she said. 'And I'm glad we've come away.'

X

Other people are not specimens in a zoo. You can't gaze at them without speaking to them. The nun, the smart mother and her little girl carrying her illustrated story-book, settled opposite us in the seats reserved for them and Marian at once began to stare at them in a trance of benevolent intensity that I felt obliged to break. The train shook with a burst of speed as I pointed westwards, inviting her attention.

'That must be Monte Amiata,' I said. 'Unless it's Monte Cetona.'

Marian made no response. She was absorbed in her study of the little girl and the perfection of her appearance: beautifully dressed, beautifully behaved. It was a picture and I was inclined to resent and disparage it. Why should I have to sit and watch the smooth intimacies of understanding between mother and daughter: note the intriguing resemblances of olive skin, dark blue eyes and long eyelashes and fleeting smiles. Were they advertising perfumed soap or bourgeois Italian virtues? Their unspoken affections drew them closer together so that the nun, who was a large bony woman, seemed to spread the blackness of her habit protectively behind this fashionable Madonna and Child.

'*Amiata* has the same root as *heimat*,' I said. 'So Muzio tells me. He says when we see it we should have the feeling of returning home. I don't know whether that goes back to the Goths or the Lungobardi. I don't quite see how that lot could have felt they were coming home.'

Marian must have heard but she paid no attention. Earlier she had been cheerful enough chatting about the exhibitions in Venice. She even began to elaborate a theory about the underlying unity in the ancient world of the concept of Otherworld and Underworld. She began to list the myths available for comparison, from Arthur to Hercules, until this travesty of Madonna and Child arrived with their black escort and genteel bustle and took possession of their side of the compartment. I made another attempt to engage her interest.

'When you come to a place like this,' I said. 'You are more aware of it, aren't you? I mean the primaeval substratum you were telling me about. The levels and the layers and so on. It must be as true of the history of peoples as it is for geology. Here one is more aware of what still exists just under the surface, and on it for that matter...'

Marian wasn't listening. The little girl had begun to return her stare. It was impossible to guess what each saw in the other, but whatever it was it excluded everyone else. I saw the fragile innocence of the little face disturbed. She lifted her hand and drew her mother closer to her so that she could whisper in her ear. It was about Marian. I looked at Marian's face and saw tears springing up in her eyes and beginning to run in silent parallel down her cheeks. I wanted to say something and yet there was nothing I could say. All I could do was retire rather noisily to the corridor as though I needed to smoke a cigarette. They could have been tears of some kind of happiness. The features of her face were so still and expressionless: tears running down cheeks of stone.

I became aware of the musty smell of the nun's habit at my shoulder. She was talking to me with professional concern.

'Forgive me, signore. I do not wish to intrude, but I could not help noticing. You carry a burden of sadness.'

I must have looked more distressed than a woman with tears running down her face Was I going to ignore this woman? Other people. Other people. Where do we draw the demarcation line between "us" and "other people?" I caught a glimpse of unstinting benevolence behind the steel-rimmed glasses. I had to respond: it would be easier to say in another language.

'We had a daughter,' I said. 'She died.'

The nun's face glistened with sweat and compassion.

'What a sorrow,' she said. 'A small daughter like our little Luciana?'

'No. She was twenty years old.'

Now I was able to look her square in the face. What would she have to say about that?

'It is hard,' she said. 'It is impossible for us to understand.'

I felt suddenly frivolous and ready to say something rude such as 'You can say that again, sister.' Or, ' And what would you know about it?' And I was mildly shocked that such thoughts should have occurred to me. My nature was to withdraw into myself and take refuge in my inherited reticence.

'I shall pray for you,' the nun said.

I repressed any further frivolous comments that presumed to bubble up in my mind. Out of the cavernous folds of her habit the nun extracted two small leaflets. I glimpsed the lurid picture in red and gold of the Madonna on the first page with a star-like firework over her head and a cross above that.

'One for you. And one for her.'

With elaborate tact the nun withdrew to her seat in the compartment. The bulk of her blackness hid the exemplary family from my sight. What could I do except retire to the toilet, hang on to the rail and stare at my own unpalatable image in the mirror. I wanted my tears to flow from my stubborn eyes. The leaflet was covered with unhelpful pieties. It seems that we have sinned in thought and in word and in deed and the fact was we had not loved the almighty and most merciful God with all our hearts which was what we should have done and I suppose it was for that reason among a million others that my only daughter was found rotting in the ferns. There was more to it than that. We had failed to love others, i.e. other people, in anything like the manner in which our Lord had loved us and we had to be permanently sorry for it and keep on confessing our sins right on to the end of the road. I pressed my foot on the flush pedal and dropped the leaflets into the pan. Looking at myself in the mirror and waiting for tears to flow was a repulsive exercise. There was nothing I could do except return to my seat in our compartment.

There everything had been transformed into sweetness and light. Marian was teaching the perfect child a Welsh nursery tune that she had supplied with Italian words. The nun was clapping her hands to keep time and the beautiful mother was smiling a beautiful smile.

'*Se avessi un bel muletto...* If I had a little donkey / And the donkey wouldn't budge/ Would I smack him and beat him / No I would not....'

I couldn't bear it. I could see Marian sitting on the edge of Rhiannon's bed and the little girl's eyes shining as she clutched her stuffed toy and they sang this very rhyme together in a soft duet because the donkey was wearing slippers on his way to bed. I stepped back into the corridor and turned to look at the view and waited for my eyes to fill with tears. We were pulling in to Orvieto before the miracle could happen.

There was no time for elaborate farewells. Marian kissed the little Luciana on the cheek and I took care of our hand-luggage. Muzio and Prue were down there on the platform waiting for us. I spotted them among a restless crowd of tourists, conscripts, elderly travellers, and railway staff more interested in each other than in any of the passengers. Prue was wearing dark glasses with white rims. In no time she and Marian were weeping in each other's arms even as people on the platform surged around them. Muzio embraced me briefly and then struggled to take charge of our luggage. I looked up and saw the ideal family in the window of the compartment we had vacated. The large nun stood behind them and raised her hand in a gesture of benediction.

FOUR

i

It is hard for me to accept that Marian's rate of recovery is more
rapid, more successful, more positive than mine. She seems to have
shed her share of the blame of what happened. Blame is the wrong
word and so is responsibility, but I can't help remembering that it
was her lapse into primitive emotion that drove them out. This is
unjust but it persists in my mind. I have put away such false accusation but I know where it is hidden. I know everything and I know
nothing. I go through the motions of restrained and civilised behaviour while I am still floundering in a fog of despair: trudging
through an emotional quagmire where metaphors are mangled and
the meaning is sucked out of the simplest words: loss, grief, death.
I can't go on staggering about like the victim of a soundless explosion. We are guests, after all, and we were brought up to
demonstrate gratitude bordering on the effusive for all kindnesses
bestowed upon us. Yet at the most unguarded moment, in a
narrow street on the way to buy more film for my camera, or waiting for the caretaker to open the gates protecting an excavation, I
have to stop myself throwing back my head and howling at the blue
sky.

Marian was being cured by some healing process not available
to me. We are both recipients of Muzio's care and attention. Can
it be that Prue's relentless pursuit of enjoyment, her raucous zest
for life, has a beneficial effect that passes me by. In their separate
styles they both put themselves out for us. We are adopted: something between lame dogs and surrogate children. We are nursed
along. Marian is showing a depth of interest in Etruscology she
never showed before: and an equal absorption in the minutiae of
local gossip and politics as transmitted through the chatter of Prue
Bianchieri. My wife is being nudged back to normality by a
comfortable routine, by a privileged interesting existence.

It is pleasant to listen to Muzio's voice. From one excavation to
another he exercises his mastery of the subject in his own inim-
itable relaxed and elegant style and I admire him for it. Yet there
are still whole surfaces of my damaged psyche I cannot bear

anyone to see, let alone touch. Somehow Marian no longer has to suffer the strain of covering up the successive emotional shockwaves I am obliged to endure.

That evening at the *castello*, as the sun went down and we were allowed to assume we were exempt from any prospect of redundancy and the mundane preoccupations of earning a living, in the silence before Prue rang for coffee to be brought in, Marian spoke out as if she wanted a sympathetic world to hear what she was thinking. *She is with me all the time.* Mercifully it was too dark in the room for Muzio and Prue to see my hands and my lips trembling. How could our girl be with her at any time? Rhiannon was buried for ever in that chilly extension of consecrated ground higher up the slope facing the immutable sea. I would have preferred her to be closer to the ancient church dedicated to a saint who my girl had once described to me as being "cuddly". It amused me at the time but I never asked her exactly what she meant. *I'll never lose her.* How could she speak so calmly. *She'll always be with me.* How could a woman of such intelligence bring herself to make such a confident claim? It was more irritating than the trance-like assurance of an illiterate adherent to some fundamentalist faith. It ignored my existence. It brushed aside the entire territory of rational qualifications that was my natural habitat. In which case she was saved and I was lost. And this was the woman who gave way to an urge to murder that wretch, a fellow human being all the same, dazzled by the lights of her vehicle. What could I say that would not descend into a hysterical denunciation of her inconsistencies?

In *San Pietro* a row of late Etruscan sarcophagi had been left to slumber solidly along the south wall of the cavernous basilica. Prue Bianchieri was wrinkling her nose with disapproval as she patted the stone paunch of a reclining dignitary.

'Disgusting,' she said. 'Showing off his belly. What a travesty of the Last Supper. Talk about conspicuous consumption. This lot ate themselves to death.'

Muzio interrupted his exposition of that late phase of Etruscan history to smile at his wife's antics. Marian smiled too. She was concentrating on absorbing everything there was to know. The star pupil of the seminar. I had to detach myself from them in order to give myself a chance to breathe: escape from my own petty malevolence. Marian was insisting on some precision in the chronology of distinct phases in the development of the Etruscan world view. Muzio was hesitant and yet more than ready to respond. I contrived to shift backwards until I hovered above the broad steps that led down to the crypt. It was a necessary underworld to be explored. An ante-room for disorientated displaced persons. I found myself in an artificial forest of dead marble columns: petrified sterile sanctity supporting groined vaulting until the next earthquake.

An empty underworld. The cold light from the narrow windows pierced the perpetual twilight. I was counting the pillars a second time when I caught her face smiling at me. It was her smile. Fleeting, unforgettable, untouchable. The glance, the eyes, even the dark hair along which I once drew my hand. She moved and I moved to keep her in sight. I had descended those broad steps in order to play hide-and-seek with my dead daughter. It was as it should be. The teasing that belongs to a loving relationship. She wanted to hide so that I would be compelled to come and look for her. She was the messenger with something vital to reveal. Maybe a few whispered words that would release me from my iron cage. I would dare to speak to her. Before I could move closer she was gone.

In the world above, on the floor of the basilica Muzio was still absorbed in his discourse, spurred on by Marian's undivided attention. The girl, it had to be the same girl, was crossing the vast empty floor. Even her walk seemed familiar. Jaunty, confident, a clean pair of heels. She joined what had to be her family, not mine. Was that her father who looked as self-important as a visiting senator? He was pointing out to his wife and smaller children, the faint outline of an avenging angel hurling the damned into the faded flames of a fresco cracked by the earthquake of February 1971.

He had a great tale to tell, a role to play. The girl joined them, even at a distance sure of herself, contained in her own beauty.

'Where did you disappear to, you naughty boy?'

Prue was murmuring like a serpent in my ear. I stiffened and protested my innocence with too much emphasis. My thoughts and feelings were private and had to be hidden at all costs. I took her arm, which made her smile and insisted on drawing her attention to serrations in the Romanesque arches which seemed to me to be distinctly Etruscan. Muzio summoned her attention.

'Prue! That was Guidatti and his family. How long have they been in here?'

'My dear. How should I know?'

'They must have seen us. I'd better go and say hello or he will be mortally offended.'

Muzio's tall figure hurried across the patterned stone floor, determined to overtake the Guidatti family before they left. I longed to accompany him in order to take a closer look at the girl. Was the resemblance so startling? That fleeting smile between the marble columns seemed all approval: a permit to stay and haunt this place. Some kind of message. It happened. I saw it with my own eyes. Or just another pretty girl, eager to meet the world, and to be met.

'Bless him. He's so anxious not to give offence.'

I listened to Prue and kept an eye on the cordial encounter at the cathedral door. The girl had moved ahead of her family and was a black figure waiting in the sunlight of the empty square. I would say nothing to Marian about it. How could I speak of what could not be put into words without making myself ridiculous. What are the sounds that describe a signal from the underworld?

'I don't want to sound like a snob but I find with these people it's better to keep your distance.'

'Why do you say that?'

How cool and impartial my wife sounded. If only I could find a strength that would correspond to hers.

'They always want something,' Prue said. 'They think you have influence and it's your duty to exercise it on their behalf.'

She put her hands together in a gesture of operatic supplication, and began to whine.

'"Ah Signor Marchese, dearest Don Muzio, our true friend and protector, be so good as to give our boy the letter of recommendation for the softest job you can find him...."'

'What about "our girl"?' Marian said.

She was ready to enter the spirit of the game.

'They haven't really caught up with that yet,' Prue said. 'Girls are still marriage counters. Pawns in the great game of family aggrandizement. I tell you this place is still living in the days of the Papal States....'

Prue Bianchieri specialised in disparagement. She liked to bring everything down to her own cynical level. Marian couldn't see that. She just took pleasure in her bluff Yorkshire manner.

'There isn't much about this lot I don't know, my love, and the trouble is what I know is not worth knowing. Did you notice the girl? A beautiful specimen. But quite a handful from what I hear.'

True or false it did nothing to impair the impact of the smile. An encounter with a ghost had restored my sense of purpose, given me a new sense of direction. Somehow I would control this season in Etruria. I would not be redundant here. Muzio was on his way back and rubbing his hands. He was an image of goodwill and innocence as he passed through the sunlight that streamed with spectacular power from the massive rose window down to the mosaic patterns on the basilica floor.

'If there's anything you want to know about the living around here, my dears,' Prue said. 'Apply to me. About the dead continue to direct your enquiries to my learned husband.'

She reached out to take Marian's arm and shake it until she was willing to join in her laughter. Muzio stood before us.

'We are all invited,' he said rubbing his hands together.

'Oh, my God....' Prue demonstrated mock-horror.

'Peace between the fish and the fields,' he said. '*Corrigone* and white wine. It will be interesting for them. We must preserve the old customs Guidatti said. He's right too. Basically he is a very decent fellow. He's someone you can count on. That means a lot when all is said and done.'

'Your mother won't like it.'

'Why not? Why shouldn't she?'

'She'll say, you're bending over backwards again to please the *cafoni.*'

'She can say what she likes.'

Caught between two formidable self-willed females. No wonder there was a pallor on his cheeks. I needed to try and forget my private pain and make more of an effort to ease his. Together we would further his plans for the Study Centre at Fontane. That would give the edge of purpose I was looking for. Under the influence of that smile my strength was flowing back and what better use to put it to than fostering peace and reconciliation.

ii

My feeling was that we should humour the old girl. Marian was less accommodating.

'This is absurd,' she said looking at her wristwatch. 'Who does she think she is? Who does she think we are? A pair of peasants coming to pay the rent?'

'For Muzio's sake....'

I made a conciliatory gesture. I wasn't in control of the situation, but at least I had attained a fresh ability to control myself. And this was underwritten by an encounter with a ghostly smile. I was more aware now of the life going on around; more confident that I had a positive role to play in it.

We were comfortable enough in the leather armchairs of what was more of an ante-room than a salon. Through the wide door-way we could see a table near the open window already laid for three. Between the patterned warmth of the roof tiles there was a view of a blue corner of the lake and above, Montefiascone shimmering in the haze. The old Marchesa suffered from an arthritic hip that made her move about with an exaggerated military stiffness. She was taking her time to make an impressive entrance. This was her private apartment on the first floor of the *castello*, and here she was looked after by a married couple, notable, according to Prue, for their sullen efficiency. They came from the Italian Tyrol and had been imported, again according to Prue, because the old Marchesa still had neo-Fascist connections in that area and knew something about the Fambini that ensured their absolute loyalty. Any tendency they might have had to take advantage of an old woman's frailty was inhibited by a lack of local connections. Carlo appeared in his striped jacket to ask whether he could offer us an aperitif. He glided around like a man who had spent a lifetime serving in old-fashioned Tyrolean hotels. He was reputed to understand English and German. Marian was confident our language was one he would not understand.

'I suppose we must put up with it,' Marian said. 'For his sake. I never saw such a difference between mother and son. He must have spent years going out of his way to make himself as different from her as he could. *Grazie.*'

She took the lemon and soda-water Carlo had prepared for her and sipped it thoughtfully.

'One can only assume he takes after his father. The same kind of rare cultivated flower. Refined, reserved, scholarly and so on. But then the question arises, how did two such different characters come together? The love of opposites or another dynastic marriage?

'Other people.'

She could see I was teasing her and she was pleased. She held up her glass and released one finger to point at me.

'Exactly. In this old world there are two mysteries: other people and ourselves. And there are no prizes for guessing which mystery is the bigger. My goodness. I've just invented an aphorism. It will be epigrams next! Pass me a note-book. I must put it down!'

Our laughter must have seemed immoderate or even immodest to Carlo. He probably knew the strange couple had lost a daughter and were still unpredictable, unbalanced. Well-trained servants knew so much more than they ever let on. He barely smiled as he bowed and withdrew. He had heard the Marchesa approaching, her walking stick tapping the marble floor with ominous regularity. But she welcomed the sound of our subdued merriment and was already expressing her approval before she came into sight.

'How splendid to hear guests laughing,' she said. 'Even before I offer them my limited range of pleasantries....'

The severe black dress she wore had shoulder pads like epaulettes that accentuated her effort to carry herself with authority. Her skin was mottled and her hair dyed an unprepossessing black. The string of pearls around her skinny neck supplemented her toothy smile of welcome. Under her left arm she was carrying a large photograph album which immediately aroused my curiosity. There would be photographs surely of Muzio as a boy and of his father, and we would see him in a depth of context that could only enhance and enrich our friendship.

'How very kind of you both to visit me. It is a work of charity to come to lunch with a cantankerous old woman. I'm sure my reputation has gone before me.'

This last was addressed directly to Marian. I was impressed with her steady response.

'Forthright,' Marian said. 'Not cantankerous. A lady who likes to say exactly what she thinks.'

The Marchesa held her mouth open briefly before giving an explosive chuckle.

'What a splendid answer,' she said. 'My dear, you should join the diplomatic corps. Heavenly. Quite heavenly. Let us go and eat shall we? Not that I eat anything but I shall enjoy watching you. Erminia has a limited repertoire, but at least the fish comes direct from the lake.'

It was pleasant eating by the open window. I was prepared to enjoy the meal in every detail from the finger bowls to the skillful unobtrusive service provided by Carlo who was now equipped with white cotton gloves. The wines were from the reserved selection of the *Co-operativa* of which Muzio was either the president or the chairman. Marian was less at ease.

'You have heard of course that I am an unrepentant Fascist? I freely admit it.'

She was exerting a charm like the perfume of old face powder.

It would have been impolite not to smile back at her.

'People should not be afraid to declare where they stand. You know. Like Martin Luther. *Ich kann nicht anders.* There's too much ambiguity about these days. People shilly-shally. You never know where they stand.'

She rubbed her hands to signify her satisfaction and for the first time I thought I saw a glimpse of her son in that unconscious gesture. Marian was toying with the sliced fish on her plate. The Marchesa noticed at once.

'Is there something wrong with that?'

Marian shook her head and declared with some enthusiasm that the fish was delicious.

'He made mistakes,' the Marchesa said. '*Il Duce* definitely did not *a sempre ragion...* But there was more to Fascism than poor Mussolini. These are a people that need discipline above everything if they are to hold their heads up in the world. Order and discipline. Without them civilisation sinks into chaos and anarchy. There. I've said my piece. Now can we indulge in more relaxed pleasures. I have brought some photographs to show you. A surprise. You see. I am historical and I have pictures to prove it! You are Welsh? You come from Wales. Of course you do. What I have to show you are pictures of your prince. And I am of the company. Those wonderful summer days. On the Adriatic. I was so young then. Just a slip of a girl. He was so charming. The Prince of Wales. Prince Charming.'

'Our last prince was killed in 1282,' Marian said.

I looked at my wife with wavering admiration as she mumbled into her plate. The Marchesa was puzzled.

'I beg your pardon?'

'He was killed by the English. They stuck his head on a pole and exhibited it on the Tower of London.'

'Ah,' the Marchesa made an effort to show understanding. 'Battles long ago.'

'Unless you count Owen Glyndwr,' Marian said.

She frowned as she threaded her way through a familiar litany.

'And we don't count the Tudors,' she said. 'At least I don't. The best you could say for them would be that they were opportunists. But then I suppose all politicians are opportunists. The trick is to be on the winning side when the final whistle blows. It was a bit like that here, wasn't it?'

They were gazing at each other with sudden hostility. It was time for me to make some reassuring remark: something light-hearted, if only it would occur to me. Not so much a joke as a pleasantry. Something perhaps about lesser breeds without the law, couched in amusing self-deprecating style.

'Separatist,' the Marchesa said.

It was an ugly word that she used with patent disapproval.

'You see it happening in Yugoslavia,' she said. 'That way an entire Imperium collapses. The seeds of anarchy and confusion. The first sign of a new age of barbarism. Let us be frank about this: inner weakness and the delicate fabric of civilisation collapses from within. Now mark my words....'

Marian's knife and fork rattled on her plate.

'Excuse me....'

She pushed back her chair. The Marchesa took time to abandon her thesis and show a degree of concern appropriate to an experienced hostess.

'Something didn't agree with you?'

'No, indeed. The food is excellent. I just don't feel well.'

I escorted Marian to the bathroom adjoining the Marchesa's bedroom. She was pale and ready to vomit. She wanted to be alone. She sent me back to the table. The Marchesa clutched the photograph album as she made an effort to be understanding.

'I am too combative,' she said. 'I am too fond of argument. I get carried away. I should not do it. Especially with a mother who is grieving. You must forgive me.'

She was staring at me with such intensity. I had to assure her that she had given no offence and there was no occasion at all to ask forgiveness.

'One gets so old, one forgets these things. My heart has been broken so many times I suppose it has gone hard.'

She opened the photograph album briefly but seemed so displeased with what she saw that she tossed it to one side. The past was over and done with and the sepia mementoes were dispiriting to look at. Her two hands crept over the white table cloth in my direction. They had taken on an independent life of their own, like a pair of crabs.

'My Muzio you know is so trusting and so innocent. I think you know this, Dr Morgan, as well as I do.'

'Aled,' I said.

'Ah yes, of course. Aled. Such an unusual name. Suggests the deep sea to me you know. I don't know why. He is so exposed you know. Unprotected. I know how much he values your friendship. That brings me great comfort. Now tell me about these plans for the old farmhouse at Fontane.'

I had to tread cautiously. For all I knew the old woman had the power to veto the project. The farm and the buildings were part of the estate and I assumed they were within Muzio's gift. My university and his would provide capital grants for the restoration and extension, and the *Soprintendenza* of the Province would contribute to the running costs. It would become a Centre for Archaeological Studies and Excavations and, I managed to hint, with an unskilled combination of soft soap and amateur diplomacy, bring fresh renown to the Bianchieri name.

'You don't have to worry, my dear Aled. It has my blessing for what my blessing is worth, which is very little. All I suggest is that you don't confine your efforts to those degenerate Etruscans. As you know Rome was always my ideal and always will be. That was the true pinnacle of our glory. But I mustn't go on.... He is so unworldly you see. My Muzio. Just like his father. He was born like that. A child of the angels. But one can not always rely on the angels. They have other things to attend to. Can I be frank with you?'

'Of course.'

Her large eyes were scanning my face with unnerving intensity.

'He relies too much on Luca Puri. He gives him too much freedom. Too much power. This is a serious weakness. My boy is conscientious, of course I know that. He has a fine sense of duty. Just like his father. But he is too trusting. Luca Puri is merely the *fattore*, the farm manager. Nothing more. Will you please see that this new project does not fall into Puri's hands? I am not saying he is dishonest. And I accept that he is a very hard worker. But he has a taste for power. And with a new enterprise like this, temptation may set in. You look at him closely, my dear Aled, the next time you are near him. You look at those eyes. Sly. Shifty. And for that matter the shape of his head. Are you interested in phrenology?'

I shook my head.

'Ah now, you should be. My uncle Dino said *Il Duce* never took a man into his confidence without first studying the shape of his head.'

She raised her finger suddenly.

'Do I hear someone crying?'

I listened. I heard nothing.

'Your wife, grieving. Tears are like flowers on the loved one's grave. Ah my friend, I know what I'm talking about. When I lost my sister and my Guiseppe in the same dreadful November, for

101

three years I moved through the world like someone already dead inside. Go to her, my friend. Go to her.'

I found Marian sitting on the toilet seat in the Marchesa's bathroom. She was fully recovered with a determined look on her face.

'We've got to get out of here,' she said. 'I can see now what's going to happen. I'll be trapped between two women who can't bear the sight of each other.'

Marian looked at my puzzled face.

'You have no idea what's going on,' she said.

I tried to defend myself.

'She didn't even mention Prue,' I said. 'Not once. And I was listening.'

'She was testing me. Poking with a stick. I couldn't bear it. It was enough to make me throw up. And that's how it will be. It's like a war and you can't be neutral if you're housed under the same roof. If we stay we've got to find an apartment.'

I was ready to agree with her.

'Yes. We shall,' I said. 'Why not. Somewhere within easy reach. Marta perhaps? Or Capo di Monte. With a view of the lake.'

The Marchesa was on her feet when we rejoined her.

'Will you excuse an old woman?' she said. 'I must take my siesta. A bad habit I acquired when Giuso and I were in Sicily in the fifties. You must make yourselves at home. Ring that little bell and Carlo will bring you whatever you want. My house is yours.'

iii

The dog started barking and leaping about as soon as he saw us approach.

'That bloody dog,' Muzio said. 'Just look at him.'

It amused me to see the determined look on Muzio's thin face and to hear him swearing in English. 'Bloody' was a favourite adjective: suitable for a whole range of occasions such as this unexpected emergency at the heart of his domain. Muzio was a natural liberal obliged by circumstance to exercise conservative restraints. His 'bloody' was quaint but it relieved his feelings. This dog demanded notice and total indulgence. Imposed from within or from without, civilisation depended on restraint. Discipline was essential: nobody had ever attempted to discipline this bloody dog.

'Turco! Turco! Shut up will you.'

The dog barked even louder than ever. The gate was wide open but he bounded about inside the confines of Fontane as though it were his function to welcome rather than ward off intruders.

'It's too ridiculous,' Muzio said. 'He's here because he kept biting his mistress and when the test comes, he licks the intruder's boots. Shut up you useless beast!'

Muzio was furious with himself more than with anyone else. While work was in progress at the proposed Study Centre, and making good progress under his supervision, thieves had broken in and made off with expensive tools and recent archaeological finds, temporarily stored in cardboard boxes. The farmhouse was in an isolated position on the brow of a hill overlooking the lake and nothing of the slightest value should have been left lying about. We had been together to report the break-in. I moved in Muzio's shadow like some pale plenipotentiary from a distant land and he used me to underline the international nature of the enterprise at Fontane. As long as thieves could break in and burgle such an important property with impunity, the reputation of the commune was under a cloud and the good name of the province besmirched. The *Carabinieri* listened alertly and were delighted to demonstrate their efficiency. That very morning they had located a stolen van abandoned in a ditch on the old road to Arlena. It contained a few archaeological objects probably too heavy to carry off by hand and they were engaged on compiling a list that they would like us to examine. A haphazard affair, said the *maresciallo*, very probably the work of unemployed vandals from Viterbo. He had one or two leads. He would pursue the case with the utmost vigour and get in touch with the Marchese as soon as he had anything vital to report. I stood in the background listening to it all like a keen observer in the back row of the stalls appreciative of the orotund projection.

'That bloody dog,' Muzio said, 'should have been strangled at birth.'

Turco belonged to Prue and it was she who had spoilt him. The white fluffy puppy had swollen into a white fluffy monster that snarled like a wolf and still pranced about with infantile abandon. He had bitten his mistress in the arm and in the leg before being handed over to the muscular regimen of Luca Puri, the farm manager. It was Luca now who slapped the dog down as he walked to meet us. Turco took no offence. He slobbered around Luca's powerful legs and at the first opportunity reached up to lick his bare forearm with salivary adoration. Muzio gave a succinct report of our visit to the *Carabinieri* and Luca took it in with a concentrated stillness that gave me the chance to study him with the close attention the old Marchesa recommended. His eyes were small but it didn't follow that they denoted slyness. On the contrary one could argue that they lent a bucolic honesty to his rugged looks. Her distrust of the man could be due more to her own impotent envy than any peculiarity in the shape of his head. Up on the roof of the loggia two of his men were laying tiles, fitting the convex part of each piece over the concave portion of the next in the way in which it had been done in this classical landscape since the days of the Etruscans.

'I know the horse has bolted,' Luca said. 'But I'm having the locks on the stable doors changed all the same. Mauro will see to it. This place will never be safe until someone lives in it.'

A man who pondered on problems and emergencies before they occurred was best equipped to deliver considered remedies in as few words as possible. Muzio showed complete confidence in his *fattore*. It was pleasant to see the respect they had for each other. Luca was expert in his business and 'Don Muzio' as he called him was the kind of enlightened master to whom he could demonstrate loyalty without losing an atom of his evident sturdy independence. His smile was a comparatively rare event. He pursed his lips and stared intently with small suspicious eyes as he weighed both the practical worth and the consequences of whatever was being put to him. His solemn statuesque manner was plainly an aspect of his resolve never to be ingratiating: but when he did smile, there was an abrupt transformation from grave senator to a country clown capable of dionysiac abandon.

'I have to go over to San Magno to inspect the terracing,' Luca said. 'There are cracks there after the rains. Could be five days work. I'll take this brute with me.'

Turco barked with joy when he sensed he was about to be taken on a trip. Luca slapped him into panting silence.

'My grandfather used to say working dogs should never be allowed near women,' he said. 'Especially ladies.'

He expected us both to appreciate his humour.

'Robberies are acts of God,' he said. 'As far as Insurance companies are concerned. That's me speaking, not my grandfather.'

He collected his jacket and made the dog jump into the back of his pick-up truck. He shouted his last instructions to his men on the roof. Luca was younger than Muzio, but his attitude was that of a protective older brother. His grandfather had been *fattore* under the old system that resembled the Tuscan *mazzadria* where the tenants were liable for a rent as much as half of what they produced. By now Luca's office in the *fattoria* had become the nerve centre of a considerable agricultural co-operative. Muzio remained the chairman and the titular head, and his approval had to be sought for any major project, but I could not imagine it being withheld as long as Luca remained manager. We watched his dusty truck bumping up the track that led to the main road. He went about his business with something of the visible confidence of a hero in a Western movie.

'He's a good fellow,' Muzio said. 'A first class manager. But he has some pretty appalling ideas.'

He smiled and shook his head like a parent amused by the wayward antics of a cherished offspring.

'He was mad keen on turning this place into an hotel. *Albergo Fontane*. With stables turned into a restaurant specialising in regional cooking. There you are. That is the limit of their creative imagination.'

We walked around to the front of the house and stood on the terrace among piles of building materials. Muzio pointed to the uncultivated slope immediately below us strewn with boulders.

'He wanted to dig out a swimming pool down there,' Muzio said. 'He couldn't wait to bring in the earth movers. I had quite a job to restrain him. "Listen Luca" I said. "These will be young people. Students and post-graduates. They like exercise. If they want to swim they can run down the couple of kilometres to the lake. And collect an appetite on the way back." "I'm not talking about students," he said. "I'm thinking of rich old ladies who want the whole world on a plate." The ideas they have. The mentality!'

He meant the ordinary inhabitants of his territory. I wondered if he realised how paternalistic his attitude sounded. They were all his wayward children, living by courtesy of his ancestors in a suitably modified version of the earthly paradise. Eons ago the earth had heaved expressly for their benefit and the volcanic pit of hell had been covered over with the awesome tranquillity of the wide waters of the lake that stretched before us now permeated with the enchanting dazzle of the morning sunlight: all for their benefit. Just by being born here, they had inherited the earth.

'They don't need to think,' I said. 'They've got everything. Much better to keep their distance from the Tree of Knowledge. Just look at it. Is there anywhere that gives you a stronger sense of an earthly paradise? And on top of that, layer upon layer of history and if you care to look, prehistory. A palimpsest of the human condition.'

He was amused by my enthusiasm.

'Look at it,' I said. 'On a day like this. No wonder they painted the walls of their tombs in such bright colours.'

'On a day like this, my dear chap, this place was burgled. There is always trouble in this paradise. Because it is infested with snakes and bandits! Wild beasts and dangerous humans. Just like the rest of the world.'

I was curious about Luca.

'Is he married?' I said.

'Divorced. Luca is a self-centred pagan,' Muzio said. 'He has a wife and a couple of children in Manciano. His idea of heaven is driving down to Port'Ercole in a fast car and lying on the beach with his ageing pals watching the talent and discussing prices. To be quite honest he hasn't much conception of anything beyond profit and loss. But I mustn't sound ungracious. He's an excellent manager and that makes my life much easier.'

I heard Prue calling our names in the empty building. Her musical tone reverberated in the vacant rooms. She emerged to tread gingerly over the unfinished threshold.

'How are my boy scouts? The scholar detectives. All the riddles solved I have no doubt.'

She showed signs of impatience as Muzio reported on our visit to the *Carabinieri*. Even the mystery of the deserted van in the ditch only briefly held her interest.

'Have I got news for you, my dears!'

She smiled triumphantly and pointed at me.

'Such a stroke of luck. We've found the perfect hide-out for Herr Doktor.'

Prue liked inventing nicknames for me. They didn't seem to stick. Muzio was disapproving.

'He doesn't need a hide-out,' he said. 'He's perfectly alright where he is.'

She ignored the protest: this was something she and Marian had worked out between them.

'On the second floor of the *Palazzo degli Adami*! With a balcony overlooking the lake and the *Rocca* protecting your right flank. A reasonable rent. Cheap in fact. What more can you ask? No room of course for the *macchina in casa*: they didn't allow for cars in the fourteenth century. But a parking space on the *piazzale*. Who could ask for anything more?'

'I honestly don't see there is the slightest need for them to move,' Muzio said.

'None whatsoever.'

'Don't worry,' Prue said. 'Your playmate will be no more than seven kilometres away. And his dear wife will be able to sleep more peacefully at night.'

Muzio turned away. Embarrassment put an end to his objection. It pained him that the open hostility between his mother and his wife made it impossible for a woman he admired and respected like my Marian to stay in his ancestral home with its many rooms and secluded gardens.

Prue was studying the boulder-strewn slope immediately below us.

'You know what would be just right down there, don't you? A swimming pool. And a second terrace lower down. A flowery terrace you know, overlooking the olive grove. I can just see it.'

She made film-director's gestures with her outstretched hands, framing her view of an embellished landscape. Marian was making her way carefully towards us. My heart stopped as I saw the girl from the Basilica take her arm to help her over the building debris. They were like mother and daughter and Marian looked so pleased and happy.

'This is Grazia,' she said.

She was delighted to introduce her and account for her unexpected presence.

'I'm in the process of giving her an English lesson!'

They were looking at each other and laughing like old friends.

'She saved our lives didn't she Prue? It was amazing. I was about to be landed with a very dubious arrangement when who should come in with a message from her father but Grazia. She was so quick and so intelligent. I saw her whisper to her friend Adriana who works in the agency and before you knew it we were saved and we were redirected.... Mind you I haven't said "yes" yet, have I Grazia? I said we'd find you right away, Aled, and you could come and give it all the seal of approval. Exciting isn't it?'

They were smiling at me. I was being given time for the shock to sink in.

'Did you see the old stables?' Prue said. 'Or the dining-room I should call it. These beastly students are going to be thoroughly spoilt.'

A plasterer was at work on the scaffolding at the gable end of the long stable-room. Prue greeted him as 'Michelangelo'. He raised his trowel and the room reverberated with their humorous exchanges. Marian took me aside to whisper in my ear.

'Do you see the likeness?' she said. 'I saw it immediately – even from the side. The line of the neck and the ear. Did you notice? And the smile. It isn't the same. And the eyes. They're not the same. But the effect, the overall effect is so similar.... You think I'm making too much of it?'

It gave me an excuse to stare at the girl: I had to conceal how fast my heart was beating. Muzio was being nice to her. Showing her where we planned to put up full-size facsimiles of Etruscan tomb paintings on the walls. She was paying him the closest attention, just as Rhiannon would have done. Why was I so intent always on concealment? Joy should be spontaneous, open. This was a disturbance bordering on madness that had to be contained.

'A bit of kitsch,' Muzio was saying. 'But it should help to create the right atmosphere. Stimulate a spirit of enlightened inquiry. After all, lots of museums have done it.'

She was local. Did she understand what he was talking about? Of course she did. She was listening with a bright intensity that enhanced her charm in exactly the way I remembered Marian, when we were young, listening so intently to our professor that he would expand his exposition for the sheer pleasure of her graceful attention.

Prue was examining an enlarged tracing of a detail from the Tomb of Orcus stacked against a bare wall.

'Hey,' she said. 'Just look at this. Now who does she remind you of?'

Muzio tried to respond to her high spirits.

'*Tu mi fai rimembrar, dove e qual era / Proserpina nel tempo che perdette la madre lei....*'

'Purgatorio!'

Grazia spoke up like the brightest pupil in a class. Muzio showed he was pleased and impressed by the speed of her response. I could see it also made it easier for Marian to dote on her image. The girl completed the quotation.

'*Ed ella primavera.*'

'Never mind about that,' Prue said.

She insisted on all our attention.

'Who does she remind you of? Apart from the snakes in her hair?'

There was no immediate answer.

'It's Persephone,' Muzio said, rather half-heartedly.

'I know that. But who is she like?'

She seemed to consider appealing to the plasterer on his platform, but he was in the middle of exercising his craft, transferring wet plaster from the mortarboard to the wall with a series of dexterous movements with his trowel.

'Me of course,' Prue said. 'Who else? What a head-dress. It would have to be made properly of course. Not so easy to sing with a thing like that on your head. We could put on a marvellous performance in here. Build a stage that end. You can be Pluto, Don Muzio. You look gloomy enough. And Grazia here can be Euridice I suppose. Where can we find an Orpheus? Um? How about Herr Doktor? Aren't all Welshmen supposed to be able to sing?'

Prue took in the frown on Muzio's face.

'O My God. Just think how wonderfully annoyed your mother would be.'

Prue always brought things down to earth and that brought me relief. I saw Muzio's resentment. It was indiscreet of Prue to bring up family conflicts in the hearing of the girl, who would quite likely carry it all back to the *trattoria*, which as Prue herself said was equivalent to a broadcast on local radio: not to mention the plasterer who had begun showing off his singing voice as he reloaded his trowel. Prue moved closer to Marian and myself so that she could pass on a comment in English for our ears alone.

'Singing is for servants.'

We had heard Prue repeat this odd proclamation of her mother-in-law's many times before: and her comment: ' "So is living, I suppose," I said to her. My God what century is that woman living in?'

iv

We were pleased with the apartment. Marian said it was exactly what we needed. It would encourage us to integrate, become part of the circumstances in which we found ourselves. The heavy furniture surrounded us with the impartial cordiality of an old-fashioned hotel. Our neighbours in the *borgo* acknowledged our presence with regular greetings. An amiable woman called Aurelia came in to clean three mornings a week. She accepted any stale bread we could spare her to feed her six hens cooped in one of the roadside caves carved out of the tuffo. She sang softly as she worked. Our privacy was respected with a traditional politeness we studied and admired. We were in the oldest part of an ancient town. The people were like the buildings. They contrived to be medieval and modern at one and the same time.

Marian had a mission. She undertook to give Grazia Guidatti lessons in English literature. They had become fast friends. Marian had no need to be embarrassed by the intensity of her interest in the girl. They could spend time together. They could sit in the shade and the most dilapidated garden could take on an arcadian radiance from their presence. Even at a distance the sounds they made were appealing: when they laughed it was an instant addition to the music of the landscape.

For my own part I was compelled to work up a new interest into an obsessive academic pursuit: a piece of research I could claim entirely my own. Muzio's archaeological projects required little from me except regular assent. I would cherish an enterprise of my own. I had an uninterrupted view of it from the narrow balcony of our apartment that overlooked the lake. The spinsters who owned the place had left a pair of German binoculars which I used to contemplate the small island of Martana where the subject of my researches was caught in a silken trap and murdered. With my elbows on the balcony I could stare at the island through the binoculars and see Amalasuntha walking again through the ruined gardens. It had to be part of the glory of the place: a presence of the past. That murder engineered from far away Constantinople had brought about the collapse of Gothic power in Italy. There was a case to be proved – death by conspiracy not misadventure – evidence to be sifted, and the enterprise would allow me to live in the past as a ghostly refugee from an awkward present.

The balcony with binoculars was a fine and private place to ruminate. It was also liable to unexpected interruptions. Below me, where a uniformed street-sweeper was pacing his labours, a noisy open-topped vehicle in lurid colours drew up and the youthful driver stood on the seat and waved to attract my attention.

'Dottore! Doctor Morgan! I have a present for you. Can I come up?'

As well settled-in residents we already knew about Giorgio what everyone else knew. He was the spoilt son and heir of the Lido, a chrome and glass hotel further along the lake. He had copper-coloured hair, terracotta skin, a smile as wide as his face and a voice hoarse with interminable crowing. I sometimes bumped into him at the bakery first thing in the morning. 'Ah Giorgio!' The baker's wife always expressed her delight at seeing him. I was never so pleased myself.

'Can I, Dottore?'

I could drop a flower pot on his smirking face. For one reason only. His passion for Grazia Guidatti. Aurelia knew about this. I suppose everyone knew. Aurelia pointed out to Marian the advantages of an alliance between two families that in the not so distant past had been on opposite sides in the struggle between the Black and the Red. There was more to it than that. Aurelia played on Marian's curiosity with dark hints in the lower register. Anything concerning Grazia she was quick to realise was of deepening interest to the foreigners resident in the apartment for which she had certain responsibilities.

'Look, Doctor Morgan. Look!'

He was exhibiting fragments of sculpture and pottery. Then from the pocket of his modishly crumpled jacket he produced what looked like a pair of false teeth and flashed them up at me. He considered his gifts and his jokes like himself, irresistible. A brief nod from me and he was on his way up. When I opened the door and he entered the cool of our dim vestibule carrying a canvas bag, he was already bowing and dipping merrily as though miming in an unresponsive mirror the kind of warm welcome he felt was his due. He put the bag down in order to offer me a brief glimpse of the false teeth.

'Etruscan!'

He chuckled happily.

'Not everyone knows that the Etruscans invented false teeth. "Look" I say to them. "These come from the tomb of Lars Porsena." That, they are quite prepared to believe. But not the historical fact that the Etruscans invented false teeth. What can you do with such people?'

Here too, it was standard practice for individuals to despair of the failings of their tribe. Was he referring to the entire population, or to the habitues of the bars around the lake that he chose to frequent? He was a notably social animal liable to turn up wherever there was promise of excitement. He made up noisy vehicles in order to roam further afield in search of diversion. A spoilt child determined to make his mark on the world but uncertain yet exactly how to do it.

'There must be more than these.'

He opened the canvas bag so that I could inspect the marble and terracotta fragments inside.

'It's quite amazing,' he said. 'I happened to be in a quarter of Viterbo I never visit. Such a dull corner. Very boring. But we needed a new valve for the garden pump and my mother knew these people. I had to wait so I dropped in the bar across the square and who should I get talking to but these three scruffy cowboys. I couldn't give you their names. I knew one of them by sight. Ruggero something. He used to be an apprentice with the plasterer working in Fontane. He sacked him for being lazy. They had these bags under the table. "Hey, you fellows," I said. "What have you got down there, last week's laundry?" They were full of innocence. Bits and pieces they had collected on a building site. "Now look," I said. "I wasn't born yesterday. Would they by any chance be part of the stuff that was stolen up at Fontane? If I buy you something to drink, you can tell me all about it." This Ruggero, he went as pale as death and pushed back his chair and mumbled something about an urgent message he had to deliver in Civitacastellana, and before you could say "stop or go" they were gone, all three of them, and leaving this bag behind. Just like this.'

He was staring in my face with the innocent cordiality of a painted cherub: a categorical assurance that there was nothing to disbelieve in his story.

'I'm not an expert,' I said. 'You should take them to Don Muzio.'

His manner changed abruptly. His head hung down.

'You are quite right,' he said. 'I confess it openly. These are an excuse to come and see you. To speak to you. Forgive me for asking. Is Grazia here?'

He was frowning hard with the effort of imposing on his cheerful features the aspect of a love-sick swain. He expected my sympathy and in theory I would have been inclined to give it. In ancient societies, after all, there were forms of love that were acknowledged as afflictions along with pneumonia or scarlet fever. The truth was at the moment I found him more objectionable than Buddy Thwaite.

'She's with my wife,' I said. 'In the old garden. Do you want to speak with her?'

Giorgio shook his head sadly.

'Ah, the lesson,' he said. 'Everyone wants to learn English. Why is that, Dottore?'

It was a good question and it took me unawares. Giorgio seemed to know the answer.

'To get away,' he said. 'That's what it is. And why is that? I say we make a terrible mistake running away from the place we belong.'

Had I seriously underestimated this young man? He seemed capable of wisdom. I should not allow middle-aged prejudice against youth to blind me to his merits. I should invite him to sit down.

'Would you like me to call them up?'

I glanced at my wrist-watch.

'I should think the lesson would be over by now.'

He was not ready for a confrontation.

'If you would tell her one thing,' he said.

It was easier for him to ask a favour now that I had shown a degree of sympathy and an inclination to oblige him.

'Tell her that I forgive her,' he said.

This took me by surprise. I responded as delicately as I could.

'Isn't that the kind of thing you'd better tell her yourself?' I said.

'I saw them with my own eyes,' Giorgio said. 'In each other's arms. I could have killed him. But I'm not that sort. I'm modern. I don't believe in vendetta. And as for women. You can smell it when they are full of the instinctive lust for mating. I don't think he had her. I don't think so. Not when I was watching. I could see down into the grotto when I spied on them. He had the smell of her on his fingers. I saw enough to torment myself with a jealousy I thought would kill me. Tell her I forgive her. Tell her I will honour my pledge.'

He gave a deep sigh to indicate the weight of the burden he carried. Now he was ready to smile again. He would take his leave as politeness demanded, on a cheerful note.

'They say love turns every fool into a bit of a poet,' he said. 'Now I know it from experience. You were so kind to listen to me ... it all tumbled out.'

As I saw him to the door he turned to me again.

'Mind you, Dottore, I'm not such a fool as all that. When I saw what I saw, I turned it over in my mind of course, and as soon as I cooled down I knew what to do. I went straight to her father and I told him. "This is going on," I said. "Are you going to stop it?" And fair play to him, he put a stop to it. You have to know what's going on, Dottore, or the whole thing becomes unmanageable.'

In the dim vestibule his face shone like an Etruscan mask: half animal, half human; repulsive and fascinating. Did he understand me better than I understood his pagan depths? I struggled to assume a benevolent manner.

'Tell me Giorgio,' I said. 'How old are you?'

He smiled as if he were responding to a far more subtle question.

'Twenty, Dottore,' he said. 'But they always said I had an old head on these shoulders.'

He demonstrated the truth of the received wisdom by sharing with me a final confidence.

'In less than ten years my mother will retire,' he said. 'And I shall own the Lido. Grazia will be glad then. Queen of the Lido. Mistress of the Palace.'

It was a relief to be rid of him. The light became gloomy, the apartment unfamiliar. What were we dabbling in? It is dangerous to intrude into the lives of other people. Altogether better to retreat into ourselves and cherish an independence no matter how sterile. Hide in that cloak of self-protection that can go under the pious name of polite restraint.

From the kitchen window of our place I could peer down into the dried out garden to watch Marian nurse her knee as she listens to Grazia reading, correcting her gently as she went along. I don't know why my fevered imagination chooses to see her as a protective deity watching over a young and beautiful nymph. Arid academics need arcadian images. An earth not defiled by the Fall. It was a dream and a dreamer is always condemned to stand outside his dream. My interest was outside their innocence. Their soft voices snared the summer morning and turned me into a stone spy.

V

There was no one to whom I could turn to unburden myself. I had to think more than twice before opening my mouth. I couldn't ask Marian what it was she and the girl were talking about without betraying an unhealthy interest. She was amused by the intensity of my devotion to the minutiae of daily living. Shall I get some more wine? Do we need more olive oil? I had to guard against asking the same question more than once on the same day. I made it my business to get the fresh bread first thing in the morning, to contact the fishermen on the lake about the first catch. I knew where to get everything we needed and hurried around like a boy-scout doing messages to make Marian's season in the apartment as untroubled and as comfortable as possible. I must have been a familiar figure on the cobbled side-streets as I went up and down, from the *borgo* to the more recent town centre closer to the lake.

But we arrived in this place to heal our wounds in private, not to lick them in public. While we swam in the lake, tramped in the forest, inspected ruins and out of the way churches, we would be soothed by the stately progress of an Italian summer sauntering on beyond the measured season. In this way the pace of living would slow down to give us a fresh awareness of growth in stillness: a capacity to draw into our bruised psyche enough of the creaturely strength of the earth around us to bring us renewed vitality. The soil itself exudes messages as well as thin mists and fertile vapours. Just so. Just so.

I might have taken Muzio into my confidence if I had had more to reveal and less to conceal. In any case he was preoccupied with a sequence of small crises that had come up in estate management. We had to postpone a week-end exploration in Selva del Lamone which might have given me the chance at least of enjoying the comfort of one of our quasi-philosophic conversations. When I returned the fragments of the finds that Giorgio had left with me, Muzio set them out on the desk in his study and stared at them as though they were pieces in a game of chess. 'These are the least valuable,' he said. 'But how did they know?' He brooded at length over the problem. 'Human behaviour,' he said. ' Is so darkly unaccountable. No matter what restrictions you put on it, the evil will wriggle out.'

I was uneasy as I listened. Was my behaviour so visibly unsavoury to bring such sadness into his husky voice. 'I use the term "evil",' he said. 'I suppose some would call it the aggressive power of the life force. Like weeds breaking through concrete.' He smiled at the comparison. He could hardly be referring to the pilferings of a bunch of young vandals from Viterbo. He could have been talking about some animal instinct struggling to free itself from the gravitation pull of death and carrion corruption. 'When you think, Aled, of the sheer weight of supernatural restraints in pre-industrial civilisations....' For my own part I was still puzzled as to why he should want to think of supernatural restraints as he stared at the haphazard fragments on his desk.... 'Hellfire, torments, eternal damnation, all that sort of thing, what little effect they had on human behaviour....' When he looked up at me I sensed an urgent plea for sympathy as well as understanding... 'You realise how thin the thread of reason, thinner than the thread of fate, that is supposed to hold together what civilisation we have left.'

I concluded it was private rather than public behaviour that gave the melancholy edge to his musings. He must have been thinking of his wife and his mother: present discord and the deeper conflicts of the past. The boldness of his mother's neo-fascist pose could be an effective cover for more serious crimes committed in a past darker than she was prepared to admit. Prue more than hinted as much. She had shown Marian a tattered photograph of a fascist reception committee greeting Adolf Hitler at Orvieto station with flowers and a red carpet. Marian said the young Marchesa was a conspicuous presence in a smart black uniform.

To show solidarity and to please him, I attended a day conference on environmental issues in the Province. The meeting was held in a secularised church off the piazza in the lower town. I sat in the back and Muzio sat on the dais in the restored apse of the church along with the guest speakers. There were four of them and the microphone was passed between them along the table. The bare walls of the church were hung with posters and slogans. It was in every way a praiseworthy occasion. I sat there alone, fingering leaflets and a pamphlet before I realised that Grazia was sitting a few empty seats away from me, industriously taking notes.

To whom else could I turn to unburden myself but this girl? She was so busy taking notes as far as I could understand she hadn't seen me: or if she had she had cancelled out my presence with Marian's absence. What she should be busy writing now would be a record of the confused confessions I longed to make. If I moved closer to her she could hear my thoughts. It took a supreme effort of will on my part to return my attention to the lecturer. Of course, I heard him argue in his monotonous voice, in a civilised society it has become imperative to modify, for example, the individual freedom of the hunter, and compel him by law, to re-adjust his attitude to a whole range of aspects of what we call for convenience sake, the animal kingdom.

He was not arguing that birds and fish and insects had intrinsic rights in any anthropomorphic sense: merely that the sheer pressure our bulging species was bringing to bear on nature demanded an urgent re-assessment of values. Amen to that I say and if I were closer to the girl, I could explain in simple terms that the daughter I loved with a consistent untainted purity was eaten by maggots and insects, and that I didn't seek to blame them. All I would argue would be the reinstatement of angels in the great chain of being which had to take in life and death, if only to avoid the pitfall of sanctifying the fierce sub-terrestrial agonies of insects.

A neighbour from the *borgo* was trying to attract my attention.

He was a retired dentist and he wanted me to witness his interest in the environment and his public spirit. I returned his salutation with restrained cordiality. Had he noticed my avid interest in the girl? I was brought to earth from the contemplation of angels with a sickening thud. I no longer fitted in with this assembly of responsible citizens sitting patiently within the bare walls of this secularised cult centre. The stone slabs under my feet changed from cool to cold and I needed an exposure to the sun and the mundane concerns of the piazza. I could stand outside as if I were waiting for someone, or go in a bar and order the inevitable cappuccino or a campari and soda.

When I moved to the shade of the church Grazia came up to me. Her eyes were large with sympathy. Her face was as serious and as perfect as an angel of annunciation and I was struck as speechless as a green youth with admiration of the way she held her head slightly to one side.

'I admire her so much. She has such courage.'

It took me time to realise it was Rhiannon she was talking about, not Marian. This sobered me a little. I began to concentrate on the differences, and the superficial resemblance vanished. They couldn't be more different, so what was the nature of the illusion that led me to believe even for an instant that they were one and the same? What is the nature of a smile beyond the exposure of well-cared-for teeth? Was Rhiannon and her accumulation of posthumous virtues all they talked about, when the sound of their mingled voices was as soothing as the murmur of hidden doves and the intermittent hum of bees at work in the flower beds?

'You think I am like her?'

She was inviting me to study her. I would need to walk around her, examine her delicious profile and then that full face where the plumpness of adolescence had left the smoothest traces and the perfect shape of the lips curved in an incipient smile. Could I tell her I had this painful need for beauty while my foot was over the threshold of middle age? Did I appear such an obvious father figure, licking his wounds in the shadow of a former church and passing his hand nervously over his grey hair?

'I would like to be like her.'

I was listening so intently to her words I must have appeared to be memorising them as they fell from her lips.

'She was a free spirit I think. That is what I want to be. To dispose of myself. I'm not going to be disposed of.'

She was laughing. Like Rhiannon she was determined not to

117

take herself too seriously and this added to the enchantment. But it also pushed me further down into the dungeon inside myself. How could I ever confess that it was the need to worship love that I longed for? She was holding up her notebook for my attention so that I had to stop staring at her face.

'I am making notes for Franz,' she said. 'He wants to know everything about our region. That is how the Germans are. So thorough. I like that. They get down to work and they get to the bottom of things. Did you know about the prophet who lived in a cave on Monte Amiata? In this century.'

I was charmed by the innocence of her question. Rhiannon was like this: wide-eyed, smiling, asking questions like musical phrases.

'I had no idea. And I live here. But Franz knew. That is how he is. He looks into things. He studies. He learns languages. An hour and a half in the mornings and an hour and a half at night!'

She expected me to share in her wonder. This Franz was already clothed in glory. She had no idea of the quantity of surplus love that was weighing me down. All she had to do was reach out her hand and I could transfer it directly to her.

'When they came here, his Italian was so poor. It was so funny but he worked at it. An hour and a half first thing in the morning and an hour and a half last thing at night. If you need to communicate, he said, language is a minor problem.'

She smiled at me with such innocence, she could have been leading me to worship with her at the same Teutonic shrine. It would be a way of being at her side. I had to make a rigorous attempt to hold on to my common sense.

'Did my wife give you the message from Giorgio?'

The frown brought a severe aspect to those too immaculate features and restored a degree of order to my seething emotions.

'That one,' she said. 'He can keep his hands off me. I won't let him touch me. I would rather die.'

She searched my face anxiously to gauge the impact of her vehemence. It seemed to me a strange bond was being established between us: not the bond I desired, but something was at least better than nothing. Across the piazza, in the doorway of a jeweller's shop, someone was trying to attract her attention. She would allow nothing to intervene at such a vital juncture. There were important things she had to explain.

'How can I protect myself except by making myself hard? I don't want to be hard. A woman shouldn't be forced to live on just what men want from her. Why should a blessing become a curse?

What a girl has is what so many men want that it becomes danger-
ous for her to walk out of the house. This is unjust. Like slavery.'
  'Of course it is.'
  I was eager to agree with her.
  'Franz understands,' she said. 'We are so open with each other.
Here that is impossible. They are all like that Giorgio. They think
of one thing only. A woman as a chattel or a toy. One or the other.
Something to use and then toss to one side. Do you mind if I talk
like this?'
  She surmised that my attention had begun to wander.
  'No,' I said. 'Only there's someone by the jeweller's shop trying
to attract your attention.'
  She gave me a last smile before she left me.
  'There is so much to talk about,' she said. 'You and your wife.
I am so comforted, talking to you both.'
  I continued to smile as she crossed the square. In my mind I
would go over every word she uttered for the rest of the day.

vi

I was quite wrong about Amalasuntha. She was as much the victim
of her own machinations as those of the unspeakable Empress
Theodora. I suggested to Marian we should make a trip to
Ravenna to study the idealised image of that woman and her sinis-
ter court in the mosaic of the apse of the Basilica of S.Vitale. She
didn't take me seriously. 'Why don't you stare more closely at
those reproductions in your book,' she said. 'Count the *tesserae* and
come to a conclusion about the petrification of earthly power.' She
was right of course. As usual. The whole edifice was paid for by
an imperial spy and it was begun while Amalasuntha still imagined
she reigned in Italy. This is the reality of politics. What can I
conclude, except the platitude that politicians, whether patrician or
proletarian, ancient or modern, are faced with the same perennial
problems. It is their machinations combined with their ruthless
manipulations of the baser instincts of their constituents that bring
the glory of one garden after another crashing to the ground.
Marian is not in the mood to appreciate the pleasures of the historical chase.
  Through Muzio's influence and good offices I have gained
access to the works of Cassiodorus and Procopius in the archiepis-

119

copal library. In these deeply silent rooms the dust has been allowed to settle as if it were a delicate part of the evidence that was on no account to be disturbed. In a glass case by my elbow, eleventh century vestments in faded threads of crimson and gold hang waiting for the last judgement. This is the place to be. The further away in time the dread events to be studied, the older the record, the more fundamental the lessons to be extracted from them. There are standard nightmares for tyrants, for example, and they recur like decimal points through any calibration of history – like the head of a great fish on a plate on which Amalasuntha's father at dinner the night before he died, saw the open jaw and accusing glare of his last innocent victim. Here history cannot be abolished. Out of an ecclesiastic silence the past emerges, like a giant stirring in the mist, and cold as it is, it does not crumble to the touch. These rooms provide a refuge where the image of Grazia Guidatti does not flicker constantly in front of my eyes. Here a middle-aged man need not listen to his bones rattle inside his flesh as he attempts a grotesque courtship dance in front of a radiant girl who is looking straight through him at the image of her own fair-haired Teutonic hero, her private Dietrich von Bern.

Not that there is any warmth or comfort in the sour scandals of Procopius' secret history. Jealous of a woman she had never set eyes on, Theodora conspired with Theodatus to destroy Amalasuntha. So much malice and malevolence and unremitting rancour.... Why should I be poring over these bilious records of human frailty through the ages? Chiefly in order to avoid the even more distasteful task of examining myself.

Next door to the library were three spacious rooms of this private museum which had no need to ingratiate itself with the visiting public. Items from a range of periods were exhibited together. They were intermittently dusted, consolingly disordered. Muzio had told me to look out for a glass case in a dim corner containing the mummified body of an unknown desert saint reputed to have been brought back from the Crusades as a gift for a twelfth century archbishop. Some inquisitive scholar had proved it was not the glamorous champion of third century orthodoxy previous generations had claimed, so the church authorities had it quietly shunted into the comfortable obscurity of its dim corner. As a small boy Muzio said he used to look at it for hours convinced that it was due any moment for resurrection. Then he would go home and the saint would visit him at night with his jewelled head-dress slipping over his left eye and the sounds of an unknown language hissing through ivory teeth. More that once he woke up crying to find his mother bending over him with exactly the same fixed smile on her face.

In the bright light of the open doorway leading from the museum to the courtyard I saw the figure of a man in a chauffeur's cap standing at ease, waiting for instructions. I recognised Carlo, the old Marchesa's loyal retainer. Here he was exercising yet another function. I was not eager to encounter him. I began a fresh circuit of the exhibits, paying particular attention to a large amphora in a case by itself. The decorative figures on it were black and particularly clear. A young woman was being pursued by a lustful centaur. I was trying to remember the legend when I looked up and saw the dowager Marchesa on the other side of the glass case smiling at me grimly.

'It's a fake,' she said.

I stared at the amphora and tried to see it in a new light.

'I remember the man who made it,' she said. 'He had a cramped little workshop behind his watchmaker's shop in Perugia. A clever little man Zappatoni. The family still have the business. But the son is a clumsy creature. He could never turn out a thing like that.'

While I was in the library she must have been sitting in the back of her ancient limousine with the sun-blinds drawn, waiting for me to emerge. Carlo was at her beck and call. She would dispatch him across the street to fetch her squeezed lemon and ice water and to check on my movements. She was a cunning old woman and she was Muzio's mother. There was the same morose world-weary look in their eyes: the same stubborn resolve to face up to unpleasant realities. She indicated the leather-covered locker-seats between the windows. I should sit down and listen to her. Carlo stood in the doorway exercising the seasoned patience of a hotel trained servant.

'You realise my charming daughter-in-law would like to kill me?'

She was smiling calmly as she said it, not displeased at the expression of shock on my face.

'She has her reasons. But you wouldn't expect me to respect them. She has a lover. She would not have children on any account, but she is quite happy to have a lover. Perhaps more than one.'

I was tense with the effort of restraining a wave of nausea rising inside me. Between the shining floorboards and the high ceiling of this airless room, I was overhearing echoes of the determined malice that drove Procopius to compose a secret history in order to demonstrate the depravity of an imperial master and mistress he had spent so much of his working life supplying with unlimited fulsome flattery. Not that this old witch would condescend to flatter anyone: the source of her venom was an accumulation of frustrated hopes and the disappointments of a long lifetime.

'Does the truth embarrass you?'

She had observed my discomfort.

'It does most people. She claims she visits her music teacher. Judging by the results he is not very good. He is so old he doesn't hear very well or see very well. So she does what she likes. Recently I have had her followed. You understand my motives, my dear friend? I will not allow her to harm my son.'

As her head moved in the light from the window, it was dangerously youthful eyes I saw glowing in a withered face. She wanted to put my loyalty to Muzio to the test. She would compel me to take sides: prise me out of any comfortable neutrality.

'It gives me no pleasure to touch on the subject of my appalling daughter-in-law, I assure you. It is not one of the comforts of my old age. All I ask, my dear friend, is that you do not allow your wife to become an accomplice in my dear daughter-in-law's machinations.'

'Good heavens!...'

I had to register a protest before I could itemise the things I was protesting about. Prue was an independent person and she went her own way but I could not imagine that she was conducting a clandestine love affair. Where was the evidence? Was it Carlo who followed her checking out on the length of time she spent with her ancient music teacher? And it was even more absurd to suggest she had more than one lover. Perhaps her free and easy English ways had given rise to gossip. If they had, it was unworthy of the old Marchesa to pay it any attention. And worse than unworthy to suspect my wife, Marian, of all people, of being any sort of accomplice to what she, as a minister's daughter, for heaven's sake, and still an uncompromising Puritan, would classify as treachery as well as adultery. Prue had been a particular comfort to my wife after a bitter bereavement and we, Marian and I, had no reason to be other than devotedly grateful to Prue and Muzio for all the help and comfort they had given us. I stood up. The choice was making a long speech or remaining obstinately silent. The old woman was watching me with the close amusement of a behaviourist peering through a two-way mirror.

'My dear Doctor Morgan,' she said. 'I have hurt your feelings. That is the risk I always have to take. And you cannot believe me.

I suppose your loyalty does you credit. But I have the evidence. All I ask is that you make your wife aware of the unhappy situation. Would you be so kind as to give me your arm? It is so much more difficult for me to get to my feet than to sit down. Old age is too ridiculous.'

vii

The top of the exposed tomb made a convenient table. It was also big enough to accommodate Prue Bianchieri. She was wearing a tattered straw hat and her bare legs stuck out at an ungainly angle like the legs of a rag doll. That was probably the effect she wanted to create: girlish, careless, a free spirit. Marian offers her the last slice of the delectable pie she made for this outing. They both laughed so easily. I lurk in the shade of an ilex tree, studying their behaviour. In spite of myself I record their most trivial utterance as evidence for the prosecution. With her mouth full of pie Prue speaks even more loudly.

'You see I'm just an uncomplicated Yorkshire lass! I knows what I likes and I sees that I get it!'

Hardly damning evidence. And why have I held back from telling Marian about the old witch's malicious accusations? The old *strega*, as Prue calls her, had the nerve to warn me against allowing my wife to become her daughter-in-law's accomplice in her devious pursuit of extra-marital infidelities. Had I mentioned it, Marian would have exploded, and what good would that do? Since we landed here she has moved closer to Prue than ever before. I was the one assumed to be devoted to Muzio. There was supposed to be no wall between us. But we never exchanged confidences in the way these two seemed to be doing these days. On the score of fidelity I suppose I myself had something to hide. As for Muzio, he had retired inside himself and raised the drawbridge. Only when we discussed Etruscology and the cherished project at Fontane did any degree of warmth enter our conversations. In the end was that all we had in common?

Muzio had gone across the hillside to photograph dubious restoration work going on alongside an ancient bridge, with, he assured me, authentic Etruscan foundations. Protecting the Etruscan heritage was after all a passion: a relentless campaign. He was mixing our pleasure with his business.

Prue brought the invitation. She was bright and generous and pressing.

'My dears, what is the point of living in a place like this unless you seize every chance you get to dress up in the brightest colours! Make sure of a big share in the sun and the booze! Who can live on books, for God's sake? We'll be on the dusty shelves soon enough. Tomes and tombs, my dears! Gather ye rosebuds and wine bottles and hunters' sausage and cheese and your delicious pie and off we go!' Muzio's camera case is at my feet and his cherished *tascapane*, that ancient leather satchel that accompanies him on every expedition. The circular rock on which Prue is sitting is the roof of a sunken Etruscan sepulchre, noble family size. At the mouth of an extensive necropolis we are surrounded by trees that give us as much shade as we need from the mid-day sun. In the storm last night the heavens opened and in the valley of the tombs the vegetation had miraculously renewed itself. Yesterday after cooling themselves in the lake, these two women were lying close together on the black sand and I could overhear their conversation muffled as it was in the humid air. 'Oh I was quite clear about it, my dear.' Prue spoke with the assurance of a female deity choosing to divest herself of a degree of power. 'I would make myself immune from the biological treadmill. Indeed I would. Just a little snip. That's all there was to it. Then I could devote my whole attention to being an artist. Even a failed one if that's the way it would turn out.' I heard Marian make noises of polite disagreement before asking a delicate question. These middle-aged women who prided themselves on their capacity to speak frankly: so why should I be so hesitant to let them hear about an old woman's slanderous spite? I could not take refuge much longer in the stuffy virtue of not retailing gossip. 'With my husband's consent? Of course old thing. Consent? What am I talking about? Wholehearted agreement. He had his reasons. I had mine. We planned twin-track careers you might say, as opposed to being a pair of cattle in harness. What's wrong with trying to plan a rational way of life in this vale of tears? It can't be any worse than any other and might well turn out to be better.'

She was a woman quite pleased with the sound of her own voice. Her confidences were like public announcements. Did that mean she had nothing to hide? Not necessarily. It could be the most effective camouflage. She could parade about, swinging a wide selection of broad-brimmed straw hats making herself conspicuously immune from suspicion and all the time conducting an illicit affair with byzantine ingenuity. But where and how and when and for that matter with whom? And who am I to investigate the mystery? Infatuation in any form is a dangerous topic. As I strain to analyse their chatter I have the unpleasant sensation of the old Marchesa squatting on my left shoulder and baring her teeth like a short-tempered simian.

It had never been easy to see any resemblance between that autocratic unnerving old woman and her considerate thoughtful compassionate son. So what could you call his birth except a miracle? A happy accident then: a stroke of luck, an evolutionary leap, an uncovenanted blessing; the inadvertent fruit of what could have been no more than a dynastic marriage engineered to shore up the cracking foundations of the Bianchieri inheritance. So much for romantic sighs and whispers about a better race born out of the ecstasy of erotic love, like silver music on a mossy lawn. What gave the gaunt old woman the right to sow doubt and discord in my insecure mind?

'Is Doc-torr Morr-gan doon in the doomps?'

Muzio tried to deliver the stupid phrase he had devised years ago with a Scots accent. It had been funny once. There was a German version that amused him even more. He sat down beside me and held up a limp handful of autumn cyclamen he had gathered on his way back through the trees. He hadn't the slightest idea that the state of his marriage and the malice of his mother were the source of my despondency

'Was it these?' he said.

I stared at the blooms already drooping over his fingers.

'Were these the flowers that Proserpina was gathering when old Dis picked her up?'

'I don't know,' I said.

'You don't know!'

He stared at me so challengingly I had to make an effort not to reveal what I did know.

'We've shrunk the myths,' he said. 'That's our trouble.'

My trouble, or his trouble? Engines against understanding would be a good name for worn figures of speech. What was he being so triumphant about?

'Why do people call psychiatrists "headshrinkers"? Because Doctor Freud and Co. have reduced the myths to pocket roadmaps that allow us to explore nothing more than the underworld of our own emotions. A nice little private exercise to divert us from public concerns, you could say.'

'Well, that's quite a lot,' I said.

'Myths were meant to be so much bigger!'

He waved his handful of flowers about.

'They should incorporate the entire structure of a society, the life-cycle of a species. They should be elaborated in a new context, my friend, to provide towers and pyramids of satisfying concepts and all embracing meanings to the processes of life and death. Eh?'

'Muzio! Caro! Where did you get those?'

The excitement in his voice had attracted Prue's attention. Her interest was in the bunch of flowers in his hand and not in what he could be saying.

'For you, my dear!'

If I were asked, I would say that you could no more re-cycle a myth by an act of will than restore life to these fading flowers. They may have been grown from seed in the greenhouses of hell but our ladies were not discouraged. They scrambled to their feet, eager to penetrate the *burrone* to gather the cyclamen growing in their shaggy beds between the mossy tombs. They called us and we were obliged to follow them. Like schoolboys at play we slithered down a slope grasping rotting branches that snapped under our weight. There were brambles to avoid and the paths were hidden among the myrtles and the mastic shrub, and when we found them they were muddy with the overnight rain. The few clouds left in the blue sky looked so distant above the trees. We arrived in the green and purple gloom of the underworld before reaching the necropolis. On the stouter tree-trunks it was a relief to see faded arrows pointing to the more notable tombs.

Muzio was in his element. He had identified fragments of a wall of interlocking stone he believed had been displaced by an earthquake years ago. In the open fields above the gorge there had once stood an Etruscan city of noble proportions. There was a strong case for new excavations to be made in the area. I wanted to be infected with his enthusiasm. An intense exploration of the past was still a remedy against the discomforts of the present. He was wielding his camera with a will. 'Science', he muttered as he focused on the formation of the blocks of stone. He shifted his ground like an expert cameraman to capture the spontaneous enthusiasm of two women in straw hats bending low to pick the secretive purple flowers, and he grinned as he whispered, 'Art.'

Strange what happened to my camera. Before we left Maenhir I went to look for it. It was gone from the shelf in my study where I always kept it: where it had lain in fact from the day Rhiannon had stormed down the lane in the wake of her bearded lover. Marian could have hidden it or given it away. I didn't ask her. Yet another example of a failure of communication? In any case, had I found it, I would have been faced with the decision whether or not to bring it. I could have taken pictures of Marian and Grazia together. At least a photograph is evidence. One twenty-eighth of a second could provide a clue to the elusive nature of a relationship. In a dream I deliberately left it on a cliff-edge in the hope that someone would take it. And indeed when I returned it was gone.

'Just look at this!'

Muzio stood in the centre of a muddy amphitheatre and drew our attention to the symmetry of the shapes carved into the rock. An impressive semi-circle of tombs had been carved out of the tuffo to resemble town houses with noble doorways and ornamented capitals. Jagged holes above and between the tombs made by the tomb robbers centuries ago remained as evidence of their savage greed.

'It would be here they would lay out the funeral banquet,' Muzio said. 'Imagine these *tombe* brightly painted! Imagine the delicacies on the tables. Turtle eggs. Jellied fish. Venison. Wild boar. Heaped fruit. And the dancing. The pipes and the castanets.'

'Like this? Or this?'

Prue gave her bunch of flowers to Marian so that she could attempt some of the dancing poses that were familiar from the walls of the painted tombs.

'Lovely idea isn't it? The living dancing for the dead. Passing on the joy and delight of one world to the next, the feasting as well as the furniture.'

She couldn't resist the chance to show off, twisting her wrists, bending her knees, making large balletic gestures with her arms. In my eyes she was far from being as graceful as she imagined herself to be. But Muzio was full of approval, like a teacher watching a favourite pupil perform. He took as much pleasure in her inclination towards vulgarity as in her instinctive enthusiasm. The attraction of opposites.

'There was this, wasn't there?'

Prue's wrist was over her forehead and one hand suspended awkwardly over her face.

'Martha Graham stuff,' she said. 'And the painters were right you know. Weren't they Muzio? Bare feet and bare hands are enormous when the dance draws attention to them. And you need to be half naked in those lovely diaphanous red and blue robes and the laurel leaves in your hair! Not slopping about in the mud. Where's Marian got to?'

Through the jagged hole made by a tomb-robber I had a glimpse of my wife standing motionless in front of a pair of stone chairs carved out of the rear wall of the largest tomb of the group. It was a dry intriguing interior, stripped bare and every detail carved out of the rock: the parallel beams of an Etruscan ceiling, stone beds arranged against the walls and equipped with stone pillows. There were only slight traces of colour left on the walls: but it still had the dignified proportions of a family habitation. Marian was lost in thought. Her eyes were closed. It was my duty to be alongside her. I stepped carefully through the muddied entrance and took her hand. Prue peered in from outside.

'This desirable residence for sale,' she said. 'Hundred per cent mortgages available. Better than Cerveteri I think. More private. No bus-loads of tourists. Look. Why don't you two sit in those chairs? Just made for you. Muzio! Come here and take their pictures. The king and queen of the underworld. Pluto and Persephone. Positively their last appearance!'

Marian was perfectly willing to obey her, so I had to follow suit. A shaft of sunlight poured down from a hole in the roof and fell between us. Prue was delighted with the effect: as if the last of the light were searching us out as we sat in the semi-darkness. Marian stroked the pitted tuffo of the arm of her chair with the palm of her hand. I did the same to try and understand why the sensation pleased her so much. Muzio was having trouble with the flash on his camera.

'Don't move,' he said. 'I shan't be a second.'

Prue was impatient.

'Do hurry,' she said. 'That stupid old camera. You'll miss that lovely beam of light.'

'That won't come out with a flash,' Muzio said. 'It's one or the other.'

It was in the beam of yellow light that I made out the faint outline of a girl's profile on the wall behind Marian's head. There were hands raised in dancing posture: long fingers stretching towards and away from the hair of the head. It was Grazia I could see: her profile. I clutched the arms of the chair and the coldness of the rock spread through my body. The tomb grew darker.

'Oh God!' Prue said. 'I see I shall have to get one of those Japanese magic cameras for your birthday. Honestly. Look. The beam of light.... Where has it gone to?'

128

There was no trace of the girl's image on the photographs: no elongated fingers, no black hair band. Therefore it had only existed in the disordered heap of theories and suppressed desires littering the floor of my mind. Or the walls. Internal graffiti scribbled by my own hand. Muzio had wasted too many frames, carried away by enthusiasm for the subject, egged on by his *donna tremenda*. In every shot Marian and I appeared as lifeless as wax effigies and in none of them was anything visible on the wall behind our heads even when I pored over the prints with a magnifying glass. In a couple of them Marian's eyes were closed. She looked equally drained and absent when they were open. We are never still enough to examine ourselves, let alone each other. My eyes were wide open and the pupils were red as though I were practising to be a demon from the infernal regions.

If there are angels there must be demons. Procopius attributed Justinian's abnormal lust for power and wealth to a demonic origin. The mother of a tyrant sometimes confessed to the visitation of a demon on the night of his conception. How else could the emperor rise abruptly from the imperial throne and allow his body to glide up and down over the mosaic floor while his head vanished from sight? I am sick of Procopius's byzantine scandals and his relentless bile and, for that matter, Cassiodorus's sententious pomposity is too much to put up with.

Between them they have succeeded too well in smothering what scintillae of immutable truth lie in the events of a distant past: their Greek and their Latin are tight bandages around a shrivelled mummy. So I shall blame them for my own incapacity to bring Amalasuntha's anguish back to life. 'The source of all Amalasuntha's misfortunes was being born a Goth and dying to be a Roman. Discuss'. The best I am capable of is tinkering with a reduced number of verifiable facts and using my own sanitised academic bandages and mincing scholarly conjecture to regurgitate the episode on the pages of some obscure journal. I need to improve my score of publications for the next issue of the college gazette. It is one of the few documents, I am often told, that Sir Kingsley Jenkins reads with rapt attention. So the only history that really matters is one's own.

I held on to the library chair and restrained myself from giving up too easily. Self-disparagement ranks high among the effective excuses for doing nothing. I launched myself on this research as a life-giving inspirational activity to justify our prolonged leave of absence in the rich autumn sunshine of Etruria. I needed such consolation. Muzio at least understood that I was driven by the desire to expose a trace element of historical truth, in the hope that a spark of light would bring back direction and meaning to what was degenerating into a rudderless redundant existence. But I had to come up for air, escape from the unnerving silence of the ornate library where the only signs of life were the motes rising and falling with cosmic calm in a single beam of light. Outside the solemn silence there was a secular world bustling and shining in the sun. The stones of the ancient city were all warmth and welcome and the streets loud with a life that seemed capable of renewing itself for ever. No wonder people were so eager to wander about and bathe themselves in an illusion of diurnal springtime and perpetual diversion.

I had access to a shaded balcony above the library that over-looked the piazza in front of the *Municipio*, and a curved terrace with a view of the open countryside falling away abruptly from the city wall. Beneath the terrace the remains of a Roman villa had been excavated. Across the valley to the south west the apse of an abbey church had been thickly buttressed after an earthquake, but it still leaned at an angle that gave it an endearing vulnerability. In the terraced earth beneath it, small figures were visible harvesting the vines. Other people's labours in a season of fruitfulness and visual perfection are balm to a troubled spirit. The tables on the terrace had been set out so that customers could sit under the awnings and parasols to enjoy extended vistas of the fertile coun-tryside. I was surprised to recognise Marian and Prue at a table on the edge of the pavement. They were wearing dark glasses and enjoying cold drinks. I didn't draw attention to myself. Marian was not due to collect me from the library until closing time. It had been my understanding that she was taking Grazia on a visit to Acquapendente to interview an old woman who remembered the martyred prophet who lived in a cave on Monte Amiata. And yet she was here already with a Prue who looked at her most sophisti-cated. I saw the English marchesa abandon that pose as a truck drew up against the pavement alongside them. It was driven by Luca Puri and she was eager to greet him. He was in his shirt-sleeves, as purposeful as ever. He leaned out to give his instructions. Prue was avidly attentive. I was appalled as I saw the old Marchesa's suspicions confirmed in front of my eyes; appalled because Marian was sitting there, taking it all for granted, clearly an accomplice. Spectators from a balcony should not be obliged to inhale the dust of the arena. I suppressed a cowardly urge to return to the sanctuary of my mahogany table in the library. The present was pulsating with problems far more intractable than any intrigues and infidelities buried in the distant past. I breathed deeply before clattering down the exterior staircase to the *cortile*. I told the ancient porter in his cubicle next to the massive door that my things were in the library and that I would be coming back. I dashed across to the cafe tables on the terrace.

All that remained on their table was stained glasses and a torn bill. The truck had vanished. I hurried across the piazza and caught a glimpse of the two women turning into a church that had no obvious attraction to the tourist. They vanished like startled deer that had caught the scent of hounds in pursuit: or a pair of rabbits escaping down a hole. Were there other spies abroad? Prue was hardly famous enough to be scandal-sheet fodder. It was absurd, ridiculous to a point of degradation, that I should be shadowing them. They were behaving like imitation resistance heroines making their way through a town under enemy occupation. What roles we thrust upon ourselves to disguise the urge to satisfy our less legitimate desires. Because of our need for sordid secrecy the rest of the world becomes a cloud of hostile witnesses. How did the hymn go?... Hide my weakness from the people....

And where better to hide than the dark interior of a church? It took time for my eyes to become accustomed to the gloom. I am all in favour of churches no matter how many of them or how strongly they stink of incense. Down the ages they have provided shadowy oases in cities obsessed with getting and spending, and refuge from indifference and sunlight. I groped about until I saw Marian sitting by herself, watching with rapt attention, a woman in a side-chapel praying to the Virgin among a small forest of candles. There was no sign of Prue.

I expected her to be startled when I touched her shoulder. She behaved as though she had been expecting me or someone like me to whom she could murmur a conclusion at which she had arrived.

'It's easier talking to an image, than conversing with the air.'

She could have been thinking of her father, in the old days, standing in the pulpit his face raised and his eyes closed. An admirable man. He had a notable sermon on a text from the first epistle to the Thessalonians: Prove all things: hold fast that which is good. Or was she referring to our own hesitant exchanges?

'Did you see him?'

'See who?'

It was silly that we should be talking in whispers.

'I think I saw him. You didn't?'

I insisted that we went outside. Once in the street she looked up and down to see if she was still being followed.

'Prue says this place is infested with spies.'

She smiled at me to make sure I understood she was repeating an amusing remark. Had she reached the stage where she was prepared to accept every remark made by Prue Bianchieri as uncommonly witty?

'I thought you were taking Grazia to Acquapendente,' I said. 'I thought you said you'd be there all day.'

'Her father wouldn't let her come.'

'Why was that? I thought he was pleased she was taking lessons from you.'

'I think he is. Up to a point. He's a bit of a tyrant if the truth be known. He wanted her to work in the *trattoria*. One of the women had been taken ill. That's what he said anyway. She was very disappointed.'

This was all very well, but not a real explanation. I felt she was nervous. Her head was held back as though she were poised to justify herself.

'Where's Prue?'

I tried not to sound like an investigating magistrate.

'We were being followed,' Marian said. 'I told you. This creature Agostino. Like a character in a play, Prue said. One of the gravediggers in ... I can't remember the name of the opera. Which one was it? Anyway we popped in the church and Prue popped out through the further door.'

'Why should he be following you?'

'My goodness, how should I know? What is it that makes an informer tick? Second nature, Prue says. It's a way of life here. She says it's the last twitches of a massive patronage system that ran everything in the Papal State for centuries. For all I know the old Marchesa employs an army of spies.'

We stood opposite the terrace where I had seen them together obviously waiting for Luca Puri. I took hold of Marian's shoulders and turned her around to draw her attention to the recessed balcony on the archbishop's palace.

'I was up there,' I said. 'I was watching you. I saw everything!'

'Oh dear....'

132

She was smiling at me with maternal tolerance. This made me angrier.

'You of all people,' I said.

'Let's sit down, shall we?' she said. 'So that you can recover from the shock. Let's pretend we are tourists, enjoying the beauty of the place. This is Arcadia after all. Or a version of it.'

She was so calm and relaxed. In her forties a female wields an exceptional degree of resilience to cope with upheavals of physical change. Marian remains in command of her self: cool and elegant, sipping her campari. I could only guess at the depth of the impact of her personal grief: at the exertions needed to hold together the fabric of her being after the catastrophe. She was looking at me with such quizzical objectivity as though I were a creature so self-absorbed that I had never really touched the raw edge: as though all my life an innate self-concern had softened every blow.

'You could hardly call him a *cicisbeo*, could you?' Marian said. 'Or a *cavaliere galante* ... but there we are....'

What I took to be an attempt at cynicism set my teeth on edge.

'Adultery,' I said. 'It's an old-fashioned word. A fact all the same.'

I stared at her accusingly. That damned old woman had been right. My wife was an accomplice in this sordid business. Helping this loud English woman deceive her sensitive, thoughtful husband; my friend, to whom I was so deeply indebted, who never appeared so vulnerable and unprotected as at this moment. I was entitled to be angry and to be hurt and disappointed.

'He knows. Muzio knows.'

She spoke to console me but it had the opposite effect.

'I don't enquire too closely,' Marian said. 'They are good friends. Devoted to one another. But as far as I can gather the physical side isn't an essential component....'

She saw me pull a face at so much superfluous delicacy and this amused her too.

'He is impotent.'

I saw her fingers close into a small fist on the white plastic surface of the table.

'That's what it amounts to. And he does not grudge her the sexual satisfaction she needs, so long as that awful mother of his doesn't get to know about it. What's the matter with you?'

She sat up in her chair, concerned suddenly for my well-being, staring at my white face. I was experiencing a revulsion against my whole surroundings. Arcadia was a dungheap of corruption. How

133

much could I tell her? It was choking me. I would be trapped in it. I was overwhelmed with a yearning for sea-spray and sand and seagulls and windswept simplicities. I found it difficult to speak more than single words.

'Morals,' I said. 'Your beliefs. And so on.'

'Prue hasn't got any religious beliefs,' Marian said. 'As for Luca, he is a complete pagan. His life is totally seasonal as far as I can gather. He's a kind of licensed bull. There is a code of course. Ritual and ceremony. Custom and practice. I don't pretend to understand it all. But Prue is a kindly soul. And I can't restrain her with the restraints I use on myself.'

My mouth hung open. If there were more shocks to come I had no defence against them. Marian was smiling. I must have looked foolish. She leaned over to pat the back of my hand. I had to blurt out what I was feeling.

'Oh God, I want to go home.'

This was funnier than ever. She burst out laughing. She had no idea of the tragic depth of my feelings. In my mind's eye I was visiting a grave on the hillside, within sight of the sea, and dropping on my knees alongside it. The ceremonies that belonged to innocence had to be simple and sincere.'What about your research?' Marian said. 'How is it going?'

'Arid,' I said. 'Barren. Pointless.'

'What about poor old Amalasuntha?'

'I'm not saying she deserved what she got but it was inevitable that it came to her. And the reason is so banal it's not worth repeating.'

'What was it?' Marian said. 'You've roused my curiosity, Doctor Morgan. Go on. Tell me.'

'She wanted to be what she was not,' I said. 'She was born a Goth and literally died to be a Roman.'

'That's interesting enough,' Marian said. 'Can you extrapolate from that and arrive at ... shall we call it a universal historical truth? Born a Goth, you should die a Goth. Something of that sort.'

She was not taking me seriously and I couldn't blame her. It was worse than being out of my depth. I was being confronted with the stark image of my own inadequacy and it was unbearable to suffer this so late in life in alien surroundings.

'We've got to get out of this,' I said.

She could see I was gritting my teeth.

'I can't do anything here,' I said. 'I can't rebuild my life on endless recriminations and resentments. We have to go back to our own. To a place where we are needed. Where we belong. All we can do here is cultivate habits of betrayal.'

I was forcing her to be serious and to listen to me. What was bad for her was bad for me and vice versa. We had to get out to preserve what we had left of our integrity. These things weren't easy to put into words and yet we had lived more than the entire lifetime of our only daughter together; we were supposed to have areas of understanding that had no need for being put into words. She considered my proposal and rejected it.

'I think Grazia needs me,' she said.

I had to hold myself back from crying out "Do you think I don't?"

I needed her. I was being thrust outside a magic circle of feminine friendships: I was being forced to hover helplessly outside an exclusion zone: left to my own devices when I had no devices worth owning.

'In a way the poor girl is dreadfully isolated,' Marian was saying. 'She is in a very difficult position. I'm sure you've noticed, Aled. The child sees herself condemned to a life of servitude. I've got to help her.'

And who is going to help me? If anyone is isolated, I am. Locked up in a prison of my own making no doubt, but that does not make it any less constricting or less painful.

'You ought to know this, Aled. She has a real aptitude for study. An appetite for literature. And a depth of human understanding unusual in one so young. She's only eighteen. She applied for a place in the Modern Languages School in Rome. I'm sorry to say Muzio wouldn't help her because he was afraid of offending her father. I said I'd ask you to talk to him. Once we've made out a good case, I told her, I'm sure he would listen.'

I could only adopt an attitude of critical detachment. The girl's career in the real world was one thing: the ache of my imagination quite another. To me she was never a child. More an unattainable woman.

'What about the German boy-friend?' I said.

'Surprisingly she doesn't talk so much about him. I think she writes him endless letters. Endless. I've posted one or two for her. Letter writing gets it out of her system.'

I wondered if it would get it out of mine. My problem was I had no one to write to.

ix

Taste is a strange business. Every available space on the walls of the Guidatti *trattoria* hung with pictures, some for sale, some to hide patches of damp. They vary from timid landscapes, often local with corners of the lake a conspicuous motif, to crude attempts at abstract expressionism. Is this the centre of her world? And what attaches her to me more than a fantasy painted inside my skull? Each night my head on the pillow is filled with the same silent fruitless debate: is it possible to love two people, and if so, equally or differently? The fury can stretch into the small hours and burn my eyes in the darkness. Is one a youthful re-incarnation of the other: or have my affections like my wits so to speak broken loose? And does that mean I am about to explore a new channel, even engage in a second life?

Of course I am disorientated. Life is more difficult to account for than death. I am distressed and disillusioned that Muzio should condone his wife's affair with his farm manager and that my wife should be able to tell me so. "You know, you can spend a lifetime pondering your relationship with your wife." Had he said that or had I dreamt that I heard him say it? It was certainly his voice. "Many people do. I decided not to. That way we can both get on better with our lives". When did I hear him say it? And why had I not understood. It seems to damage our friendship in a way I cannot fathom. Marian finds me naïve, as if naivity were worse than ignorance. Perhaps it is in middle age. Therefore I am entitled to set an agenda of my own if only to prove that I too am capable of duplicity.

Both the dining rooms are empty. An artificial rose propped up in a thin vase stands on every table. It was Marian's idea that we should arrive early: make an opportunity to beard the lion in his den. I could hear his voice now somewhere in the kitchen regions. I listened intently to catch the drift of his mood. It sounded like pater familias laying down the law. Would he emerge rubbing his hands and bowing agreeably? That was our best hope. We were Don Muzio's particular friends and we were worthy of his solicitous attention. It was Grazia's younger sister Silvana who eventually arrived in the expanse of restaurant to register plump surprise and then delight at our presence. This was her father's favourite, Marian said, fourteen, fat, submissive and pleased to see us in our usual place with a good view of the lake. Marian took a benevolent interest in the whole family. There was Gianni, aged nine also plump and spoilt by his mother. To me the whole tribe were a serious impediment impinging like crude reality on the sensitive tissues of a dream.

'But you must take something....'

As she whined persuasively close to my ear, the girl peered into our faces as though we were in imminent danger of starving to death. To set her mind at rest we accepted water, red wine and bread. It gave her something to do. It got rid of her from the fringes of my imagination. Through a frame of red leaves on the wild vine growing around the pergola I could see the purple waters of the lake swaying in the evening breeze, and the last rays of the sun burnish the tops of the towers of the Monaldeschi fortress above Bolsena. It was a view I had become accustomed to cherish. It made me feel at home in Muzio's territory which was also the girl's provenance. All the same it is an abysmal weakness in a rational man to insist on idealising a young woman.

'Don't look so worried, Aled. "Have confidence in your mission." Remember?'

Something her grandfather said years ago when Marian was contemplating her first protest. The way she remembered it now suggested she was harking back to the adventurous spirit of her youth.

'You don't really favour the idea?'

'I never said that.'

'What are you saying, then?'

'Only that one can't assume that our Cymric obsession with education is a universal preoccupation. Especially in this neck of the woods.'

'Isn't it curious,' she said. 'That we should allow a myth to fade and cease to function at the very juncture in history when it could be put to really good use. Remember what happened to the Etruscans. Their myths ceased to function and in no time they faded away.'

Café conversation. I was content to listen to her. It was so much easier here than in the confines of our hired apartment. Soon the diners would start arriving making their way in dressed in their own styles of vociferous animation, fuelled with the prospect of a good meal, making note of a foreign couple by the window deep in private discussion. Dining in public is the most effective privacy. Marian was able to expand one thesis after another about education and I was bound to agree with her. There was no sign of

Guidatti. He had not made his entrance to exercise his repertoire of salutations and courtesies. When we were last here with Muzio and Prue he positively took the floor to enlarge on the role of what he called good taste in the delicate operation of incorporating antiquity and history and art into the burgeoning network of tourist attractions around the lake. So where was he now? Where was he lurking? In the shadow of his growing suspicions? He knew we were here. Had he guessed we were on a mission?

Grazia appeared behind her as silently as an apparition. She had glided through the dining room without my seeing her, and now she was bending down to kiss Marian on the cheek. Her smile in my direction was like a benediction. It had to be resisted. She wore a dark blue dress that shimmered in the evening light and the ringlets of her short dark hair gave her oval face the confidence of a renaissance angel. How could I resist? Her slim expressive fingers restrained me as I struggled to get to my feet. Marian more than pressed her to sit down. She refused.

'If I come, I come to serve, not to talk,' she said.

It was an enchantment. She was so much more than the outline of a painted face on the wall of an Etruscan tomb. Only the living had eyes that searched out the world with such wary eagerness: indentations at the corner of those generous lips forecast her smile. She was so sensitive and tactful as she begged us not to bring up the subject of her academic career with her father this evening. Marian was disappointed. She demanded an explanation. She would take a stand for what she believed in.

'It is a bad time,' Grazia said.

'And when is a good time?'

It was true. A man could love more than one woman. My infatuation for the girl increased my love for Marian. This was a minor miracle and a major inconvenience. It could involve me with including the entire Guidatti family.

'He thinks this morning he has been cheated in Viterbo. This makes him in a bad mood. But he has to hide it. You know? For business and for social reasons. So he pushes it down inside and that makes him worse. And on who can he take revenge except his family, his servants, his dependents. Most of all on his eldest daughter who gives him such displeasure with her disobedience. Like Eve in the garden. Do you think God must be masculine to give the male so much authority?'

Marian was won over. Grazia suggested a plate of *prosciutto crudo* and peeled figs to begin with and then *coregoni* with rosemary with a tomato salad and the wine from Pitigliano. It was more than affability. She had this gift of putting people at their ease with every gesture she made. She was so young and yet possessed with so much unforced grace. Was it the land that she lived in that gave her this capacity to renew the joy of living? My fevered imagination invested her calm beauty with uncanny powers.

'It's up to you,' Marian said.

Grazia had left us and Marian was giving me close attention. It wasn't possible she knew what I was thinking, but her challenge startled me all the same. More lights were switched on. People were beginning to arrive in groups. Guidatti emerged to receive them. He seemed deliberately to keep his back turned. As soon as a party of six were settled, he disappeared.

'You've got to persuade Muzio to bring pressure to bear. That's the way it should be done I suppose. He has to set it all out as attractively as possible. It would cost Guidatti nothing in effect, and it would bring honour and renown to the family. We want nothing except to help. While she studies in Wales she could live with us, and we could still help if she decides to go to Milan afterwards instead of Rome. The plan is completely flexible. And entirely for her benefit.'

It was what I wanted to hear, but I had to make a show of trying to resist it: lashing myself to the mast of probity in order to subdue the charm of the siren's song.

'Here more than anywhere else we know about, my dear, the family is an organism,' I said. 'A living organism. And in a time of transition like ours, an era of unprecedented change, it's such a delicate balance. Part of a threatened ecology.'

Marian had her elbow on the table and her fist under her chin as she listened to me. I was spurred on by the sceptical look on her face.

'There are things here that remain unchanged since the ancient world....'

'Aled! Come off it....'

Marian was smiling with a degree of affection at my naïvety.

'There's a television set in every *trattoria*. And a football match on every night. What's ancient about that?'

'All I am saying and it isn't much I know, but to me, here, the primaeval sub-stream remains very close to the surface....'

'Tread softly because the earth may quake?'

As usual she was mentally ahead of me: but I had made my neutrality apparent with a burst of unusual cunning. There was nothing I wanted more than to have Grazia near me. The possibilities of her continuing presence lit up a future with colours I had begun to believe no longer existed. Marian was smiling at someone and lifting her hand in tentative greeting. I turned in my chair and saw Luca Puri and three of his cronies settle at a table near the door with a good view of the television set. He was carrying bottles of his own wine. He lifted one so that we could see it and showed that he would like to bring it over as a gift if Marian would permit him. I had to make an effort to be as amicable as possible. Marian invited him to sit with us as he placed the bottle on the table.

'For a moment then,' Luca said. 'A brief intrusion.'

He lowered himself with elephantine grace to the edge of a chair and extended a large hand to lift the bottle so that he could study the rose-colour of his wine in the pale light. It was something he hadn't tried before, he said, and he was moderately pleased with it. The grapes were a mixture he had cultivated on his own little plot on the outskirts of the village. He would be happy to hear our opinion of it, without compliments. He shifted on his chair to engage Marian in a more intimate exchange that I was allowed to overhear.

'That dog you see. It bit her again. It's dangerous but she won't let me put it down. What should I do?'

He was turning to my wife for advice on an urgent problem. In a sense I was being set aside, or more precisely, being given occasion to see her in a new light: the woman of exceptional wisdom to whom people could turn for worthwhile advice. Luca expected Marian to intervene with the English Marchesa on his behalf or somehow to contrive to get a message through to her that he had failed to convey himself. She seemed quite ready to take on the combined roles of advocate, go-between and confidante. Luca was eager to unburden his honest misgivings.

'It was a mistake, Signora. One must be frank about these things. A woman needs children. Dogs are no substitute. It could be said of course that I am a poor specimen of a father myself, a failed father in effect. A selfish brute no doubt. But I live close to nature and from there, how shall I put it, acquire a certain understanding, stupid as I am.'

Marian was paying him close attention. I suppose that meant that I, too, had to accept that Luca Puri was a great expert on the deeper needs of the female. He was addressing himself with the seriousness of a physician to the condition of a favoured patient: this was too like the fashionable charlatan Doctor Pan, with his repertoire of priapic cures. I was able to stare closely at two thirds of his sunburnt face and the mask I saw suggested his treatments were available to any woman who chose to take advantage of them. In his own modest way, his vestige of a smile suggested he was a public benefactor. He was something of a hero and on occasions he needed to be recognised as such. Statues had been erected before now to such a force of nature. When Grazia arrived balancing our plates of *prosciutto* and figs, he was able to reach out to her waist and sketch out an avuncular hug because both her hands were preoccupied.

'Here's a girl,' Luca said.

He spoke like a connoisseur at a cattle auction. This was the choice woman of the day. The pearl of great price. The bride that had to be garlanded for sacrifice.

'The flower of Etruria! The rose of our existence!'

When her hands were free Grazia elbowed his arm away with a rough vigour that delighted me. It was a declaration of independence that made me want to cheer. She pointed at the bottle Luca had brought.

'That's not wine,' she said. 'That's sour grape juice.'

Luca did not take it as a joke. The girl had to skip away from the range of his fist. On the television the highlights of a vital football match were being transmitted. Luca's friends were calling him. Apparently he was the only one of their party who would be allowed to turn up the volume. He seemed to me more surly than polite as he left us. Grazia's description of his precious vintage had hurt him.

Marian detected an expression of distaste and disapproval on my face. She leaned forward over her plate of *prosciutto* and whispered as though someone near could understand what she was saying.

'You have to take them as they are!' she said.

I smiled as she forked *prosciutto* into her mouth as a reward for giving me a thin slice of the wisdom of the ages.

'I wouldn't dream of doing anything else,' I said.

Our table by the window was wrapped in prolonged silence. The right side had won the football match. Each goal had been shown more than once in slow motion; and each one had made its contribution to an audience of animated gaiety. We were among a people who knew how to enjoy themselves. From the days of the painted tombs each generation had inherited an ability to disburse its fund of accumulated joyousness whenever the least opportunity presented itself. It seemed a measured, serene and good-humoured affair with the conspicuous absence of excess or hysteria.

And how would they see us if they bothered to notice us and use the same critical and yet sympathetic objectivity? A pair of foreign academics marooned at a silent table by the window, trying their best still to be enchanted with the lights trembling on the waters of the lake, and the distant floodlit towers that were the commonplace landmarks of their daily round. They saw northerners trapped in the pressures of their obscure studies and characteristically inhibited, unable to sit back and relax. Perhaps Guidatti had let it be known, in his own delicate combination of word and gesture, that we were bereaved parents on some form of compassionate leave? It was also true that we were guests of the Marchese and should be allowed to wander around unhindered with our grief draped like invisible cloaks from our bent shoulders.

We were convalescing, and where better to indulge in that process than here? I breathed deeply with the desire to disgorge a sentiment, however vague, about our surroundings, and therefore by implication about our situation, with which Marian could wholeheartedly concur. We owed it to each other to express solidarity.

'You know, within their limits, and we all have our limits, heaven knows, our home-made ramparts that so easily turn into stumbling-blocks, these people are in touch with the essentials. They know about life, what there is to be known, what we are allowed to know....'

'And they know about death,' Marian said.

I reached out to cover her hand with mine. I was moved to the brink of tears by the calm sadness I saw on her face. It was there for me to share and I reached out to touch it. For that brief moment our understanding was all.

Grazia brought us the fish and Silvana followed in her wake with the tomato salad and a single portion of fried potatoes that she insisted we share between us, with her mother's compliments. She withdrew so that Grazia could lavish all her attention on us, particularly on Marian. I saw the understanding that passed between them, and the way Marian raised her head to smile at the girl.

'Do I hear music?' Marian said.

There were antique figures with their instruments playing on the verandah. I turned my chair and saw Luca and his friends urge the musicians to come inside. The visitation was so unexpected and colourful that everyone stopped eating to watch and listen. Three youths stepped in straight out of the eighteenth century. They wore breeches, buckled shoes, white stockings, and brown velvet tunics and caps decorated with red and yellow ribbons. They played a pipe, a flute and drum as they marched up and down between the tables and the diners clapped their hands in time with the old-fashioned tune. I overheard Grazia whispering in Marian's ear about a local attempt to revive an old custom to celebrate either the beginning or the end of the wine harvest.

She was pleased that Marian was pleased, but she wanted us to understand that it wasn't all that authentic. Just a jolly gesture, a folklore stunt. The diners in general were more enthusiastic. Signora Guidatti appeared in the shadow of the archway leading to the kitchen, wiping her hands on her apron, her face glistening. Her husband took up a position in front of her, his right hand poised to deliver an episcopal benediction at the appropriate moment.

The musicians stood in the middle of the room and the youngest began to sing a song in Roman dialect about a girl and a glowworm. His voice, the plangent tune, filled the air with the scent of a nostalgic happiness as if someone had broken a box of precious ointment and poured it over our heads. Here life could become more amenable like music in the dark. Then they marched again making a more discordant sound that was still a celebration. While they were marching, Giorgio emerged from the verandah to collect his share of the applause that was bound to follow. He had brought the musicians in one of his made-up vehicles. They were making the rounds. In the raw electric light his face was like a terracotta mask, his wide mouth stretched in a fixed smile of self-satisfaction. He would acquire a reputation as a restorer of ancient custom and the exhibitions he organised would make his more flamboyant excesses socially acceptable. He bowed when the three boys bowed. I was surprised to see him walk directly towards our table.

'Did it please you, Signori?' he said.

What could we do except praise the event extravagantly. He was ready to accept the credit. I murmured something about the spirit of the Middle Ages, but his gaze had already settled on Grazia. It was she he really wanted to talk to: but in our presence. He needed us as witnesses: guarantors of his openness and seriousness and sincerity.

'I have brought you a gift, Grazia. I made it for you myself.'

From the pocket of his loose jacket he extracted a necklace with metal tassels that glittered temptingly in the light. He raised it to suggest that Grazia wear it now around her neck. She stepped back as though it was a halter. Giorgio showed the necklace to Marian inviting her to examine it in detail. He took her into his confidence and she had no alternative but to listen to him politely.

'It took so many hours. Copied from an old Etruscan style I can say. My cousin Naldo he is an expert in these matters. I admit he helped me. But it is good, and it will look well on her. Grazia, please try it on. I made it for you.'

'Keep it,' Grazia said. 'I do not want it.'

It was total rejection and it was magnificent. Every movement she made met with my silent approval. Guidatti arrived at our table. This was after all his *trattoria* and in every corner he had the right to know what was going on. He had authority and he was prepared to exercise it. Grazia had shifted so that Marian was between her and her father. Giorgio was quick to demonstrate tactical skill in the way he played for the father's support. He narrowed his shoulders to make a blatantly obsequious apology.

'Forgive me,' he said. 'I should have sought your permission and I do so now. It's the only right thing to do after all. A small gift for Grazia. I have made it with my own hands, with some help from my cousin Naldo who as you know is a superb craftsman. As a sign, shall we say. As a symbol of some value....'

Guidatti took the necklace and examined it with a critical eye. He treated it with the respect due to artistic effort.

'It is good,' he said. 'An object of beauty. Very well made.'

Giorgio continued with his humble petition.

'All I wish,' he said. 'Is that things should be as they used to be....'

He had to divide his address between the father and the daughter, and he was succeeding with impressive oratorical skill. And our presence was necessary: the fulcrum of the discourse more than the eye of the storm. Each one of them had something to demonstrate.

'Wear it.'

Guidatti exerted his authority over his daughter. He required her obedience.

'Put it on.'

He held out the necklace.

'You have no reason to refuse such an excellent gift. Accept it in the spirit in which it is offered.'

'With your permission,' Giorgio said. 'The first of many.'

It was a tactical mistake. There was too much triumph in his smile. Grazia snatched the necklace and hurled it across the floor. Guidatti and Giorgio were equally appalled. Some of the diners had already noticed a scene was in progress. I saw a middle aged woman put down her fork and lick her thickly painted lips in anticipation of tastier fare.

'The first and the last,' Grazia said.

She had reached the archway leading to the kitchen before her father caught up with her. His dignity, more precious than riches or honour was at stake. He caught the girl by the arm and shoved her into the shadows, out of sight of most of the diners, but not out of my sight. I saw his arm rise to strike her across the face and I heard her cry. It brought me to my feet. There were no fetters that could hold me to my chair at our table. I moved under the archway and I saw the scene in the kitchen. The mother too was joining in. Guidatti's gestures to heaven were attempting to justify his brutal behaviour. Grazia was cringing by the back door, her hand still covering her cheek.

She had to listen to her father asking heaven and earth why he had to endure the plague of misfortune and punishment brought on his head by an ungrateful and disobedient daughter. What could I do to help the girl? She forced open the kitchen door and ran out into the night.

X

Their lives could go on without hers: mine couldn't. I couldn't leave her wandering alone in the darkness along the shore of the lake. She was out there beyond the reach of the outside lights of the *trattoria*, nursing her sorrow. I stood on the uneven surface of beaten earth that served as Guidatti's parking ground and listened to the lake water lapping the roots of the cane reeds that grew at the water's edge. It was like the sound of sobbing. The stars and the moon in its last quarter were bright above the black canopy of umbrella pines. She was out there alone in her agony, and I would find her. The stupid brute had no conception of the pain and anguish of losing a daughter. Guidatti was everything he claimed not to be: an unreliable, obsequious, money-grabbing materialist squatting on the fringe of the Garden of the Hesperides; a human ape waiting for a golden apple to drop into his gaping greedy mouth. It was absurd that Muzio should give him so much attention. As I trudged through the volcanic sand along the margin of the lake I could only conclude that Guidatti had some negative political pull: a private force of gravity, a convenient store of inertia that only an earthquake could dislodge. Guidatti was an insect nesting under the petrified centuries: and I would be nothing better unless I found her quickly. The prime function of living was searching out the chance to love. The day it was bereft of the last flicker of loving compassion, this world would be a dead planet.

She was clinging with arms outstretched to the high wire fence protecting one of the narrow strips of land reaching from the old Via Cassia to the lake. These gardens were intensely cultivated and jealously guarded by their owners. Grazia was locked out; her escape route cut off. I could see her knuckles gleaming where her fingers clutched the mesh of the wire. Her head, her hair, her body, hung down with the erotic desperation of a crucified figure: or so it seemed to me. I was here to take charge of the deposition. We were alone on the edge of existence and I was her only hope of renewal as she was mine. She sank down into my arms. She was no longer crying but she desperately needed comfort.

There was a feverish hunger in the way she responded to my comforting caresses. Her fingers clutched at the back of my head like signals of unrestrained devotion. Her tongue slipped between my lips and I was stung into a degree of passion that I had forgotten could exist. This was the impossible sweetness of youth that swept the years away. A tender sensuous heaven was not out of my reach. I was as young as she was and we were absorbed in that loving that touched on worship. Everything that separated us melted away and we trembled together on the threshold of a new creation. The last vestiges of the cage and the prison and the iron bars dissolved and we were caught in the yearning naked embrace that brings lovers close to immortality. She had to know that my love was unconditional and that I would do anything for her. I could hear her whisper that we had to be careful. This was more rational than my endless repetition of the same sacrificial avowal: *ti voglio bene, ti voglio bene*. There had to be restraint and she had the strength to restrain me.

'We must think of Marian,' she said. 'Aled. Aled. Think of Marian.'

I thought of Grazia. Only a barbarian could take advantage of a virgin in acute distress and leave her pregnant. Weeping needs comfort. Loving is too easy. There has to be an erotic basis to my benevolence. Comfort her indeed. Honour her. Sin needs to be sweet to offer temptation. She left my side to cool her hands in the water of the lake. She splashed water into her face and turned to speak to me with a new authority. I was pleased: filled with admiration. The romantic fever need not subside; only change direction.

'She is my friend,' she said. 'How can I betray her?'

I could hardly account for my own behaviour. I could not begin to provide her with an alibi for hers. What fantasy in her mind coincided with mine to produce this dangerous reality? What I needed was some theoretical justification for transforming a dream into this crisis. Talking was important. I lifted her wet fingers to my lips. They were rough reminders of kitchen work and domestic tyranny.

'We must accept this,' I said. 'As a stretching experience. To give us a deeper, wider understanding.'

'Do you think so?' she said. 'Is it possible?'

I was captivated by such open unstinting charm. There was consolation in confidences. She had become the person I had to speak to. And before that I had to listen to. Her secrets I could accommodate comfortably alongside my own.

'My mother,' Grazia was saying. 'She is the worst.'

She gripped my hand tightly as she spoke. The concerns of her life were being transferred to mine. We would have so much to talk about, this evening would last a lifetime. There was the moonlight on the lake and her distinct voice mingling with the lapping water.

'She is so weak. That is what I detest. Her mouth is full of platitudes that mean nothing. I am a disobedient daughter because he says so. The great Guidatti. He is in charge of her mind and she chatters on about beauty and love and how I should be like her. She understands nothing. For her it is right that I should be engaged to that horrible Giorgio, so that when the Lido comes under his control, my father will become the most powerful and important man on the north side of the lake. And what good will that do her? And yet that is all she thinks about. Can you imagine it?'

I had to show I could. It was no time to be making a defence of the virtues of motherhood, or traditional values. It was my sympathy and understanding she craved, and I had to be ready to give them in full measure. Intimate confession would replace and even transcend physical intimacy. I nodded and squeezed her hand.

'At first I was only determined to show them that I was not just a pretty pawn for them to use. You understand?'

Of course I understood. I understood everything. I wanted to take her in my arms and smother her with understanding. She held both my hands and I listened with all my heart.

'I told you about Franz?'

Everyone seemed to have told me about him. Love among the tombs. The excavation's Romeo and Juliet. There were remarks I wanted to forget. Giorgio being modern, wallowing in his synthetic magnanimity. He had the smell of her on his fingers. Was it a grotto or an excavated tomb? She unwittingly encouraged men because she was in heat. Did he say that? The egregious Giorgio. I had to cast off the weight of middle-aged cynicism and recapture something of the generous idealism of my youth.

'I went to Franz just to show them I would be with a mind of my own. Then love grew between us. How can you tell about these things? He respected me for what I was. You understand?'

I was pledged to understand.

'They could not bear to see my happiness. When Giorgio told my father, he beat me. He said I would bring disgrace on the family. Can you imagine that?'

What better way to encourage young love than to put obstacles in its path? That was something I knew about. Hence those letters Marian so kindly posted. If only she had been as accommodating with her own daughter. Was there no word of advice I could give this girl from the depths of my bitter experience?

'She must love you, Grazia,' I said. 'Your mother, I mean. You must allow for that, my dear.'

Grazia was trembling. It was more with anger than with cold.

'She knows,' she said. 'My mother knows exactly what he's like. And she can leave me like an animal in a trap, you know, a living bait.'

'He?'

'Luca Puri. Who else? He is the master of ceremonies. You don't know these things. I know. My mother knows. That idiot Giorgio and his family are in Luca Puri's pocket. So how can I escape? If I were married to that idiot Giorgio, that Luca will be waiting to add me to his collection.'

I showed indignation, horror, distress, but I felt guilt. A weak and milky academic sharing the same goal as that priapic pagan. Animal lust driven by animal cunning. How far could I descend into this subterranean Etruscan world? There was nothing romantic about the girl's situation. The victim of a sacrifice as cold as the horizontal figure in a fading tomb fresco. We had to move back to the weak lights of the *trattoria*. I was already too concerned with making my own excuses to work out how best to help her. Hypocrisy after all is my way of life.

'What can I do? How can I escape from them?'

She repeated these questions so quietly and yet so insistently while I told myself that love meant protection. I had to find ways and means to save her. I had to engineer an escape. And what better path to freedom than education? It was after all an article of faith. Why should repeating it make me uneasy?

xi

They had insisted on coming. Prue said she wouldn't be left behind. She made Marian come along. It meant I was losing a chance to talk privately to Muzio. And now the woman was bending back her left leg to consider the condition of the heel of her shoe. Muzio had told her more than once high heels were ridiculous for the kind of expedition we were now embarked on. The path from the river was overgrown with brambles and dwarf thorns. Prue had been grumbling steadily as she brought up the rear: a bit of a lark had turned sour. We were in sight of the rock tombs and the hermitage and sanctuary that we had convinced ourselves had been occupied by Irish monks in the early Middle Ages. In the bleached tuffo cliffs ahead of us we could see the carved apertures and caves open their black mouths to the sun.

'Look,' Prue said. 'God knows what they were after and God knows what you two are hoping to find. I've had enough, thank you very much. This is as far as I'm going and that's flat.'

'My dear,' Muzio said. 'What a pity we can't say the same about your heels.'

His shoulders shook with restrained appreciation of his own wit and Marian laughed obligingly. It was soothing, the way they approved of each other, Muzio and Marian, without demanding too much: a point of stability in the emotional turmoil of my inner world. Prue searched about for a suitable resting place. The midday heat was too much for her. We were all sweating. Muzio led the way, his *tascapane* bouncing on his back as he beat down the thorns and brambles with his heavy stick. The flies followed us like the smell of the myrtle brought out by the late autumn burst of hot weather.

'How was I to know the damned place was so inaccessible,' Prue said. 'If I'd known I would never have come.'

She waved the flies away with a gesture of exasperation.

'Patience,' Muzio said. 'Only another half kilometre and we

reach the gorge. All dark and wet. And the waterfall where the monks had their perpetual water supply.'

'Not another step.'

Prue squatted under a wild olive tree and pulled off her shoes. Her toes looked cramped, distorted and strangely aged. She massaged them with steady affection.

'Just leave me mineral water and a nibble and I'll wait for you here.'

'Me too.'

Marian elected to join her. There was room for two of them in the shade. They smiled at each other, demonstrating female solidarity. Once our backs were turned there would be no limit to the territory their tongues would cover or to the decisions they would come to. They were practical women and for them to discuss was to decide and to act. Why could I not talk to Muzio with the same unfettered freedom? There were questions buzzing in my head with greater persistence than the flies; more disturbing than mosquito bites. The women were smiling and waving us on our way with gestures that to me reflected an open conspiracy.

'You boys run along. Then you can come back and tell us all about it. Shoo!'

They were in such close unison they could have been singing a chorus.

'No need to hurry. We've got lots to talk about.'

Would it involve Grazia? I suspected it would. It wouldn't be easy to talk to Muzio. Words became scarcer when there was more to conceal than reveal. In our different ways, he and I were chronically evasive. It seemed now as if it had always been so: from the beginning a process of polite evasion had been built into the foundation of our friendship. After all these years, what we had most in common was little more than an exaggerated respect for privacy. This was too absurd and I would have to say so. The Latin and the Celt needed a strong dose of Anglo-Saxon frankness. Just let us imitate for once that bluff outspoken English bluntness that Prue Bianchieri was inclined to glory in. Not that she in reality was any less devious than the rest of us. Ostentatious straightforwardness was in the end a more effective cover. She sat in the shade of the wild olive shaking her shoe at me like a woman who knew exactly what she wanted and proclaimed her inalienable right to have it.

'My dears,' Muzio said. 'You really don't know what you're missing. A Rosetta. Traces of twelfth century frescoes. Statues if they're still there. And the chance of finding something to confirm the Irish hypothesis. And ... and ... a passage that leads directly to the Etruscan necropolis.'

He turned and pointed dramatically to the cliff face in the distance emerging from the green scrub like a magic fortress, burnished with sunlight.

'During the war, partisans hid up there,' he said. 'And there are work-rooms carved out of the rock with shelves and cupboards.'

'Wonderful,' Prue said. 'Next time we'll bring a team of Sherpas.'

They were laughing at us as we left them. 'Boy Scouts' they called us. Marian wanted us to give their regards to Pluto, if we should bump into him. I followed in Muzio's footsteps and their giggles faded into the uneasy silence of the wilderness. Above our heads rooks circled in the azure sky. I only had to look at Muzio's brown boots to realise how much he was in his element. Trudging through the undergrowth was much to be preferred to estate management or the tedium of academic colloquia.

Here he was part of his chosen landscape, where rocks and plants and wooded heights merged with ancient and medieval ruins. He was an accredited ambassador from the Present, allowed unimpeded travel among the tombs where the long dead slumber with magnificent indifference among the detritus of their vanished civilisations.

At the bottom of the gorge the roots of thin trees, as much as eighty feet above us, clung like unkempt hair to the wet outcrops of rock. A persistent finger of water had worn its way down, before tipping into the pool at the base of the gorge. Muzio was more agile than I negotiating the slippery causeway that led to the narrow steps carved out of the tuffo. I saved my breath as we emerged from the damp shadows into the white heat of the mid-day sun.

The remaining climb up to the carved entrance to the Hermitage was hazardous. Steps had been worn away by the weather and by landslides and earthquakes.

'Muzio,' I said. 'Let's sit for a minute. I wanted to talk to you about the girl in the *trattoria*.'

It sounded a feeble attempt at objectivity. He was looking at me with critical curiosity. I needed to speak with the firm conviction of a moral tutor advocating a better deal for a misunderstood student. Muzio leaned back against the cliff face and closed his eyes.

'Marian tells me she is a very promising student,' I said. 'As you know Marian's standards are extremely high. If she says the girl is good she must be very good.'

Muzio nodded sagely.

'That may well be,' he said. 'But education isn't everything. I seem to remember hearing you say that yourself.'

He wanted an abstract discussion with amusing undertones. He wasn't prepared to consider that a girl's entire future was at stake. I had to be more assertive.

'We can see the circumstances,' I said. 'We are outsiders of course. Marian and I realise that. But we both feel very strongly that a person of exceptional promise shouldn't be restricted and shackled in this way. You know what I mean?'

Muzio was rummaging in his *tascapane* for his pipe and tobacco. This was a hopeful sign. At least it meant he was prepared to argue a case.

'If this European business is to move ahead on the highest cultural level,' I said. 'Then surely people of talent, gifted young people, should be free to move; to go where they need to go to develop their gifts and their talents.'

'Elitism.'

He grinned at me slyly, trying to quote me against myself.

'She has promise,' I said. 'Surely promise should be allowed to fulfil itself?'

'We can't afford that illusion.'

The ceremony of lighting his pipe appeared an exercise in protracted sagacity. It exasperated me.

'What's that supposed to mean?'

'Just that we poor old Italians cannot afford to indulge in your British illusion of individual freedom particularly your Welsh extension of the notion. "The divine right to get on in the world.... Onward and upward"....'

He was quoting me again: using critical remarks made in entirely different circumstances to undermine my present argument. I had to rein in my anger.

'It's not what I'm talking about,' I said

He ignored my indignation and waved the stem of his pipe at me.

'You lot are uniform by nature and by nurture. We suffer from an excess of individuality. Or selfishness, to use an unkind word. You form a queue. We stage a riot. So you see the strength of our society is the extent to which we can curb this dangerous tendency.'

'I'm not discussing social history,' I said. 'I'm discussing the fate of one single little individual.'

Muzio spread out his hands as though he had established an equation.

'Can you separate them? We are all cogs in the same machine and if we don't get out of this sun, old friend, our brains will be fried.'

To follow him, I had to concentrate on the climb. To miss a foothold would have meant a nasty fall. The roots I tried to grab hold of were not always strong enough to hold my weight. It was a relief to arrive at the damp stone shelf in front of what had once been a window. Above it the circular remains of a rosetta gave the ruin its name. Muzio was waiting for me to take an intelligent interest in the place.

'You realise we are standing on earth and rubble,' he said. 'Within a few feet of what was the roof of the oratory. Can you see the colours still? And it was all carved out of the rock. Can you see the fingers of a Christ figure holding a cup? Over there. The rest has gone. Black and wet. It must have been a last supper.'

He was willing himself to be carried away with the excitement of the centuries. He had extracted his camera from the *tascapane* and was ready to clip on the flash apparatus. I had to press forward with my case.

'You can do something to help her, Muzio,' I said. 'I'm sure you can. By way of recommendation. Nothing more. If there were need for financial assistance, then Marian and I would be delighted to help. You can understand why.'

He made a polite effort to show that he could understand our interest, even our enthusiasm: at the same time he wanted to advise caution to dissuade us from any precipitate action.

'We have a responsibility, old friend,' he said. 'To look at these problems in the wider context. I know that sounds pompous, but it's true you see. What have we been saying all these last few months? Eh? The uncontrolled movement of peoples: Europe's most pressing problem. Immigration. At one end of the economic scale the pressure of impoverished East Europeans, and at the other, well-to-do settlers in the regions of France and your Welsh heartland and all the lush corners of the West: from the Algarve to the Hebrides.'

'That's not at all what I'm talking about!'

I had to raise my voice to interrupt him.

'Oh but it is, old friend, it is. People in constant transit, rich or

153

poor, will never settle long enough in one place to cultivate a tolerable civilisation. Weeds in the wind sow nothing but more weeds. You've said it yourself, Aled. This age will ruin the planet with the sheer force of shifting about.'

We bent out heads to burrow more deeply into the network of chambers carved by successive generations out of the tuffo. Here the living and the dead had co-existed for centuries, sheltering from war and famine, pestilence and invasions. Muzio insisted I took a lively interest. We used our torches. A shepherd had spent the night in a niche carved for a coffin and there was still grease from his candle in a solid puddle on the stone. Under a carved arch with traces of red and blue patterns, stood twin pedestals of sacred statues, removed Muzio said, by German soldiers in the second world war and now safely housed in a museum in Cetona, or was it Chiusi? He seemed concerned with the fate of everything and everybody except Grazia Guidatti.

'So you won't help her?'

I didn't know whether or not he had overheard my mutter. His hand descended on my shoulder.

'I can't interfere, Aled. I really can't afford to. You must understand. It's not my fault that the father is what you might call a closet tyrant. It may sound absurd and unjust but I can't risk the damage to the social fabric. It's all so delicately balanced. You have no idea. You pull one brick away and the whole wall collapses. That's inexact. You interfere and before you know where you are, you've started a family feud, launched a vendetta. That may sound melodramatic and maybe it is to save myself an embarrassment I am exaggerating a little. I can't afford to be too self-critical. I still have a position to hold. The unwitting keystone of an invisible arch.... Oh dear, listen to me. They must stay as rooted as circumstances allow. If you and Marian do anything, for the sake of social harmony and parish-pump peace, old friend, it is better that I know nothing about it.'

And that was that. The subject was set aside so that we could continue to explore with uninterrupted concentration. I couldn't tell him about the threat to Grazia's freedom and integrity and independence without revealing the full extent of my attachment to the girl. And was it possible that my attachment was in itself as illegitimate as Luca Puri's lustful interest? The only safe criterion was what Grazia herself wanted. In other words her freedom of choice; which was precisely what my friend Muzio, the Marchese Bianchieri, was prepared to withhold from her. So much for academic friendship. I scraped my knees in the rubble as I scrambled through a hole in response to a call from Muzio. He had found something. His voice was trembling with unexpected excitement.

'Look at this!'

Around a crude workbench there were torch brackets in the wall. A pencil of sunlight filtered through a hole in the roof. On the bench there were pottery figurines, a bronze cauldron, a bowl mounted on clawed feet and two vases in *buccero* covered with Etruscan letters.

'Stolen.'

Muzio was trembling. I had rarely seen him so angry. He was examining the stuff closely in the light of his torch.

'What can you do with a people like this?'

'Shall you notify the police?'

'Fakes. Forgeries. Look at this.'

He picked up a jug by the handle.

'A famous wine pitcher....'

I stared at the detail: a pattern of armed riders with shields and spears and long noses circling the belly of the vase. To my inexpert eye, it looked genuine enough. He snatched it from my hands and hurled it against the rock so that it shattered into many pieces. He bent down, picked up his stout stick and swung it at the row of objects on the bench. I wanted to restrain him.

'What else can you do,' he said. 'It would be a waste of time to bring in the *Carabinieri*. It would take too long and they would get away with it. You see what happens. Debasing the currency. Falsifying the records. Wilful distortions. Worse than tomb-robbing. I'm sorry but this sort of thing drives me mad.'

I was disturbed for a different reason. It seemed to me that my friend had a greater concern for things than for people. These were fakes; but it was also a false analogy to compare them to counterfeit currency. Their circulation only affected the lives of a limited well-to-do clientele of collectors. I was concerned with the defence of a girl of flesh and blood in the first bloom of her beauty, a threatened human treasure, a soul above price.

xii

What else could my heart do except leap up when I recognised Grazia's handwriting on the sheets of paper on the side-table. The bold round regular script flowed along alternate lines leaving room for the corrections Marian would make in green ink. Her writing was a surrogate presence: the sheets lay under the oval mirror and in a moment Marian would settle down to reading the essay. The reflection in the mirror and the reality on the table were equally dear to me: just to stare at them was a soothing substitute for touching her face. The vision was sweet and painful. I had to move further away and put more of the heavy furniture of the room between us. Any moment Marian would come in and sit at the side table to correct Grazia's work. I would see her reflection too in the mirror: her fist against her mouth and a smile perhaps on her lips at the quaint charm of some expression or other involving the impulsive wide-eyed honesty and innocence that shone out of the girl. I had to turn away in case Marian looked in the mirror and caught a glimpse of my absurdly guilty secret.

'Aled. I thought you were going out.'

'Yes, of course.'

She settled into the chair and took possession of Grazia's papers in exactly the attitude I had anticipated. The girl was in her hands not mine and I had to bend willingly under the yoke. It was as much as I could manage to keep incoherence at bay as I went into unnecessary detail about the chain-smoking priest Don Franco, the worker priest with a harsh hoarse voice, who had summoned me by name across the street in Capo di Monte to ask if he could take half a dozen of his youth club to visit the alterations at Fontane, and perhaps go on to explore the mediaeval ruins behind Farnese where Muzio had some work going on for the *Soprintendenza*. Without crossing the street, the little priest in black mufti enlarged on the importance of instilling the youth with a sense of history while he greeted passers-by, accepting invitations to drink coffee in the nearest bar, and patting infants in push-chairs on the head. I hardly needed to say anything except that I was sure Muzio would be only too pleased. My chief business in this part of the world appears to be the role of benevolent listener. My neck became stiff with automatic nodding.

I glanced in the mirror and realised that Marian had stopped listening to me. She was absorbed in Grazia's inspired writing and concentrating on the most effective correction to make in green ink. As I left the room she barely lifted her head when I said I would be taking the Fiat to Angelo's garage to see what he could do about the red light that kept on flashing on the dashboard.

It would have been an absurd over-statement to claim that I had been turned out of the earthly paradise as I waited for Angelo to check the electric circuit under the bonnet of our second-hand car. All the same I felt abandoned: marooned on a rocky comfortless island of middle age. Marian was at home absorbed in Grazia's manuscript which was the next best thing to her living presence. Some kind of writing from her in my own hands would have been a comfort: a mere mention of poetry or literature or philosophy seen with dewy freshness through her young eyes: a glimpse of the world as she saw it inscribed by that affectionate hand. Whether she was at the *Trattoria* or helping out at the Agency, Grazia would not want me hanging about like a moonstruck adolescent loon. There was always work to be done at Fontane. In less than a week there would be celebrations there to mark the completion of the roofing and the out-door repairs. I could do some physical work or walk up the path to the woods. It was time I had a more rigorous private conversation with myself. The business of thinking was to break out of the silken cords of fantasy and arrive at the hard high ground where existence takes on a clear and uncompromising outline, the immemorial truthfulness of rocks and stones and trees.

I had not gone a hundred yards from the gate at Fontane when I heard my name being called.

'Aled! Dottore!'

I looked up and saw Luca Puri taking boyish delight in his precarious position at the top of the tree. He waved his electric saw at me as though it were a toy sword and I had to smile and wave back. This was his strength after all and I had to acknowledge it. He said without boasting that he would never ask any of his men to do anything he was not capable of doing himself. I could see for myself that they were at full stretch tidying up the approach and the environs of Fontane ready for the celebrations. All around they were at it, cleaning ditches, filling potholes, burning brambles; and I had barely noticed, they were so much part of the landscape. Luca reserved the more hazardous tasks for himself and how could I not find that wholly admirable? Here was an opportunity to exercise rational detachment. Around the bole of the tree, Prue's idiotic Maremma shepherd dog was panting about, his tongue hanging out with a foaming admixture of anxiety and admiration for the human god who could climb so high, and slice off large branches with the touch of an electric wand. He could bark ecstatically each time a cataract of leaves and branches struck the ground.

Luca possessed a functional nobility so long as he was contained within his allotted habitat: which included tall trees from which he could grin down at lesser mortals to instill in their fainter consciousness something of the exuberance of his manifest strength and skill and daring. This was after all the human energy and power that tamed the wilderness. Without it in full measure, what could have subdued the inhospitable forests, the stubborn soil and made the stony fields and hills of clay blossom like an extended garden? Sour wine notwithstanding, Luca was a fair example of a breed of man that grew out of the place for the express purpose of sculpting a landscape calmly punctuated with Etruscan cypresses. His remote ancestors had ploughed that deep furrow out of which emerged the miraculous figure of a child with white hair to teach them the signs and portents and the way to live with the seasons.

He landed near me with a thud that made the earth tremble. The dog was delighted, licking Luca's trousers and boots and stretching his neck to reach the butt ends of his master's fingers.

'Don Muzio tells me you are interested in Amalasuntha.'

There was a cheerful expression on his face announcing he was about to make me an intriguing offer.

'Would you like to see her grave?'

He was amused by my excited response. I couldn't suppress it. Any residual scepticism was swept aside by the bright hope of discovery. It was possible it existed. Stranger things have happened. I didn't mind if he laughed at the eager way in which I accepted the invitation. It was obvious that he did not take my researches too seriously. It would be useless to describe to him the vaulted emptiness of Theodoric's mausoleum at Ravenna. The Goth raised it in his lifetime to be his imperial last resting-place and his obedient and pious daughter Amalasuntha finished it and saw him buried with Roman pomp. And yet not so many years after her death, Catholic monks in a frenzy of orthodoxy hurled his body into the canal. It was thirteen hundred years later that labourers widening that same waterway uncovered a golden cuirass adorned with precious stones that could well have been Theodoric's: the rude mechanicals were arrested in the act of stuffing their booty into a melting pot. It would be a lightning flash of coincidence if something similar happened to his daughter the queen's remains. Was it any use asking Luca whether Amalasuntha's corpse was decently buried or tossed into the lake with a millstone around its neck, to sink to a depth of one hundred and forty-six metres? Did he know that she lay in her bath listening to the court poet's second-hand hexameters in praise of the island gardens, when the silent boats of the murderers landed? It was in her bath the silken cord was tightened around her neck.

'Are you saying she is buried on the island?'

He was grinning at the stress I put on my question. An event fourteen hundred years old could hardly be treated as an urgent priority.

'Tomorrow,' Luca said. 'A good excuse for a picnic. Bring your wife and I shall bring Maria Luisa. She wants to check something in the ruined tower.'

It was all arranged in his mind in the short time he had seen me wandering up the path: between shifting his position to lop off another branch. Management after all was his forte. And this Maria Luisa: a worthy spinster who packed herself neatly into a navy-blue business costume and a white blouse and made up her face with what looked like a film of pink and white wax. Prue passed remarks about her but Muzio said she was notably efficient and reliable, and that without her a whole facet of the work of the *Camera* would collapse.

'Maria Luisa has the keys. And she is my cousin. I tell you she is not as formal as she looks and she can dance like a gypsy when she feels like it.'

Luca slapped my arm to show he was my friend and would do anything for me within reason. The fluffy dog started to leap about infected with Luca's geniality. Luca was obliged to smack him on the nose to calm him down.

'This grave,' I said. 'Where is it then?'

'Just a hole. The old folk would say it used to be a well. I suppose they chucked her down the well like a dead cat.'

He grinned again and peered at me through narrowed eyes with cheerful indifference while he waited for me to make up my mind. How could I accept his offer let alone his friendship without betraying Grazia? The girl feared this man because the system he controlled would put her at his mercy. I could see the sly neutrality in his smile. Amalasuntha was a woman and therefore a disposable object: something to be used and cast aside, and he saw no harm in it: a living girl or a dead cat. He moved through the breeding grounds of nature to offer a range of opportunities his guests could accept or reject, his liberality concealing a web of ulterior motives. Whatever he had in mind, being familiar with foreigners gave him a certain prestige among his own kind: *i stranieri* found him interesting and collectable and sought out his company and therefore his intrinsic worth was even greater than they had imagined. This would be a visible trip to the island: nothing clandestine about it like his assignations with Prue Bianchieri. A different display of potency and effortless power.

'I don't know about Marian,' I said.

It was my polite but cautious response. I looked for a way to squash the idea of a picnic and Maria Luisa dancing in her tight skirt, without losing the opportunity of identifying what he claimed to be Amalasuntha's grave. At the moment he seemed to be standing astride of it, controlling any reasonable access. I could take it up with Muzio of course: but that wouldn't be so easy now without giving this man what would appear gratuitous offence. He had no idea about my inclination to treat him as potentially a dangerous enemy.

'You must make her come,' Luca said. 'Tell her how much she will enjoy it.'

It was quite lordly the way he moved off with the dog obedient at his heel. He assumed that I had accepted his invitation. There was of course much he had to supervise. Muzio gave me to understand that Luca was uniquely qualified to carry a vast range of responsibilities. He had to keep an eye on everything: not only the oil, the fruit, the animals, the wheat, the crops, the vines, but a variety of employees and dependents: day labourers, craftsmen, contract workers, tenants under various agreements. Without him Muzio said the estate would soon collapse. He was a present-day Atlas who carried a small world on his shoulders. He turned to award me a last greeting.

'*A domani!*'

It would have been churlish, and a lack of respect for his bucolic virtues, not to have waved back.

xiii

The facade of the Basilica began to shake and then crumble in slow motion. There should have been a warning, the earth rumbling, but I heard nothing, and in my dream, the silence was more terrifying. Bits of marble were dropping off and my duty was to run around and catch them before they smashed to pieces on the ground, but my legs refused to move. Fragments of pagan and Early Christian and mediaeval carvings mingled together in free fall like stone snow flakes: carved sections of the massive rose window turned into lethal petals. There was a greedy god with a face like Luca's and a

160

long tongue hanging out and the sight of it made me realise that Grazia was crouching alone in the crypt, hiding there, with no one to rescue her. Should I sacrifice my own invaluable life in what could well turn out to be a vain attempt to rescue hers? I was in the grip of this agony when the sound of Marian laughing woke me up. She was in her dressing gown, standing on the narrow balcony outside our bedroom and waving a hand in the direction of the lake.

'Oh dear,' she said. 'Aled! It's gone. Disappeared. And the islands have gone with it. I'm so relieved, I can't tell you.'

I stepped out on to the balcony, rubbing my eyes. Marian was clapping her hands with excessive jubilation. My head was still aching from drinking too much wine the previous evening, and the after-effects of what was after all more a nightmare than a dream.

'And thereupon a fall of mist and the castle vanished ... and the tomb of poor old Amalasuntha with it.'

It was true. The lake was hidden in a thick white mist. Visibility was so bad the tower of San Francisco wavered like an unearthly hangover in the stubborn mist. I could hear voices; women at their windows, people in the street, twittering with the agitated clarity of birds assembling for migration. The mist was disturbing the humans of our *borgo* in their cosy nests. In this weather the fisher-men wouldn't venture out and all the day's menus would need to be reconsidered.

Marian shivered cheerfully inside her dressing gown.

'Strange, you know. I dreamt we were caught in a sudden storm like those engravings in the old bibles, only there was no one to still the tempest ... and I was standing up and rocking the boat and screaming, What do I care about Amalasuntha!'

It would have been pleasant to respond with some colourful account of my own dream. But how could I without revealing my obsession with the girl and her fate?

'Oh dear, Aled. I hope you're not too disappointed.'

I made toast and coffee and Marian squeezed oranges on the noisy little machine. As we settled to breakfast she pointed her piece of toast at me.

'Listen,' she said. 'I don't want to sound alarmist but we've got to do something about Grazia.'

She was staring closely at my face and I had to make an effort not to show either guilt or alarm. She had to assume my concern for the girl was disinterested and at the most paternal. The secret of my infatuation was buried too deep inside me for anyone to know about it except Grazia herself and I was confident she would never mention it to any living soul. Even to that German boy to whom she wrote so regularly and at such length she would never reveal the secret that was after all such a central part of the love we shared.

'It's just possible that young man of hers will turn up next week.'

It was safe for me to raise my eyebrows and demonstrate concerned surprise. Marian was absorbed in her own calculations and permutations.

'Prue bumped into Don Franco. Didn't you see him yesterday? Didn't he tell you anything about it?'

'About what?'

'Obviously he didn't. He had a letter from Professor Helms. The old boy was bringing a party of students to visit the Swedish excavations at San Giovenale. We think it's very likely that Franz what's-his-name will be one of the party. Apparently he was one of the Professor's favourites.'

'Who's we?'

'Prue and I of course. The point is, does Grazia know about this? She hasn't said a word to me. And she gets letters from her Franz addressed to Adriana, her friend at the Agency. You didn't know all this?'

'No,' I said. 'Of course not.'

It was legitimate for me to listen to her intently and encourage her to speculate. What I could not do was show any of the longing I felt to see the girl and question her for myself.

'The thing is,' Marian said. 'What do we know about him? Precious little. I've made a few discreet enquiries as it were, between conditional clauses, but apart from smiles and glances suggesting a Teutonic super-hero gleaming with all the virtues, all I've been really able to find out is that Franz's father is a school-teacher who drives a fifteen year old diesel Mercedes, and that there are other children all younger than the great Franz. Which doesn't suggest great riches.'

'Nothing wrong with that,' I said.

I had to say something. It would have been as absurd for me to be jealous of this boy as for Grazia to be jealous of Marian. Things had to be kept in perspective and unflinching good will towards all concerned was the only way to do it

'Prue had a worst case scenario,' Marian said.

I would have preferred Prue Bianchieri to be left out of it. We were indebted to her, I suppose, and I had to be grateful to the part she had played in our healing process, especially Marian's. But it would be too high a price to pay for peace of mind to see my Marian being transformed into a tough experienced lady-of-the-world in the mould of the Marchesa Bianchieri. Time passes and wounds heal but we don't have to change out of all recognition.

'Suppose he turns up. Like a young knight in shining armour. We have to be prepared for that. Will she run away with him?'

She didn't seem to be aware of any parallel with our previous experience and it would have been gratuitously cruel for me to talk about the possibility of history repeating itself. If I was so appalled at the extent of Prue Bianchieri's influence over her, it was time to begin thinking seriously of leaving this place.

'We've got to be prepared,' Marian said. That's all I'm saying. The young are capable of anything!'

My heart was heavy and all I could do was shake my head like a greybeard contemplating a world of interminable folly. Time passes so that one pain can replace another.

I jumped in my chair when the telephone bell rang. I still was not used to the way it bayed excitedly throughout the apartment like a visitation of ghostly hounds.

'That will be Master Luca cancelling the excursion,' Marian said. 'You can answer it. I'm going to take a shower.'

It was in fact Maria Luisa. I listened intently to her prim and deliberate voice. She spoke with the precision of a civil servant explaining to some untutored member of the public the meaning of yet another official form and how it should be filled in.

'This is Maria Luisa speaking. Luca is confident the mist will lift before mid-day. In the meanwhile he suggests that I should call on you in my little car and bring you to his *cantina* about eleven o'clock. He has much to show us, he says. Mysteries and surprises. You know how he is.'

She might know, being his cousin and loyal admirer. I didn't. Luca himself was enough of a mystery to me and I had no appetite for surprises. I said as much to Marian as she moved in and out of the old-fashioned bathroom drying her hair with impatient vigour.

'I don't know about a mystery,' she said. 'He's pretty obvious really. Just a manly man. Of course he has his uses.'

For a moment she stood in the bathroom door draped in a towel with a knowing look on her face that was most unsettling. More echoes of Prue Bianchieri. What was a "manly man" for God's sake? Apart from something I manifestly wasn't. And what were the uses he could be so conveniently put to apart from assuaging the sexual hunger of his employer's wife? Muzio and Prue could keep up the pretence of being contentedly married if that was what they both wanted. In practice the convention as far as we were concerned was a trap. As they took their separate ways they were creating separate camps leaving Marian in one and me in the other.

'Oh dear,' Marian said. 'A whole morning of Maria Luisa. When she gets in here she will have made a complete inventory of the contents within fifty seconds flat. Prue calls her the ultimate Nosey Parker. She knows everything about everybody. By the end of the day if we survive it, we will have our biographies printed in triplicate on the back of her mind. Prue says there is nothing that woman doesn't know about this place. She probably knows the exact whereabouts of Amalasuntha's last resting place.'

Marian was resolutely cheerful. This was one of the fringe benefits of spending so much time in Prue Bianchieri's company. When the worst has happened to you like losing a daughter, a new confidence in confronting the world becomes available to you. Was that all Marian meant when she made gnomic utterances about Heaven being Other People? They take you out of yourself.... I must have been watching her get dressed with an unblinking gaze of canine fidelity. She was my mistress after all and a faithful hound always waits to be told what to do and think next.

'Do you know what I think?'

She could see how eager I was to hear what she had to say. This was the easy exchange of confidences that I cherished and had characterised our unique relationship from the beginning. If we lost this we lost everything.

'You should have stuck to Boethius.'

'There are always clues,' I said.

While I welcomed criticism, I had to demonstrate that I had a purposeful point of view.

'History leaves indelible marks all over the place,' I said. 'If you can be bothered to look closely.'

That sounded eminently solid and sensible. As far as I knew I wasn't quoting anyone. It was as well to remind Marian that I was still capable of original thought.

'I think you've let yourself get carried away with the sound and fury of great events and the glamour of the House of Amal,' she said. 'The aphrodisiac of supreme power and all that.'

'The view from the balcony,' I said. 'How could I resist it? Isola Martana. The last act. It's the world we still live in.'

I tried to sound even more vigorous.

'Power still flows from the barrel of a gun. The only difference is Theodoric won his way to the top by inviting his rival to dinner and splitting his skull with an ornamental sword. At least he did his own butchering. And you could say it was more colourful....'

I was warming to my theme when she passed behind my chair and ruffled my hair.

'Stick to Boethius, my love,' she said.

'Why? When it's all part of the same relentless pattern?'

'I don't know ... because you are fundamentally a gentle person.'

'Timid you mean.'

She didn't correct me.

'I'll wear my black shell-suit,' she said. 'The weather and Master Luca are equally unpredictable. God knows where he intends to take us.'

I could have demolished any proposition about the inadequacies of a scholar's character limiting the scope of his studies. That would undermine the whole basis of impartial inquiry. It wasn't in any sense a sound philosophic position. All the same in my case it was true. The verdict had been given with such casual affection, the only response could be a bowed head and silence.

xiv

Maria Luisa drew up her shiny new car outside the Porta Romana so that Marian could get out and follow the steep cobbled passage that led to the dressmaker's apartment. The new car fitted the proud owner almost as tightly as her navy-blue costume. There was a fixed smile of maternal possessiveness on her face as she played with the gear lever with one hand and let the other rest on the steering wheel. One-way traffic passed through the ancient gateway. If the glitter of her new car was noticed, that could only enhance the pleasure of ownership.

'I shan't be long,' Marian said. 'But you know how it is. If you don't make regular visits, Guiseppina will just set it to one side and get on with something else. Not that I'm blaming her. But that's how she is.'

'Don't worry,' Maria Luisa said. 'There's no hurry. The mist is lifting. We must make today a holiday.'

From the quick glance Marian gave me I saw how she was

escaping from Maria Luisa's perfume and advising me to wind down my window as far as it would go. Maria Luisa was an admirable woman, well-informed, reliable and well-intentioned and we had no reason to be anything but cordial towards her: but in such close proximity one was forced to conclude the sickly sweetness which mingled with the unpleasing smell of the interior of a new car could only have been intended to mask more pungent bodily odours. I sat like a graven image secretly ashamed of my own fastidiousness. Some well-meaning friend should tell her that a woman with a weight problem should not wear tight clothes. Alas, we are not so easily separated from the self-images we choose to adopt. No one should be more aware of that than my own hypercritical self. I should compensate for my disparaging thoughts by being agreeable. Taxing my brain to discover what we could talk about next increased my discomfort. I myself began to sweat and that in itself was a form of approximate justice. Maria Luisa was confidently at home. She could nod graciously to the passers-by who recognised her with respect and this made me abruptly conscious of being a stranger in a foreign land. She belonged here. I didn't.

'Luca hasn't seen it yet.'

She patted the steering wheel like the lady owner of a winning horse.

'He'll have something to say, no doubt. I bought it without consulting him.'

I tried to look interested but it wasn't of any great moment to me whether Luca Puri approved or not of her impulsive purchase. Her unexpected decision to spoil herself was a topic that had already been exhausted before she embarked on her circumspect descent of the flights of stone staircase down from our apartment. She was preparing to repeat herself now perhaps without being aware of it. It was a habit she had acquired from the nature of her occupation: outlining the same precise answer to the enquiries that flowed in all day long from a steady stream of anxious and impatient and ill-informed taxpayers. To be relentlessly repetitious was an essential qualification for the job. It would also account for the muted insistent tone of her delivery. She never raised her voice, and thus each interlocutor had to calm down and pay closer attention to her exposition of the intricacies of the case.

'Of course you know that Luca is Don Muzio's half-brother?'

Both her hands were resting on the steering wheel. There was a distinct change in the nature of her smile due to the movement of her head as she waited for my reaction to a piece of privileged information. That too would be material to be classified and appropriately stored.

'No. I didn't know,' I said.

Maria Luisa sighed with what I suspected was simulated regret.

'Perhaps Don Muzio did not want you to know. Perhaps it is easier for him that way. There are still many conventions he has to observe in his position. I wanted to explain something. For Luca's sake. It is why the old Marchesa hates him so much. I wanted you to know this.'

My head was nodding sagely but I was deeply uncertain how to react. There were contradictory warning signals flashing in my head that made me frown and sweat until I felt my buttocks sticking to the passenger seat. I could raise a hand to stop her and say these were things I had no wish to know about: but that would only have drawn attention to my confused emotional condition and given the woman cause to ferret out its origins. My only defence was silence. I would have to let her assume I was intrigued by the romantic detail of her story.

'Luca's mother Rosanna was the love of Piero Bianchieri's life. She was the daughter of a peasant. An only daughter. She left school at twelve to work on the little farm. She was beautiful. But for the sake of the estate, Don Piero had to make a wealthy marriage. When Rosanna became pregnant with Luca it was already too late. So she was married off to Renato Puri, the old *fattore*'s son. Renato was a bit simple. Backward you could say. He doted on Luca as if he was his own. Now they are dead: Rosanna, Renato, Don Piero, so what does it matter? These things happen everywhere. Luca is a strong man. But the old Marchesa is still bitter. Hate is a dangerous thing. That's why I wanted you to know. There are those who know, but they know it is better to be quiet about these things.'

It occurred to me that she was taking me into her confidence in the hope that I would take her into mine. I was not short of secrets. But it would never be in her card-indexed cabinets that I would choose to deposit them. Marian came bustling back.

'Guiseppina,' she said. 'Her son wants to get married. I had to listen to all the shortcomings of the prospective daughter-in-law. She smokes all day and hates cleaning and thinks this is the most boring town in Italy. She wants to drag Guiseppina's son to Turin and make him work in a factory.... Oh dear.'

We were all smiling as we drove off. How easy it is to be impartially sympathetic to other people's troubles and how comforting to contemplate them at a safe distance. Did Prue know her lover was her husband's half-brother? Of course she did. She was the kind of woman who made it her business to know everything. Then I had to ask myself whether or not she had told Marian. It would have been part of her general policy to drag her friend and companion down to her level. If she wanted Marian to know about the affair and act as her accomplice she would never have been able to resist adding spice to her confidences: just as the knowledge would inject additional spite into her feud with her mother-in-law.

Our progress was slow. I found the mist depressing. Visibility was still down to a hundred yards and that seemed too accurate an index of my mental condition. I felt trapped in the car with the perfume and Maria Luisa's obsessively cautious driving that she assumed to be deserving of consistent encouragement and admiration. Marian was so patient and forebearing I had a sudden longing to share with her memories of our Rhiannon. I suffered an acute bout of nostalgia for home, our house on the island and the grave-yard by the sea where our girl was buried.

Luca's *cantina* was tucked away beyond a row of unsightly huts and lean-tos opposite what I took to be strips of market garden allotments on the southern outskirts of the town. The huts seemed packed with rusting tractors. There were hens and guinea fowl and ducks in squalid pens as well as fierce dogs and bitches with their puppies that barked their heads off as Maria Luisa cautiously reversed her precious car down the muddy dirt track. Her smile showed she was already anticipating the pantomime of Luca's reactions when we arrived under the vine arbour protecting the entrance to his private winery.

He came to greet us. The sleeves of his clean shirt were rolled halfway up his powerful forearms, his hands were on holiday in his pockets and he was smiling, freshly shaved and shampooed, a glowing picture of health and vitality. He kicked the tyres of the new car and Maria Luisa giggled with the thrill of so much seigneurality.

'Luca will do anything for me,' I heard her mutter as she swung her legs with surprising agility out of the small car. What it really meant was that she would do anything for Luca. She was shivering with delight as he examined the car in detail. Regardless of his clean clothes and clean hands he poked about knowledgeably under the bonnet. He dragged out a low trolley so that he could pull himself under the chassis to examine the quality of the anti-rust sealing. It could all have been superfluous: play-acting to impress a pair of foreign academics and Maria Luisa, who claimed to know nothing about cars. On the other hand, a man so much in charge of his habitat would need to reassure himself of the quality of every machine and device allowed to move into his territory. There was a solidity about his existence that made mine seem febrile and transient. Everything that surrounded him had to be an extension of his own solid self.

Luca had hosed down the floor and set a broad barrel to function as a table with smaller barrels around it so that we could sit and sample his attempts at a *rosé*, as he said, in the right atmosphere. We were surrounded by the clean smell of diluted vinegar. I thought I detected an uncharacteristic vulnerability as he leaned forward and awaited our verdict. He was anxious for praise, so we gave it, although the wine was commonplace enough. It was a ritual that had to be gone through. Afterwards Maria Luisa could express a girlish desire to turn the handle of Luca's private grape crusher and we showed an intelligent interest in the state of his vats and the detail of the processes such as the use of olive oil to seal the demijohns. While he gave a demonstration Marian was able to pour away the contents of her glass into the soil of one of the luxurious pot plants that flourished in the arbour. This was well calculated, since Luca insisted on refilling our glasses. We still had to sit and go through the motions of discussing the political situation and shortcomings of the economic life of the country that Luca had long concluded were endemic.

'What do you do? What can you do with a country that prints money to get out of all its difficulties? What do you do with political parties that will stoop to any device to remain in power?'

Marian and I listened politely to the received wisdom of current political discourse. It was all we had to contribute. Maria Luisa showed intense support with much nodding of the head and interjections of approval. She also kept an eye on Marian and myself to confirm that her cousin Luca was a serious and responsible person capable from his own efficient practice of knowing how a prosperous and self-sufficient country should be run. He was resolutely opposed to unbalanced budgets and iniquitous devices such as the *scala mobile*, the index-linking of salary system that was no more than built-in inflation, and a disincentive to hard work: also as a loyal citizen who had enjoyed his military service he was deeply disturbed by the "noises from the north" and the threatened cantonisation or worse of a great nation that had suffered so much in order to attain Unification. When he raised a hand and declared himself a devoted *Garibaldino* and we declined another fill of the *rosé*, there was a sense of another formality satisfactorily completed. It made me wonder whether an inclination towards ceremonial was inherent in his nature or whether it was some subconscious compensation for his illegitimacy. He watched me stretch my legs as I rose to my feet and saw me smile at my own eagerness to concoct a theory based on a piece of information acquired for the first time barely an hour since. Luca smiled back at me and raised a sinewy finger.

'My mystery! Follow me my friends!'

Luca led the way down a staircase which had been carved out of the rock that formed the rear wall of the *cantina*. He raised his voice cheerfully to warn someone we were coming.

'Massimo! No need to hide, old comrade. Only friends approaching.'

The little man, almost a dwarf, sat cross-legged like a tailor on his bench. He was at work repairing a small votive figure with the help of an instrument that looked like a metal palette-knife and the flame of a bottle-gas burner. He wore oval spectacles on the end of his nose and in the light of the reading lamp he was using, the skin of his face had the consistency of brown paper. The sound of Luca's voice reverberated between the stone walls of what would have looked like a dungeon but for the clutter of Massimo's equipment. In the corner, a black kiln shaped like a coffin was plugged into a large power point. Luca pulled a switch and the whole room was flooded with a bright white light that made Massimo blink and cover his eyes with his sleeve.

'Here is a great artist at work, eh, Massimo? The unknown Michelangelo. The Leonardo of the lower depths. Just look at this.'

With a flourish he plucked a cover from a clay bust on a low wooden plinth.

'A work of art! Nothing less.'

Maria Luisa clasped her hands together under her chin and murmured her admiration: '*che bello*'.

'Originality isn't everything,' Luca said. 'Pure craftsmanship is just as important.'

Marian was peering more closely at the features of the clay head.

'A Roman senator?' she said. 'Is that what it's supposed to be?'

Luca tapped his chest and winked.

'An ancestor. That's for certain. A direct ancestor.'

He bent his knees and ranged himself alongside the bust so that we could see the resemblance. Except for the molding of the sparse hair, it was close. He had been the model.

'Boldness has run in my family for two thousand years,' he said. 'Here is the proof for you! Who said "I found it clay and I left it marble"?'

He was in high spirits. I suspected he wanted to show Massimo and Maria Luisa how much at home he was with these foreign friends of the Marchese. And to us, perhaps, he wished to lift a corner so that we could guess at the extent of his underground empire. His power was less conspicuous, but it reached further than that of his half-brother.

'Massimo is a great artist,' Luca said. 'I have to tell him that every other day because he doesn't have faith in himself. He was abused as a child. Terribly abused. He won't mind me telling you. They tied string around his ankle and sent him down the holes into the tombs like a ferret to carry out whatever he could lay his hands on. That's how he learnt to see in the dark.'

'How terrible,' Marian said.

Massimo was blinking and grinning. His false teeth for some reason did not fit properly in his wide mouth and this made him look much older than he was.

'Massimo, tell them about the earthquake.'

Massimo showed that he would prefer not to. What we heard of his voice seemed rusty from lack of use. He was too shy to speak, or rather his teeth were giving him trouble and it would be easier for him not to go on at length.

'When was it? Maria Luisa, when? The earthquake that struck Tuscania?'

'February, 1971,' Maria Luisa said.'How can I ever forget it?'

'And how old were you then, Massimo, eh? Fourteen, fifteen maybe? Because you were small they were still using you. Imagine it,' Luca said.

'There he was underground, and the earth quaking. It's all very well to say we are used to earthquakes in this region. They still kill. Twenty three dead, a hundred wounded, five thousand made homeless. All in less than a minute. And that same evening this little boy alone in a tomb. And what happens? A miracle. A new crack in the wall and he looks through and like Aladdin he finds treasures in the cave. And what happens? His wicked masters take the lot. But they get caught and the state grabs the lot. And what does Massimo get? Nothing. Except one ancient pot he managed to hide in a sage bush. And there on that shelf is an exact copy.

Only of course, it's better than the original.'

Since Luca was laughing and so pleased with his story and the happy ending we were all obliged to laugh too.

'Now then,' Luca said. 'You must take a little souvenir with you. Only please, you must promise not to tell Don Muzio. Or the lady Prue. They would not approve. Let this be a strict secret between us, eh? And when you are far away in your cold north country, you can take this god in your hands and he will keep you warm.'

He was at his most charming and it was embarrassing. Marian and I looked at each other. How could we refuse to accept a fake figurine of a guardian of the long dead. A double-faced male figure. Muzio would be furious. Luca was masterful. He could sense our hesitations and brushed them aside.

'Massimo wants you to have one each. So we can no longer dispute the matter. They are his handwork and his gift. He breaks no law and therefore neither do you.'

Leading the way up the stairs to the *cantina* I was still troubled by what I was carrying away, small as it was and relatively insignificant. Muzio was my friend and in a sense our benefactor. He was capable of going on at great length about the ethics of art and the moral laws of authenticity. I consoled myself that there was still time to refuse the gift or even to "accidentally" leave it among the pot plants where Marian poured away her drink.

I heard her let out a sudden cry of alarm. I turned around and saw Luca holding her with both hands on her breasts on the excuse that she had lost her balance and he was saving her from falling and injuring her back. He was looking at me and at first I thought he expected me to be grateful. Lying back and supported by Luca, Marian looked extraordinarily youthful and vulnerable. She was my wife and I loved her and felt a need to be strong and protective. He had thrust his face alongside hers and was peering up at me with a mischievous challenging grin. Marian's alarm was turning into embarrassed laughter. He was not going to let her go. Behind him Maria Luisa seemed to be taking an unhealthy interest in the proceedings.

'So! She's mine now, Dottore. How can I let her go? It's impossible!'

He saw it all as a big joke: a cheerful indication of the extent of his mastery. The cool impudence of a woodland deity snatching a partner for some unholy orgiastic dance. Maria Luisa was there specifically to witness it and report it.

'You will lend her to me and we will all be happy!'

172

Out of her helplessness Marian was looking at me and surely she expected me to do something. Her embarrassment was becoming more acute by the second, and yet she was obliged out of a false sense of politeness to laugh and smile. I dropped the figurine I was carrying to free both my hands and moved down the steps to take hold of Marian. I snatched the figurine she was clutching and pulled at her arms. Luca had to let go of her. Marian protested mildly.

'Aled,' she said. 'Don't be so rough. Look. My little mascot is in pieces.'

I breathed deeply to control my anger. Both the figurines were broken.

'People are more important than things,' I said.

Luca and Maria Luisa stared at us in some bewilderment as we snapped at each other in our own language.

'In any case, they are only cheap little fakes,' I said. 'Cheap and nasty. We have no business to be carrying them away.'

XV

The new dining hall of the Centre at Fontane reverberated with the cheerful chatter of important guests. I wandered about clutching the stem of my wine glass too tightly as I tried to look responsible and approving of everything I saw and heard. The Etruscan reproductions on the plain walls were a success because they had been enlarged and hung with restraint and discrimination. This was something I could say if someone should ask me. Marian and Prue were avoiding me because they were intent on enjoying themselves and maybe they saw me as some sort of homesick skeleton at the feast. I watched them glide in and out of the kitchen apparently waiting and serving, but each time they appeared it was some fresh phase in a game that made them smile at each other with conspiratorial hilarity. At least it was a way of living with a shining honest surface.

It was a celebration. I was the one who had least to celebrate. Sir Kingsley Jenkins's pompous letter made it quite clear that our College Council had nothing more to contribute in the way of capital expenditure which is what the Centre had most urgently needed. The letter made me feel I was here on false pretences. It was time to go home. For some reason Marian was in no hurry.

She would smile as she listened and then add something like "all in good time." "Other people" had so taken her fancy. There was no question about it. Professor Helms and his little party were present and he had brought a firm offer of generous collaboration from his university.

Deutschmarks were in and Helms was *der haushohe Favorit*. He sat next to the old Marchesa at what was in effect the High Table, and his trim white beard wagged as he engaged the old witch in solemn conversation. Not that she was listening all that closely. Her eyes were everywhere, darting about with what I was inclined to consider malevolent intensity. The old bitch was trapped in her own unquiet self just as much as I was in mine. Above her head the enlarged reproduction of dancing figures from *La Tomba dei Vasi dipinti* demonstrated an equilibrium that could last for ever. What was I to conclude? Did things only get better after we were safely dead? Alive, everyone was keeping a jealous eye on everyone else and we were incapable of relaxation, not to mention serenity. Correction. I looked at the painting instead of the old woman and I decided that individuals, and maybe societies, flourished better when they had the capacity to accept death as the portal of unalloyed delight. I looked around for Marian. She was lost somewhere in the kitchen. Perhaps she had no need to test the hypothesis. It was what she meant when she claimed like a circus-tent clairvoyant that Rhiannon was "always with her". This was the illumination that eluded me because I was too self-obsessed and possessive to listen to anything except the repetition of my insecure inner voice.

I needed to drink more wine, to strengthen my awareness of the unique Italian genius for modulated social gaiety: that innate gift for celebration and geniality without excess. They did not need the quantity of alcohol I was bent on consuming in order to enjoy civilised contact. They weren't driven by an incessant questioning restlessness, because they put their trust in the tried and tested steps of ancient routines that made it possible for them to dance on ground that could heave and tremble like molten lava at any moment. Different habitats produced different species.

'Dottore, Aled, can I talk with you?'

Grazia had made her way towards me. The new dining room was comfortably full. This was a sound democratic cross-section of local people, archaeologists and people of influence in the province. From the corner of my eye I could see Grazia's father's chest expand like a male bird in a courtship dance as he outlined in slow motion Italian, his pet theory about the protection of ancient monuments to a Frau Doktor with rimless spectacles and gleaming teeth who gave him her earnest and undivided attention. The grimace on her face suggested she was congratulating herself on comprehending everything he was saying. My spirits lifted without alcohol. There was an opportunity for intimate conversation with Grazia in the chattering commotion of this public occasion. Our words could swim towards each other borne up by the sound waves of conviviality. We could sit down at one of the tables and bring our heads closer together.

We gravitated towards a corner and sat down. Above Grazia's head there was an enlargement of a Schulz drawing of male and female Etruscan heads. It was the man who extended his elongated fingers under the delicate line of the young woman's jaw in order to bring her comfort. It was certainly what Grazia was looking for. The Helms party, bringing news of financial support, did not include a single undergraduate. So there was no Franz present to delight and excite her. His absence was painful. She would have to make do with me. It was to me she turned for solace.

'Franz has to work.'

Her large eyes were searching for sympathetic understanding and I was ready to give it.

'His mother is ill. He does extra hours at the Computer Centre. Long hours. It is bad for his eyes.'

I had to take in the details of his tribulations. Marian could have done it better. I had to concentrate on not allowing the girl's transparent devotion to her German boy to diminish my attachment to her.

'Franz says I have natural gifts as a writer. He says I am a poet.'

I nodded as though I entirely agreed with him. The slightest remark this girl makes seems to get etched on my heart. Why should the way she was smiling at me now render me weak at the knees?

'How can he tell?'

Her laughter tinkled like a celeste above the cacophony that surrounded us.

'He doesn't know enough Italian to really judge.'

'Show me something,' I said eagerly. 'Show me something you've written.'

Marian said she was talented. She was perfectly entitled to harbour immense literary ambitions. Her beauty had to be more than an inanimate icon for God's sake. I needed to take a deeper more objective interest.

'You said I was like her.'

She leaned across the table as though giving me another chance to study the resemblance. I couldn't tell her how completely that first shock of recognition had faded. Few things are more uncomfortable than a guilty lover's attempt to cancel lost illusions. I want to be honest but the wickedness of the desires that lie so deep inside me stirred like a nest of vipers. The more I stared at her the less Rhiannon I saw. This was a radiant living girl whose form could blend with mine and restore more than my youth: bring me visions from the deepest fountain of life. My daughter was a distant sorrow.

'I think of her so often,' Grazia said. 'I put myself in her place. Because of you, because of Marian. I feel her a part of myself.'

The tips of her fine fingers were stretched towards her breast and her dark eyes were enlarged with imminent tears. Too much sensibility made her suffer. This was love of a rare purity. I had to understand it before I could share it.

'Was her voice like mine? Do you hear her voice when I speak?' The effort was painful. Rhiannon's voice was childlike, innocent, distant. When I tried to hear it again it faded like a colour setting on the horizon. This voice was warm and vibrant and close to me. No two voices could be more different or further separated in time and space. No two voices could ever be the same in any case. Established fact.

'Franz says, since it means so much to me I should write about it. Like a prose poem. An elegy. You tell me so little about her. I am afraid to ask Marian too much. For a mother it is still too soon. Too painful. I understand that. I can ask you. We are close. A father feels. Of course he does. But he feels in a different way....'

She wanted emotional excavations. That was the brutal truth. For her literary composition. The fingers of her hand on the table crept closer to mine. I looked down at them, predators trying to ingratiate themselves. This is what they wanted from me. Details. Notes. Biopsies. Authentic recollections. Raw material.

'Where are you going?'

I shook my head and blew my cheeks out as I failed to reduce my confusion into words. On the trestle table by the kitchen entrance there was a generous supply of those wines from Pitigliano. She didn't realise she was probing into areas still too tender to touch because she was consumed with a vulgar urge to convert our fathomless sorrow into a piece of fancy prose. I stood up because she was forcing me to become aware of a hard core of ambition hiding behind that pretty, sympathetic exterior. It could only be driving ambition that caused her to be so indelicate.

'Only if you can bear it, Aled....'

I heard no more as I moved away to get at the wine table. My shoulders sagged as I attempted a moving portrayal of a man numbed by an inner pain. It was better that she should think that; and be left to realise the extent and even the source of her insensitivity in her own time. My need was more wine and plenty of it.

The polite back of the Marchese Bianchieri was a barrier across my path to the consolation of red wine. He was refilling the glass of Horst Gruner, a genial specialist in proto-Villanovian culture whom I had already met twice and avoided once. Now I held back to avoid my erstwhile best friend. Was it Muzio or I myself who once fervently declared there was no wall between us? If I stretched out my hand now I could encounter unbreakable glass several inches thick. And whose fault was that? I could never tell him I knew of his blood relationship to Luca Puri, because he had never told me. Any more than he has mentioned his resentment or disappointment or irritation or whatever it was to my expressing a wish to go home. That came via Prue and Marian. The same route I suppose that my complaint had taken to reach him in the first place. I hadn't even brought up the vexed topic of Amalasuntha's non-existent tomb or Luca Puri's tom-foolery in that connection. If I did, I could not expect much more than some tautological comment about the earth being both our cradle and our grave. Was he aware of his half-brother's predatory lusts? How much did he expect me to tolerate? And yet I loved the man. My affectionate admiration was unimpaired and a substantial further intake of wine would certainly increase it.

'Aled! Do tell Horst about your discovery in the museum at the Archbishop's library.'

His role was the cultivated host. What was left of our friendship would have to survive on a thin diet of anecdotes and shared interests. I could seal off my threatened feelings with conversational rubble such as how the Jews in the Papal States nipped over the frontier-river to Pitigliano every time his Holiness had a bad headache. All I had seen in the museum was a piece of fourteenth century manuscript showing a miniature Passover Celebration and we had concluded it must have come from Pitigliano.

With practised ease Muzio detached himself from Horst Gruner and left me stuck with him. Very properly the Marchese made no distinction between one guest and another. All had to be made to

177

feel at ease and entertained, especially the Germans who brought financial gifts. Towards me politeness was a distancing process. He left me in his place close enough to Horst Gruner's plump adhesive presence to hear the rumble of his stomach. Gruner was proud of his smooth idiomatic English. He shifted even closer to me as though his fluency entitled him to greater frankness and intimacy. His bulk stood between me and the wine. His eyes glittered out of folds of flesh like those of a rodent peering out of his burrow at an enthralling dangerous world.

'Tell me,' he said. 'Old chap. Who was that pretty girl you were chatting to? Or should I say chatting up?'

He wanted me to appreciate that he didn't miss a trick.

'Is she local?'

More colloquialisms flowed out in a plaintive monotonous note at odds with the glint in his eye and the smirk on his lips.

'Quite a girl,' he said. 'I suppose you could call her a stunner. An absolute stunner. A bit of alright. Very much what you fancy....'

In its own insidious way it was developing into quite an attack and I had to take evasive action.

'She's my daughter,' I said. 'Would you mind moving a bit so that I can get at the wine.'

He jumped to one side. To soften the blow I lobbed a conciliatory cliché back at him.

'Let the dog see the rabbit.'

He shifted away when he saw Prue wanted to talk to me. She caught my arm as I was in the act of refilling my glass. I could see she was excited and pleased with herself.

'Professor Helms wants me to sing,' she said. 'Do you think I should?'

As though anything could stop her. What did she want from me except encouragement to do what she pleased, which is what she is accustomed to do. She was looking at her mother-in-law sitting alone at the corner of the table on the dais, clutching the ivory handle of her stick. Helms had managed to get away from her.

'Show her what cultured people really think,' Prue said. 'The stupid old sow. Arrogant old snob. Living in the last century but one. She'll be absolutely livid.'

Prue's lungs were already expanding with the prospect of displaying her talent and discomforting her mother-in-law at one and the same time. The old Marchesa looked miserable enough already. The price of her pride was isolation: parked at the end of an empty table with nothing to do except view the cheerful proceedings with what looked like contemptuous disapproval.

'Mozart or Schubert,' Prue said. 'What do you think?'

I felt the wine making me inclined to be witty.

'This year anything but Mozart,' I said.

Prue gave me a hefty nudge that almost spilt my drink.

'You Philistine,' she said. 'I was thinking of *Der Zauberer. 'Ihr Mädchen flieht Damoten ja!'* And I could pretend Helms was the Magician.'

'Well I suppose he is,' I said.

She didn't hear me or take in the sarcasm.

'They'd like that. And maybe end up with *Nacht und Traume*. If I can manage it. That always brings tears to their eyes. Frau Morike will play for me.'

Her excitement was making her brain work faster. Her eyes were bright with the prospect of staging her own apotheosis. She had an audience all around her waiting to be captured.

'Marian wants a word,' she said. 'She's with the fish lot in the kitchen.'

On this democratic occasion willingness to work was a conspicuous virtue.

'Don Franco and Luca are building a bonfire. Where I always said the swimming pool should be. And there'll be a fish barbecue. Luca's in charge. Marian would like you to lend a hand.'

That meant it was Prue who wanted me to lend her precious Luca a hand. That would suit her purposes. After her glittering performance there would be revelry all round, spilling out on the terrace and she and her muscular lover could retire into the shadows – outside the blaze of light. She wanted to conscript me in the name of archaeology and academic democracy to her team of stage hands. I despised the woman. A lie would be good enough for her.

'I've promised Muzio to have a quick word with his Mamma. We felt she looked isolated. "All alone and no telephone."'

Prue looked at me suspiciously. I smiled with pleasure. It was a smart move. It never pays to be too naïve: not even for a simple soul like me.

I approached the old Marchesa seated as she was several inches higher up than anyone else. Her eyes were red with disapproval of the sight of lesser mortals enjoying themselves. Her slack mouth twitched with a desire to interfere and stir up hostilities. I bent down as though it were my function to placate an ancestral spirit. She was all that was left of the uniformed Fascist Furies among the party welcoming the archangel of chaos at Orvieto station.

'I wondered if I could get you anything.'

That sounded civil enough. She swivelled her rheumy eyes up at me and gave an unexpected smile that was if anything more alarming than her frown.

'I see you are paying attention to the Guidatti girl.'

It is a dangerous illusion to assume that one's behaviour ever passes unobserved. There is always someone watching: the living and the half-dead. This old woman was in contact with infernal powers. She sat up here watching and brooding and biding her time to summon up the spirits of discord.

It appalled me to think I could look so besotted from such a distance. It was a remark I had to ignore and yet a clamped jaw would be an admission of guilt.

'Marian is giving her lessons,' I said. 'She is very bright. Very intelligent. Marian says she reads a great deal.'

The old witch was much amused by my confusion.

'You people from the north,' she said. 'You are so absurdly romantic. You take this erotic business far too seriously. What do you think she is? A damsel in distress? Just because she happens to be pretty.'

Being pretty could never have been a condition she suffered from. She was what Muzio's father had to put up with. Her chest began to wheeze as she prepared to deliver another humorous comment. A ringed finger beckoned and I was obliged to bring my head closer to hers.

'You know that before you can rescue a maiden in distress, first you have to kill the dragon. I don't suppose that appeals to you.'

She was looking so pleased there must have been panic showing in my face. Luca Puri was the monster I would have to destroy. She was a dragon herself and in her baleful glance she saw a father who had lost a daughter comforting himself with a nubile girl who would be certain to manipulate his infatuation to her own advantage. She sat up here waiting for me to commit some act of irredeemable folly. I needed more wine to fortify myself against the fear of folly and against fear itself. Large as it was the dining hall was becoming too hot and too noisy. Every door and every window should be thrown wide open. Outside, dogs were howling but no one seemed to be taking notice. There were warnings everywhere. I seemed to be the only one to hear them.

In the kitchen my wife was enjoying herself, cutting up vegetables. There was soup being made on a large scale, the smell of fresh bread and fish being gutted. All the women looked flushed, laughing and smiling, bonded together by joint effort and an enviable affection for one another. Marian spared me a moment to chant their praises.

'You were right you know,' she said. 'They have got a talent for enjoying themselves. And for mutual comfort. It is a form of goodness really. It radiates from a firm moral centre. And that is a very comforting thought. Where's Grazia?'

I wouldn't have called it goodness. Colour. Gaiety. Style even. Unbroken since the age of the painted tombs. Very well. I suppose I had gone about that at too great a length. Life enhancing et cetera and so on. Now all I wanted was escape.

'Don Franco wants to talk to her.'

And so he would. Above suspicion. Marian said she adored Don Franco because he was so transparently good. He certainly liked to talk to everybody. A bright spark of goodwill darting about, his little face gleaming above the black cloth as he delivers his telegrams of hoarse encouragement and comfort. He pops outside for a quick cigarette and keeps an eye on the barbecue and the bonfire, giving Luca Puri ritual pats on the back before diving in and weaving through the bodies in the dining hall like an outside-half practicing side-steps.

'We shouldn't get too romantic,' I said.

It seemed a sage comment to make. I meant we should not allow ourselves to become too deeply immersed in the seductive life of this place. I don't know whether she heard me. Women's cheerful voices reverberated around the bare walls of the kitchen.

'I tell her quite seriously that work is the best remedy for the lovelorn. Work and plenty of it. She agrees with me, bless her. She always tries her very best. Go and find her if you've nothing better to do. Tell her Don Franco wants to have a word.'

'I expect he has already,' I said.

'And don't drink too much or you'll be sorry in the morning.'

I could hardly be sorrier than I was already. It couldn't be folly alone that accounted for the pain in my head and in my heart. I wanted to ask Marian if she had noticed how much the dogs were barking but her friends were calling her and she was drawn back like a smiling recruit into a fresh configuration of the dance. It was bitter and sweet to look at her regain the exuberance and exhilaration of youth. This was the girl who went marching and protesting and stood up in court to be reprimanded and fined when we were young, and I had been part of the same idealism that for some reason was painful now to recall. What had I lost even before I lost a daughter? A purity of idealism could you call it without sneering? The unsullied pleasure of devotion to a cause that was self-evidently greater and better than the sum of our little selves. Where had all that gone to? Marian was the only one who could tell me; but at the moment she was otherwise engaged.

There were faint lights of fishing boats like fireflies on the waters of the lake. The stars in a windless heaven were in place and all I had to do was sip my wine, listen to their music and set my brief existence in some kind of context. The trick was stillness so that the pain of all time could shrink inside my skull. The same calm constellations shone in their courses when Amalasuntha built her father's tomb. They made no distinction between a daughter burying a father and a father burying a daughter and there was no reason why they should. Poor Grazia. If I loved her why should I indulge in an hysterical reluctance to talk about Rhiannon's death? Love demands honesty. What was the difference between positive and passive resignation? Would the girl tell me? I barely understood it myself.

The dogs were calming down under the influence of the balmy Mediterranean night. Luca Puri and Giorgio and his young friends were dragging the branches Luca had trimmed from the surrounding trees, to throw on the bonfire and bring fresh colours and sparkle out of the flames. They also cleared waste wood from the restoration work on the buildings and I was happy to leave them to it. Grazia appeared on the terrace following Don Franco. I raised my hand but she didn't see me. I was sitting in the shadow. It was the bonfire she and Don Franco were staring at. I wanted to tell her she was entitled to make use of me more than I was entitled to make use of her. She had a right to make use of my pain. The little priest was talking. Virtue is spelled in words of one syllable. If we can't transmit erotic love into disinterested goodwill, life sinks to the level of the jungle.

Inside the dining hall the guests were listening to Prue Bianchieri singing. In the clear evening air her voice throbbed with deep emotion. Something about bitter misgivings, sighs, and the torments of unrequited love. The music was revealing enough whatever the words. It lent a magical quality to the night, like the flames of the bonfire. Luca and his crew stopped work to listen. Giorgio put his hand on his heart and his shadow grew on the slope to grotesque proportions as he mimed exaggerated devotion. The moment the applause came, Don Franco began to wonder aloud if the barbecue would be ready in time, and was there enough aluminium foil for the fish? He left Grazia standing by the barbecue clutching an empty basket.

She was without protection. In no time Giorgio and his gang had scrambled up to drag her down to the bonfire. It seemed playful enough at first. Prue had begun singing again but now the lads were more interested in persuading Grazia to dance with them around the fire. I couldn't make out the degree of her reluctance. Luca seemed to be ordering the boys to keep quiet. He was on the side of attentiveness to civilised behaviour. Then abruptly the situation changed. His large hard hand closed around Grazia's wrist and he was trying to drag her away from the firelight. Giorgio and his friends stood back afraid to intervene when they could see quite plainly that Grazia was resisting.

I was taken by surprise by my own reaction. I stood up so suddenly my wine glass shattered on the terrace floor. My body was taken over by a storm, an explosion of irrational fury. This man was an enemy and it was my duty to attack him. At least he was restricting the girl's freedom and in the darkness he would take her by force, and such was his power no one would stop him. Except myself. I flew down the slope almost into the flames and snatched up a burning brand. As I raised it above my head Luca's shepherd dog attacked my legs. I pushed the flame into his face and his hair sizzled as he yelped and shot away. Luca had let go of Grazia and was shouting at me to drop the burning brand. I swung it around my head and shouted at her to get back on the terrace. The sense of triumph was more intoxicating than the wine. If my hands were burnt I didn't feel it, berserk as I was. I was forcing Luca to retreat before me when the ground gave way beneath my feet. It flashed through my mind that I had somehow encountered an earth tremor. For a moment I was conscious of treading air before I stepped in a black void. My head hit a rock and I lost consciousness.

FIVE

i

I was still in the living world. The sunlight sparkled on the inside of my eyelids because the sparks of the sun pierced the close weave of the blind drawn half way down the window of the compartment. It was generally assumed I had been very drunk. A deplorable condition but, in a foreigner, forgivable. Giorgio swore I had been yelling unintelligibly as I plunged down the slope towards the fire. He said I was like a man seeing things: or pursued by the furies. The longer people listened to Giorgio the greater his inclination to draw on his imagination. I never said 'Teodorico', or 'Amalsuntha', or anything of the sort. They also claimed they saved me from falling in the fire, which was rubbish. If I had had a sword instead of a piece of wood in my hand I would have split Luca Pura open from shoulder to groin. That might have shown he hadn't an honest bone in his body: but the bloody mess would have turned me into a herbivore and Marian says I eat little enough meat already.

It was also alleged that in my delirium I raved about some nymph or other being pursued by a satyr and in danger of being bitten by a snake. That could have been true. For an unspecified period of time my mind had boiled with a vision of the unchanging treacheries of the human condition. As for the girl I imagined I was defending, she had seen it all and could have come forward as a reliable witness, but instead, she retreated into what I took to be a frightened silence. What happened was I recovered some form of consciousness and I was treated by a chain-smoking doctor with a Portuguese name and a twisted grin. He drove me home and helped Marian to put me to bed. I woke up with my right wrist in a splint, and every bone in my body aching and my head dulled in an analgesic haze.

I was declared harmless and I was forgiven. Or rather quietly demoted to that lower level reserved for individuals whose odd behaviour transforms them from grave responsible citizens into fodder for sniggers and incidental jokes. At the Centre, the great project of Fontane, Professor Helms ruled. The Goth had ridden in, loaded with Deutschmarks, and the locals, Roman or Etruscan, were falling over themselves to collaborate: and if any of my suggestions were to be considered it would be on a basis of grace and favour. I saw myself as an inadequate representative of an impoverished power, and since that was the way in which the wheel of fortune turned, there seemed to be very little I could do about it.

When you are ill and indisposed you cease to be responsible for anything, not even yourself. From a horizontal position you gain a view of the ebb and flow of a sea of faces. We live in a world with an infinite capacity to settle down after large and small upheavals: earthquakes or minor insanities. In no time at all it was business as usual. Selected delicacies were sent from the Guidatti *trattoria* together with home-made get-well cards from the smaller children. Luca Puri called with a few litres of his wine and his best virginal olive oil which he claimed was efficacious for the massage of sprains and bruises. It was judged I was too ill to receive him. The egregious Giorgio delivered a colourful cake from the Lido that I would never dream of eating, and he managed to give Marian several new interpretations of my unexpected eruption before she was able, politely, to get rid of him.

Marian was merciful and tender. She frequently held my hand and she managed to make Prue Bianchieri keep her voice down as the mezzo-soprano's expressions of curiosity reverberated around the apartment. "What do you suppose..." I heard; and "Do you think?..." and "Could it be?...". Meanwhile I would lie in bed divested of responsibility, and the great tide of the dreams that lap the shores of our existence, has helped me to get away on a train going north with a sneaky little song in my heart and my lips sealed.

Marian arranged my escape in comfortable stages. There was an exhibition of Ancient Manuscripts at the *Trivulziana* in Milan, she announced, it was my absolute duty to visit. Rare Roman codices and papyri that had not been exhibited before. There might even be something there copied from Boethius. She showed a new and tender concern for my interest in ancient writing and calligraphy: I could see she believed the renewed practice of the craft might bring a degree of composure to a troubled soul. She booked me a room in the old Locanda in *Via Castelfidaro*. She would join me there in a few days when I had had time to see and take in every-thing I needed. She would be in constant touch and she wanted me to enjoy the first steps of freedom inside the comforting context of being fully taken care of.

I was also touched by the quiet and still remote way Muzio showed his concern for my welfare. He would drive me to Florence along the Via Cassia not only for old time's sake. He said it would give us time for a proper chat. There were also agricultural improvements for poor soils he wanted to visit beyond Radiocofani and we could stop at Chiusi for a quick look at the new excavations in the catacombs of Santa Mustiola. A particular gesture of goodwill and friendship was a fruitless attempt to locate the traces of a Celtic settlement that was supposed to have left its mark north of Chianciano. We were almost at the Porta Romana before Muzio revealed what was really on his mind.

'Look,' he said. 'Put it this way. I can't let you go back empty handed. I'll put it all on paper of course so that you can wave it under your Principal's nose: but we could certainly offer a two year, postgraduate course and an agreed number of undergraduate residencies for the excavation seasons. With the Deutschmarks and so on we could go half way to meet the costs, scholarships, awards, or whatever. There are endless possibilities and as far as Kingsley Jenkins is concerned, you are our one and only accredited intermediary.'

My heart warmed towards him. He wanted to secure my academic niche. It seemed our friendship was after all unimpaired. But then he went on and spoilt it even as I stared gloomily at the murky waters of the Arno.

'Helms is in full agreement. Did I tell you by the way he has bought an old farmhouse outside Gradoli? Did I? Luca is guiding him through the quicksands, so to speak, and giving him valuable advice and directions. And the Herr Professor's Swedish wife is jumping up and down with excitement. There's a lot of work to be done on the place, but she can hardly wait to invite some member or other of the Swedish royal family to tea!'

It would have been churlish not to smile at his little joke. There could not, however, be a more conclusive demonstration of my reduced status.

This train was travelling north, my wrist in a splint, I was still black and blue down one side of my body. I was redundant: being transported, shipped out, not escaping. A foreign body, wrapped up and discharged. The young man seated opposite was even more insulated from other people than I was: immersed in his pink football newspaper: a complete universe concocted daily to orbit around the hot pursuit of a leather ball. He was totally absorbed and for him I did not exist, and that, by and large, was a comfort.

The other occupant of our compartment was more threatening and I had to avoid his hungry glance. His aluminium crutch was stored along the lower luggage rack and he wanted the world to contemplate the stump of his left leg that had been amputated above the knee. Was he too poor to afford an artificial leg: and was he a Sicilian, an Albanian or an Arab from North Africa travelling north with a small black volume clutched in his right hand which could have been a Koran or a Bible? There was rope tied around his battered suitcase, holding it together. I drew the sleeve of my jacket over my wrist. The sight of my injury could only draw attention to his. It was uncomfortable to be reminded of how much I had to be grateful for. The blue pinstripe suit had been made for somebody else. It was too big for him. The empty trouser leg was folded around the stump like an untidy parcel. He was young. His lips moved in his dark face before he spoke. He could keep silent no longer. His harsh fairground voice filled the compartment.

'When I had two legs I played mid-field for Kugar-Delvino.'

The football enthusiast emerged from his pink dream and his *Gazetta dello Sport*. He frowned as he seemed to notice the other man's missing leg for the first time. They were both young. They both had the same dark curly hair. They could both talk football. They had a lot in common.

'The Lord took away my leg!'

The cripple lifted his black bible. He sweated even more exultantly. I would never ask him but I wondered in what sense he spoke of the Lord taking away his leg: a disease, an accident? Did he equate the Deity with fate or Fate? Should we all?

'So that I should give my time – which is all the time we have got let us remember – to the study of his Holy Word. I have lost a piece of my earthly body in order to gain my heavenly soul. Who would dare say I do not have the best of the bargain?'

I suspected this was an oration he had made many times before. He was an itinerant evangelist determined to make capital out of his disability.

'Excuse me.'

The football enthusiast leaned sideways apologetically.

'I never heard of this team. But where is this Kugar...vino?'

'Albania. Where else.'

The answer was unacceptable. The football enthusiast withdrew his polite attention and muttered into his paper.

'I have to say this. We don't want any more Albanians. We've got far too many already.'

'I am an Italian citizen.'

There was a note of triumph in the harsh voice.

'I was born in Agrigento. I have my passport. Let me show it to you.'

' It doesn't matter. It's none of my business....'

'Oh but it does matter. You can't let a small thing like this come between you and your immortal soul.'

The cripple's face gleamed with a fierce amiability. This was an encounter very much to his taste – I could see a loud altercation developing. I closed my eyes but that did nothing to discourage it.

'Time will roll all that stuff away. Don't let that pink paper come between you and your salvation, my good friend....'

The football enthusiast was roused. His face flushed.

'Listen,' he said. 'I am a good Catholic. And my immortal soul as you call it, that belongs to me and to no one else.'

The cripple waved an unwashed finger in the air.

'Wrong,' he said. 'You are wrong my friend.'

He was seized with a remorseless delight.

'It belongs to Jesus! Your immortal soul belongs to the Lord Jesus. Not to you. Not to the Church. Not to the world. It belongs to Jesus!'

He opened his bible and held it out like a plate.

'This book, my friends, is in three languages. Italian. Greek. Arabic. I speak them all. And they all carry the same glorious message. I also speak Albanian. I have the gift of tongues.'

He was offering to read aloud to prove his linguistic abilities. The noise filled the compartment. The football fan did not want to listen and neither did I.

'Excuse me,' the fan said. 'But this is not polite....'

He wanted my support. I was about to give it when I saw the figure of a nun appear in the window of our compartment door. She could have been drawn by the noise the Sicilian was making. If a religious revival was about to break out she was already clothed in the vestments of indisputable piety. She moved more by curiosity than approval. She looked at me and through half-closed eyes I caught a glimpse of that haunting smile I had seen between the cold pillars of the crypt of the Basilica. It was a visitation to frighten me out of my hardened insulated state. The smile was a summons. I stood up, ready to follow her. I don't know whether the Sicilian thought I was moved by his scriptural eloquence. It was a familiar passage about suffering little children to come unto their master since they were the composition of the kingdom of heaven.

The Sicilian held me by the sleeve as I struggled to open the stiff compartment door.

'I can read them all, Signore. Not because I am a scholar. Because I am saved!'

He wanted me to look at the columns of different print in his book. It was certainly worn with use. His fingers shuffled the pages. He was offering to read any page I should choose.

'Did you see her?' I said.

He didn't seem to know what I was talking about. The nun had moved away. She looked so young. Was it a child dressed up to look like a nun and radiate innocence? There was no one in the corridor. Outside, the power of the sun was chasing away the remnants of mist that clung around the rows of poplars on the Lombardy plain. I could have been hallucinating. God knows what that grinning Portuguese had mixed into his pills. He struck me as being a bit of a charlatan and yet Prue Bianchieri spoke of him with a unusual degree of respect. He had cured her once of some obscure liver complaint and his local reputation was made for life. Should I stagger up and down the train looking for her or return to my seat and endure the verbal barrage of the evangelical Sicilian? In a train, choices are always severely circumscribed. I could wander up and down these corridors for ever.

I almost stumbled over a girl sitting on a bulky suitcase in the space outside the toilet. It was Grazia. She seemed to be hugging herself with an obscure delight. She looked so young. Both her white hands were stretched out as though they were enjoying their unaccustomed idleness. She showed no surprise at seeing me. Her smile was as brilliant as ever. She had a velvet cap on her black curls and although she was sitting in such an undignified position she could have been looking down at me like one of those angels that peer down at us from a painted Renaissance heaven. She was making an unsuccessful attempt to stop herself laughing.

'Grazia! Where on earth are you going?'

'To Milan,' she said. 'Like you. Where else? You see. I have made my escape. *Voilà!*'

I was caught up in her laughter. This was her adventure and she was determined to enjoy it.

'You were right, Aled. You were right.'

Whatever it was I had been right about, it was an unalloyed pleasure to be with her. We stood side by side clinging to the chrome bar across the window. The fertile plain outside in the sunlight was being rolled up like a carpet of unreality. We made up a universe of our own.

189

'I must live first,' she was saying. 'And then I shall write about it. Not her experiences you understand. But my own. You were right. I must make my own search for truth. And what I write will be more dear to me than my own eyes.'

They were dear enough and near enough to me now. This was as close as lovers ever came to each other: being carried away and yet absorbed in stillness. Whatever she chose to say would fall from her lips like a profound truth I was hearing for the first time.

'I am in flight from darkness and in search of light....'

Out of the noise of the engine it was her voice. They were her words. It was my privilege to receive them: to nod, to agree, to approve, smile and applaud.

'We need a certain love to exist,' she said. 'To break out of the darkness. With that power you make your own way. You take responsibility for yourself. Why should a woman be a slave? Always meek, always suffering. To be young and free is wonderful. You understand that, Aled?'

Of course I understand it. I stood alongside her to understand it even better although I was neither young nor free.

'What kind of love? You have to find out. Only experience can tell you. In people, in nature, in an unconfined world.... You understand what I mean?'

There were things that I could add about the progress of the soul, but swaying alongside her excitement, clinging to the rail, they would sound pale and theoretical.

'How did you get away?'

She put a finger to her lips and managed to look demure and rogueish at the same time: an adorable child incapable of wickedness.

'My amazing escape.'

She wanted to share with me her delicious naughtiness.

'Disguised. They disguised me. For the sake of her operatic past,' she said. 'The nun's habit. I could have sung too, I was so happy. And Marian said her Aled would help me.'

Whose fate were they deciding, those scheming women? Marian talking about me as though I were her pawn. Grazia could see how disturbed I looked. The train accelerated and we clung to the chrome bar as if we were clinging to each other.

'Too much deception?'

She was peering intently at my troubled face. She perceived more than I did. We learn so little as we grow older. She was wise and mysterious and I was fluttering like the page of an open book.

'Don't worry. I am not a wild person. I have thought about things. I have thought a long time. They don't know this, but I can tell you. I cannot act without telling him. He is part of my life. You understand, Aled?'

It was becoming clearer what I was here for.

'Franz will meet me in the Brera. I will bring him to you. You shall see. And I will take my life from there.'

This was well beyond Marian's plan for the girl to live in our home and go to our university. Grazia was in charge of herself. Her hand slid along the metal bar until it touched mine. This was more than a bid for freedom. She wanted to bend the world to her will and was prepared to take any risk. She could see I was alarmed and despondent and she had sufficient strength left over to comfort me.

ii

The Locanda was a comforting nineteenth century oasis in the heart of a furiously modern city. Guests were expected to sigh with relief as they passed through the antique portals to relax in the golden gloom of the interior. Grazia was empowered and eager. I sat helpless to the point of impotence. She had four currencies rolled into four separate cylinders, provided for the most part by Marian and Prue and carried, on their advice, very close to her person. She was armed she told me. Suspended like a necklace was a small container of disabling gas and in her handbag, alongside a pocket edition of Foscolo's poems, a knuckle-duster provided by an aggressive Prue Bianchieri. The girl was smiling but she was serious. This was a fierce feminist fairy-tale concocted by the three of them. It would be unkind to say the girl burbled. Her excitement was too charming for that. It was something to admire and envy.

'It is a new era,' she said. 'For the first time in history a girl alone, a single girl, can be a wandering scholar, a pilgrim, even a troubadour. Why not? Europe will become one again and we shall be free women. It is a miracle when you come to think of it.'

What was my wife up to, aiding and abetting a young girl to run away from home? Marian of all people. Her inconsistency took my breath away. Prue Bianchieri I could understand. She was getting rid of a presumptive rival. Her game was bridling her over-amorous stallion. But Marian. My Marian. She should be here now so that I could cross-examine her across the brass-topped coffee table. The girl was leaving me to digest my disabilities and discontent alone in this quiet backwater, while she made her jaunty defiant way to the *Palazzo di Brera*. There she would be united with her Franz, and the young lovers would wander arm in arm through the galleries to gaze at pictures lovers always gazed at. And what would they be plotting? I was left alone with my ignorance. I had nothing better to occupy myself with than struggling to pick out defects in the girl's character and appearance. Strictly speaking her eyebrows were too thick. She had this habit of giggling. Her teeth were uneven. There was no evidence to show she was capable of submitting herself or her motives to rigorous analysis. I could ask her nothing without sounding insufferably priggish and pompous.

What will you do? I wanted to ask her. And what do you expect your gallant Franz to do? And why didn't you let Marian know you were arranging to meet him?

'I sent him a plan of the *Pinacoteca*. He is to wait in Room 24 near to the Raffaello Marriage of the Virgin. So there.'

The pleasures of conspiracy. I have to smile while she giggles. What makes me seize on her most trivial remarks and ponder their significance? These creatures created to look like renaissance angels in order to conceal depths of feline cunning. Off she went. As free as a bird. And I lay back in chains. All thanks to my wife who never did as much for her own daughter. This girl's escape could not have been mounted at a moment's notice. I saw nothing. How much the self-absorbed miss of all the machinations going on around them. They could have been muttering about this enterprise when Muzio and I laboured like pack-mules up the cliff to the inaccessible Hermitage. All males condemned to be kept in the dark. What was I supposed to feel, planted in this modest hotel of old world charm and character, except impotence and humiliation?

I was being made to suffer. I was being punished. Marian was putting me to a test. Since our very first meeting, way back in the days of protests and marches and defiant meetings, she took pleasure in exerting moral authority. Over me and over anyone else who would listen. It was always meet and proper to submit. I was being deputed to look after her protégé. And this was on an assumption that my sexual drive was only fractionally stronger than Muzio's. She was prepared to conspire with her friend Prue in an exercise calculated to emasculate an unsatisfactory male. For how many shortcomings was I being made to pay?

The girl was a step ahead of them. She had sent a plan with

instructions to her German lover. She had youth and beauty on her side and they would guide her through the darkling streets. Outside a late afternoon Milanese mist was gathering. I was alone among the rustic antiques and early nineteenth century prints, like the last patient left in a doctor's waiting-room. There had to be a prescription and a cure.

When the happy pair finally arrived she would expect me to greet the young man with kindly warmth. Love me, love my boyfriend. What was I going to say? Make a ghastly repetition of my effort to be agreeable to Master Buddy Thwaite. Young men were no longer a species I was enamoured with. I would settle for my station in life as a harmless and humdrum academic. As my grandfather used to say, if you aim at nothing you can't miss it. In a spasm of impatience I moved to another reception area in search of a change of scene. It was hopeless to attempt to read a book.

I dozed as though anaesthetised in front of an open fire. When I opened my eyes I turned my head to see her face in the window looking in. It seemed small and forlorn. I jumped up. I saw her pay the driver of a yellow taxi. I saw the taxi speed away and leave her on the pavement as if she were undecided whether or not to come indoors. I saw her shoulders sag. And in the artificial light I caught a glimpse of what she might look like twenty years hence. She aged as she stood alone on the pavement.

When she came in the room she was smiling, resolute, positive: hardly the same person that stood outside in the street. She shivered slightly from the autumn cold, rubbed the end of her nose with the back of her hand before approaching the open fire.

'Franz is in Turkey,' she said. 'Isn't that amazing?'

I suppose for her it was. The great adventure had stalled at the end of the first day. At least I was at hand. She was not alone staring into the abyss.

'I waited, ' she said. 'I waited a long time. Waiting is always a long time, isn't it? The custodians were very suspicious. Was I there for stealing something?'

She managed a giggle. That was enough to overwhelm me with love and sympathy.

'So I telephoned. What else could I do? I spoke to somebody. An aunt I think. My German went weak at the knees and at the mouth. This woman kept saying 'Turkei.' 'Die Turkei.' It was too ridiculous. I could make no sense. And that was it. I put the phone down and I walked that Via Fiori Chiari until I took control of myself.'

She raised both her hands, closed them tight, and shook them.

'So I telephoned again. With my mind in order. This time I spoke to his father and we understood each other far better. A colleague fell ill. At very short notice he was offered this place in the team. Excavations in Lydia. Possible proof of the "eastern theory". So you see he had to choose. A trip for nothing to Turkey and possible archaeological triumph. Or pay the travel to Milano to meet some girl. Which would you choose?'

I restrained myself from giving a fervent answer. I was here as the only person she could turn to.

'Where have you been?' I said. 'All this time.'

'I walked,' Grazia said. 'Like a tourist. In and out of churches. There was a church devoted to the Virgin and I sat and stared at a great forest of candles wondering what to do. It was simple. I would climb to the roof of the *Duomo* and stand on those marble slabs and face the east and wave towards Turkey. That's what I did and that's where I've been. I stretched my heart two thousand miles.'

Franz was a shit. That's what I found out: that he was not good enough for her and probably never would be. Who was I to judge? And what alternative could I offer?

Grazia became concerned for my condition. She caught me wincing as we made our way up the narrow stairs to bed. Her tenderness was delightful.

'You are still not well,' she said. 'You are in pain. I can see it. How can you forgive me for being so self-absorbed?'

At the turning of the stair I stood to smile at her, to show her I could forgive her anything. She had wisdom beyond her years and the cool sculptured beauty on that upturned face would keep a painter occupied for a lifetime to capture the elusive concern in those eyes and the parted lips. My response was to mutter like a besotted idiot.

'Two of us,' I said. 'Here.'

I wanted to say something profound about the chance that had marooned us together, just the two of us, in the centre of a great city. Not that it was chance: part accident, part plan in which I had no part. The enthusiasm was there, but not the capacity to unravel the mystery and set it out in so many words. I made light of my bruises and the state of my wrist. They were nothing alongside the privilege and the joy of being with her, our rooms next to each other and the sense of revelation, like the soft glow of the light behind her head.

The bedrooms were small and furnished in the same comfortable antique style with the early nineteenth century prints marching on across the faintly copper coloured walls. Grazia came into the room resolved to see to my comfort. The hand she laid on my forehead was maternal. So was her kiss on my cheek. This was an eighteen year old girl putting a man of fifty to bed: an easy source of ridicule, except for her strength and competence and my state of blissful content. I should have telephoned Marian. That was the arrangement. In this room at this hour life no longer seemed to need arrangements. Equilibrium was an accomplished fact. I considered stretching out my arms and drawing Grazia down to me, but it was Time and Place that settled on my chest and the weight of a segment of the earth that stretched from the roof of the *Duomo* to an un-named site in Asia Minor. I could accommodate it all and that in itself was a triumph. I closed my eyes and sank into an easy sleep.

Late in the night or in the early morning, I felt someone shivering with cold in the bed alongside me. Grazia's breath whispered in my ear.

'Aled. You were groaning in your sleep.'

My head filled with clarity like a white light. This was the visitation I had longed for. Her hands were so cold.

'I couldn't sleep. I've been writing. No. Not letters. My journal. And it's just the beginning of my journey. It is better than crying.'

I could feel her laughing at herself again. As always, that made her more remarkable. She was at my side and she was wonderful. She was the centre of the world. I thought I could hear her murmur that we were here to comfort each other and keep each other warm. This was bundling. The kind of courting that went on in the stable lofts a hundred years ago: or in alpine ski huts when the young cuddle from the cold. I wanted to feel her closer in all her naked smoothness. I discovered then that under her night clothes she was still bundled and bound in her winter underwear. She resisted my effort to undress her.

'No,' she said. 'Aled. No.'

At first she calmed me as though I had a fever. My voice croaked with disappointment. She could barely hear what I was muttering.

'Are you keeping yourself then? For your beloved Franz?'

It was spiteful and crude but she forgave me. I embraced her again and all the clothing that clung to her body. The clothing was there to guard and preserve her chastity like a marketable commodity. I had to accept her for what she was and be grateful for the privilege.

'Aled. You must be the poet of tenderness.'

She whispered as she restrained me. What did she think I was?

'I'm no poet at all.'

'Yes you are. Ungrasping. Generous. wise.'

'Old. Worn....'

'Not so old, I think.'

Her voice seemed to tease me. I took it as a challenge. We create idols in order to tear them down. She struggled to defend herself.

'Listen. Aled. Now listen. In a way I would willingly give myself to you.'

I lay still and listened to her as if she were the priestess of the Oracle.

'Virginity is of no account. In a way of speaking. A woman has as many lives as the menstrual cycle. Are you listening?'

I hear every single word and memorise each one.

'She has many lives and she may have many loves. I can believe that. But in my case, as I am now, in this life that has a number eighteen stuck on it, I must have control. I must not become pregnant. I must not carry a child. Not on any account. In the future everything can be different. But now I begin my journey and I must control my destiny. I must not have a child.'

She seemed to think she had convinced me. I could accuse her of planting the seed in my head. She had activated a latent desire I had been unaware of until that very moment. Over and above all, my excuse could be, it was a child I wanted. To take the place of the precious child I lost. And this girl whom I was supposed to love with an ethereal tenderness, it was this girl who could give me what I wanted. She could satisfy a dominating desire that had sprung to life in the depth of my being. I had the right to master this girl and make her submit. She didn't realise at first how determined I was. Her laughter gave way to anger as we struggled. I tore at her clothes. To protect herself she kicked me and knocked my wrist so that the pain shot like a fire up my arm. She scrambled out of bed and switched on the light. She was hurt and she was angry. She stretched out her arm towards me accusingly.

'You are not my friend,' she said. 'How can you be? You want to destroy me.'

She left me in my despair. As if I had destroyed something. I lay alone in the room unable to sleep and wondering how if ever Grazia and I could be anything like intimate again. I should never

196

have touched her. In the morning I would apologise and she would forgive me. But the trace of something precious would have gone for ever. The loss was mine, not hers.

iii

It amazed me to see how completely Marian took the girl under her wing. All I could do was hover guiltily on the fringe of the circle of light they created between them when they were together. In Grazia there was no discernible trace of the disappointment that had devastated her only thirty six hours or so ago: or of the abortive encounter in my bed. Whatever she felt and whatever conclusion she had come to I could only hope she confided to her journal, not to Marian. Here in the Locanda I could only watch with envy the way they exercised their affection for each other ... they had nothing to hide and everything to gain: a new strength, a youthful confidence and enthusiasm. Everything they said and did proclaimed a zest for life. The city of Milan was at their feet.

'We are here to enjoy ourselves,' Marian said not once but many times. Each time they managed to laugh as if she had just coined a witty phrase. Together they were strong enough to reduce the ruthless and impersonal mechanism of a great city into the interior of a gigantic toy shop. Marian was ready to march about with a panache that recalled our days of protest; and Grazia followed in her wake not so much as a protégée as a matching illumination. I was excused sight-seeing and shopping expeditions. My frail condition was also the subject of repeated humour. A fine excuse to leave me behind. I wasn't well enough to work in the *Trivulziana*. It was left to Marian to put my dazed existence to better use.

'Aled,' Marian said. 'I am about to ask you the most enormous favour.'

'Anything,' I said gallantly.

'If you could fly to Manchester,' she said. 'That's the easiest way. And the quickest. And get the house ready. Fires in every room. A warm homecoming. And make some enquiries at the college. See if we can get a place for Grazia. I thought History would be a possibility. Rather than English. Or a joint honours in French and Italian. We can manage the tuition fees, can't we?'

I wondered very tentatively about raising the girl's hopes. As to fees, they went up year by year. She would need four years surely in a foreign language. Marian looked so resolved there seemed little point in anything except a show of responsible acquiescence.

'What will you two do?'

'We'll come by train,' Marian said. 'Via London. She hasn't said it in so many words, but I know she is dying to see London.'

Marian had thought it all out. She was motivated by unshakable benevolence. London had never been one of her favourite places.

'She's told me twice that Foscolo died at Turnham Green. I think she fancies a sentimental journey. He's a great hero of hers. You know she keeps a journal?'

'She does?'

My eyebrows went up and I shivered inside as I assumed an ignorance that could pass for innocence as well. Was I in it? Had Marian read it? That journal suddenly acquired the status of an ominously vital document.

'I don't know how we figure in it,' Marian said. 'If we figure in it at all. I have the feeling she only makes use of everyday events as a stimulus to allow her imagination to take flight. You know, prose poems, not data. That's why she is so interested in Rhiannon. There's talent there. No doubt about it.'

I thought of that girl and her journal as we flew northwards high above the Alps and the cloud-covered peaks. The things young persons write in their diaries expose many of the secrets they keep securely hidden behind their eyes. Those luminous eyes of Grazia had the gift of looking at life as if it had never happened before. It was not a case of having taken a girl too seriously: I hadn't taken her seriously enough. Marian was right to send me to prepare a way for her. It was at least a purpose in what was rapidly deteriorating into a purposeless existence. I had resolutions to make and I had to be resolved and not dissolved to make them. I was still alive in this metal projectile as we shot through the stratosphere each of us docketed and in place, as motionless as corpses with tickets in our pockets instead of tied to our toes. The mountains below us, the stars above us, and nameless mysteries inside us.

There was a groan alongside me and I heard the occupant of seat F13 mutter he was gasping for a drink. He had already seen the cabin crews approaching. He barely touched the wrapped food in the plastic containers on the table-shelf in front of him, but he ordered a sequence of brandies and sodas. He was slumped in his segment of seat, his collar and tie loosened and his waistcoat buttons undone, weary and plump with the shadow of his beard darkening in the early morning light. He had things on his mind and he was ready to confide in me.

'I'm not a racist,' he said. 'God forbid. My maternal grandfather was a Manchester Jew. But my God, those bloody Japs are hard to stomach. They buy themselves in and they sit tight in the board room learning the bloody balance sheet off by heart, and then one fine day they pounce and you're voted off, and you find yourself outside the front door of the family firm where you've worked all your bloody life and if you're lucky, clutching a tin handshake ... and they're still ruthlessly polite as they shut the door behind you....'

He had a poor opinion of the state of the world below us. In his opinion it had no idea how to look after itself. He had been in textiles all his life. His great-uncle had a combing machine with patent laps and rollers named after him, and he himself in the full-ness of time had inherited the chair of the company: until the Japs moved in.

'They say you've got to move with the times,' he said. 'And what does that amount to? Making yourself redundant. Talk about the Yellow Peril. And what were they after? A foothold in Europe. And that's what Old England has become. A back door for the Yanks and the Japs to use without even wiping their bloody feet. And where does it leave me? Sales rep for an Iti company flogging exactly the same old product. A wife and three kids and a mort-gage in Alderley Edge. I spend half my life in bloody aeroplanes. Look at this.'

He fingered a red miniaturised calculator he kept in his waist-coat pocket.

'I keep a check on my mileage,' he said. 'Just in case I can get in the Guinness Book of Records. Next week its Buenos Aires, Rio, Valparaiso. That'll add on a bit. Mind you I don't know what the hell else I get out of it, except indigestion.'

He had supple lips and a velvety voice and talking generated more talk. It is a myth that north-country Englishmen are taciturn. Out of an autobiographical ectoplasm emerged a thread of dreams. There was the one in which he was a fish in a tank on an airport bar in danger of running out of water. The same blue light grow-ing hotter and stronger. This was amusing. He gurgled for some time before he said how much more serious it would be if the bar ran out of brandy. When we landed and our feet made their way through the maze to re-establish contact with familiar earth, he gave me his card and said in case we meet again, you never know, ships that pass in the night *et cetera*. It was only later I realised he had not even asked me my name.

iv

You leave a place in flight from intolerable grief and embarrassment and you return to find the whole place un-nervingly the same. You walk through the college precincts as if you had never been away. The same green tiles. How could they change and remain in place? The same echoing footsteps, even the same pale light falls in the same way between the pseudo-Gothic arches to relieve the Stygian gloom. Fragments of comments never meant to be overheard and happily forgotten return to linger with intent on the damp air.... *Poor chap.... Poor old Morgan. Only child ... spoilt mind you. Spoilt rotten. Ruined. All the same, poor bugger. Hate to be in his place.* I see myself making my last exit from the Senior Common Room. Head lowered like an animal on its way to an iron pen, making a futile effort to escape and facilitating its own capture. *They were always on about the language as if it were some kind of panacea ... the first chance they get, they shunt her off to Cambridge.... Best of both worlds ... always turns out to be the worst.... So you can't win, can you?*

Back you come. The same old place. The same old smell. As if history had never happened and even your continuing existence was in doubt. Until you come face to face with the familiar grain of the surface of the door of your room and discover it has become someone else's academic horoscope. On the white card inside the snug little brass frame, someone else's name is printed. Not Dr. A. Morgan, Classics, but Dr. G. Ogwen-Spinks, T.R.S. – namely Tourism Research Studies.

Not that I was ever attached to the beastly room. A cold and impersonal corner, badly lit. Still, a convenient refuge in times of stress. A suitable sulking chamber, for licking real and imagined wounds. It seemed the appropriate spot to which I should return. And it had its comic side. I stood with my nose within inches of the panel, like love locked out.

'Good God! since when have you been back?'

Sockburn's voice came rolling down the corridor followed by the clap of his marching feet. His heels and toes were tipped with steel to give his locomotion force and authority. The long approach should have given me time to prepare an account of myself. Why had I come back before the end of my Sabbatical? What would be an acceptable excuse? When he was within reach he would slap my back in comradely fashion, and I needed to measure the extent I would show pleasure at seeing his rugged face and grizzled hair. Whatever I said he would take his customary pleasure in bringing me down to earth and, as he would put it, face to face with reality. Had I been away a hundred years or transformed into a six foot frog, he would not speak any differently.

'My God! You've got no idea what's going on in this place!'

That was something he had been saying ever since I could remember. The expression on my face must have suggested something fresher.

'I tell you Morgan, you made the same mistake as Trotsky.'

He was pleased with the humour of it and delighted to expand.

'He went away. Old Joe Stalin never left his desk. They've turned this bloody place upside down, I can tell you. Look at this.'

He stuck a finger at the name of G. Ogwen-Spinks.

'A failed philosopher, but the slimiest fixer you should ever wish to meet. He'll go far, that lad.'

He lowered his voice so that it no longer echoed defiantly down the corridor.

'Mind you, you'd better get on the right side of him. He might have a place for you. And you might need it. Latin doesn't live here any more.'

It was expected and still it was a shock. Sockburn was right about the urgency of finding a niche in the new regime. I would prefer to be attached to Old Welsh and Celtic Studies than get involved with G. Ogwen-Spinks: but beggars can't be choosers when redundancy looms. Sockburn was looking uncharacteristically humble: even crestfallen.

'I was bought off,' he said. 'Didn't put up much of a fight. How could I? Nobody here to support me. It wouldn't have been any good anyway. The choice was between taking umbrage or taking whatever was offered. Which is no choice at all. You are looking at a Careers Counsellor, with a special responsibility for mature students east of Suez. It's quite as bad as it sounds. But what can you do? I've got a sick wife to support.'

His manner towards me warmed. The thought of his wife and her disabilities had put him in mind of our lasting bereavement. He demonstrated his concern for my welfare.

'Listen,' he said. 'Since you're back. See you get a word in with the Head Man as soon as possible, if not sooner. Things are moving with an unhealthy speed around here. It may seem quiet at the moment but in reality the place is seething with discontent and incipient revolt. Everything is up for grabs. Dozens are being made redundant. But you've got a trump card, haven't you? And the sooner you play it, the better, believe me.'

'What trump card?'

'There's no such thing as security of tenure. Unrestrained market forces have taken over. The checks and balances that have been the bedrock of my political and social life have been abandoned. It's time to take to the lifeboats.'

'What trump card?'

Sockburn's eloquence sounded hollow in the echoing corridor. I felt obliged to restrain it.

'Your *Principe* or *Marchese* or whatever he is. He's your meal ticket, Morgan. You wave him under the Principal's nose. And his wife's. Send them into ecstatic orbit. There's a word to the wise. The best advice I can offer. Unless you fancy a job east of Suez? How about Dubai?'

He was trying to give the impression that the campus was in the grip of revolutionary change: a place overrun with strangers and spies. To my eyes, it all appeared exactly as it had always appeared in spite of the new name on my door. A wet day early in the autumn term. The leaves beginning to fall. On the hillside beneath the halls of residence, brown bracken bending its head in mute surrender. A lachrymose widowed season that fitted in only too well with my mood. Sockburn jerked my arm and I could see he was more than happy to have me back. It was even possible he had missed me. Over a drink he would fill me in, he said. He wasn't utterly without connections. He would introduce me right away to Miss Hughes-Davies, the Principal's new secretary, a buxom motherly young woman, sympathetic to the older man and an ally worth cultivating.

'I don't know about you, Morgan,' he said. 'And all your southern exploits. But I'm a changed man, I can tell you. Forget about the rockery builder and home repairs expert. The scholarly recluse. Forget about all that. I have become a dedicated and assiduous committee man!'

He took pride in being a joint secretary of the Faculty of Arts sub-committee on the New Prospectus, and in being a member of six other sub-committees. He also had a foot in the door on the

House and Fabrics. It was the only way. His voice quivered with a conviction I did not recall hearing before. The place was being infested with pushy young academics festooned with theses on utterly worthless subjects. Joining sub-committees was a vital element in his defensive game plan, his crusade. It was the only reliable way of getting to know what plots were afoot.

'Phyllis doesn't like it,' he said. 'I may as well admit. She feels it means I've got less time for her and for home improvements. But there you are. As I keep on telling her, if you've got a power-struggle on your hands your only chance of winning is to enter the fray well prepared and with relish. Nil desperandum.'

He could see the morose look on my face and he assumed I was still grieving. He would make it his business to see I snapped out of it.

'Now then Morgan. Roll your sleeves up, old man. Into battle and all that. Don't let's have any of your Celtic Twilight. Onward and upward! We're here to win, not to lose.'

For me it was a season of retreat rather than advance. I was like the hedgerows in our lane, drained of vitality and ready to retire to those buried roots for the long and presumably nourishing sleep that awaits another spring. What I needed most was to visit the cemetery. Rhiannon's body was buried in that extra piece of consecrated ground higher up the slope facing the open sea. It was attached by a new wall to the old churchyard that was full to overflowing, where we used to joke there was standing-room only. The church itself had been locked against vandals for many years. A solid but modest stone affair, quietly boasting of areas of stained glass made in Louvain in the early sixteenth century and bought by a local squire from some smuggler in the early nineteenth century: an open secret that was a cause of quiet local pride. She always loved it. Or was it our love that rubbed off easily on an impressionable only child? Her great great grandfather's grave we found subsiding and overgrown with brambles. It was she that insisted we should have it restored and tidied up. We were so impressed, Marian and I, with the wisdom that floated in the open air out of the mouth of our own babe and suckling. This is where we belong, isn't it? she said. Where our ancestors are buried.

There had been a recent burial just two yards from Rhiannon's grave. The muddy mound was still covered by a variety of flowers in transparent plastic covers, hot-house red roses, bronze and yellow chrysanthemums saying goodbye to summer, loyal long-legged carnations in pink and white and written messages on cards blurred by rain not tears. The condensation inside the cellophane and plastic made the flowers look distant and unreal.

Mud and rain were the abiding reality and that was how it should be. She always understood the wisdom of the seasons. In the field behind me the air vibrated with the excited twitter of a myriad small birds in some stage of migration. I stepped back over the wet grass to look at them. They were almost invisible in a wild hedge of thorn choked with bramble: an extraordinary assembly, all sound and excitement, the dead and the living could hear.

I would come here often. It was an essential element I had been missing. Here I could converse with her as peasants always communicated with their loved ones, alive or dead: not necessarily through words. I could see her now, in this season of change, as she had once been, a solitary child playing on a summer afternoon in the churchyard and stopping to stare at inscriptions on head-stones as though they were the pages of a story-book. Somehow or other our imaginations would persist and communicate and thrive. If the stars and the astronomical computations of the sky at night wished to join us, they were welcome too.

It was getting dark when I arrived above the top gate of Maenhir. Crows were alighting on top of the standing-stone in the field behind the house, like aeroplanes arriving on a tight schedule. The leaves of the sycamore trees were shrivelled by the salt sea breezes and were ready to fall. The crab-apples were rotting in the grass. What pleased me most was the sight of the red berries of deadly-nightshade glowing on the bars of the gate. The wreaths must have been created by children from the village. Their imagi-nation too was part of the scene. It could have been a welcome home.

V

It was getting dark too, when they arrived. The standing-stone in the field above the house was a black silhouette against a red sky. I switched on every light I could see as a sign of welcome. Grazia shivered and hung back, overawed perhaps and even frightened by an unfamiliar scene or by having reached at least the end of the first phase of her adventure.

'Is it what you expected?'

Marian was in a state of subdued excitement herself. She had the girlish enthusiasm of a young person introducing two people she loved who had never met before. I hung about the doorway and on the narrow verandah like a lay-figure that could be placed in any position to improve the picture. A farmhouse of this age has a personality of its own and we had modernised it with care so that it remained as pretty as a picture in any season and at any time of the day or night. The thick limestone walls were responsive to every change, willing to be occupied and re-occupied, offering a constant south-facing refuge. Grazia stepped back to look at the outbuildings and the walled orchard in the thickening light.

'So beautiful,' she kept repeating. 'So beautiful. So charming.'

She shifted about out of doors, apparently reluctant to come in. Her feet crunched on the gravel and the security light kept coming on and off as she passed through the beam. The mechanism alarmed her until she got used to it and began to laugh. There seemed to be so much she had to say and yet she was lost for words.

'I alighted here,' she said. 'Just here. In one of my dreams. Right in front of your door. I had transparent wings. I had flown over the sea.'

They both laughed hilariously and I felt obliged to join in. There was no point in cross-examining her about the dream. If she ever dreamt it. Or was it a fancy that had just crossed her mind at that moment, that she was eager to share with Marian? The bond between them had been drawn even closer in my absence. In the living room Grazia raised her hand to feel the uneven surface of the oak beam we had so laboriously exposed and treated above the inglenook. The firelight flickered on her enchanted face and I saw her eyes close and open as her finger-tips moved along the beam: a delicate process of adoption.

'It is as if we had been waiting for each other.'

She was murmuring for Marian's benefit, not mine.

'It is so strange. How do you behave coming to a place you have dreamt about so often...?'

Grazia slept in Rhiannon's room. Before she fell asleep she would fill her journal. The owl hooting in the branches of the sycamore would be recorded and the silver path of the moonlight on the bay that she could see from Rhiannon's bedroom window. The girl from the *trattoria* was articulate and confident in these new surroundings. Soon she would have the scent of success about her. It wouldn't matter in the end that her Franz was too obtuse to cherish the lyric strain in her impressionistic writings. She had made the landfall my daughter had failed to make and Marian's breath rose and fell as she slept undisturbed at my side.

Everything had to be arranged and re-arranged and yet at breakfast alongside the warmth and comfort of the Aga stove there seemed to be no hurry. The situation at college was by no means as black as Sockburn had sought to paint it. In the matter of Grazia's enrollment I had already had a quiet word with Lloyd of Romance Languages and he had been glad to welcome me back and indicated his desire to be helpful in any way he could. The rules could be bent, he said, without breaking them, and it would be fun to boast of a native Italian coming all the way to our corner of Wales to read a degree in her own language and in French! Lloyd specialised in being calm and urbane and admitting to an intense interest in the visual arts. He carried a watch in a fob pocket at the end of a silver chain and in my case he always went out of his way to be agreeable. For Grazia he suggested an impromptu test: say one hour and a half to answer three questions in Italian, French and English. He would be glad to invigilate himself. As far as registration went, if the test proved successful, as he was sure it would be from all I told him, her passport would do instead of her birth certificate for the time being.

All went reasonably well with Kingsley Jenkins. He was well-dressed for some formal occasion. His bald pate was reflected in the polished surface of his desk and his brow furrowed as he took his time to recall the circumstances of my prolonged leave of absence. His hands were clasped in fleshy embrace on the surface of the desk and each thumb took its turn to twitch as they resisted the temptation to twiddle. Our Principal would have liked the world to believe he was presiding over unprecedented academic upheavals with Olympian competence and calm. Only an uneven pulse at the top of the right side of his jaw betrayed what was developing into a chronic anxiety state. The greatest strain was remembering all the things he was terrified of forgetting. I tried to make the possibilities of our fruitful connection with the *Centro* at Fontane as simple and as clear as possible. It became necessary to repeat them and introduce Muzio's title and position several times so that Jenkins could memorise them before coming to any conclusion.

'We must talk again, Morgan,' he said. 'It looks promising, but as I say we must talk again. And we have your future to consider and to take care of. We are living through difficult and delicate times. But I have to say this, off the record of course, quite off the record, in these troubled times, it's not a case of what we can offer them Morgan, but of what they can offer us. Do you think you could summarise the proposals on half a sheet of paper? Then we'll talk again. Maybe I should bring Travel and Tourism in on this? And Business Management. And maybe not. We'll see.'

Marian wanted Grazia to see everything while the good weather lasted. They crossed the Straits and made a pilgrimage to the very spot where Math and Gwydion had conjoured a wife out of flowers for the youth who aimed and shot an arrow between the sinew and the bone of a wren's left leg. On the west coast of the island they climbed a sand dune to overlook the shore where the starling had landed on the giant's shoulder and ruffled its wings to reveal the message pinned there by the princess imprisoned and humiliated in an Irish kitchen. Grazia said it was a story she could write about. Then she blushed at being so openly naïve and for a moment I saw how her youth was protected by its own poetry.

When they visited the restored burial chamber on the headland overlooking the same bay, they found the gate locked. A mysterious stranger appeared with a key. From the saddlebag of his bicycle he produced a box of white candles which he lit and placed at specific points among the upright stones, so that the women could see the chevrons, spirals and zigzags carved on their uneven surfaces.

'Don't you want to know who he was?' Marian leaned across the table to smile at me. Since I seemed to be a joke they both had in common I felt obliged to try and be witty.

'Taliesin?' I said. 'Or it could have been Efnisien? Did he smile or did he frown?'

Grazia could have had little idea what I was talking about but she laughed just as loudly as Marian. Perhaps she felt it was the least she could do. Love us, love our landscape. Not to mention our heritage of myth and ancient history. It was all part of a process of absorption.

'He was a post-office clerk from Birmingham,' Marian said. 'He had this marvellous hobby. Cycling around from one megalith tomb to another. Such a nice young man, wasn't he, Grazia?'

'Oh yes,' Grazia said. 'Very quiet. He could have been a poet.'

'I don't want to spoil your fun, ladies,' I said. 'But Professor Lloyd is ready to give Grazia a private test. It's all been arranged. A little bit of French and English as well as Italian.'

I would soon be in harness. I had no difficulty in sounding academic: all set to re-start paying tithes of mint and anise and cumin. I was also quietly resentful of the ease with which Marian was transferring the familiar consolations of our existence to the new arrival: jealous in my suppressed fashion: and therefore more than ready to bring them both down to earth. There were procedures to be followed and Grazia Guidatti would have to follow them just like anyone else. It was right and proper there should be no exemptions for individuals however gifted, however exotic and beautiful. When she listened her lips were tight with concentrated restraint.

She was launched on a sequence of quests and explorations. These voyages of discovery were exciting and admirable and I resented being left out of them. More often than not I came home to an empty house. I made amusing remarks about the meagre role of a house-husband. More often than not they chose not to hear them. They were too busy burbling about the exalted function of women in Celtic mythology and the trace elements of matriarchy in local customs. They were covering so much ground in so short a time I had no idea where they were when the telephone rang, and I heard the voice of Prue Bianchieri asking for Marian and speaking in a rapid excited whisper. She was acutely disappointed not to have Marian on the line.

'You had better tell them,' Prue said. 'The game is up. Muzio knows where she is. And that means it's only a matter of time before Guidatti knows. Then he'll be across there with Interpol before you can say cop.'

'How does he know?'

It seemed to me that Prue Bianchieri sounded displeased with herself and even guilty. This was pretty unusual.

'I must have let it slip out,' she said. 'Quite by accident. Anyway it's done now. And I'm ringing to warn you. I suppose it had to happen anyway, sooner or later. It's always the same when you're naughty, Doctor Morgan. Sooner or later you have to face the music.'

She was telling me! Prue Bianchieri of all people. In what sense had I been naughty, compared to her? And in what way was I responsible for Grazia's flight? Any residual guilt I harboured had nothing to do with the girl's escape. What I needed was some simple uncomplicated relationship like the one I used to enjoy with Marian, where we could discuss problems of responsibility and integrity for hours on end, and even compare these concerns with the way our immediate forebears agonized over sin and innocence and deep religious doubts. How could we have left ourselves so exposed that an entire situation, more than that a way of life, could be transformed, reversed, upended by a whisper on the telephone?

It was late when they got back. The dinner was in the oven getting dry. They were laughing so much when they came in, Grazia had to hang on to Marian's arm. At first I thought they were laughing at me. I was still wearing the glossy white apron with a Southern Comfort label enlarged on its front to protect my clothes while I prepared the meal.

'You are not going to believe this,' Marian said.

They hadn't been drinking and yet in some way they were intoxicated. Their eyes shone like clandestine lovers enjoying the stolen hours of each other's company. I was being allowed to witness their effervescence and I should feel privileged.

'This second-hand book shop,' Marian said. 'We were looking for a copy of Racine, so that Grazia could freshen up on Berenice. It was Berenice, wasn't it?'

Grazia smiled and nodded eagerly. I began to suspect those smiles and nods. They were like the emblems of sincerity used by good-looking young actors in American films. They were part of a commercial blanket of imposed cultural modes and they had penetrated into every *trattoria* with a television screen from one end of the Italian peninsula to the other.

'I hadn't looked at the sign over the door. The place was a mess really. But that is part of the attraction of second-hand book shops. If you could call it a shop. A book tip would be more like it. We browsed around and we found an odd volume of Racine going for next to nothing. There was an assistant perched on a stool with a paper-back glued to his face in a way I have to admit now I found vaguely familiar. Guess who it was?'

'Yes. Guess.'

Grazia cried out over eager to join in the game.

'Buddy,' Marian said. 'Buddy Thwaite.'

How could she utter that name with such benevolence? Only six months ago she tried to kill him. The smell from the oven began to make me feel sick.

'And the book in front of his nose. Like this.'

The pantomime was on the verge of being repulsive. And Grazia had to copy it.

'Guess what it was?'

'A horror comic.'

I spoke as flatly as I could in an effort to bring them to their senses.

'No!' Marian was absurdly triumphant. Did it please her so much to have me at a disadvantage?

'No! *Welsh Made Easy*. Buddy Thwaite is making an all out effort to learn Welsh. Can you imagine it?'

There were too many things in the world I couldn't imagine. People were too unaccountable. The longer you knew them the less you understood what made them tick. I was listening to my wife and looking at a stranger.

'It was too absurd. And yet it was true. And truth is stranger than fiction. We had a long chat.'

'Don't you want to eat?'

It was a way of stemming the tide of revelations. I had to be given time to digest unpalatable facts and to formulate an appropriate rational reaction. Grazia seemed to understand this better than Marian. She helped serve the food with professional dexterity. I made a fuss about the wine but neither wanted to drink. Marian sat in her chair as still as a medium prepared to receive and transmit an extraordinary message.

'We had a long chat,' she said. 'About Rhiannon. One sees so little. I have been at fault. She left an indelible impression on him.'

I had to look away from Grazia, her smiling and nodding were getting on my nerves so much. They were no help to me as I tried to cope with a tidal wave of irrationality that threatened to submerge the very room we were sitting in. Marian was eating nothing. It struck me again how thin she was. I had read somewhere that visions were symptoms of under-nourishment. Loss and grief could leave people permanently unbalanced. I felt a wave of panic as I racked my brains for some nostrum to stabilise my own condition.

'The Megalith builders and the Celtic Saints,' Marian said. 'He's obsessed with them. And he wants Y Gymraeg in order to bind himself to the rocks. To the earth that sustains him.'

'Like Prometheus....'

I ignored Grazia's excited interpolation. She could keep it for her journal.

'We gave him a lift home,' Marian said. 'That's why were were so late.'

I refrained from asking her whether she had been tempted to run over him. Anything I said would betray a mood of profound scepticism that gripped me. It was more than scepticism. A frightening spasm of hatred and fear. I hated them. I hated the world. I hated myself.

'You never saw such a mess,' Marian said. 'An absolute pigsty. Ash and cinders spilling out of the grate until it was under your feet. Spider's webs over the windows. Brambles growing as high as the eaves. A single cold water tap and no indoor sanitation. He was pleased with it he said, because the rent was next to nothing.'

'It was wonderful,' Grazia said.

She could no longer contain her enthusiasm. Marian was smiling at her fondly. To me her words sounded like the besotted outpourings of an idiotic female.

'The place of an artist. This is how an artist must live. No conventions. He has the courage to be different. To live in his own way. To give up everything for the sake of his art. This is what an artist must do. Risk everything to play with fire. Like Prometheus. Steal a spark from heaven.'

'Yes, well....'

I spoke in measured terms as soberly as I could.

'I'm not an artist, so I wouldn't know about these things.'

They were in no way deterred. Marian spoke and Grazia nodded. They had been there to comfort this artistic hero. And what had he ever done, I would like to know? What had he ever achieved except the death of my daughter? The wind turned outside and drove smoke down the chimney. It billowed out of the fireplace. The women took no notice. Nothing could interrupt their dithyrambic trance. I saw wreaths of smoke wind around their heads as they spoke. They looked beautiful and dangerous.

'She will be part, always, of whatever he produces.'

Marian lowered her voice to express her conviction. Grazia was nodding.

'In wood or stone. In music or in words. He has dedicated his life to Rhiannon. Not just her memory. To her living spirit. She is more than his inspiration. She will speak through him.'

Was I supposed to be grateful for that? They both looked so elated. Grazia was listening to the wind in the chimney as if it were the most mysterious sound she had ever heard, bringing wonders and revelations and new directions the world had never heard of before. At some point it would be my unpleasant duty to tell them about Prue Bianchieri's telephone call. The hounds were closing in. Not now. It would be unkind to spoil their fun. I knew something they didn't know and knowledge was a substitute for power.

'Anyway,' Marian said. 'I've asked him to tea tomorrow. It's his day off. It's important for you to meet him.'

vi

The fellow could never have been without his attractions. It was simply that I had not noticed them before. He had a wide asymmetrical smile that clearly appealed to women and there were dimples lurking behind the sparser hairs of his beard which had grown again, more Rasputin than Christ, and led a dance of its own as his jaws worked their way methodically through Marian's cooking. The pony-tail was a new feature. As he consumed one scone after another, watched over by two admiring females, in training for a parallel remorseless attack on a plate of cakes, I studied him with an intensity that disturbed me more than it seemed to disturb him. I suppose the kind of life he had chosen to lead made him immune to hostile stares. He was as thin as ever in spite of an elephantine capacity for the consumption of food. That at least was something to envy, even admire.

'It's amazing the things you come across,' he said. 'Keeping a second-hand book shop.'

He had brought Marian a book of photographs of aboriginal rock engravings from New South Wales. She was still nursing it on her lap in spite of its grubby condition.

'They are so beautiful,' Buddy said. 'And like everything beautiful, looking at them gives you a fresh view of the universe.'

Marian and Grazia had adopted the attitudes of disciples, ready to transform his truisms into pearls of wisdom once they had fallen from his sticky lips.

'Aboriginal is a good word,' he said. 'It's what we need to get back to. That sense of one-ness with the living world. Easier said than done, of course. We have too much luggage to discard, Rhiannon used to say. Where's the eye of the needle? The point of entry? It was something she'd picked up somewhere. She had a genius for picking things up. You move in quietly, and you move in among the simplest and least and lowest of those who tread lightest in the world, and take the least out of it. Like mice and sparrows. A new order of existence.'

'That's wonderful,' Grazia said.

Her eyes were shining with enthusiasm. For her, this man swallowing scones and cakes was a remarkable discovery. A genius. Of course in a miraculous world it is never easy to distinguish one miracle from another. Rhiannon had certainly picked him up. He seemed to be taking this fugitive girl and the magnanimous welcome equally for granted. What instrument can register the difference between the confidence of the charlatan and the inner calm of the prophet? Why should this creature be exempt from my chronic state of unease? He is marketing illusions as authentic visions. It was time to inject a note of reality into the proceedings.

'Tell me,' I said. 'What happened to your friend Pete?'

He was not at all put out. He chewed and swallowed before answering.

'Poor old Pete,' he said. 'Wandering around Scandinavia. Roadie and part time fiddler with a five man group. Six man if you count Pete. He's still hoping to get into Germany. He sounds wild but he's got a heart of gold.'

'Anyway you parted.'

I tried to sound relentless without being impolite. He smiled his new wistful crooked smile that I had to admit changed his pale bearded face for the better. In the kindest way possible he wanted me to appreciate that academic measures of success and failure were irrelevant to the business of living.

'He got fed up with me talking about Rhiannon all the time. In a way you could say he resented her message. It cut across all the plans and dreams he had made up to keep himself going.'

'So much for the brotherhood of man,' I said.

I rewarded myself by popping a small cake whole into my mouth. Buddy sighed deeply. I saw an identical shadow of sympathy flit across the women's faces. A prophet's image emerges out of a mosaic of large and small sorrows.

'It's not easy,' he said. 'You have to begin by being totally alone.'

Nobody could be more alone than my Rhiannon in her grave. Out of the silence and the expression on my face, Buddy Thwaite showed he took this also into account: her death, my despair. Somehow it helped him to sit in this house once again – where she had been so tenderly brought up – eating her mother's cakes. He could count on an illumination he had inherited from her and it gave him a serenity, a state of quiet happiness, that was denied to me. It was unjust that I should be haunted by the loss of my daughter, while he could claim to be inspired by her: that she could have weaned him off horror comics and put him on a steady diet of Welsh and meditation and the unflinching contemplation of the miracle of existence, and left me nursing a dull ache. From me she had withdrawn her presence and the emptiness had filled with the sour breath of disappointment. Marian and Grazia acquiesced in this unfairness. They listened to him with rapt attention and smiled at me with pitying indulgence.

'You know she used to say trying to be good was the supreme adventure.'

The charm of a captive audience was making him garrulous. He managed to dispose of the cakes at a steady rate without seriously interrupting the flow of his discourse. Having his cake and eating it.

'It need not be less exciting than trying to be thoroughly bad, she used to say.'

Did she indeed? In that case, Mr. Thwaite was it good or bad that she left you? When she was pregnant with your child as we had to assume it had to be. Or was that a dangerous experiment that went wrong? An infatuation with someone else that turned out to be a mistake. That could easily happen as I knew to my cost. Good and evil were two sides of the identical coin. What if Grazia had been as unrestrained as I was on the side of the lake that warm night when she fled from the *trattoria*? When does the novitiate stop being thoroughly good? The tips of my index fingers met as they pointed in his direction.

'She left you,' I said.

He stopped chewing to consider the accusation.

'I don't think it was because she thought I wasn't good enough for her. I wasn't of course. But I don't think it was that. I think she was above that sort of thing.'

'Well, of course, we can think anything we like,' I said. 'It's facts that are hard to come by.'

His pale blue eyes were looking at me as though he wanted to understand and sympathise with my barely veiled hostility.

'She had to find out for herself,' he said. 'My childish difficulties were an encumbrance to her. I can see that clearly enough now. At the time I was heart-broken. I was weak of course. And obsessed with myself and my own little problems.'

'Find out what?'

I was not comfortable. It was my weaknesses he was addressing, not his own. He was beginning to make invocatory gestures that would soon get on my nerves. It was an effort to sit still and listen.

'There is this terrible expanse of solitude like a desert that has to be crossed before you reach ... "oasis" isn't the word.... What are the words ... before you cross the language barrier, let's say?'

Grazia was excited by the concept, vague as it seemed to me.

'That's it,' she said. 'That is it exactly. They shouldn't be barriers. Words. They should be steps towards understanding. That is why each generation has to find a language and recreate it. Do you know what I mean?'

'Out of the silence?'

Buddy was looking at Grazia as though she were delivering an urgent message. They would talk to each other and we would do our best to pick up the crumbs that fell from the table they alone were sharing.

'Out of the stones if necessary,' Grazia said.

Buddy closed his eyes to make another effort to recall something Rhiannon had said.

'We have to learn outside the rule book of preconceived notions and received opinion, that's what she said. We have to learn to live with a benevolent detachment and participate without judging. Accept the kindness of the stones.'

The words meant far more to them than they meant to me. All I could take in was the warmth of the communication growing between them. I could not bear to look at it. It was as if they were falling into each other's arms. I had to go outside. At the end of the orchard there was a view of the mountains across the straits. I fixed my gaze on an isolated patch of pale green sunlit slope that appeared out of the cloud and the mist. I stared at the bright upland and the rolling cloud that threatened it until the west wind made my eyes smart. I turned to contemplate the silver fronds of the giant pampas grass waving in the corner of the orchard as though they were signs and symbols that had some explanation to offer. There was a scattering of curlews in the field below the orchard. These were not inclined to migrate. They would winter here along the coast and keep in touch with their fluted melancholy cries. Melancholy to our ears of course. The birds were perfectly content to circulate and keep their distance. I thought I could hear laughter coming from the house.

vii

Cled Celtic Studies rang up to ask whether I could drop into his room for a chat. He never gave much away on the phone: brief but cordial whispers as if it were always possible a third party could be listening. Years ago we had been involved in campaigns of protest together: removing road signs, daubing government offices, even climbing television masts. Maybe he had developed a conspirator-

215

ial style then and it never left him. He was short-sighted too and that made him frown as though with lingering suspicions. We had both long long since abandoned the thorny paths of protest in order to concentrate on our careers. Cledwyn had moved much further up the academic ladder than I had, through shrewd specialisation and a punishing schedule of publication. I had been so slow in finding a nice patch of territory to cultivate: wasting too much time playing about with styles of calligraphy. As Marian used to say, fiddling instead of getting on with it. At least my wife was brilliant and she had always tried to point me in the right direction. It wasn't our fault that civilised standards were crumbling from inner exhaustion and the classics being tossed on the scrap-heap.

At least Old Cled had rung me up. Old in the affectionate sense. He was a good two years younger than me. I took it to be a promising sign: an essential preliminary to chartering a fruitful area for my kind of expertise somewhere between Brythonic and Old Welsh. Myself, I fancied concentrating on *De Excidio Britanniae* and maybe some *Hisperica*. We could discuss forms of attractive presentation that could slot into the New Prospectus that Sockburn was so excited about. Even lend it a touch of additional distinction. I had a positive sense of academic renewal as I crossed the suspension bridge. I could still enjoy the rights and privileges of a citizen of the Republic of Learning. I felt borne up by the warm air of confidence: until I was confronted with the cold rock face of reality.

Dr. Cledwyn Dodd was engaged in a damage limitation exercise. He tried two approaches. At least two. The first was jocular, avuncular. Too much intensive immobility at his desk had given him a pregnant paunch which he both protected and paraded inside a plum-coloured waistcoat. He used an old M.A. gown as a convenient prop in which to attitudinize in front of his seminars. His hard stare through pebble lenses recalled the moment he grinned down at me through the struts of the television mast challenging me to climb higher when my fingers were already as brittle and as unpliable as icicles. The same old mocking grin that classified me as an ineffective operator. If I fell it would be the awkward tumble of a clown. He had a nice room at the top of the college with an enviable view.

'Some people have all the luck,' he said.

How could he possibly be referring to me. The insensitive bastard. He smirked away as he prowled behind his desk. There were photographs of college groups from his Oxford days framed on the pale green wall behind him. Chaps who crossed their legs and folded their arms and waited for the passing years to garland them with preferment.

'Morgan's Hellenic tours,' he said.

He was liable to be convulsed by his own witticisms at any moment.

'I can see you now old Al. Spelling out inscriptions for rich widows and American culture vultures. Do you realise a quarter of the population of Western Europe will be in permanent transit by the end of the century? You'll be there to give the Department of T.R.S. a touch of class, a bit of tone....'

'So you've got nothing for me?'

He was about to become penitentially sorry for me and that would be even harder to bear. He flopped down in his swivel chair and gave out a prolonged sigh that did nothing to diminish the size of his paunch. His next pantomime was designed to express helplessness, frustration, followed by the last vestiges of righteous indignation. His shoulders sagged with the weight of his responsibilities. I began to anticipate his phrases while I turned my chair to study the view from the window: the old slate harbour, the blue waters of the bay, the long headland on the horizon like a petrified prehistoric monster.

'What can I do?... My hands are tied ... it's hand to mouth old boy, hand to mouth. Short time contracts, research fellowships and no tenure ... it's all the rage ... the sounds that Kingsley wants to hear are pressure-cooker theses exploding and PhD's being fired off like human cannon balls.... It's not for me to decide, old boy, but if I were you I'd get my feet securely under the table at T.R.S as soon as poss. Oggie Spinks is your man. He's not so bad. At least he's firmly bi-lingual and in that sense you could say his heart is in the right place.'

'Even if he never climbed a television mast,' I said.

It took Dr. Dodd a little time to catch the reference. When he did he became one of the boys again, chummy and expansive, pleased with his room, his little pinnacle of power, and above all relieved at having broken the bad news and having disappointed me without a trace of blood on the floor. Well worth the trouble of one quick unrecorded telephone call. He saw me out with a climatic barrage of goodwill and unspecified invitations.

'We must get together,' he said. 'We really must make time for it. A good old chin-wag about old times. Those were the days, eh? We'll never see their like again.'

I arrived home to find Marian in quite a state. She did not even ask me what it was Cledwyn Dodd had wanted to talk to me about.

'Muzio's coming,' she said. 'He's bringing Guidatti with him.'

It was a threat of invasion and she was looking at me as though it was all my fault. I was tempted to point out that whom the gods wished to destroy they first make mad. Instead I made a noise that I knew she would condemn as reprehensibly feeble.

'Oh dear,' I said.

I tried to sharpen my response.

'At least it's better than the police,' I said.

'What's that supposed to mean?'

She was blaming me. It was unjust but I felt too dispirited to protest. Marian hadn't begun to appreciate the strength of the tide of troubles we were facing.

'Grazia isn't under age, if that's what you're implying,' Marian said. 'At least I had the sense to look into that side of things before we embarked on the venture. She is eighteen years and eight months old and it seems to me she has a perfect right to take charge of her own destiny. Or at least as much right as anyone else. What was perfectly clear to me, and still is perfectly clear, is that father of hers had absolutely no right to deny her the opportunity of a higher education. She has a duty to her own talent.'

Marian's cheeks were flushed. In spite of her righteous indignation, she was feeling uncomfortable pangs of guilt. She had after all conspired to separate a young girl from her family and it must have felt a bit like robbing a bird's nest. The more her attachment to Grazia grew, the greater her responsibility. Her mind raced as she rehearsed her arguments to herself and paced restlessly around the living room. What worried her was the prospect of having to take on Muzio as well as the father. She had to summon up the strength to face them both. Marian and Muzio had always been such good friends; always so pleased to see each other and enjoy each other's company. I had seen with my own eyes the pains she had taken not to allow Prue Bianchieri's intrigues and machinations to impinge on her friendship with Muzio.

Now there was much more at stake. She was ready to wrap herself in a feminist flag and mount the barricades. She would fight to defend Grazia's liberty. The ramifications of my relationship with Muzio would never be allowed to get in the way. As I watched Marian, I saw with alarming clarity the threat to my links with the *Centro* at Fontane. The ideological element is always the most destructive in a conflict. So long as what she saw as Grazia's rights were being defended, it wouldn't worry Marian all that much if my association with Fontane was broken. I wanted to make clear to her the threat it all meant to my status and prospects; it did not seem the appropriate moment. Her efforts were being mobilised to protect Grazia's interests, not mine. Everything that happened seemed to conspire to drive us further apart.

'Where is she anyway?' I said.

'At Buddy's.'

How swiftly the re-bearded Buddy had come to occupy a pivotal position in our domestic arrangements. And he had acquired a physical energy that had not existed when Rhiannon was alive. He was even taking a smiling pride in being a hewer of wood and a carrier of water. Muscles had appeared where they never existed before.

'The shop or the cottage?'

I couldn't use the title of either site without sounding sarcastic. Marian has always considered my sense of humour excessively juvenile.

'She intends to hide in the cottage,' Marian said. 'While they are here. As long as they are around. She's gone to make up a corner where she can sleep. She's determined not to go back.'

I could see it had not even occurred to Marian that history was repeating itself. She didn't even see that she was operating as an involuntary matchmaker. It was difficult for me to make a comment that would not cause offence.

'Elective affinities?' I said.

Marian was instantly defensive.

'They understand each other,' she said. 'They have a great deal in common. It's quite remarkable to watch. You have this sense of something new and important growing in front of your eyes.'

I drifted to the kitchen to make myself a cup of tea. Why should every change in the course of history have to appear in the guise of an elopement? It was possible I had grown too old and too arid to appreciate springtimes of the spirit. Perhaps I could if Marian helped and I made a special effort. At the moment all I could do was worry about Muzio's visit. The whole point of friendship was to dispense comfort not impose distress. I heard Marian's voice behind me: distant, cold, challenging.

'You could give her away if you want to,' Marian said. 'You have that power. After all she's only a girl. A chattel to be used.'

It was the coldness and the contempt that shocked me. She had been aware of my infatuation all along and it meant nothing. She had treated it as an infantile aberration, allowing it to run its course like a child's fever, it mattered so little. And now her affection for Grazia had outgrown whatever affection she had left for me. For days now, for weeks, I had been watching these two reach levels of loving consciousness I could not aspire to. Did that mean it was a state of being from which I was for ever excluded?

'You don't need to worry,' I said. 'I won't betray her.'

viii

The weather had turned cold. The train was late. I wandered up and down the platform tormented by questions I seemed to have lost the capacity to formulate and face up to, let alone answer. People shivered and warmed their noses in their mufflers as they waited for the train's lights to emerge from the tunnel. Marian was so positive of the justice of her cause: but she still needed to make Guidatti out to be a monster in order to reinforce her resolve. Grazia was a slave she had helped to escape, fleeing across the ice-floes from the clutches of a cruel taskmaster. Guidatti was a petty tyrant who had crushed and battered his wife into submission and was now determined to put his eldest daughter through the same unholy process. It was, she insisted, a classic example of the abusive tyranny of patriarchal power. Grazia was not allowed to be more than a chattel, a piece of property her father could dispose of as he wished. This was slavery. She rummaged around the study until she found a blue pamphlet that summarised the United Nations Declaration of Human Rights. I had to keep a straight face as she read aloud what she considered to be the relevant clauses.

She hadn't been so entirely out of sympathy with the Lazio way of life when we first went there. In fact I could remember complimentary phrases she used about customs and practices that had stood the test of time. She had an even more elaborate thesis about Italian family life being developed through the centuries to withstand chronic political instability in order to preserve the basic essentials of civilised living. Where had all that gone to? Into the same pool of oblivion that swallowed her vendetta versus Buddy Thwaite. The extent of the disruption we – or should I say she? – had caused did not seem to cross her mind. I had to be on Marian's side of course. I had no choice.

There lingered all the same a residue of guilt. That relentless tribunal in permanent session at the back of my mind could set up a case and accuse me of having abused the girl's bid for freedom to attempt to gratify my own desires. If the defence argued that she was making more use of me than I made of her, that did not absolve me from the responsibility of wanting to make her pregnant in order to satisfy a fantasy of replacing the child I had lost. The control of sexual appetites remained at the heart of all systems of morality because it was at this point animals and humans came closest to the potency of creation. The cold approach of freezing fog did nothing to clarify my confused thoughts. Muzio's imminent arrival was in itself one simple question. Why did we have to interfere?

Muzio was my best friend and it could be argued my patron. If Muzio was prepared to take it up there had to be some residue of justice in Guidatti's cause. So where did that leave me? During the greatest crisis in my life I had drawn heavily on Muzio's goodwill and now I needed to do the same again to save my academic career. The mere fact that he was prepared to escort Guidatti all this way suggested we had repaid him for his kindness and concern by disrupting the delicate balance of a social fabric that depended for its well-being on his devotion to a tradition of benevolent paternalism. My hands were stuffed deep into my pockets as I slouched up and down the platform. Perhaps they should be carrying a great bouquet of flowers? What was needed was a peace conference, not a declaration of war.

If the train did not arrive I would not be displeased. A crisis postponed is a crisis averted. Given time, their inexorable advance could be halted by a barricade of clichés. The essence of the academic approach is infinite postponement – *As regards the future of the department no decision will be taken until further information has been made available.* The train crept out of the tunnel with a deliberation calculated to prove that the human race was a species doomed to be overtaken by events. The two men descended from the train like an accredited delegation from a foreign power. Guidatti turned up the collar of his overcoat and drew down his black homburg until the rolled brim was touching the top of his ears. Muzio wore a scarf and a voluminous raincoat of the latest style that reached down to his ankles and made him seem taller than ever. He greeted me warmly so that I longed to share with him my comic impression of Guidatti as a furtive mourner arriving late for a mafia funeral. It would have been a silly joke anyway and quite out of keeping with the strains of the occasion.

All the same, Guidatti was overplaying the role of a distressed parent. He choked with emotion as I greeted him and his hands played around his throat to indicate that he was too overcome to speak. Inside the protective collar of his overcoat he was a man, I was to understand, reduced and scorched by heartbreak. Without the unwavering support and succour of the excellent marchese so noted for his selfless regard for the welfare of his people, he would have been led off to an asylum or carried down to his grave. Certainly he stuck to Muzio so closely he could have been begging him to hold his hand and guide him through the chilly perils of this barren foreign land. The tyrant of the *Trattoria* had shrunk to a small figure ready to panic the moment Muzio started to drift out of his sight.

Indoors, Guidatti occupied the left corner of our inglenook with his knees as close as they could get to the open fire. He kept his overcoat on and nursed his hat in his lap to indicate he was not staying. His cup of tea was on the floor by his feet, untouched. He took no interest in his surroundings. He made no effort to listen as Muzio and Marian chatted amiably and exchanged the latest news. Prue had accepted invitations to sing at Bergamo and Brescia. Under her own name so as not to embarrass her mother-in-law. This was an old pleasantry they could share with the warmth of renewed understanding. 'Prudence Cooke – the well-known mezzo-soprano from Yorkshire, England.... The English Nightingale,' Marian murmured, and this was another old joke that would help to improve the atmosphere. Muzio said they would take a little holiday and explore Val Camonica and what a pity we couldn't make a trip of it together. As I listened my hopes were raised. We were old friends after all. There had to be a way to resolve our difficulties. There they were, Marian and Muzio, cheerfully confronting each other in the warm light of our living room. Neither of them had real reason to be difficult. There was too much to lose. Particularly for me.

Guidatti caught me looking at him. His patience suddenly gave out. He seized the moment to break his silence.

'You must know how a father feels, Dottore, to lose a daughter!'

It was strange to hear his stricken voice in our living room. He was drained and reduced like a man who had speculated unwisely and lost a fortune. Who were we to judge the extent of his love for his daughter and to prevent him approaching her?

'You haven't lost her, Signor Guidatti,' Marian said. 'She has just exercised a choice to leave. Young people do that.'

Just as he raised his voice, she raised hers. But he ignored her. He did not take his eyes off me. We were men: heads of families bound by responsibilities with duties to fulfil and obligations to honour. We should be ever mindful of the well-being of the souls a beneficent Providence had seen fit to commit to our care and not pay too much attention to the unconsidered and impulsive utterance of women. In fact, at times of crisis we had a duty to hasten to each other's aid. As Don Muzio had done in this case, setting an example that I should follow in the name of friendship and honour.

'She is not here.'

Guidatti stood up so that he could challenge me directly.

'So where is she? I am her father. I should speak to her.'

I could feel my eyebrows twitching as I tried to decide what I could say. Muzio was watching me. Evasive action would appear despicable. Outright lies would make me sweat visibly and therefore be impossible to conceal.

'She has a right to her own life,' Marian said.

She had tried, without success to keep a shrill note out of her voice. Guidatti still behaved as though he hadn't heard her. He appealed to Muzio who sat exercising judicial calm and drumming his fingers on the arm of his chair.

'Do I have a right to speak to my own daughter, Don Muzio? After travelling all this way? Am I to be denied this? Is it for this I came all this way?'

'She has been here,' Marian said. 'I am not denying it. She is very well and very happy. If she comes again we shall do everything in our power to help her. We love her as if she were our own daughter. But she is not here now and we do not wish, we do not try, to control her movements. We are here, available for when she wants us.'

Guidatti was shaking his head as though Marian's voice was a buzz in his ears he wanted to get rid of.

'My daughter,' he said.

He was still addressing Muzio, pleading his case.

'She is my daughter. Why should she be taken from me?...'

'No one took her.'

Marian was raising her voice again.

'She went away of her own free will.'

'And who gave her money? Who helped her run away?'

Guidatti's eyes were filling with tears that could represent anger as well as grief. He addressed me with increasing ferocity.

'Why do you hide her? Why do you keep her from me? This is a crime, I think. A serious crime. Don Muzio! These are your

223

friends. You brought them to our place. Please. Ask them where I can find my daughter and speak to her.'

Muzio raised a hand to pacify the man. He looked first at Marian and then at me.

'It isn't much to ask....'

It was a note of quiet appeal I could easily have responded to.

'Maybe,' Marian said. 'But it's more than we can give.'

Muzio sucked his lower lip in silence before rising to his feet. His presence dominated the low ceilinged room. He was the negotiator and the opposing positions had hardened.

'Look,' he said. 'We all need a good night's rest. If you could come around to the hotel in the morning, Aled. We could arrange to see your Kingsley Jenkins. About Fontane. And then maybe things would come clearer.'

'There's no need for you to go to an hotel,' Marian said. 'You can stay here. There's plenty of room.'

Muzio looked meaningfully at Guidatti. He was already making for the door.

'I'm not alone,' Muzio said in English. 'And he's very upset. I have to keep an eye on him.'

'Of course you do,' I said.

Marian was still keyed up and it was the only thing I could think of saying.

ix

Purpose and direction. How are things to be between the gates of birth and death? Either we shape events or we are shaped by them and so forth. In the midst of life there is never time for dispassionate discussion, even between two level headed academics also bound together as man and wife. There were considerations of great moment we should be discussing. What had this foreign girl got that she should cause all this disturbance? An impossible father liable to be made more impossible by being wrenched from his natural habitat. I could understand how Muzio felt, and too much understanding reduces a man to dithering indecision. Marian and I were alone in this house of ours and the distance between us was so great we could barely hear each other.

'Shall I make you some hot milk?' I said.

She said she was determined not to take a sleeping tablet. It

224

would make her snore with her mouth wide open and she would wake up with a headache. I went in and out of the house and up and down our lane in search of the consolation nature was supposed to provide. The winter was closing in. The lane was muddy and uneven. We needed to speak frankly with each other. The girl had gone. There was little more to conceal. *Si fallor sum* If I misbehave, I exist. Did that mean in this state of pale neutrality I no longer existed? I am more than a speck of cosmic dust at the mercy of any breath of solar wind. I have a responsibility to myself and to my wife. We had to consider each other. Our own future. It was ridiculous not to talk.

I found her sitting up in bed, unable to sleep and apparently reduced to debating aloud with herself.

'It isn't their decision. It isn't our decision. It's her decision.'

She derived satisfaction in repeating the proposition like a mantra. She would have liked one to make noises of approval. It wasn't a seminar I wanted to take part in. The girl was gone. We were left. We ourselves were the problem.

'I have this feeling she has immense original talent.'

I was prepared to confess. Marian was more inclined to eulogise than to listen. Confession was important. The gap between what we are and what we should be is the main justification for our existence.

'Of course you know I'm no authority on Italian literature. Or any literature if it comes to that. I don't claim to be anything better than a nit-picking philologist. I just have my paltry share of a woman's intuition. There was a force there. A power. If it's there at all it comes out early. Especially in a woman. She is one of these rare specimens that illuminate experience. Every literature needs its exiles as well as its natives. Imagine her saying that. A slip of a girl. She had it all worked out. She certainly woke you up.'

I could tell her nothing. Confession was good for the soul of course but if I submitted to Marian's cold analysis, I would have no soul left. My sins were shreds and tatters I needed to hang on to. I could take refuge in being obtuse and inadequate. I shrank back to a shadowed silence.

'You think I am to blame.'

That's all she said and we knew what she was talking about. It was our dead daughter that created the gulf between us not the wonder-working Italian girl.

'Of course I don't.'

It sounded too vehement. I would have liked to repeat the denial in a different tone of voice: but that would have made it worse.

'You drift around this place like a constant reproach.'

It was unfair and I had to submit to it. She was absolving herself with a wave of her hand.

'At least I try to learn from my mistakes. I was at fault. Do you think I don't know it? Terribly at fault and I admit it. At least I have tried to learn my lesson. Some things are fixed, some things flow. Grazia must be allowed to flow at this juncture in her life. That's all I'm saying.'

She didn't understand nearly as much as she imagined she did. That's what I stopped myself saying.

'You had better tell me just how she got away,' I said.

I sounded calm and judicious. I was the one who had to face Muzio and Guidatti, devising defences and excuses.

'Prue dressed her as a nun and we drove her to catch the feeder train at Zapponami.'

Prue was the prime mover. I could see that. Marian had collaborated. I was guilty by association. Muzio would always consider us more to blame than his wife. That's how it was and that's how he was willing for it to be. While he was here, she could do what she liked with Luca Puri, and then return to the music room to belt out her scales *fortissimo* to annoy her mother-in-law. That was their life and that was the way they wanted it.

'Get me a glass of water,' she said. 'I'll have to swallow that damn tablet. Otherwise I'll never get to sleep.'

She took it and within minutes she was snoring. I lay still in the darkness. I needed to think. The function of a trained intelligence is to anticipate permutations, not cringe in a trance of foreboding. Muzio and Guidatti had travelled all this way to talk to the girl and they couldn't possibly return without achieving that object. The father probably dreamt of bundling his daughter into a sack and carrying her home on his back. Muzio in the politest way possible would threaten to bring pressure to bear on me to reveal her whereabouts. Lead me to her, old friend, or I'll make it crystal clear to your Principal, that your influence with the *Centro* at Fontane is minus zero.

The miserable Guidatti had some hold over Muzio we knew nothing about: could not even guess at. A stranglehold means the capacity to strangle. No wonder Muzio preferred to mess about with the ancient Etruscans. They were safely dead and not liable to spring up and take a grip on your windpipe. The living are always more dangerous, more mysterious and unfathomable and impossible to know. As for Marian and myself, we were academic fools who had blundered into territory where intelligent angels would think twice before treading. I felt a deep need for the soothing exercise of recording the wisdom of the past in the most elegant script I could manage.... *Late patentes aetheris cernat plagas / Artumque terrarum situm.*

The vastness of the heavens, the narrowness of the earth, the brief candle of our existence and so on. It wasn't merely a question of perspective. There was enduring comfort to be found in the shadow of a great spirit and the strength of his phrases. At the lowest level however bad things may seem to me I can bear in mind they were a damn sight worse for him. In a damp cell he could still engage in polite conversation with that angelic lady Philosophy. To write in a dark tower, alone, under the shadow of execution, a work of genius to console the tortured thoughts of fifteen centuries. This house is warm and I can creep down to the study, get out my equipment and reaffirm the value of the lines by copying them as skillfully as I know how. Even to the least gifted here are consolations of craftsmanship. I was in my dressing-gown when I heard the creak of a footstep on the stairs. Grazia had a key. I was using my torch so as not to disturb Marian. It was important for her to sleep.

The beam from my torch caught the tantalising smile on Grazia's face. It held that same insubstantial promise in the ghostly light. A false goal made visible by a foolish fire. She was wearing the long winter overcoat Marian had given her and she carried a small haversack slung over her shoulder. She raised a finger to her lips and went into the room she occupied that used to be my daughter's. By the bed she turned to see me standing in the doorway. She whispered Marian's name.

'She is sleeping,' I said. 'She took a sleeping tablet.'

Grazia opened the drawer of the bedside table and took out a plump diary with thick black covers that were made to last.

'My journal,' she said. 'I can't live without it. Or leave without it!'

She giggled in that charming way she had, but I knew it was true. She was ready to gamble her entire existence for the sake of whatever entries it would occur to her to scribble on the next blank sheet of that damned book.

'Listen,' I said. 'They were here this evening. All you've got to do is talk to them. That's all. We can do that tomorrow morning at the hotel where they are staying. Come to an understanding. Not a compromise. Just so that they won't feel they've travelled all this way for nothing.'

'You have been so kind to me,' she said.

She was looking around the room, memorising every detail, every trace of Rhiannon's life that remained in view. My heart sank as I realised with awful certainty that she was about to run away again. What she was doing was in no-one's best interest, especially not mine. I should tell her that running away could easily become a habit, a way of life in itself.

'Buddy said something wonderful this evening,' she said.

How could he not. His father was in advertising. He had bequeathed to his son the gift of striking an empty utterance before expiring from over-indulgence. This creature was a shambling all-purpose penny-ha'penny prophet with the singular gift of attracting gullible young females into his orbit. Would it have been any good to shake her until her teeth rattled?

'It was the way he said it.'

'Of course it was.' She was being expressive with her fingers again. A gesture that once enchanted me did not enchant me any more. It only made me conscious of pain for my middle aged romantic folly. In any case there is nothing like an academic anxiety neurosis for snuffing out the flames of lust.

' "Life is a delicate network of friendships and we must use it." That's what he said.'

I was supposed to be impressed. Such profundity. And I was to understand how she regarded this somewhat droll creature with comradely affection. She was directing me to observe her depth of understanding, witness her generous response and to share these privileges as a parting gift.

'You see, Aled, what he meant was that if we don't make use of it, this network, it will blow away like a spider's web in the breeze!'

Once again her fingers fluttered. To be so pleased with herself and this preposterous rebirth of fraternal values. They would be embarking on the most fatuous adventure since the Children's Crusade. Spider's web indeed. I was the fly not the spider. Friendship indeed. Had she any concern for me? How could I talk to her? Or to the egregious Buddy. They were a new species outside the range of my ability to communicate. They had succeeded in insulating themselves from comprehending even the simplest propositions. She could perfectly well do her degree in Rome if I persuaded Muzio to bring the right kind of pressure to bear on Guidatti. She was old enough to start learning the first steps in the art of compromise that in the end were essential to any form of social cohesion. Nightmares could be brought to an end by waking up. Consideration for others, for God's sake, took precedence over diary entries and artistic aspirations. There could be a happy issue to all these difficulties over a cup of luke-warm coffee in the lounge of that hotel tomorrow morning. It was all so simple. A modicum of compromise and co-operation and we could all dance in the streets. It was a part of being human to understand that the canons of public and private behaviour were not so dissimilar. How could we enjoy the sheer magnitude of the promises of grace if we remained trapped in our man-made selfish desires?

'It's so warm in here,' she said. 'So comfortable. I do love this room.'

She sat on the bed and then lay back as though it belonged to her. The bed and the room and the previous occupant would be woven into a sequence of one of her artistic dreams. It was this that made her hold out her arms to me. I was being included in the work of art; being rewarded with her own potion of affection and forgiveness.

'Dear Aled,' she said. 'Hold me.'

It was easy to give in. I held her and I kissed her. She fingered the back of my head and I was strangely comforted. Her fingers were capable of restoring my youth. I should open Marian's overcoat and bring myself closer to the young body underneath. She sighed and shook her head with some show of reluctance to deprive me of my prize. She was strong and it was her strength that was there to restrain my lovesick ardour.

'You know I love you both,' she said. 'I can't tell you how much. Something for a whole lifetime.'

She was dispensing consolations as she stood up ready to leave.

'You must kiss her for me. Dear Marian. As she sleeps.'

It came as a shock and yet I could never have been unaware of the truth. We had served our purpose. The strange couple who arrived at the lakeside with their burden of grief and loss. My career, such as it was, the price that had to be paid so that this apprentice genius could arrive at the first stage of her manifest destiny. And what was she for God's sake except a pretty young woman? Just another nice looking creature carrying the seeds of good and evil. In this harsh world, good was liable to be trampled on and evil in league with greed and avarice would invariably triumph. In all the tired centuries nothing really changes.

'Give her my love and give her all yours.'

She had so much nerve. It made me burn to realise how much stronger her young will was than mine. I had forfeited the power to be positive through a sterile combination of academic inertia and romantic illusion.

'It is important to me,' she said. 'You understand that, Aled.'

To defy her father? To act as if the future was her exclusive domain? Was there nothing I could say to persuade her at least to talk to the man?

'My freedom,' she said. 'Not for its own sake. For what it will allow me to do. I have a duty to myself.'

And that was it. The supreme reason for egotism lurking like a steel spring behind that pretty face.

'And I am tough,' she said. 'And practical.'

She laughed and tapped her solar plexus as if it were the appropriate centre from which all existence radiated. I spluttered to disguise my anger as anxiety for her well-being.

'For God's sake, girl. How will you manage?'

This seemed to make her laugh even more. She put her fingers on her lips and rebuked herself.

'I shouldn't laugh. But it is absurd. A trick of fate.'

'What else.'

She missed my sarcasm or ignored it.

'You know the stamp collector. Buddy's rich step-father. He hated Buddy. You know that.'

I restrained myself from asking how anyone could possibly hate Buddy.

'The stamp-collector left all his money to Buddy's mother. Now she has given him half. Half of all her wealth. Can you imagine?'

She wanted me to understand she understood about money. It was there for the taking. So adult. So worldly wise. And what about my job? Could I just say that one word and would she understand?

'He has the power now to go in pursuit of visions. And he wants to share it. We will go together to Germany. He will pick up Pete and I will pick up Franz. A new life will open before us.'

I was supposed to admire all this and accept the cold reality of losing my job in order to allow her to join the bearded Buddy in pursuit of visions.

'That is the plan. I have deep faith in myself. When we are gone you can tell them. Make them understand.'

This was my ultimate function. Just to hurl myself on the sacrificial pyre. Had the girl any idea of the extent of the devastation she was leaving in her wake?

'Oh Aled. I have caused you so much trouble. Now you are beginning to hate me. I feel it. We must be friends. Closer than brother and sister. That's what love means. I have my vocation. You know that. One day you will be proud of me.'

'Your father is breaking his heart.'

I wanted to accuse her. Her mouth was tight and stubborn.

'He wants a slave. A daughter in chains. You know all that. You said it. You helped me escape.'

'They love you. They are your family. At least talk to them.'

'I love them more because I am free. One day I will come back and they will be proud of me. Tell them that. You are my messenger.'

'You know what happens to messengers,' I said. 'They get shot.'

X

Next morning Marian came down in her dressing gown. She sat close to the Aga clutching a mug of tea in both hands. As she had predicted she was suffering from a headache. She said it was made worse by the sound of her own voice. It was a pretext for prolonged silence. Her eyes were more often closed than open. There was no Grazia and the kitchen was alive with her absence.

'Why didn't you wake me?'

I barely heard her mutter.

'She insisted you would understand.'

Marian's eyes were shut and I couldn't judge whether she understood or not. I had to steel myself to renew a concern for my wife and forget the girl.

'Thoughtless little bitch.'

It was a spurt of momentary spleen and I saw the vestige of a smile on Marian's pale face. I was still making the noises of a man who had made an irredeemable fool of himself.

'She doesn't exist just for our benefit.'

She meant my benefit. It was more than a gnomic utterance. So much criticism flowed from it. I belonged to a much lower circle than the one reserved for grieving parents. I was a creature of the male menopause, infatuated with the state of infatuation. Her silence was too much for me, driving me towards unbearable self-revulsion. I had to defend myself. If it came to apportioning blame she could be accused. She allowed her affection for the girl to be exploited by Prue Bianchieri; that frivolous pampered would-be Diva, warding off middle age with amorous intrigues: just as I had tried to do. That woman belonged to the same circle of contempt.

I wanted to redeem myself by being attentive and considerate to Marian. I could prepare her breakfast but I knew she couldn't eat anything. I yearned to make amends and there was nothing I could do.

'Strange,' she said. 'How old and useless one can feel.'

'Useless,' I said. 'You're not useless.'

All we had to share was the old grief and misery and despair of losing our daughter. This adventure with Grazia was an empty substitute. This was a trial that would recur in one way or another for the rest of our lives. Time was a static snare and delusion. It never progressed. If only we could believe there might be another life we could look forward to, or at least find refuge in....

And I had this uncomfortable test in front of me. Marian could ruminate as long as she liked in the warmth of the Aga. I saw her stretch out her thin fingers as though something precious had slipped between them. She barely raised her head when I told her I had to go to the hotel to meet Guidatti and Muzio. Her mind was so far away it wouldn't have surprised me had she asked me who they were.

The wind had turned to the south-west and it was pouring with rain. In front of the picture-window of the hotel, Muzio and I stood to look at the view of the motorway. The stream of vehicles had their headlights on mid-morning and they created their own spray as if they were semi-aquatic animals condemned to perpetual motion. Anywhere in the world traffic was the same. This seemed a suitable topic for an abstract discussion concerning the value and virtue of hanging on to where we belong; the sanctity of the original square mile and so forth.

'People come and go,' I said. 'That's the way it is. A frenzy of movement. It's become part of the nature of things. There's very little we can do about it. There isn't a single anchor left to keep people in one place long enough to take root. Unless you count a television set!'

Muzio was in no mood to listen to vapid theorising. He looked trapped by the wet weather. Guidatti was slumped in a bulky hotel armchair groaning to himself like a man suffering an unjust fate. I was right about the coffee. It was lukewarm.

'The disgrace,' Guidatti kept repeating. 'The disgrace. What will people say? What will they think of us?'

'This man Thwaite,' Muzio said. 'Is it the same man? The one they call "Buddy"? I thought he had gone. Disappeared. Gone away from here.'

'What can you do? He came back like a dog returning to his vomit.'

I had not meant to sound so vehement: I wanted to sound more philosophic.

'A way of putting it,' I said. 'This time he had money. He's got a second-hand bookshop and a broken-down cottage. I've no idea where they've gone and I have no idea what they have in mind.... It's too ridiculous.'

I couldn't make him smile at the absurdity of the situation. This comfortless hotel, the rain pouring down outside, the endless flow of traffic with lights switched on mid-morning, Guidatti slumped in his chair and, one could only hope, his wife in the kitchen of the *trattoria* twelve hundred miles away enjoying the blessed relief of his absence. Would it be too much to expect that when he got back, the worm in the kitchen would turn and at the very least throw a wet dishcloth at him?

'Our lives are ridiculous enough already,' Muzio said. 'No need to add to the folly.'

The comment was quiet but heartfelt. It made me wonder what Prue might be up to. Were she and Luca Puri planning to strangle the old Marchesa in her bath and drop her in a black hole during her son's absence? Muzio looked despondent enough to lead one to think that anything could happen. Certainly some cherished political plan had already been blown off course. Guidatti was piling up reserves of resentment. I had to sound as helpful as I could. It wouldn't be any use at all trying to shift the blame for what had happened from Marian to Prue. His wife was enough of a burden to him already. All very well to make trips to Brescia and Bergamo. Most couples get on well enough when they are on holiday. It's what happens when they are trapped behind bedroom doors that really matters. It would please Muzio best if I could contrive to bring some comfort to the deflated Guidatti. He was still moaning away. 'What will people say? They will say, here is a man who has no idea how to bring up a family. How to control his own children. So how can he claim any authority in the councils of the community? How can he hold his head up so high? I see ruin staring me in the face. Ruin and disgrace.'

'Listen,' I said. 'You can say she is living with us. And studying. Studying in Wales, which you have been to see for yourself. Your brilliant daughter is happy living with good people in a beautiful country.'

His eyes were dark and huge as they stared at me. They accused me of having a talent for losing daughters. I half expected him to say it. He held me responsible and hated me for what had happened. Whatever I managed to concoct in praise of Grazia and her abilities he would take as a personal insult. If I were less ingratiating I could be brutally frank and point out that families were meant to be broken up. It was a genetic necessity. A truth to be universally acknowledged. It wouldn't have helped. The truth is never convenient.

Muzio made no mention of visiting Kingsley Jenkins. If there were penalties to be meted out for this sequence of mistakes and misfortunes I was the first in line to receive them. The Marchese and the local politician became as silent as judges considering a verdict. It struck me then that all Mediterranean concepts of justice turned on retribution: and part of the punishment had to be the end of my valued friendship with Muzio. Where there had been warmth, comfort, understanding, from now on there would be only distant politeness. There was no useful purpose served standing like a tailor's dummy in this hotel lounge. I felt my presence was unwanted. They had their own emergency plans to make and there was no role in them for me. In fact they would not want me to know about them. I had proved myself an unreliable ally. I murmured something about my concern for Marian and that she wasn't looking too well.

'You know where we are, anyway,' I said. 'If there is anything we can do.... Anything at all....'

I made all the right noises. In Muzio's gaze I read pity and reproach. People who were irritating and indecisive in their private lives were unsuited to wider responsibilities. Guidatti's mouth hung open. He was at a loss what to say as he stared at a barbarian foreigner whose behaviour could never be accounted for. The gap between his way of life and mine could not be crossed or closed.

xi

There have to be consolations. Broken hearts, they say, can be mended. Clouds can lift and from the west as I drove home, the pale sunlight broke through and my heart lifted as it gave a distant view of our home, Maenhir, in its noble position on the brow of the hill. We had chosen it and cherished it together. It was Marian who saw it first and pointed with the gesture of a traveller catching sight of the promised land. The original shining brow! It's the position that counts, Aled. The position is everything. And the position hadn't changed. I had to remind her of that. The past was a quarry out of which we were entitled to dig precious memories which we could handle and polish. We were obliged to console each other. It was our proper function. I could even go so far as to claim we would not have lived and lost in vain if we could transform this one good place, which had been our daughter's cradle and nursing ground, into a spring and fountain of new life.

What if I did lose my job. I had health and strength. We should allow ourselves, encourage each other, to become imbued with her spirit and even inspired by her adventurous example. We could recover those halcyon days of the great good cause. I could climb a mast again and put my life in jeopardy: regain the exhilaration that can only come with risk and fear. There was no limit to what we could still achieve together. The sooner we resolved to make a fresh start, the better. I drove up our bumpy lane like a man sent on an urgent errand. A pair of marauding magpies just had time to scatter out of my way. Nothing except our own shortcomings stood in our way. That needed to be said. Theories about the immediate past and the remote past were bubbling in my mind when I turned the last corner and saw thick smoke billowing out of the open half-door of the outhouse that used to be a stable.

It was a dangerous fire that could too easily spread. Immediate action was called for. I was arriving home in the nick of time. The hose-pipe and the tap were inside the stable. It was where we stored the books and magazines we had no room for in the house. I shouted Marian's name and soaked my raincoat in the ditch between the lane and the orchard. With the wet coat over my head I felt my way to the hose-pipe and managed to turn on the tap. I brought the fire under control and I was exhilarated by my own effort. I had responded effectively to a challenge. The smell of the smoke in the stable would last for ever. On the cobbled floor I could make out the remains of files and papers among the charred books; which suggested the fire had been started deliberately. As the water gushed from the hose-pipe my excitement turned to foreboding. Behind me Marian stood wearing a woolly cap and a long overcoat. From a deep pocket she took out a box of matches to shake it in the air before stuffing it back.

'Marian. What's going on? What do you think you're doing?'
She sighed deeply and shook her head.
'Setting the place on fire,' she said. 'What else?'
I began to shiver. There was water trickling down the back of my neck. Some of the stuff on the floor was research material. Left over from the days when she had dreamed about her daughter collaborating with her on a substantial contribution to Celtic philology. I began to tremble with delayed shock. Marian led the way back to the warmth of the kitchen. She found me a towel. This was a more acceptable form of reality. I said as much. The warmth of the Aga was the warmth of the family hearth. She shook her head and my heart sank.
'This place was always designed to keep reality at bay.'
We knew each other so well, she must have known that word reality was reverberating in my head. Proof if proof were needed how much we belonged to one another. She had something disagreeable to tell me and the expression on her face told me she was searching for the best way to go about it.
'People latch on to each other because they are incapable of standing alone,' she said. 'They devise a purpose and call it a design. What happens when the purpose is gone?'
'What are you talking about?'
I knew and I didn't know. Grazia Guidatti had been the substitute purpose and she was gone. Very well. Good riddance. Now we could approach the subject of a fresh start. I had so many things to say about it, but Marian contrived to be ahead of me. As always she was there occupying the higher ground.
'I have to ask myself, what am I good for?' she said. 'Ideals and illusions. We need them because we live on them. One illusion gives way to another and they all go up in smoke.'
'It's obvious,' I said. 'We need each other. Surely now more than ever.'
She had no right to disagree with me. It made me angry. I had to contain my anger, but the effort was cancelling out all the arguments I wanted to make before I could formulate them. This was no way to conduct a discussion.
'We can't do each other any good,' she said. 'Not any more. A mirror image is a blank wall. It shows you nothing. It just blocks off your bit of sunlight.'
'I don't know what you are talking about.'
'This place is empty,' she said. 'There's no point in worshipping the container when it contains nothing.'

'Rubbish,' I said. 'That's rubbish and you know it.'

'An empty nest,' she said. 'If that's all you've got all you are doing for the rest of your life is worshipping your own comfort.'

'Listen,' I said. 'I've been going over in my mind all the things we should be doing here.'

'I'm going away.'

I didn't want to believe what I was hearing. I cried out.

'This is where we belong!'

She had delivered her announcement. She left me to go upstairs. I stood still to listen to her moving about in the bedroom. I had been thrust out into the cold. If only it were some form of punishment or revenge. It was worse than that. I tramped up the stairs after her, stamping my feet with infantile insistence. There were suitcases open on the bed. She was already packing as calmly as though I did not exist.

'This is total madness.'

I tried to work myself up into a frenzy of indignation. It was either that or sinking on my knees to the sides of the bed to plead and beg. I failed to do either.

'I've got to look for something else.'

'That bloody girl....'

I was stung to inarticulate fury, spitting out sacrilege. She stopped to look at me and I knew what she was thinking. The end of an infatuation. So much less dignified than the end of an affair. A middle-aged clown infatuated with infatuation. She could be sorry for him. At least it kept him going when he needed to be kept going. It was a general not a particular absolution I saw in her eyes, as she considered my pitiable condition.

'She could have had this place,' Marian said. 'That was always a possibility. One more ideal. It might have given the place an injection of meaning. She didn't want it. Didn't need it. Any more than she needed you. Or needed me. So there we are. A comprehensive demolition.'

'You can't talk like this,' I said. 'I need you.'

I had to resort to begging. Her concern was so detached it unnerved me.

'Why do you go on like this?' I said. 'I need you. You know I need you.'

'We have to learn to stand alone.'

If I had any reasoning power left it was draining away. She spoke of teaching and nursing. Working in the west of Ireland or the Hebrides. Why there more than anywhere else? She had this need to serve. Some kind of missionary urge I could barely understand. Punishing herself on the edge of a jungle or in some war zone. Somewhere remote as far as she could get away from me. She was talking and being reasonable in an irrational world, but I could barely hear her. All I wanted to ask was did she think as much of me as I did of her. Did we not share the same ache, the same unbearable despair.... Was I so far outside the limits of redemption? I could have attacked her physically but nothing I could do would ever beat her into submission. I left our bedroom while she was still talking. The house was drawing in shadows. Whatever Marian chose to do she would do. This had always been the case since I first knew her. I had no means of stopping her.

xii

In November, when all the leaves have been washed off the trees, our island reverts to a primordial condition: a dignity that puts it back at the rocky centre of the universe. In the afternoon it exudes its own numinous power between weather-fronts, when the muscular sun exerts itself to create a crack in the clouds and transform the western sky into an extended slit of penitential fire. There are a few humans about. Beams of light and pillars of vapour ascend and descend like angels' ladders from the molten sea to the golden door in the sky. This is the time for the indolent and the introspective to emerge in gum-boots and assume that the universe has been created for their benefit. I was still drawing comfort from copying out Boethius. *Quisquis profunda mente vestigat verum....* Whoever seeks out the truth in depth of thought ... must turn on himself his inward sight. All true enough. Across the western water a range of hills blacker than bibles have reclaimed their mythological status and the solitary scribe can also write himself in as the direct descendant of Adam.

I was out to hunt down megaliths. There can be no question that in the history of our island they have a tendency to move or be moved. It is not for me to question the inventories prepared by dedicated scholars over the last century. They acknowledge that more have been destroyed than survive. It is still not easy to distinguish between circles, standing stones, tombs, and the natural rock outcrops that, like messages from the underworld, thrust themselves to our notice at the winter solstice. That is what I am

238

concerned with: the messages. There are many that remain and more that are overlooked. And even when they are found and carefully recorded they are never deciphered. It has occurred to me in my indolence that this disability is due to two factors that are impossible to calibrate: the exact time of the year and the day when the light from heaven illuminates the markings, and the emotional state of the scholar as he hurries to attempt his reading.

I walked along the familiar farm road for half a mile and trod the muddy path to the restored tomb covered by its smooth grassy mound. I was in a state of subdued excitement since all the omens seemed propitious. I carried my powerful torch but I hoped I would not need it. The space between the uprights on the west side of the tomb had been designed four thousand years ago and had been left intact by the restorers in the hope that the setting sun would send in its sparks to light up the subterranean darkness. It was a temple and a tomb, belonging equally to the living and the dead and therefore it constituted a great human triumph over nothingness and silence. It was intended that the dead and the living in this place should continue to communicate with each other. The markings were made on the underside of the stones so that the dead could be consoled by reading the chevrons, and the spirals and the zig zags, just as a scribe enjoys the exercise of calligraphy and the glance of the eager reader dances over the printed page.

I heard childish voices behind my head. And then adult voices. A nuclear family was abroad armed with guide-books. A little girl's voice piped into the still air. Her brother was dashing up and down the grassy mound declaring himself to be king of the castle and waving an imaginary sword. I could hear the parents laughing.

'This place is nothing to do with King Arthur, David.'

The father's voice was firm with tolerant authority.

'Or the Druids. It's much older.'

I banged the side of my head on the jutting stone as I turned to look at the little girl's head in silhouette against the setting sun. She was peering in at me. The twist of hair on top made the outline comic and I smiled at her as I rubbed my head. My smile frightened her.

'Mummy! Daddy!'

She had a piercing cry for one so small.

'There's a man in there and he's not dead.'

The mother's voice was an older replica of the same penetrating sound.

'Alice! Come away from there. You'll get your feet wet. David!'

The brother had arrived alongside the little girl, avid with curiosity. He carried a junior camera with a built-in flash. He jerked up his arm and in less than a second he took my photograph. He scrambled away shouting and waving his trophy.

'I took his picture! I took his picture! The man in there.'

I suppose he had. If it came out, in years to come they would peer at it and wonder who on earth was smiling at them out of the tomb. Meanwhile I am alone and unentangled as a single stone.